THE PROPHECY

THE PROPHECY

SARAH LUDDINGTON

Mirador Publishing

http://www.miradorpublishing.co.uk

First Published in Great Britain 2010 by Mirador Publishing

Copyright © 2010 by Sarah Luddington

All right reserved. No part of this publication may be reproduced or transmitted, in any form or by any means, without permission of the publishers or author. Excepting brief quotes used in reviews.

First edition: 2010

Any reference to real names and places are purely fictional and are constructs of the author. Any offence the references produce is unintentional and in no way reflect the reality of any locations involved.

A copy of this work is available though the British Library.

IBSN : 978-0-9567111-0-6

Mirador Publishing
Mirador
Wearne Lane
Langport
Somerset
TA10 9HB

For David,
my husband to whom I owe everything. My best friend and my solace (except for the cats...), you just get it....

And Heather,
wherever you may be my friend, this one is for you. If you hadn't said, "I want to be a bad guy in your book." I would never have started this journey.

And the music,
please check my website www.darkfiction.eu for the list of bands who influence my work.

Many thanks have to go to so many people but these folks will never forgive me if they don't receive a special place in the first novel—My family (Mum, that's you, Abi you too and in the interests of family peace—Dad, Sandy, H and Becky), how you put up with my madness I'll never know. My friends at our dojo (Eleanor and Jo my special girls). I know you all think I'm nuts but you also put up with my wittering. Bernie for being the only one to help with spelling errors (I hope the vodka made up for the hours it took) and Lampeter University for giving me the education I needed to lend me the courage to finish the first version of this book. Interesting place Wales!

PROLOGUE

AS DAWN STARTS IN THE EAST, SO WILL DARKNESS...

THAILAND – SIX YEARS AGO

    The muscles in his arms screamed for release from the chains that bound his hands above his head. Alak would have risen from his knees, but they had placed a bar over the back of his legs, preventing him. He dragged his sweat soaked head from his chest pushing it back between his arms. He hoped this would at least change the pain in his shoulders. It did, but it also brought into view the true implications of his current situation.
    Worshippers filled the caverns under the ancient temples of Thailand. Members of all races had come to partake in the final destruction of one of Thailand's most powerful beings. Places of worship were always vulnerable to corruption.
    Alak saw his friend and companion of long standing not three yards away. The two men had been together for the whole of Alak's life. Everything he knew about the world derived from his friend and now his friend would help to destroy everything for which they worked. Darkness would finally fall.
    The tears came easily. Not because of the beatings and pain Alak endured, but for the loss of love and for the lives of every one of their friends that had been

destroyed. He was truly alone. He had no power left. Nothing left to fight this final agony.

The words of the ceremony's leader washed over him. He no longer listened, no longer cared, he just wanted the end to come. He had begged for it and hoped his God would forgive him.

Alak began to realise his captors had changed their focus, to him. The moment had come. He hoped it would be swift. Though somehow he doubted it, they would need to feed upon his pain. Using it to further corrupt his friend. Alak looked hard at his companion. He tried to find a way into that now alien mind, begged for his friend to at least acknowledge their connection. But there was nothing, no-one left in there for Alak to connect with. In that moment all hope died.

The priest moved forward to stand before Alak. Thailand's humidity made the white ceremonial robe stick to the priest's pale Caucasian skin. The priestess, splendid in her arrogance, walked around behind Alak and grasped his hair, forcing his head back between his arms. Alak lost sight of the people. He found himself trying to focus on the dark ceiling, the hanging stalactites were like shadowed daggers.

He felt the woman's thumb in the joint of the right side of his jaw, another finger in the left side. She pushed. Alak fought, but the pain increased, he opened his jaws. More words flowed around him. Then his beautiful and now terrible companion drew a knife across his own arm and thrust the wound against Alak's mouth. The hot coppery fluid spilled into Alak. His companion's dead blood. He couldn't breathe, the liquid suffocating him. He screamed as he swallowed, choking. He felt it spill down his chin, over his chest, he gagged but still it poured down his throat. Alak thought he would drown in the terrible flow.

Then the pain started deep inside him.

As the first wave of agony struck, the chain's holding him bucked under his thrashing movements. The cavern had gone quiet and still while Alak's mindless screams filled the stagnant, humid air. All had gone to their knees before his cries of agony, as his companion's blood burned through his all too human body.

The pain eased and Alak's head fell forward once more. An expectant hush filled the cavern. When he once more opened his eyes, Alak felt bloody foam dripping from his mouth. Nothing of the pure spirit had been left within him. His new eyes burned with lusts and hungers never to be sated. The congregation went wild as their leaders and the human's companion rose. They displayed the degraded Guardian who would no longer maintain the ancient traditions, no longer be able to keep the darkness at bay....

NORTH AFRICA ONE YEAR LATER

Carthage had been good to him. Africa had been good to him. In this cycle, he had learnt so much and had accomplished so much good. That's why the ending of his life seemed so cruel. Nabil gradually became conscious of vast amounts of pain in his arms and legs. He soon realised he had been suspended several feet above the floor of the cave, by his ankles and wrists, his body held taut, but his head able to move. As he twisted, he gasped at the sight of hundreds of people from all races surrounding him in a tight circle. They sang dark hymns that undulated around his stretched form. Nabil felt glad his body had always been strong and fit. If he had been heavier, he would have dislocated his major joints for certain. Despite this positive approach, sweat bathed his dark skin.

Nabil twisted once more as the crowd parted. He watched as a white couple in white robes approached, with them came his vision of beauty. Her dark skin glistened in the torchlight and Nabil began to cry out to her, but the words tied themselves up in his parched mouth. This was not the woman who had spent decades teaching and loving him. Her face had been twisted into a dark mask of hate, forming a sadistic parody of beauty. Nabil shut his eyes, unable to understand the corruption of all he had loved.

The hymns rose around him as he watched his long time love move with her unearthly grace between his legs. She raised a dark blade above his suspended body. Nabil screamed her name over and over as she began to carve into his flesh, her eyes flashing with joy at every stroke. The heat of Africa filled his lungs with tortured breath; just as it filled those around him with the power to sing, louder and louder in that small cave in an ancient city.

An eternity later the knife stopped.

Just as Nabil felt the safety of unconsciousness once more descend, the woman in white grasped his head. She prised his jaws apart.

Hope no longer flickered in even the lightest part of his soul. Nabil knew he would welcome the madness that came with the blood he'd been forced to swallow. As the pain rose from the pits of his body, Nabil did not fight. Could not fight. His fight ended when he had gazed into the eyes of his love, as she forced her death dealing blood into his fragile human body. He knew it was over and only hoped the darkness descending within him would be stopped somehow, somewhere.

NORTHERN TIBET – LAST YEAR

Priest and Priestess smiled at each other as the raving beast was led away by her lifetime companion. Neither cleric felt the cold as the wind whipped across the tundra of Tibet. Six of the Guardians had been destroyed. They had corrupted the companions and teachers. Murdered their support networks and turned each Guardian from powerhouses of light and love, to vacuums of darkness and hate. A lifetime of planning had neared completion and the siblings were pleased.

Just one more, one more pair to corrupt and the seven would become their creatures. It had taken six years to reach this level of power. Just one more year and they would reach a plateau none of their predecessors had even dreamt about; but this could not be rushed. They would leave this place and travel to London finishing what had begun many months before. Tightening their circle of followers and bringing their power to bear on the strongest and oldest of the Guardians.

Turning as one, they walked away from the tunnel's entrance and the blood soaked ground. They ignored the bodies of the victims, who had given their lives willingly once the destroyed pair had needed to feed. They walked from the horror feeling stronger than ever before, high on the dark energy they had produced and stored. The Land Rover sat waiting, with heating, wine and civilisation. Before they lifted their bodies into the leather interior, the couple watched their neophytes begin to sample the obscene pleasures of their latest corruption. With dawn several hours off, the fun would go on for some time. The couple wished they were a part of the pain, but that pleasure would have to wait for other times. The Land Rover left the area, and drove toward the West.

CHAPTER ONE

Esme winced as she gulped another mouthful of the disgusting take-away coffee. She stood outside the building that contained her office and gazed upward, allowing the commuters to brush past her with vigorous efficiency. A rubbish bin sat, squat beside her, the restless rush of humanity ignored both her and the bin. Esme stuffed the evil brew into the bin's gaping maw.

Continuing the mournful stare, she wondered for the hundredth time why she bothered. Looking through the glass front doors, she watched the security guards check the badges and bags of people they didn't recognise. Co-workers, dressed in identical dark suits to the ones she wore, milled about preparing for the cut and thrust of another wasteful day on the planet. Leaning briefly against the bin, Esme lifted her right foot, circling it tentatively, before returning it to the ground and repeating the process with the left. She regretted the choice of dark trouser suit and high heels. Her feet were already moaning.

She remembered when her dress sense had been something very different. Short skirts, big boots, multi coloured jumpers or tiny t-shirts depending on the weather, and leather, always leather somewhere. She'd even found a way of taming her hair these days.

Sighing heavily, she announced to the passing human traffic, "God, this is bloody depressing." The passing traffic ignored her.

There were more reasons than just Monday morning blues to make Esme unhappy. She shared her bed with the man who had contracted her to help build and promote his company. So, going into work meant seeing Matt, something else which made her feel sick. His company, mainly interested in mobile technology, bored her stupid. But she'd already made him a great deal of money and he paid her handsomely. As did all her business clients. The trouble started when she'd gone to bed with the idiot. She should never have done it, but it happened all too easily these days and six months later, she still hadn't dumped him.

Stepping forward, Esme finally took the plunge and went to work.

Matt's business lived on the fifteenth floor. Esme occupied an office with a view of the Thames, which pleased her, but she'd long since stopped enjoying it. She sat, staring at her computer screen wishing for a 'control;alt;delete' restart to her own life. Groaning, Esme allowed her forehead to hit the desktop. Matt's voice filtered through the door to her office. It grated. There was nothing endearing about Matt. More spiv than gent, more callous than kind, more arrogant than intelligent, Esme heard him flirt with his secretary. She groaned again.

Her office door burst open. Lifting her head off the desk, she hoped her eyes conveyed the contempt she felt for her employer.

"Are you ready for the meeting?" Matt's voice shot electrodes into Esme's brain.

"What do you think?" Just as the look melted off the man's hide so did the sarcasm.

Several hours later, Esme and Matt returned to her office, all guns blazing.

"What the bloody hell do you think you were doing in there? You cannot usurp my authority like that." Esme's hand stung as her palm hit the desktop.

She'd gone way beyond the point at which most people start spitting nails. The meeting began well enough. The clients, a company she'd worked with before, were going to help Matt hit the next level in the world of blue chip technology import and export. She'd spent weeks wooing them into dealing with Matt; they'd only agreed to the meeting because of her connections. There were also the endless hours she'd spent preparing for this, the perfect proposal. Now it lay in tatters because Matt couldn't keep his mouth shut.

The worst of it being, the whole thing left her cold. Even a year ago, this challenge would have sparked in her some divine inspiration, her adrenaline would pump and she'd have felt truly alive. Right now, she felt like shit. The work left her empty and tired. She'd delivered the proposal, everyone looked pleased, then Matt opened his mouth and it all turned to ashes.

"No one undermines my work." She flung herself down into her chair. It rocked madly. "You bloody idiot. You've ruined everything. How dare you speak to me like that."

"For God's sake, Esme stop being so melodramatic." Matt leaned on her desktop.

"Oh, so you can use words of more than three syllables. Not just the ones that make me look like, and I quote, 'The little woman.'" The words ground out like a glacier taking the top off a mountain.

"It was meant to be a joke," Matt leaned over the desk's surface, clearly hoping to intimidate Esme.

"They are Japanese. They only work with me because of my reputation. And if you don't show me respect, why should they? As far as they are concerned, if you do not respect me, you will not respect them." Esme found herself almost screaming into his face. Weeks of building resentment boiled out of her.

"If you weren't such an uptight bitch," Matt really snarled, "I'd be getting laid more often and you'd do as I tell you."

Esme realised in that moment he'd just stepped over the line. "Uptight? Me?" Esme laughed in his face. "Oh, I'm not uptight, Matt. I'm just not the slut you want me to be."

They were almost nose-to-nose. Esme saw violence in Matt's face, real violence. In a state of detachment she hit the inside of Matt's left elbow with her palm. His elbow bent suddenly, his torso collapsing in the process and air woofed out of his lungs in surprise. As his chest and head travelled rapidly toward the desktop, Esme's right hand, acting on its own, whipped his left hand into the top drawer of her desk and it closed hard and fast, trapping Matt's wrist. His face smashed against the wooden surface, Esme's right knee held the desk drawer shut, a crunching sound coming from the drawer.

Matt screamed. Esme hit the back of his head. "Shut up. Shut up and listen. I want you to leave me alone, I want to stop working for you and I want to stop sleeping with you. I resign." Her knee gave one more shove against the drawer for emphasis, before she rose.

Without looking back, she picked up her coat and the laptop. The secretary, and Matt's occasional bed-warmer, opened the door. Esme pushed passed her saying, "He'll need a cold compress on that hand."

By the time she hit the street Esme's knees shook as though she'd just completed a twelve mile run. Laughter began to bubble uncontrollably inside her belly. Freedom beckoned.

Her phone started to vibrate in her pocket. Pulling it out she glanced at the name flashing on the screen. Matt. Inevitably. The phone followed the crappy coffee from that morning and landed in the bin with a satisfying thump. Striding away, a wave of intoxicating relaxation flowing through her, Esme decided a liquid lunch would be a perfect way to celebrate.

The autumn sunlight bathed her, making her glad to be alive for the first time in months, possibly years. Sensational feelings of release made her blood sing in her heart. She passed a wine bar, hardly the perfect place, but it'd do.

Flinging open the front door, she headed for the bar. The place resembled a chic, white womb. Weird and very fashionable. Her dark suit offered a suitable contrast. She almost left to find somewhere that stank of stale beer, poured pints in glasses and had a nice nicotine stained ceiling, but they'd probably banned those sorts of places along with everything else.

Plonking herself on a nice white bar stool, covered in soft leather and chrome she ordered a bottle of their finest champagne. Her platinum card on the bar's mirrored surface ensured the barman's undying interest. The bubbles fizzed as merrily as the blood in her veins while Esme related her resignation to the attentive barman, who laughed, probably more out of fear than real humour. But she didn't care. Ten years of servitude to the great god of consumerism left her a soulless shell. Esme wanted more, much more.

Two bottles and several pick-up attempts from ex-fellow business types finally saw Esme leave the bar. Her heels were ridiculously high for walking long distances under the influence of far too many bubbles. The very nice barman, who earned himself a big tip, ordered her a taxi. Esme poured herself into it as the sunset coloured the sky in fire so bright all the buildings, which reached into it, were harsh black silhouettes. The traffic made their journey a slow crawl through the major arteries of the city. Esme laid her head back and worked on sobering up enough to leave the taxi with more elegance than she'd entered it.

"Hey, lady. We're here."

Esme's head straightened, making it pound uncomfortably. Her eyes opened, eventually, "Oh - kay, here some money." She thrust several notes into the cabby's hand and began working out how to leave the taxi.

"There's far too much 'ere," he said.

"Don't worry 'bout it." Esme finally managed to pull herself from the black cab and stood blinking, staring at the steps leading to her flat.

She lived in a nice area of London, her father bought the flat years before and it'd proved a wise investment. She occupied the ground floor of a large Georgian terrace, which even had a nice private garden. Her neighbours were nice people and the nearby park was nice too. Everything was nice, her life had been nice for years. Ever since she'd finally conformed to her father's image of the nice, perfect daughter.

The only thing she'd never managed to control was her inclination for unsuitable men. Fortunately, she'd never married any of them. With her parents now dead for almost two years, Esme realised she needed a change. Maybe the time had come to move away from the image of the perfect daughter she'd carefully created for their benefit, after her years in the wilderness of rebellion.

"These bloody shoes are killing me," Esme spoke to her feet as the cab pulled away. Dropping her laptop onto the pavement, Esme bent to remove the shoes. The world tilted at a very bad angle. "Whoa! That's not good, or clever."

Straightening too fast she wobbled, stepping backward to regain her balance. The kerb, of course, caught her by surprise. Esme liked a drink but her years of overindulgence were well and truly over, so she found herself out of practice when it came to remaining upright despite inebriation.

"Shit." The road began to reach out to grab her backside.

Life tilted crazily once more and a vice like grip grasped her waist. The road lost its trophy.

"Are you well?" a deep, dark soft voice rumbled through Esme's mind and body.

"Oh." She pushed slightly at the arm holding her waist. Her hair, always rebellious, decided to uncoil at that moment, effectively blinding her. "For goodness sake. Give me a break," Esme clawed at her hair, while still trying to stand upright.

A soft laugh greeted her attempts, "Here, let me help. Being a woman has never been simple."

"I want to take my shoes off, I hate heels," Esme almost sobbed as gentle hands began to brush hair out of her eyes.

"They are an evil fashion but be grateful you do not have to wear corsets, they are instruments of slow torture."

Esme blinked slowly, trying to process the meaning of such a strange sentiment, coming from a man.

His next words made her giggle slightly in relief, "So, I am led to believe."

Finally able to see, Esme began to really appreciate the view. Her would be saviour had deep blue eyes, thick black hair which hung just below his collar and strong facial features. Full, smiling lips finished off the ensemble. She realised, as she stood looking upward, that he must stand slightly over six feet tall. He wore a dark, thick woollen coat over a black shirt, which he filled out with a combination of good bone structure and lithe muscle. Her mind began shrieking something important to her, Esme stamped on the internal noise, not wanting anything to distract from the moment.

"I'm not certain if I should say sorry or thanks," she smiled, sobriety finally making an appearance.

"You owe me no thanks, I just happened to be passing. And maybe I should apologise for taking the liberty of holding you so close." His voice made things tighten in Esme's loins.

She coughed to hide the groan which threatened to make itself known, "Oh, no. Really, that's fine." She almost said, 'You can hold me that close as often as you like,' when her internal filter, for once working as it should, stopped her. Her feet, however, finally decided enough was enough. They wanted the same freedom her hair managed. "Oh God, I really have to take these shoes off."

"Well, at least give me your hand so I will not need to pull you out of the road once more." His amusement made his eyes shine with an internal joy, a deeply unguarded expression. Something her cynical lifestyle had lost.

Esme allowed that joy and her own sense of freedom to reach through her well-constructed barriers. She hoped her own expression shone with the same love of life. His smile broadened as he offered his hand. Evidently, she achieved the right effect.

Taking his hand, Esme balanced on one foot, trying to undo the buckle, which kept her foot in its prison. As she wobbled, he moved closer, an arm encircling her back. They both began to laugh at the ridiculousness of their situation. Finally, after her saviour's intervention, Esme stood on the cold pavement in bare feet. She wiggled her toes and groaned in relief.

Reaching for her laptop bag, she said, "I'd invite you in for a drink to say thanks, but I don't think I should be sampling any more of Bacchus's cruel brew for a few days. Coffee is definitely on the menu though." She fished her keys out of their organised pocket. Her life had become excessively organised, as well as nice. Once upon a time, it would have taken her a full five minutes to find keys in the bottom of a bag, which mirrored a hellish version of Mary Poppins' carpetbag.

"Coffee would be most welcome, but I shall have to decline." He bowed his head slightly as an apology.

"Oh, right, of course, sorry." Esme blushed. Married, gay, or uninterested in women who walked the streets drunk. It didn't really matter, she'd over stepped the mark without even thinking about it. Asking him in seemed as natural as breathing, which was odd, because Esme rarely did anything quite so dumb. Strange men and paranoia tended to go hand in hand.

Taking her hand as she began to turn away, the man said, "But I believe the term you would use is, can we have a rain check?" a level of hope in his voice made Esme stop, she turned fully back to face him. Once more, an honest expression met her assessing gaze.

"Okay, a rain check. My name is, Esme, by the way."

Still holding her hand, he squeezed it slightly, "And I am, Cursian. Maybe, I can call on you tomorrow evening after dusk?"

His terminology made her smile, "Yes, that would be lovely. Tomorrow evening."

Raising her hand to his lips, he kissed the back as though she were the most precious gift in the world. The intensity of the moment stole Esme's breath. He raised his eyes to her face, pinning her with his clear gaze. "Until tomorrow then." Releasing her hand, he turned away. Esme's heart pounded far too loudly in her ears.

"Sounds good," she told herself, turning with a confusing haze of unreality surrounding her.

CHAPTER TWO

It took a few hours the next day, but Esme eventually controlled her hangover. She spent the day playing about on the internet, drinking tea and ignoring her phone. She also managed to ignore her email. She'd decided to add Matt to her spam filter, it deleted his messages before they arrived. Petty but satisfying. By about four o'clock, Esme realised she'd spent most of the day thinking about her knight in shining armour from the previous evening. They may have spent a very strange few minutes together but Esme couldn't forget how his arm felt around her waist. How his lips, despite being cold, burnt her hand as he'd kissed it.

Pacing the hall between her lounge and kitchen for the hundredth time, she muttered to her impassive walls, "This is ridiculous, I feel as though I'm sixteen again, not thirty two."

She also wished she knew what kind of date it would be. She had no idea what to wear. Would it be dinner or the theatre? She put her obsessive thoughts and aching heart down to the hangover and her need for a new life. It left her unsettled, but excited.

Eventually, dusk darkened her lounge. Esme rose, switched off the PC and went to shower and change. Rifling through countless suits and designer frocks, she finally found some clothes she'd picked up in Camden Market on a rebellious shopping spree. Choosing a short skirt, tights, knee high boots, high-necked tight fitting black jumper and a long leather coat, she looked down at herself. Just as she decided the skirt might give the wrong impression after the previous evening and a longer one should be employed, a bang at the door made her jump.

Full dark had snuck up on her. Feeling inexplicably nervous but happy, Esme brushed her hair behind her ears and headed for the front door. She smiled as she opened it, Cursian stood there, smiling in return.

For a moment the sulphurous streetlights threw strange shadows over his face, they created an illusion of otherworldliness and danger.

He spoke, snapping reality back, "My lady's carriage awaits." Stepping aside, sweeping his arm outward, Cursian bowed slightly as he presented his car.

Esme shifted her focus from watching Cursian and trying to assimilate the flash of darkness she'd witnessed, to something which made her forget everything. "Wow, cool wheels." Esme grabbed her handbag.

A long, low black Jaguar XK8 sat in the road. Esme loved cars, her one real weakness when it came to saving the planet. She just couldn't deal with losing such things of beauty.

"I thought you would appreciate her," Cursian said, holding the door open.

Esme laughed, slightly nervous, "What made you think that?" They'd only just met how could he possibly think she would be a petrol head.

"Surely, one thing of beauty should recognise another?" Cursian replied, smoothly.

Glancing at him as he lowered himself into the car, she tried to decide if he were being ironic or plain scary. His grin as he started the car answered her concerns, ironic, definitely ironic. She relaxed slightly.

"Where are we going?" she asked.

"Where would you like to go? I have not booked a restaurant, as I do not know what you like to eat. It is also a little early I believe." The car purred as he started it up.

Esme glanced at her watch, six thirty, "Actually, there is something I would love to do and it's the sort of thing for which you need company. Though it is odd and if it's not your thing that's okay. I'd just like to do something different, first dates can be terribly dull." As soon as the words left her mouth, Esme wanted them back. She glanced at her companion who raised an elegant black eyebrow.

"Shit, sorry, didn't mean this would be boring. I just wanted to do something out of the ordinary for a change." She blushed madly wanting to kick herself, hard.

"Just tell me where you would like to go," Cursian's voice made his amusement clear.

Esme spoke quietly, her confidence gone completely. Yep, she'd definitely gone from thirty two, to sixteen, in one day. "I would love to go the British Museum. They close late on a Tuesday and Thursday. And there are loads of restaurants in the area."

"Then, you shall go to the British Museum."

"You don't mind?" Esme asked, wondering why this stranger would be happy to indulge her eccentric whim.

He glanced at her as he drove, moving the car effortlessly though the London traffic, "Why should I mind? Museums are wonderful places. They never fail to fascinate me. The interesting theories people have about the past keeps me entertained, if nothing else. And to have such delightful and amusing company will make it a great pleasure."

His voice glided through Esme, leaving her feeling as though she were being covered in chocolate and honey, so he could lick it all off later. The thought made her want to laugh, she turned away from Cursian, hiding the inappropriate thought. Esme watched as the car glided past the lights of shops and businesses, firmly telling herself to get a grip.

Sitting wrapped in her coat, held by the car seat, Esme felt calm. She really didn't understand why this man made her feel completely safe, but so jittery at the same time. Her body craved his touch, yet her mind told her not to be so daft they'd only just met. Her heart just wanted to wrap itself up and run off with him. They couldn't have exchanged more than a hundred words the previous night. Yet something in her recognised him well enough to know that riding off into the night with the guy, might end with something she regretted, but it would so be worth the ride.

She usually knew her lovers as friends for some time before bedding them, or met dates in a crowded place before deciding if they were safe to take home. And even then, she kept a baseball bat under her bed if anything went wrong. Her sudden attraction to this stranger made no sense.

"You are quiet," Cursian said.

Esme turned back to him, "Sorry, I didn't mean to be. I was just thinking."

"Anything I should worry about?"

Esme decided to explain her thought processes, "Well, I never go out on dates like this. Picking up strange men in the street isn't a habit, believe it or not."

"I do believe you, but maybe you are listening to your heart and not your head. This is not a bad thing, instincts should be trusted." He guided the car artfully between a four by four driver and cyclist who seemed to want to debate which of them had the right to the road.

Esme smiled, "That's more or less the conclusion I came too. Why did you ask me out by the way? I wasn't really at my best last night." The apology rang clearly in her tone.

He laughed, "I thought you were wonderful last night. You may have been the worse for wear, but you were utterly adorable in your incapacitation."

Esme giggled slightly, "Adorable? Me? Hum, well, hang around long enough and I am certain I'll find all sorts of ways of making an adorable idiot out of myself." No one described her as adorable. Not even her parents had been that blind to her faults.

"No, Esme. You did not behave like an idiot. You were more drunk on joy and fun than the wine. What made you so happy by the way?"

Esme explained about the previous days events. She even admitted to her relationship with Matt.

"It seems as though you have made all the right decisions. I am glad." Cursian pulled into a parking space in a side street, "After all, if you had not left him you may not have wished for my company tonight."

Thankfully changing the subject, before she made an even bigger fool of herself, Esme asked, "How the hell did you find a parking space this close to the museum?" she looked around her in amazement, as though a spacecraft had landed in central London.

Cursian grinned, "Just one of my many talents."

They walked toward the museum. Cursian offered Esme his arm. She took it willingly, enjoying the gallantry of walking with a gentleman. Once through the entrance Esme found an advert for the exhibition. She pointed to a poster covered in weird symbols and flames leaping around old hags.

Cursian said, "You came to see an exhibition on the History of Witchcraft?"

"Yep, I've been fascinated with it my whole life." Taking his arm once more Esme began to walk toward the rooms indicated on the map, "My mother raised me a very strict Catholic, until I rebelled and joined the C of E. But my grandmother, Nanna, she lived a very different life and one my Mother wouldn't talk about. But I remember tarot cards, and weird books in her house. She died when I was quite young so I never had the chance to ask her about it. My Father backed my Mother up, so I didn't even see a book on witchcraft until I ran away from home at sixteen to go to Glastonbury Festival. That was an event, I tell you. Things kind of changed for me after that. Eventually, I began to conform for my own sanity's sake more than anything else. Up until yesterday, I played the perfect corporate puppy. And now anything goes. I'm unemployed and free to do as I please." She smiled up at him and caught a glimpse of something dark lurking in his clear blue eyes. He blinked and the expression vanished instantly.

"Witchcraft certainly has some merits," he said.

"You know something about it?"

"Something," he sounded guarded and clearly didn't want to elaborate.

Esme frowned slightly. She had always maintained a spiritual element to her life. Her school had been interestingly Catholic and after her rebellious phase, Esme returned to the softer religious ceremonies and principles of a low brow church. It fitted in with her less than scrupulous life. If she had to confess and do penance for every illicit thought, never mind blasphemy, she'd never have time for work. None of her friends or lovers had ever really understood her need to attend church on a regular basis, but something in those elegant buildings made her feel safe and at home. If Cursian didn't approve it didn't matter, it would just be something she did alone, providing of course that things grew between them, she told herself firmly.

As soon as they reached the exhibition itself he clearly relaxed. Artefacts filled three large rooms, right from the earliest written examples onward. Different versions from all over the world occupied one room and an in depth analysis of the persecutions throughout Europe took up two thirds of the main room.

"Personally, I feel they have badly misrepresented the Dominican's work during this period," Cursian pointed to a particularly gruesome model of burning witches.

"Really? You surprise me."

"It is feminism which makes you feel the faith is at fault here. It never occurs to anyone that things might have been done for a reason. I have no doubt that innocent women were burned, but a great many evil ones were caught too. It was a dangerous time. Humanity had been weakened by the plague and so many wars. Evil could find a way through and this was the only way the Church could control it."

"You make it sound as though you were there," Esme stepped away from him slightly, his passion making her twitchy for some reason. "You don't have to take it quite so personally."

He smiled, relaxing instantly, "I am sorry. I dislike biased interpretations. There is no attempt to see things from the Inquisition's point of view. It may have been a blunt instrument but it did a necessary job." His gaze became distant for a moment and he became quite still.

Esme watched him carefully, standing slightly out of arms reach. Her next comment, she knew, would provoke a reaction in him. She just had to hope he liked it. She said, "Their point of view held sway for centuries, I kind of like a more upbeat perspective."

His dark blue eyes refocused instantly. He smiled, reaching out a hand toward her. "You are right, it is a different time now. Come, let us see the more recent history of this interesting social myth."

They began ambling through the exhibition once more. Esme felt her confidence return as they pointed out things of interest in the cabinets and on the walls.

"Do you know why it was nearly always women who were the bad guys? The witches?" Esme asked him in a tone which said, 'I already know the answer.'

"Yes, I know very well. It is because you are far closer to the earth mysteries and therefore more of an obvious target to those who would keep the mysteries a secret. Not for nefarious purposes but just so people would not be seduced by powers they do not understand." Cursian's tone offered little in the way of compromise.

Esme felt deflated and slightly resentful of his assumptions. Especially as she didn't really understand what he'd meant. Walking in silence for a few moments, she tried to think about his words rather than be petty over how he'd stolen her thunder. Not an easy task.

Wanting to move past the awkwardness, Esme said, "Alright, explain your thinking." She turned toward him and poked him in the chest, amazed at how solid he felt, "And I don't want any of your mystical nonsense. I want a well constructed argument."

He smiled, grabbed her fingers and kissed the ends. Esme gasped, pulling her hand back as though she'd been burned by fire brands of lust. Her reaction brought a wider smile to his face, Esme blushed, feeling foolish and cross.

"I am so glad you asked, beautiful lady. The answer is love," Cursian said.

"What?" Esme stepped back, wondering what the hell he was talking about. His touch confused her completely; who did he think loved whom?

"That is the answer to your question," he said, stopping Esme from backing into a display cabinet. "It is why women are often preoccupied with love and nurturing. There is a stronger imperative than just the expansion of the species. Women have a greater connection to the life force and therefore, understand the importance of love in generating positive energy. Men are often jealous of this connection and they wish to control or destroy it. Without love nothing in this world is possible, women understand this in a way men cannot."

Esme stood still, her head cocked on one side. This man puzzled her immensely. "That sounds deep," she examined his face for a moment. His eyes held a fathomless kindness and his mouth looked soft; he didn't seem to be taking the piss. "Okay, I'll play the game. You're intimating that women are connected to a deeper mystery in the world, therefore we understand instinctively that emotional completion between two people is important." Her academic training took the conversation instantly into the realms of intellectual inquiry rather than an opportunity to flirt. Saving her from further blushes.

"More or less." He smiled at her again.

"So, why the hell are men so damn dense about it?" Esme said with far more bitterness than she'd intended.

His expression grew sad, "Because no system is perfect and men have become corrupted over the generations. They have been dragged from the deeper mysteries and from a more sympathetic understanding of our world. It is hard to kill your enemies in battle if you can see their spirits rise in pain. Men are fighters and hunters', so losing spiritual understanding means life is less painful." Cursian shrugged as though his explanation were both bitter and obvious.

"That's assuming there is a spiritual answer to the problem and one that is affected by shifts in humanities collective consciousness. What's the explanation if one doesn't exist?"

Someone tried to pass them in the narrow corridor between exhibits, Cursian drew Esme close to his body rather than allowing her to step back. Her hands touched his chest as their eyes met; she wasn't the only one to take a sharp breath. They stepped away from each other quickly, both of them surprised by the contact. Esme's knees trembled.

"But you do not believe that and it is belief that makes all things real," his voice quivered slightly.

She laughed, "A fine circular argument."

Esme also realised the conversation had evolved a long way from where it had started but Cursian managed to force her to think about a whole range of incredible concepts. Brains and beauty, she sighed, lost in the contemplation of something wonderful entering her life at such a convenient moment.

They continued to walk hand in hand through the rest of the exhibition. Cursian making some interesting comments about some of the more recent magicians and mediums, he spoke so rudely and dismissively of the likes of Alistair Crowley, that Esme couldn't help but laugh.

After a while, they drifted off in different directions and Esme found herself drawn to a glass cabinet of lesser known witches from the last century. There, at the back, lay a small picture, an old woman sat on an old wooden chair in an old style kitchen, which Esme recognised from her childhood. Her mother had ripped it out of the house when Esme had been about eight years old. She also recognised the woman as her great grandmother. The label even named her as a witch of great renown in the area.

"What the hell?" Esme didn't realise she'd spoken aloud until her brain processed the information from her ears. Her hands stuck to the glass as though it were the only thing which mattered in the world. Esme forced her eyes to the other person in the picture.

The man behind her ancestor made her lungs stop working. Cursian stood stiffly, with his hand on the back of the chair. There could be no mistake and in no way could it be a blood relation. He was identical to the man walking toward her now.

Looking up, Esme started to back away. Memories crashing through her head like an avalanche of cinema snap shots. Images from her childhood, long dormant and seldom remembered reared up threatening to engulf her. They were so intense she stumbled, dizzy and faint. Her world twisting away from her.

"Esme?" Cursian rushed forward, reaching for her, concern written all over his face. That face. A face she had known for her whole life, one which had been absent for a long time.

"Get off me," she pushed his hands away. "Who the hell are you?"

Cursian glanced at the glass cabinet now behind them, "Oh, I see." He turned back having seen the picture, "Esme, I can explain. In fact, I need to explain. But we should return to your flat, you look as though you are going to collapse."

"You are him," Esme whispered, her memory vomiting up pictures of violence and great tenderness.

"Please, Esme. I can explain." He tried to grab her arm.

Esme back peddled, slipping out of his grasp, "I don't think so." She bolted, running headlong for the stairs. Cursian's cry echoed behind her.

She continued to run until the barrier at the nearest underground station stopped her headlong crash through the thinning crowds. Pushing her Oyster card into the machine, she ran through the underground, hit the platform and jumped on a train at random. Fortunately, her instincts, long used to catching trains forced her to catch the right one.

As she watched the stops shunt past, Esme calmed enough to think about what had occurred. Or at least she tried. It didn't work very well. A void opened in her mind and her heart. She felt betrayed, deeply betrayed for some reason she didn't understand. Her mind unable to process the jumble of memories. She couldn't find a way to pin anything down. A secret filing cabinet in her head tipped over, spilling confusion everywhere. Her hands shook violently and tears stung her eyes.

She made it home, firmly locking the door behind her, feeling in turn foolish, furious, anxious and confused. The sign at the museum indicated her great grandmother and 'unnamed companion' were powerful mages. Esme had always enjoyed the strange family stories her grandmother told her, she'd spend hours imagining the bizarre histories for real. Her father had worried about her macabre love of these tales, but her mother thought them harmless enough. Is this why she'd found it so difficult to conform her whole life? Had her parents known about her grandmother and great grandmother? Is that why her father didn't approve? Did he know what kind of family he had married? And why had her mother instilled such a strong sense of Christianity within her, if her heritage was something so different? The one question she couldn't escape rattled inside her head like a relentless maraca. How did Cursian look exactly the same now as he did almost a hundred years ago?

Pieces of a weird jigsaw began coming together. High heels and corporate suits really weren't Esme's life. And Cursian really wasn't who her warped sense of romance wanted him to be.

CHAPTER THREE

The night aged. Esme didn't really notice. She sat at her kitchen table picking at salad and chicken. Wondering how to find Cursian if he didn't turn up. Wondering if she wanted too. Wondering what the hell she'd say to him if she did find him.

Giving up on the chicken, Esme wandered into her lounge, restless and dissatisfied. Peering into the darkness for the hundredth time, her eye caught a deep shadow separating itself from the side street almost opposite. She moved back, squinting to be sure.

Esme almost ran to her front door, throwing the night back as she flung it open. Cursian stopped before mounting the bottom step. Her breath felt ragged and harsh in her chest, a lump the size of a boulder stopping her voice.

"Esme?" Cursian's voice surrounded her, filling her eyes with tears, too much compassion in one word.

She had spent several hours rehearsing what to say when he arrived and now she felt empty of coherent thought. Anger came to her rescue, unblocking the pent-up emotion, as reliable as Big Ben.

"Who the fucking hell are you?" Esme's back hunched as the snarl left her lips.

"Esme?" he suddenly sounded cautious as he mounted the first step.

"I've seen you. And it was you. What kind of sick game are you playing? The British Museum would love to know." Esme held her ground as Cursian mounted another step.

"Please, your anger is painful and powerful."

"I'll give you bloody powerful you bastard. Who the hell are you to have known my family for so long? How the hell is it possible you exist? What are you? And why do you haunt my life?" Esme's stomach clenched, and even as she asked the questions, she knew the answers, somewhere deep inside herself.

Cursian reached the top step, stopping at arm's length. His brow furrowed at her words. "Are you too angry to hear what I have to say? I wanted to talk to you tonight about me, about us. We have had so little time." He offered his hand to her, a gesture of peace.

Esme hugged herself, not wanting his touch, but needing it in her soul to ease the pain filling her heart. "Are you the, Rat Man?" her voice suddenly small, the memory almost painful.

He paused, studying her carefully, "That is how you may remember me, yes. We have known each other for many years, though you have not seen me clearly since you were a child. Can we go inside and talk?"

For a long moment, Esme looked into Cursian's face. She noticed his carefully controlled blank expression. Yet deep in his eyes she saw a different story, she recognised real fear lurking in the dark pools of blue.

"What are you afraid of?" less aggression, she unfolded her arms. His fear made her own more bearable.

Cursian blinked, hesitating, his voice sounding cautious and very controlled, "I cannot afford to create ill will. You were not supposed to discover my difference in such a casual way. Our lives are more complex than you can possibly imagine. Esme, I cannot lose you, I cannot afford to lie to you. Please allow me to enter and I can begin to explain."

She stood on the front step blocking his entrance, watching him, desperate to understand the consequences of letting him into her home. Thoughts and feelings tumbled through her, the predominant and coldly logical one screaming at her not to trust him. And why should she really? Because of some half remembered childhood dream? Esme's aggressive nature made her decision for her. It wanted to know what the hell was going on. It wanted to know how he had become connected to her family and if he was a threat. She moved to one side, allowing him entrance by assent.

"I need you to invite me in, Esme. I have never been in your flat."

She blinked at him, pausing. Bram Stoker's story filled her head, a favourite as a child. "Why?"

"It would not be so cold if you let me answer your questions inside."

"Answer mine first."

A harsh sigh of exasperation filled the space between them. Esme noticed Cursian's jaw working. "Very well, we will do it here. I do not have time for games. I am immortal. I am a mage. I have magical links to your family and have done for more or less the last six hundred years. I am not human and I am the stuff of nightmares, mainly the ones you are considering right now." He stared at her, clearly defiant, looking more like an enraged romantic hero than a monster.

Esme went blank, completely blank, what the hell do you say to a speech like that? How are you supposed to react in middle class England? She turned and shut the door in his face.

Esme leaned her head against her front door, tears falling onto the fashionable flagstone floor. She'd been trying so hard to rationalise what happened in the museum. Maybe he did resemble some relation, his grandfather or something. When she had seen him, however, she realised nobody's genetic coding ran that close. And his words, what he told her, those words hummed inside her mind like vicious electricity. Waiting to shock her the minute she tried to touch them with serious thought. She willed him to be some kind of kinky freak, or a delusional psychopath. But her mind circled once more to the picture and the evidence it presented. Her own instincts and memories wanting her to trust him, despite what her logical mind said. Along with the evidence of her own family trusting him, made her reconsider the psychopath option. She made her decision. Running a hand over her face to brush away foolish tears, Esme grabbed the door handle and yanked it open.

Her shadow filled the light from the doorway. Cursian leaned with arms and legs crossed, against the railing running down the steps. He turned his head as the door opened.

"I want to know what's going on, I want you to come in, but I warn you, the minute you try anything funny I'm calling the police." Esme backed away from the door and watched warily as he came toward her, then past her.

Several minutes later Cursian sat opposite Esme with a large oak table separating them. They both nursed huge mugs of tea. Esme had no idea if Cursian drank tea, she didn't really care and fortunately he proved polite enough to accept the drink. Neither spoke, she felt cast adrift in a reality that had little to do with the whole of the last thirty two years of her life. The world suddenly became very disturbing. How did something like this remain hidden from the rest of reality? She nodded, that was a good question and seemed like a nice detached place to start.

"How is something like you possible?" she frowned, it sounded more reasonable in her head.

"There are many things within your world that live on the edges, blending with humanity and their mundane lives. To be honest it is easier now than ever. You are all so busy, franticly looking for the next emotional fix. Often we do not even have to hide ourselves. Many of us live openly. And much of humanity wants to live the lives we offer. All these quasi faiths and alternative lifestyles accommodate us nicely. No one, nothing, makes you a freak any longer." Cursian shrugged.

"What about you? How did you come about?"

Cursian looked downward, studying his hands as they grasped the mug. "I would choose to tell you my story on another night. I would like to say here and now, I am vampire and I am mage. I have learnt to control one with the other. I am also cursed, as are you, and I think this is a more valuable conversation tonight." He lifted his eyes. He pinned Esme with the intensity of the gaze.

She swallowed the brick lodged painfully in her throat. "Okay. Tell me about this curse of yours."

"It is not mine; it belongs to you as well. The details of how it happened are not currently important, what you do need to know is your family betrayed me to your Master. I do not know how much your Mother told you, but you come from a long line of travellers. These Romanies worked for a creature in the far reaches of Europe several centuries ago. After I released myself from the creature's bondage, I hunted your family decimating the lineage. Finally, only one pair of twins survived, but before I finished what I had begun, I became bound to their lives. This happened through a process of magics I can even now only begin to understand. Your family's line and my life are bound to one mission. This is quite simple, we are to maintain the cosmic balance, ensuring evil never has a chance to dominate good. We work exclusively for neither side. However, our world is naturally inclined toward the darkness. Toward evil. Therefore, we work almost exclusively for the light, hoping to maintain the balance. Your family have always had gifts of various strengths to help me do this and now it is your turn to take up the burden. I left it as long as I thought expedient, but it is necessary to involve you and quickly."

Silence descended and stretched. Esme thought about what he'd told her. He spoke a certain amount of truth; the world did contain more evil deeds than good ones. She couldn't argue with that but why should she be responsible for this? She didn't know whether to laugh or scream at the sheer idiocy of what she heard. "You expect me to believe this?"

"Eventually, you will have no choice but believe me. Since your Mother died, your defences have been weakening. They know where you are, just as I do and they will strike."

"This is rubbish." Esme pushed violently against the table, her chair scraping the floor. "My family is part of some cosmic game to ensure light and dark are maintained in equal balance? Bollocks. I would like you to leave." She turned her back defiantly, but her internal cinema forced more memories to the fore from her subconscious.

"Esme, you have seen the evidence with your own eyes. You know I am what I confess to be, I have known every generation of your family for centuries. I cannot prove this to you, but there is so much you know, if only you would be willing to remember. Think about the, Rat Man," Cursian's voice softened.

"I want you to leave," Esme's tone told a different story.

"No." Cursian paused and spoke gently, "Esme, you are in danger, tonight and every night you deny my truth."

"What, just like that. Just like that I'm supposed to overturn thirty two years of logic and experience?" Esme turned and snapped, suddenly desperate to hang on to her mundane life.

Cursian remained mild, "No, but it is not thirty two years is it? Tell me about the Rat Man. Tell me about the stories I know your Mother told you because it was the only way we were able to smuggle your heritage past your Father."

Esme frowned, "What does that mean, 'Past my Father'?"

"Your Father didn't want you or your Mother involved. She sacrificed everything for him and because of this our efforts to maintain the balance were greatly weakened. This will make your task a great deal harder. You have also been denied the training necessary for you to control what you are and you must learn quickly otherwise harm will come to us."

"Are you criticising my family?"

Cursian paused, "Yes. Your Mother made some hard decisions and they harmed us all in the end. But she loved your Father and he was a powerful mortal. Unfortunately, he had no time for the occult. The only options your Mother had left were instilling a strong Christian faith in you, placing protection around you and your home. These have begun to collapse now she has died, leaving you vulnerable."

"What are these gifts I'm supposed to have?" Esme began to feel sick.

"You are strong, you were strong as a child. You have certain advantages others of your line did not have. But investigating these ideas is not wise currently, your talents should be developed with time and training. All I want for now is for you to help me protect you."

"That's what my faith is for."

"To a certain extent," Cursian nodded. "But it is too simplistic in your case. I think true belief in any major faith will protect you from the darker forces, but you are going to be targeted and I can guarantee your Lord has given you gifts of power to help you fight your corner. He will not want you to stand by idly allowing the darkness to take you. David fought Goliath with the Lord's blessing."

Esme sat down abruptly, "This is too much. I wouldn't swallow any of this, but for all the years I have remembered your face. The brush of your lips on my skin as you said goodbye." Pain blossomed in Esme's chest as she willingly roved through her memories for the first time. "I was so young, not even five. I remember the rats streaming into my room, three huge rats crawling up the bed. I screamed, my Mother came running, yelling in a language I had never heard. The rats ran downstairs with my Mother following. I climbed from the bed, almost falling down after them. Light from the kitchen flooded the hall, making everything clear. You," she looked directly at Cursian. "You had a sword. You had come from the garden. The three rats turned into men, ugly men, they where trying to hurt my Mother. You killed them, moving with blurring speed. The blade glinted in the light as you sliced through their flesh. They vanished. Mother began to weep. I walked down the hall; you came to the door of the kitchen and knelt. 'Cariad, I want you to remember this, I shall not see you for many years, but know I will always protect you if I can. Be good to your Mother, she is sad. Do as your Father wishes, he means well. I will always love you and never forget me.' Then you left." Esme began to cry softly, missing her family so much it felt like a weight of indescribable proportions held her down.

Arms circled her body, lifting her with no discernable effort and she felt disinclined to argue with such tenderness. She sobbed uncontrollably into Cursian's chest as he carried her to the lounge.

Eventually, the sobbing subsided. With it came a realisation she sat enclosed by a man who'd just stripped her of her reality. Besides which, could she really describe him as a man? Esme squirmed away. A thousand thoughts raced through her head leaving her feeling sick again. Her adult mind fought with childhood memories. Remembered conversations with her Mother, before her Father sent her away to school.

"Sorry, I don't know what came over me," Esme mumbled. She reached for a box of tissues, removing herself from the sofa altogether. She felt Cursian silently watching her back. "I'll make more tea." The save all conversation changer, inherited directly from her Mother. No situation too difficult that tea didn't help. She often thought there should be a tea super hero. Maybe she had become the super hero now, fighting the forces of coffee... Okay, random thoughts were not necessarily going to help.

"We have no need of more tea, Esme. Please come and sit and talk. We need to talk." Cursian's voice sent tremors through her over stretched nerves. "I understand your confusion. I too have had my world shattered by conflicting notions, paradigm shifts so vast it seems the world is never real again. I understand you feel as though you have walked into a world from a novel. Some sick reality that makes life so complex it is beyond your grasp. Let me ease the confusion, Esme. You remember enough to know you can trust me."

Esme sat.

"You do not have to sit quite so far away," Cursian smiled at her.

"Yep, I do. Being near you confuses me. You don't understand." She looked at her hands, feeling embarrassed at the words spilled from her, "You are the one I have always dreamed about. Your face I've seen a thousand times and your words have haunted every emotional relationship I've had with men." Esme glared across the room, feeling the heat in her face as she blushed. "And I always thought you a figment of my imagination, but here you are, yet just as untouchable as ever. You're not even human!"

She noticed Cursian wince, "Sorry."

"Do not apologise, you are correct. I am not human or mortal. And things between you and I are excessively complex, even beyond our family ties."

"What do you mean?" suspicion flared through her.

"We need to leave that for now. I do not want to worry you unduly."

"Frankly, you missed the boat on that score."

Silence descended, Esme considered her next move. "What's this protection you need to do?"

She watched Cursian's face fill with relief. "Thank you. Thank you for listening and trusting."

CHAPTER FOUR

A burden lifted from Cursian's shoulders as he realised Esme processed enough of the information given to her to begin to think clearly. He slid up the sofa toward her chair. The need to be physically close almost overwhelmed any control and good sense remaining. Since the moment of her birth, this vital young woman dominated his life. It had been centuries since his blood pulsed through his veins this hotly. He had missed her so much and for so long. Having her close and not being able to take her in his arms seemed cruel.

Take a breath and get a hold of yourself, he thought.

"The first thing we need to do is examine what your mother did before her death." Cursian found himself holding out his hand. Esme's small warm palm fitted perfectly as she responded to the unconscious movement. He coughed. Subtle vibrations catching him off guard, how could she do that?

"How do we do that?" Esme's green eyes snared his gaze. He started at the echo of his thoughts.

How can a vampire and master mage, feel like a school boy in front of a woman? Just an ordinary human woman. The pulse struck at him again. Cursian frowned. This wasn't from Esme; it didn't have her scent within it. Someone or thing directed this from elsewhere.

"What's wrong?" Esme asked, concern flowing from her at his obvious distress.

"Esme, I think we might be too late. Something is coming." Cursian rose swiftly from the sofa, still holding Esme's hand. He barely noticed her stumble after him. Mercifully, she remained quiet.

The kitchen of her flat looked into a small ground floor garden. Cursian knew every inch of that space. He had spent several weeks watching Esme's nightly routines, trying hard not to kill the boyfriend on sight. He even knew where she kept the key to her back door. As he reached for it, blinding light filled the garden and flooded the kitchen. Esme screamed, more in shock than pain. Cursian threw up his arm and simply smashed through the door, key forgotten in his hand.

The flash ended. Darkness swallowed the garden. Cursian's eyes adjusted far faster than a mortal's would, Esme stumbled to his side.

"What the hell was that?" she rubbed her eyes, blinking into the night.

"That is trouble. Esme, I want you to think carefully about your home and push that thought outward, away from you."

She frowned, "This is my first lesson?"

"Yes, and it is less than ideal. I believe we are under attack. I need to connect you to your home and me. Finding you through your connection to your home will be less harsh than any other way." His sense of urgency translated itself to Esme, her pulse raced, her confusion plain.

He watched her close her eyes, felt her try to breathe deeply and evenly. Obedient in the face of his fear. Cursian found his concentration slipping, as he tasted that pulse thudding in her throat. He shook his head clearing the image. In that instance Esme yelped. Cursian swung his eyes forward. Facing the two of them were three vampires and over a dozen misshapen creatures. Cursian froze recognising those gathered before them.

"Well, Cursian your strength isn't what it once was, how the devil are you, my love?"

Cursian watched the only female vampire among the group, step forward. Dread clutched his stomach at the sight of her. Long almost white blond hair reached her waist, reflecting the streetlights, making some of the long strands look like living flame encircling her. Tall and willow thin, she glided toward them, ice blue eyes fixed on Esme. Cursian moved to cover his mortal companion with his own body.

"De'hevda, take your pack of fiends and leave before someone is hurt. You have no business here, not now. Esme would not be fair game and I know how much you love your games." Ice cold anger filled his voice, anger at the creatures before him and himself. He should have seen this coming far sooner, should have approached Esme sooner, his own fear of losing her, endangered her.

De'hevda moved closer still, translucent skin firm over high cheekbones and narrow chin. Intense red lips the only real colour in her face. A dress of pale chiffons and silks brushed against Cursian's boots, moving like wind over her almost perceived body. Cursian refused to step back, forcing De'hevda to look up slightly.

"You don't mean that, lover." Her hand reached toward his face, Cursian pushed Esme backwards and stepped back himself. He didn't want contact with this fiend.

"You do not wish to fight me, De'hevda and I am not your lover." Cursian began to gather his power, slowly and carefully. He blended with every living thing around him. His talent borrowed from the trees, grass, insects and animals, even the earth itself, weaving all into a complex pattern of mage craft.

The one advantage he maintained over the creatures inhabiting this world remained his unique power source. The vampires around him derived their automation and strength from a single despicable fountainhead. He pulled from the very universe itself. His mage talents now controlled everything vampire. It had taken decades of constant control to make his natural impulses stay bound and chained within his body. The incessant checks and balances became instinct, as he grew older.

"No, Cursian, I don't want to fight you, I want to taste your new toy. I can't smell you on her, have you been denying yourself her delights?" De'hevda smiled coyly, her eyes shining.

Esme yelped from behind him as she came face to face with De'hevda. Cursian hadn't seen her move, maybe he really was becoming too old. Esme froze with shock, nose to nose with a real predator.

"You are rather lovely, Esme dear. And you smell divine. I don't know how Cursian has managed to stay away from you all these years." De'hevda raised her hand toward Esme's face.

Cursian growled, moving forward himself with the same unearthly speed. He caught her hand turning her to face him. "You want to play games, monster, you play them with me."

De'hevda smiled up at him and Cursian realised he played into her hands by allowing her this close to him. It was true they were once lovers, a long time ago, but only for a brief while. However, Cursian's already aroused body felt deprived. As De'hevda's lithe strength almost swooned into him, Cursian's control began to slip. Remembered perversions and pleasures stimulated him. De'hevda, hardly any younger than himself had welcomed the darkness and madness of vampire, adapting effortlessly to the depravation, which filled their world. His nostrils flared as he pushed the female away. He never wanted to sample those particular pleasures again, not while he held onto his sanity. The others laughed, forming a tighter circle. Cursian had allowed too much distance between himself and the house. The monsters cut off their escape.

"Enough of these games, I want what I came for," De'hevda glided slowly this time toward Esme.

A cacophony of sound rose from the gathered creatures. Their misshapen bodies wove back and forth. The beings with long arms beat the ground with their fists. Those with foreshortened limbs leapt from foot to foot. Faces gathered from the worst nightmares grinned with hideous parody. Their metaphysical stink filled the air making Cursian want to gag against their foulness.

He pulled his resources together more quickly, no longer caring if they tried to block his attempt to rid the garden of their presence. He effortlessly linked with Esme, feeling her presence beside him as a being of energy as well as a physical person. The wards of protection her mother placed around the flat came alive under her searching awareness. He realised Esme tried to allow her instinct to guide her mind, rather than conscious thought.

Just as De'hevda reached for Esme, he felt everything he sourced through his own talents vanish. Suddenly, he had nothing to throw at their enemies, but beside him, Esme began to vibrate with power.

"I want you to leave us. Now," Esme's voice sounded as though it came from a deep well within her. Cursian switched his vision to see pure energy. As she raised her hand, and before anyone prevented her, or told her such a thing should not be possible, blue flame shot from her outstretched hand. She used herself, her mother's protection and Cursian's own power. He gave willingly, not wanting to deprive her of her only real defence.

Her instinct made her reach for De'hevda, but the flame flowed around the vampire's protection. However, the creatures directly behind her were not so lucky. Ozone and burning flesh filled the night air as screams of agony rose from those caught. One of the creatures disintegrated instantly in a ball of blue fire. Its companion roasted as though caught in a microwave, its fat cooking from the inside. Now ignoring De'hevda, Cursian watched Esme concentrate solely on everything else invading her home's precincts.

Cursian watched as flesh bubbled and popped. The other vampires, both with ebony skin and lean frames, began to panic. Cursian attacked them. With a subtle understanding of magic way beyond any mortal's power, he reached for the dark energy connecting them to their Master. They were young and inexperienced. De'hevda brought them simply as a window dressing. They had no protection, so he ruthlessly severed the cords of power tying them to their Master. They began to fade in front of his eyes. Moving swiftly forward, catching the pair by their throats, he squeezed the remaining life force from them. He ripped their heads off, ignoring the gore and blood flowing round him. Turning toward Esme, he found De'hevda beginning to fade, drifting back to her Master. Neither he nor Esme could break through her defences.

Esme screamed at the disappearing figure, "If you ever come near me or mine again I'll rip your damned throat out myself. He is not your lover, Bitch and I am not your victim, you are looking at the next, Scion of the Prophecy!"

Cursian turned in time to see De'hevda smile just before she vanished, "I'll have your heart on a plate and enjoy it as supper, mortal witch. You will never be able to satisfy Cursian's lusts, no matter how he controls his needs. We will meet again, vampire whore."

Cursian noticed Esme tense as though about to run toward the ghost, "No!" he sprang forward. Covering the distance in a blinding flash, he wrapped an arm about Esme's waist and lifted at the same time. Yanking her toward him, he cut her off from the energy sustaining the burning power. The blue flame subsided. Esme fainted into his arms, instantly becoming a dead weight.

For the briefest of moments, Cursian didn't sense her pulse. The eternity ended as an erratic beat filled his head. He sank to the ground, head bent over Esme's still form in relief. He breathed in the smell of discharged power and the stink of battle, enjoying the sudden solitude, the returning peace and cleaner smell of deep night.

CHAPTER FIVE

Esme woke slowly, becoming aware of her familiar surroundings a piece at a time. Bright autumn light filled her room and chased the last of the winter night away. The changing seasons always made Esme slightly uncomfortable. She often wished it were possible to move from spring to summer, or autumn to winter without the messy bit in between, the bit that meant you never knew what to wear or where to go.

She sighed and rolled over, not yet thinking about anything but the shift in seasons. Random snatches of song filled her head. She began to try and consciously remember the words to Black Magic Woman, forcing out thoughts from the previous night. Her room slowly filled with the smell of baking bread.

Esme frowned, groaning as she sat up, the duvet fell away from her naked body. She frowned harder, sleeping naked was normal, but why couldn't she quite remember how she managed to get to bed? Esme noticed her clothes, neatly folded on the chair. This finally spurred her into full movement.

Stiffly, Esme pulled on her cream silk dressing gown, trying to run her fingers through her thick dark hair as it lay in rat's tails across her shoulders. She shuffled down the hall. Who would be cooking in her flat? Reaching the kitchen, she stood in the doorway surveying a mess of flour and pans. The one thing Esme never designed her kitchen to cope with was cooking. She stared at her beautiful rustic table and felt slightly afraid. Domesticity worried the corners of a pained mind.

"Morning, how are you feeling?" a light voice penetrated the beginnings of panic.

Esme glanced up, a small grey haired woman moved efficiently from sink to tabletop. Dark eyes smiled warmly, the perfect image of your ideal grandmother, and a complete stranger.

"Erm," Esme frowned even harder. "Um, I feel hungover and as though I've been trampled by thousands of angry dwarves. Who are you?" an edge of anger laced Esme's question.

"My name is, Brigit. I'm a friend of Cursian's. He called before dawn and asked me to come over to keep an eye on you. He's worried. He also mentioned you usually don't have much to eat in the house. One of the few good things about London seems to be you can buy almost anything at any time of day. The bread's done and the teapot is hot, help yourself."

Esme sat. Too confused to do otherwise, last night descended on her in one foul rush of noisome memories. "I think I'm going to be sick."

"No, you're not," Brigit replied lightly, "drink this and breathe. You're going to have a panic attack if you don't breathe."

Esme picked up the glass and sipped the proffered liquid. Juice, some kind of juice. She drank more heavily, the slightly sweet mixture going down with ease. She didn't have the energy to be confused by the other woman's presence in her home. To be honest the relief of having company outweighed the invasion. She missed Cursian, which made her worry about her sanity even more than the previous night's events.

"There, that'll help, juice and homeopathy, always good for panicky situations. Also, good for hangovers, of any kind," Brigit told her. Esme looked up as Brigit sat opposite, fresh bread, butter, honey and jam filling the space between them. Her dark eyes stopped smiling, "How are you really, Esme?"

Esme felt tears almost brim over. She opened her eyes wide willing herself not to cry. "Um," too late, the hot liquid spilled down her face in great long rivulets.

"It's alright, love, you're in shock, the juice will help. I've put the same stuff in the tea, just eat and drink for awhile. It's still quite early we have lots of time to talk before Cursian can come and make a nuisance of himself." Brigit smiled kindly and reached for Esme's hand, squeezing it.

Esme smiled slightly in return, the edges quivering as another wave of emotion caught her by surprise. Esme hadn't cried in months, she had barely wept since the initial news of her parent's death, now it seemed to be happening at the drop of a scone. She smiled more strongly as her sense of humour made its presence known.

"I think we have a plan, food would be great," she said, reaching for the bread.

An hour later, the two women sat comfortably in the kitchen, drinking tea and talking about ordinary life. Esme told Brigit about her school, the drop out years, university, and life in London. Brigit mentioned she owned a small bookshop, concentrating on first editions, had no family to speak of, but enjoyed a great many hobbies. Esme mentioned her own hobbies, which seemed slightly psychopathic in comparison to Brigit's knitting, weaving and felt making.

They had a lively debate about the rights and wrongs of defending yourself against attacks, when Esme went into detail about the Japanese principles of self-defence. Her martial experience covered several arts, making her reflexes sharp and her body fit. Brigit, despite her disapproval, told Esme the mental and physical discipline would come in useful. This made the previous night's events return to Esme in a rush. Never one to be a coward, she took a deep breath and plunged in.

"Okay, let's change the subject, what the hell is happening to me, and how do you know Cursian? You're not a monster are you?"

Brigit's eyebrows rose. "Interesting use of words, I wouldn't use the 'm' word around Cursian. He has a hard time reconciling what he is at the best of times. You rejecting him in such a way would hurt a great deal."

Esme snorted, "Oh, and having my garden full of freaks to which I then set fire, with some kind of cosmic power, is something I can reconcile is it?"

Brigit paused, "No, no I don't suppose it is. How do you want to do this? Me tell you all I can, or you ask questions?"

"I'll ask questions I think. How do you know Cursian? Who are you really? And who the hell is he?"

Brigit frowned, "You know who he is, and what he is, you know you are a part of this Prophecy. And there is no avoiding your destiny if you want to continue to live."

"Well, that summed it all up and made everything so much clearer, thanks." Esme sat back in her chair with a woof of silk.

"Calm down. I think me telling you things in order will be easier. At least I know where to start." Brigit sighed when she noticed Esme's scowl.

"I know accepting a different version of reality is hard. I know these creatures, including Cursian, defy logic. If vampires, goblins and werewolves really did exist, why aren't they striving for equal rights along with everyone else? The reason for this is within the darkness of the world they populate. Anything purely human but seemingly occult has become increasingly accepted, Wiccans, Satanists, mystic healers, all of them. It's all part of the same world, but they, themselves, either don't know about the other stuff or are willing to keep the secret. The world of demons and vampires is dark, the truly hidden esoteric world. Remember, a thousand years ago the world was flat, and nothing flew except birds. Even ten years ago, reaching Mars was a dream, never mind Saturn's moon. What I'm trying to explain is that there truly are more things in Heaven and Earth. However, most of us just want to ignore it."

"But people must notice these things if we've been living with this stuff for centuries?" Esme had become interested despite herself.

"Where do you think all the stories come from? They had to start somewhere. Admittedly, many of them are built on the back of earlier stories, but they all have an origin. And religion, how do people make miracles happen?" Brigit smiled.

"People don't, God does," Esme stated flatly.

"Ok, but what is God? How can this deity make himself known? How does he operate through these people, what are they tapping into? It's all part of the same thing, it's just that vampire and other creatures are made of pure darkness, whereas angels for instance are usually pure light. Unfortunately, the darkness likes to feed in this world, whereas the light tries to ignore humanity as much as possible." Brigit began buttering another slice of bread. Esme noticed her hands were covered in liver spots and wondered for the first time exactly how old this woman might be.

"So, Cursian's made of the same stuff as God?" Esme felt incredulous.

Brigit laughed, "Oh, he'd like that one. No, well, only in as much as we all are, it's all part of the same thing, we are all linked, just on different wavelengths, operating at different levels, or vibrations. God is the highest, purest vibration. Cursian isn't." Brigit had a perfect teaching tone in her voice.

"Okay, but what are you?" Esme asked.

Brigit smiled, "I'm a witch. Not to be confused with any faith orientated sect. I just study nature and have learnt to accept her gifts. I am also here to keep track of you and Cursian. He decided a long time ago he needed allies outside of this Prophecy that he could rely on to remember details and histories. Sometimes being six hundred years old you lose track of vital information. I think he's worried about the possibility of either going senile or having his mind destroyed before he can pass on all he needs to, if and when he's ever going to stop."

Esme's mouth hung open, "Six hundred years? Shit, that's an age difference and a half." Her mind rewound through the centuries, "He experienced the plague?"

"Some of them, yes, I had to learn Latin to translate the early books. It doesn't make for easy reading."

"Can I read them?" the scholar in Esme became overexcited.

"Asking Cursian directly isn't out the question. There are some subjects he won't discuss, but general histories he can remember he's happy to share."

"Cool, I could do a doctorate in medieval history."

"I thought your degree was business?"

"It is, but that's boring, imagine having a primary source at your fingertips."

Brigit smiled, "Esme, how would you explain to the academic world where you received the information?"

"Listen, this is the first bit of good news I've had, don't burst my bubble!" Esme shook her head, focusing on the now, still trying to understand. "Anyway, you keep track and write things down for him. And I'm part of some cosmic plot, but what happened last night?"

Brigit rose slowly from the chair, switching on the kettle again, "Last night you were attacked. Your mother set up some very complex defences that she must have maintained regularly, but since her death, they have unravelled. Cursian became increasingly aware of your vulnerability. But he had to go through you to fix what your mother created, hence his need to get involved so fast. It had never been his plan to introduce you to your heritage in such a way. However, he didn't have much choice, especially after the incident at the museum."

"But those things that I... that fried?" Esme's voice sounded hollow in her ears as she remembered her actions.

"From the little he told me before the sun rose, the lesser vampires and ghouls had actually manifested in your garden. They took form through some enormous amount of power, which is a good thing because it'll have drained your enemies. You apparently did something last night very few people, and I mean almost nothing mortal, has ever managed. De'hevda unfortunately is old in herself, her power is great thanks to Cursian, thus she escaped." Brigit chuckled, "But she won't be happy. Tormenting your mother was her favourite pastime, having you sending her packing will not do her pride any good."

"My mother had to deal with these things?" Esme pulled her dressing gown around her more tightly, feeling sympathy suddenly for her lonely parent.

"Yes, though her power was nowhere near yours, we were on a par and your father hated it all. He's the reason you knew nothing growing up. He also banned Cursian from seeing either you or your mother. They could have disobeyed, but your mother respected his wishes and Cursian would do nothing to jeopardise you."

"That'll explain Cursian's snippy comments."

"Hmm, I warn you now, I don't think he'll ever like or remember your father with kindness. As far as Cursian is concerned, he is responsible for your mother's death and placing your life in danger too many times to count."

Esme fell silent thinking about Brigit's comments. Having been raised believing in the supernatural ability of the Church, Esme found the esoteric mumbo jumbo Brigit described relatively easy to swallow. If God were possible, and she sincerely believed he existed, then why not demons and monsters? Besides, her own memories gave her first hand testament to much of what Brigit told her. When considering her own place in these theories, Esme shrugged, was she some kind of celestial hero? Last night seems to have given proof to some weird cosmic shit coming her way, but hero stretched it somewhat. All Esme wanted to do was destroy that smug bitch who thought she owned Cursian. And what about his lordship?

Esme's heart missed a beat as she remembered feeling him close to her, her stomach lurching to the side. She certainly remembered him from her early childhood, she certainly found him almost irresistible and she found herself wanting to trust him completely. Cursian felt right, felt comfortable. Felt dangerous and safe all at once. She felt as though he had been a part of her forever.

The 'L' word flitted through her mind. She smiled, more like lust than love surely, too soon for anything else. Besides, didn't the storybook cliché follow, the heroine falls for the dark stranger? The only trouble being, Cursian wasn't human. The thought made Esme blanch physically.

"What is it?" Brigit asked, obviously having watched Esme's thought processes.

"Cursian's not human."

"No, he isn't, why?"

Esme blushed.

"Oh, well that's inevitable." Brigit smiled, but Esme noticed the sadness in her eyes.

"What's inevitable?"

"Esme, you really ought to talk to Cursian about this, not me. I don't feel comfortable telling you about his emotional life, such as it is. He's really very private about his feelings for mortals." Brigit patted Esme's hands where they lay in her lap, clutching her dressing gown.

"But you know something."

"Yes, and it's complicated. I think it'll be harder for you to understand than everything else you are currently being asked to deal with. Why don't we stop talking about all these deep and meaningful things and go out for the rest of the day? Blow away your cobwebs, I'll show you a side of London you've never noticed before."

CHAPTER SIX

Brigit took Esme to Hyde Park. As they sat on a park bench Brigit began to explain to Esme how to view the world in a new, deeper way.

"Tell me what you see," Brigit said as a woman walked passed them.

Esme shrugged, "I see a business woman in a rush, she's a secretary her shoes aren't overly expensive and she has children. Her lunch box has Doctor Who stickers on it."

Esme looked at Brigit for confirmation. The older woman's lip's were pursed, "Try looking deeper, Esme."

Esme concentrated; slipping into the same space her mind occupied the previous night. The world changed. White coronas of light appeared around all the trees and the woman altered radically. A halo of colours appeared around her, yellow predominant with red and ugly shades of green.

"Whoa, what am I seeing?" Esme asked breathlessly.

"She is a mother, but is in emotional pain, she is angry and jealous. I suspect her husband is having an affair," Brigit sounded sad. Esme liked the old woman for being such a romantic.

They spent the rest of the afternoon spotting and interpreting different people and their lives. It brought a completely new meaning to 'people watching'. Esme had a wail of a time, finding the task both easy and informative.

Brigit finally rose as the shadows lengthened giving Esme a final piece of advice, "Just remember that all the stories are true. Some of the detail is far from the mark, such as garlic against vampires, and mirrors, but all myths exist in one form or another. Esme, you can never again take your life and reality for granted. Well, that's enough for one day. Dusk is coming and if we aren't at your flat when Cursian gets there, he'll have a fit."

The trip home on the tube proved quiet. Esme absorbed this new information, her rational mind fighting her emotional memories. She soon gave up. A lesson Esme grasped early in life had been to allow things to just roll over you. Things change and you adjust, acceptance always comes with time. Mind you, some things were a lot easier to accept than others and this lot would take a huge amount of time to incorporate.

Soon Esme sat at her kitchen table watching Brigit make chicken pie and apple crumble. She had offered to help, but after Brigit caught her eating more than she baked, Esme found herself shooed from the area. The doorbell rang. Esme grabbed the jam (damn she was going to have to do serious gym time at this rate), and wandered toward the front door.

As she reached the door Esme's stomach lurched uncomfortably. She grimaced at the jam, knowing it had more to do with Cursian's imminent arrival than the sweet sticky mess she'd been sticking her fingers into, but blaming the jam made more sense.

She opened the door, smiled and began to say hello, but faced Matt. Esme snapped her jaw shut, cold night air brought the smell of wet London streets into her flat, she shivered. She'd forgotten him completely. Her answering machine flashed quickly at the corner of her eye.

"Esme, hi, we need to talk." Matt dragged a bunch of flowers from behind his back, his hand covered in a thick white bandage. "You haven't returned any of my calls." A defiant tone laced his voice.

Esme blinked at him for several seconds. He looked as though he came from another world, another time. "I binned my mobile and I've been ignoring my machine. So, no, I don't think we need to talk, goodbye." She began to close the door.

Matt jammed his foot between the door and its closing companion. "Esme, we are going to talk, now or later I don't care."

Esme's mouth thinned, "Fine." She flung open the heavy door, catching the latch at the same time knowing Cursian would appear sooner or later. As she strode to the lounge, she heard Matt shut the door. She thumped the jam pot on a side table and took up a position in front of the fireplace.

"Well?" had it only been three days since they were lovers? When she looked into Matt's slightly florid face and remembered Cursian's, anger welled up inside Esme for having put up with the worm for so long.

"Esme," his voice grated. "I want you to come back. I need you in the business." His right hand reached for her arm, she saw bruises. Esme stepped away out of arm's reach. She found his rational tone scarier than the few rants she picked up on her machine.

"I know that, you can't operate without me and that woman you hired as a secretary is useless. But I am not coming back to you or your business." She noticed the flowers had joined the jam.

"I'll raise your retainer." Strong arms reached out toward her.

"No." Esme moved backward.

"I want you." Matt continued to advance. Esme smelt alcohol.

"No." She stood her ground.

Matt lunged forward. "I want you back, Esme and I will have you back one way or another." He grabbed her throat and upper arm, hands like a vice despite the bandage.

Esme gagged, her breath instantly cut off. She punched Matt hard, full in the face, coming across his left arm. He released her throat and cried out, reaching for his left cheek. The punch landed at a bad angle, Esme knew she should finish this quickly. Matt might now be going to seed, but he had incredible strength and durability, they play fought often. She aimed a low kick but only managed to get a glancing blow off his left knee. Matt retaliated by running at her. Esme twisted off to the side, her training making the move pure reflex. Tangling herself in the sofa, Esme hit the floor, causing a table to crash. She had no room to fight. Esme heard Brigit call. Shit, Esme didn't want to give this lunatic a hostage.

At the thought, Matt rolled toward her, catching her between the edge of the sofa and his sweaty body. Esme didn't move fast enough to get away. He rolled onto her. She lashed out, catching him another punch to the side of the face. With no room to move her hips into the blow, it lacked her true power. She aimed the next one at the side of his throat. Matt had actually listened to her talk about her training. It turned him on having such a violent girlfriend. He twisted his head enough to distort the punch, stopping it from damaging the carotid artery. Esme screamed in frustration as he became more secure across her body. Both his hands were fully occupied trying to counter Esme's training and desperation, he obviously hadn't heard Brigit. Esme's mind flew from panic, to blind rage, to cold hard detachment, to terrible paralysing fear as she realised she might lose this fight.

That fear unlocked memories she had spent years fighting, but instead of paralysis, she allowed her instinct to take over, becoming more animal than human. With both her hands held hard into the carpet above her head, she tensed, forcing her attacker to push down harder. With one desperate move, she pulled her right arm downward in an arc, her left still trapped by the sofa. It worked, his weight shifted uncontrollably to his left. Esme used strong thigh muscles in her left leg to push upward, twisting him further. He fell away, releasing her right arm but maintaining a crushing grip on her left. Esme followed his energy. She rolled onto him, but found herself unable to reach for an advantage fast enough. He continued the revolution once more. Esme screamed incoherently as the bookcase blocked her escape. Hardly hearing his threats, she felt his now free hand reach for her jeans, low hipster jeans, with completely inadequate poppers, that duly popped with one hard yank. The action spurred Esme.

"Damn it, woman, hold still and this needn't hurt either of us! You've always liked it rough, stop bitching," he grunted, spittle falling onto her face.

Esme raised her head, jaws snapping, he smashed her face hard with his free hand, her vision blurred. Her body suddenly relaxed against her will.

Just as he reached once more for her jeans, the weight and stink of his body vanished. Esme heard a cry such as you hear enraged lions make on the television. Shadows moved around her with incomprehensible speed. She curled up, spinning into a crouching position, trying to shake loose the dizziness. Cursian's back came into view and Matt's face, slowly going purple, held several inches above the vampires head, hard against a wall. She caught sight of Brigit standing in the middle of the room moving her mouth. Words slowly made sense.

"Cursian, stop! You'll kill him!" the older woman repeated.

Esme swung her head back toward Cursian. She moved with all the speed adrenaline can muster and sprang toward the vampire. She grabbed his arm and pulled down. Noticing just the one arm held Matt at least eighteen inches off the floor.

"Cursian, release him! Don't kill him here, please." Esme pulled. Matt dropped, she felt sure it had nothing to do with her pulling on the vampire's arm. Esme hadn't felt anything give. She glanced down, saw the man take a tortured breath. She turned to the vampire.

Esme hardly recognised him.

Cursian's skin had somehow hardened, pulled tight, almost like a mask. His lips were thin, pulling back, showing his elongated and incredibly wicked looking incisors, which made vampires famous. These two things combined caused him to appear other, different in a way no human would ever be, despite bad plastic surgery. Esme's breath hissed out of her body. As she looked into his eyes, Esme saw nothing of the man she knew. It felt as though she looked into death itself, if such a thing were possible. His once deep blue eyes were almost black as the pupils expanded, and there appeared to be no humanity, nothing. A void of death. Esme stepped back, instinct making her more afraid of this creature than Matt.

Cursian turned away as she moved back. Bowing his head as he did so, saying, "Don't move, control your fear. I need to hunt. I need to feed." His voice had deepened further, almost a guttural rumble.

Esme stiffened, attempting to regain control of her pulse. Matt however, began to move and whimper, trying to crawl away from the darkness before him. Cursian stiffened as all predators do before they kill. Esme heard him growl, she watched his body move toward the human figure dragging itself across the carpet. She grabbed the last dregs of her adrenaline and stepped up, intercepting the vampire.

"Cursian, Cursian, look at me. Look at me and tell me what you see, tell me who I am," her voice rang clear as a bell. Esme made a mental note to give herself several million gold stars for courage if she ever got out of this alive.

The vampire switched his attention to Esme. She locked eyes with death and almost choked on her plan. Her breath and heart rate increased almost out of control.

Swallowing, she continued to look at Cursian but said to the others, "If you want to live, Matt stay very still and stay quiet. Brigit, move to stand between Matt and the door, don't let him run. Take the lamp beside you and hit him with it if he starts to move again." She watched the older woman obey her orders from her periphery. Esme concentrated solely on Cursian. She stepped right up close, bending her head upward slightly to maintain eye contact.

"Cursian, who am I?" her voice quiet, intimate.

"You are the, Scion of the Prophecy. I must protect you," his voice cracked.

She still faced unblinking death, but Esme felt more than saw the darkness begin to shift. "Yes, I am. But I am more. You know that and I feel it. I mean more to you than simple destiny."

"You, Esme," Cursian blinked and within the beat of her heart he flooded back. His skin fleshed out, his lips covered his evilly sharp teeth, his blue eyes filled with humanity and his gentle energy washed over her. Esme almost fainted again with relief. Cursian however, looked as though he'd die of shame.

CHAPTER SEVEN

She has seen me as a monster.

The words echoed repeatedly in his head. Cursian tried to turn away but small persistent hands grabbed him.

"Don't love, please." Esme's voice sounded like the most gentle of spring breezes trying to calm his frantic mind.

He couldn't bring himself to look into her eyes. The fear he witnessed moments before proved sufficient to control his vampiric nature, but the man did not wish to confront the consequences. Then the meaning of her words penetrated the haze of self-loathing. She'd used an endearment, not his name.

Matt chose that moment to whimper. The spear of joy flashing through Cursian died. The mortal had curled into a small ball, head pulled into his neck and legs tucked up tight. He leaned into the corner formed by another bookcase and the wall. Small as she was, Brigit appeared to tower over the cringing, sniffling man.

Esme shifted position, which meant he would have to move her to reach the snivelling creature. Her intension remained clear; he would not have access to the mortal. Why that should be, Cursian couldn't fathom, the mortal should suffer interminable pain for his actions.

"What do we do with him?" Brigit asked.

"I can ensure he is never found," Cursian said, knowing it to be a fact. Esme glanced back at him, speculation replaced by understanding as she registered his intent.

"I don't think so. We simply need to leave him somewhere so he can find his own way home."

Matt's head shot up. "You do, and I'll tell the police lover boy there is a monster who tried to kill me!"

Esme crouched down, emphasising her anger. "If you do, we will deny it and I currently have the bruises to show you tried to rape me. You filthy piece of scum!"

Her anger beat at Cursian. He wanted to destroy the mortal for producing such rage and fear in his Scion. Never mind the intent of invading her body.

The thought forced a hole in Cursian's control. The vampire swimming gladly to the surface once more.

Matt opened his mouth, Cursian spoke trying to head off his imminent loss of control, "Be careful what you say, little man. I have enough control not to choke the life out of you here, but Esme isn't with me every moment of the night."

"I can create a spell to help him forget what's happened." Brigit made it sound like the most normal thing in the world. Cursian saw Esme glance at her in surprise. He kept forgetting how alien his world was to his Scion. It helped to pull his humanity back.

"I can't believe you're screwing a monster," Matt spat toward Esme.

The comment came so unexpectedly that for an instant, he couldn't believe his ears but the wave of rage from Esme almost knocked him off his feet. Cursian watched as she sprang forward, caught hold of Matt's collar, and used her anger to haul him upright. She pinned him to the wall.

Esme hissed, "Listen you snivelling, shit, you have just tried to force me to have sex with you. I want to scalp your balls right now and feed the skin to you, slice by slice. And I could get Cursian to help me do that to you."

The ferocity of her threat warmed a dark part of Cursian's heart. He smiled, a low growl of pleasure reverberating through him at the thought.

Esme continued, "But I want you gone. I don't want to see that nasty face of yours again and going to the police means I will have too. Understand this, Matt. If I ever catch sight of you, you will find yourself very slowly and painfully dead. So, don't think I won't allow you to be hurt."

Cursian moved forward to force her away from the larger man. He knew this was her fight, that she had to conquer this man for her own sake, but he would kill the mortal before allowing him to touch Esme again.

Matt stuck his face closer to Esme's, "You are fucking a freak. He's some kind of monster."

Just as she had the previous night, Esme acted with such suddenness Cursian found himself unable to control her actions. She punched Matt full in the face from three inches away, using everything she had. His nose exploded. His lips, top and bottom, split under the impact and four teeth caved in. Esme pulled back slightly ready to go again, when Cursian grabbed her arm and held her still. Matt yelled and slid once more to the floor as Esme let go. Cursian had no wish for his Scion to know how to beat a man to death.

" 'R oou ducking duts 'oman?" he screamed.

"Shut up, peasant." Cursian reached toward him, grabbed him by the hair, pulled his head forward and lightly smacked him on the back of the head. Matt folded, unconscious.

"Brigit, see to Esme. I will return within half an hour," Cursian bent, picked up the slumped figure and threw him over his shoulder.

Esme stood, hugging herself. "Just don't kill him, please," she murmured.

"Whatever my lady wishes, although I think that is a mistake."

Cursian moved quickly through the city, not wanting the stink of this mortal in his car. His speed left a strange blur on the CCTV cameras; some thing's should be left in the darkness. He arrived at the river, effortlessly carrying the body over the floodwall and down the bank. The city hadn't changed so much over the centuries, the river still supplied the best graveyard for instant disposal. Besides, old habits died hard.

Flinging the unconscious man down into the mud, Cursian paused. He stood on the edge of the concrete, watching the dark water slip past. The moon sat heavy and pregnant in the sky over his head. Its sickly form cast the shades of dead memories on the water's surface. Cursian shook his head. Now is not the time to remember, or feel the past. Now is the time for Esme. For a new life and this heaviness, this sense of impending horror, this isolation would ease. He no longer travelled alone and the Prophecy would be maintained for another generation. There would be no threat to his Scion. He would not let her down or see her hurt. Not by anything.

Reaching out, he grasped the mortal's leg to haul him back from the mud. Meticulous and tidy as always, certainly not wanting to take river mud back to Esme, Cursian manoeuvred Matt into a convenient position. Pausing for only a moment, just to listen to the cold wind as it whispered secrets in his dark mind, Cursian struck. His teeth pierced Matt's throat with ease, the other man's stubble pricked his lips. Cursian smelt Esme on the man's clothes and all doubt vanished. He fed, his senses drowning in the forgotten pleasures of the kill. This mortal tasted of violence and fear, Cursian smiled as he drank, his lips pushed against his victims dying flesh. Matt would never hurt Esme again and Cursian knew the intoxication of a man's heart stopping. The mortal's life ended in a wave of power filling the vampire's soul for long moments.

Cursian rose, pushing Matt's body away. It rolled toward the river, stopping well within the tide line. His heart raced, truly full for the first time in decades. Closing his eyes, Cursian breathed the night air and noticed the stink of the river for the first time.

"What have I done?" he spoke softly to the moon. He hadn't taken a mortal life for so long he'd forgotten how it felt to have that gift given to him. His mind reached for Esme, his only anchor in a world which seemed dark and dangerous in these troubled times. Cursian often wondered how he maintained his sanity, for some reason it had become harder these last ten years. Only Esme and watching her grow into a beautiful woman kept him focused and calm. His mind brushed hers, she unaware of his touch as always, but he aware of her pain and anxiety over Matt's attack. She needed him and this time she did not have to suffer alone, he could be there to help her deal with the pain of violence.

Turning away from the river, refusing to think about the real reason for the mortal's death, Cursian returned the way he'd come and with the same sense of urgency.

As he entered the flat, Cursian saw Brigit coming out of Esme's bedroom.

"She's been in the shower since you left, I can't get her out."

Cursian noticed his friend looked old and tired, he often forgot how long she'd been with him. "Go home, Brigit. I shall care for her from here."

Looking up at him, Brigit clearly wanted to talk, but shaking her head, she just picked up her coat and left. Cursian walked into Esme's room and waited for the shower to stop. He did not want to rush her.

The shower stopped, he expected tears, so as she appeared her quiet laughter caught him by surprise. The white towel emphasised the darkness and length of her wet hair, while making her pink skin even more alive. He'd left his long coat in the hall and suddenly felt naked without it, his soft black shirt and black jeans not enough clothing to protect him from Esme.

"I'm glad you find the situation so humorous," Cursian realised he sounded much harder than he'd intended.

Esme stopped. Turning she moved to stand opposite him eyebrow raised, laughter gone.

"Where's Brigit?"

Cursian rose while maintaining eye contact. His chest contracted painfully as he noticed her bruises for the first time. "I have sent her home. You will need her tomorrow. You should go to the shop to continue your lessons. She will need to maintain her strength if she is to be of use to you."

Again, he noticed her eyebrow. This conversation seemed to be slipping out of control.

"I should, should I? Is this an order or request?" Esme's tone caught Cursian off guard. Very sweet and gentle, he was about to answer when six centuries of dealing with women and particularly women from this family took over. Cursian closed his mouth and considered more carefully.

He coughed, "Um, request?"

"Good. Then maybe you can take that tone from your voice. The one that makes you sound like my father and we can have a proper conversation."

Damn, she was good. No argument and yet it had become entirely his fault. Cursian smiled, beauty and brains, he didn't stand a hope. Memories of the mortal's words crashed into his mind, denying his happiness, 'monster'. Beast. Cursian snapped everything shut. He felt his eyes bleed of all expression, his face too. 'A blank canvas of soulless death', someone once called it when he retreated. He noticed a small frown marring Esme's face. With all her hair wet and pushed back, her visual expressiveness became even more acute.

"What?" she asked.

Cursian refused the bait.

She muttered frustration plain, "Okay, tough guy, you've got two choices as far as I can see. I either treat you with kid gloves, allowing you to maintain your mysterious distance, as though you were some kind of precious beast. Or, we talk like friends and learn to build a relationship based on trust and mutual acceptance."

Esme's green eyes challenged Cursian for an answer. Over the centuries, he maintained a greater distance between himself and those with whom he worked. Watching human friend's die of disease and old age quickly wearied him. But loneliness tugged hard on his heart from the moment of Esme's birth. The temptation to give in and pull her close, both emotionally and physically made him ache. Yet distance would maintain the status quo. Cursian decided on distance. A certain aloofness would protect them both. Esme had to continue the family line and if she were too close to him, she couldn't.

"Right times up," Esme said.

"What?" Cursian floundered, confused.

"I can see the decision in your face and it's the wrong one. Times up, I make the decisions about us. You had your chance and didn't speak soon enough."

"I did not realise I was on a timer."

"Well you are." Esme walked quickly back toward him, towel held with one hand. Cursian stepped back slightly. Esme stopped four inches from him. She looked up. He noticed the faint scar she had on her cheek from a childhood accident, and the hazel flecks in her eyes. He also felt the heat from her body and the sound of her blood filled his head. He found he'd trapped himself unable to move back any further.

"Esme," his voice thickened. "I do not think you have thought about this, consider the implications."

"Damn the implications right now, all I want is a kiss, just a kiss. I have to know something."

He felt her hand behind his neck. He resisted for a moment, then allowed her to pull him down. Cursian felt Esme stretch up on tiptoes. Meticulously she maintained the slight distance between their bodies. Her lips brushed his, her tongue flicked out. He responded the only way a man can when he's being kissed by the woman who haunts his every waking night-cursed moment.

Cursian wrapped an arm around her waist, lifting slightly, another around her head. Supporting her weight, he pulled her close and pushed back with a kiss of his own. Her mouth opened willingly. His tongue tasted her for the first time, exploring, owning her, demanding a response. Esme duly responded. However, she seemed a little more reticent than Cursian. He pulled back afraid he had gone to far too fast.

"Is something wrong?" the words formed around a lump in his throat.

"No, nothing. I just don't want to cut my mouth on those daggers of yours," Esme smiled to take away any pain.

His eyes widened briefly, "I do not know what to say."

"Practice is all that can be said. I had a boyfriend with braces once, we managed alright."

"Maybe this is not such a good idea." Cursian released his hold.

"Oh, no, you aren't doing that, you aren't going all bleeding heart on me. Something is happening here and I don't want you running away. If you won't kiss you can talk," Esme pushed against his chest. Cursian sat back on the bed.

"Explain, why do I have this uncontrollable desire to jump your bones?" Esme had her hands on her hips. "You might be a very handsome man, but this isn't quite my style."

Cursian wondered how the towel stayed up, "From watching you over the years I would say this is exactly your style." The jibe proved irresistible.

"My sexual history is not up for discussion right now. And is none of your business," she blushed beautifully.

"Why not?"

"Because I am more interested in our sexual history," Esme stood over him.

Way out of his depth, Cursian considered his options. He'd had liaisons over the centuries, had become very experienced at playing games with lovers, but this young vital creature turned him fully on his head.

"Cursian, we both have enough know-how not to be feeling this violently attracted, what's going on? Both you and Brigit have dropped hints. Please, I can't handle feeling like this without understanding the," she paused searching for the right word, "pain," she said finally. Not the word he really wanted to hear. Esme knelt, forcing him to look down. To look down at her upturned face, framed by hair still dark from water, skin no longer flushed pink.

He gave up, Cursian puffed air outward, "Esme, there are reasons for this, but this is going to be hard for you to understand."

"Harder than what happened last night?"

Cursian smiled, "That depends on how cynical you are. Our history goes back thousands of years. Do you believe in soul mates, those that are destined to be together?"

"I'm a girl, of course I know what soul mates are. But believe in them? Not convinced," she shrugged.

"Well, start believing, Cariad. Our story begins in the desert over two millennia ago. We were young, growing up in the same city, enjoying each other's company during our childhood. When you came of age, the local priestess took you. Your parents sold you to her. Unfortunately, our love remained stronger than the pull of celibacy. They caught us.

Tortured us, for our insolence and disobedience to the gods, our death sentence was passed. We were raised high on stakes. Within arms reach, slowly being impaled as our own weight drove us downward with the magic of gravity. Our last breath cursed those who murdered our love. In that moment, our souls were taken. The very gods we were supposed to have betrayed bound us together. They heard our curse and entwined our love for all time. Every lifetime our souls have met in this plane, they have become entangled. Sometimes as lovers, sometimes as friends so close we have died in the same battles, from the same sword stroke." He fell silent and waited for the response.

CHAPTER EIGHT

Esme rose and sat beside him, all sexual tension within her gone. "That's heavy." She continued to sit in silence, considering.

After an eternity, she felt the bed move beside her, "Esme, I think I need a response."

"To be honest I don't know what to say. In some ways, it's similar to what you told me yesterday, which is equally bizarre, so why should I believe it? Yet instinct is nagging uncontrollably telling me you're right." She turned to face him, "You know life was a lot easier three days ago, you've challenged everything I know to be real and true." Esme sounded as pathetic as she felt.

"You need time, I understand. I shall leave. Protecting you from outside is as easy as it is from here now I have access." Cursian stood.

"What? No, Cursian you can't just leave. We need to talk about this, have you known me before, in your lifetime?"

He smiled, "Very perceptive, it is that connection which saved my sanity. Saved me from remaining simply a vampire. Esme, my soul has been without its partner for nearly six hundred years. It is incredibly lonely."

"Is there any chance we can be tentative? You know, take things slow, see how it goes? I mean maybe this is one of the lifetimes we are only meant to be friends."

Cursian laughed at her.

"What's so funny?" she asked perturbed.

"We can try if that is what you wish, but I do not hold much hope for such a plan. Esme, you have never been backwards in coming forwards."

"What's that supposed to mean?"

"You enjoy a healthy sexual lifestyle, which is fine and I am hardly one to criticise, although I have been around a lot longer. Why is this knowledge of us suddenly making you cautious?"

Esme frowned biting her tongue. "A few days ago I believed firmly in free will and the ability to choose for myself. Now I find my whole existence is bound up in some cosmic juggling act, to the point where I don't even have a choice about who I choose as my lover. I just want free will back, that's the whole point of life. You make decisions about faith and your actions. You break the rules that's fine, it's your decision and you know the consequences. But this is different in so many ways."

"Is that really what you think? Did you really have a choice when it came to declaring your faith? And are you sure your current decisions are not controlled by that faith? Esme, I know how Christ works within people. I have seen it often enough. My life began in one of the most religious periods in history. The tempest that is created within when Christ wants someone in his Church is too big to deny. I do not believe you have much choice. Not really. And you certainly have little choice now." He shrugged, black cotton shirt absorbing the light.

Esme considered his words. She hadn't had to examine her faith or her way of life since her early twenties. Changing her perspective would be hard and maybe Cursian was wrong. He couldn't know everything. Although one aspect was right, there had been little choice about becoming a Christian. The noise in her head had nearly sent her mad until she'd given in, then peace, until now.

"I'd still like tentative," she could feel the pleading in her eyes, the one that wasn't swelling up anyway.

"Then I suggest you dress because tentative is not going to stop me from bedding you if you remain in that towel."

Esme laughed, "Jumping my bones is a more contemporary saying. Get out of the room then and we'll talk about more important stuff."

"It may be more important, but it is a great deal less urgent."

Esme grinned and then remembered, "What did you do with Matt?"

Cursian's face darkened, "I dealt with him as a man of his kind should be dealt with. I will not have you suffer at the hands of men, not again."

"What do you mean, again?" Esme's throat closed.

Cursian's hands rose and gently held her arms, "Esme, this is not something we need to talk of."

"Is that why the police never found anybody?" Esme's voice had become fragile.

Cursian hesitated, "Yes."

"Okay. Another time." She turned away more turmoil to deal with, shattering her cosy life. The door clicked shut behind her as the vampire left. He'd killed Matt, Esme knew it and he'd killed others who had hurt her. How did she feel about it?

"I don't want to feel anything about it," she said aloud. Well used to pushing unpleasant thoughts to one side in order to continue with day to day living, Esme chose to try to forget this new nugget of information.

Once dressed, she found Cursian in the kitchen. "Brigit left supper for you and some of her magic goo for your bruises. Sit and I shall see to them."

Esme sat and Cursian applied evil smelling ointment. "Well, if that doesn't keep your hands off me, nothing will. Poo, what's she put in that stuff?"

"I do not know, but it will be one of the things she will be teaching you."

CHAPTER NINE

Esme gradually relaxed as the evening wore into night. Cursian stayed on subjects that were light and distant. Occasionally he touched on her family and his past. Esme felt too drained to pursue anything complex and deep. After she had eaten, she chose not to discuss Cursian's nutritional needs at this point, they opened a bottle of wine and retired to the sofa. Before long Esme felt light headed and relaxed enough to use Cursian as a pillow. Once he had managed to get used to the idea of having her sprawled across him with her head resting on his stomach, they enjoyed a companionable night.

During the darkest hours, she yawned and the conversation drifted. Cursian brushed hair from her forehead and smiled.

"You need to sleep," he said.

"No, I don't. I'm fine. Being with you is going to mean more night time stuff. I've need to get used to it."

"Esme, no one said you had to be nocturnal to be a part of my life, it will make you ill. Come, I will carry you to bed." He tucked an arm under her shoulders and knees, lifting her and himself from the sofa without a harsh breath.

"Wow, that's impressive," Esme murmured.

"One of the advantages of being a vampire," he laid her on the bed. "Now, sleep and tomorrow you may go to Brigit's place of work. I shall meet you there, Cariad."

"What's that name mean?" Esme felt a burning desire to surrender to sleep.

"Darling or loved one. It is Welsh." Cursian brushed more long hair from her face as she snuggled under the duvet.

"You're Welsh?"

"Go to sleep, Esme."

And she did. Deep, dreamless sleep. No violence, no death, no attempted rape, just sleep.

Esme rose the next morning, late, but feeling refreshed. She dressed quickly and left. Brigit had given Esme a card the previous day. The address of the shop on the other side of town, so she decided to do a little retail therapy on the way. Once she slackened her immediate desire for new boots, long black ones that fitted just right over her calves and ended with a flourish on the knee, the need for caffeine took Esme into a coffee house.

She sat quietly in the window, enjoying the sight of blustery wind whipping up the street. A man took the seat next to her and as one does in London, Esme ignored him. Her phone rang. She turned, grabbing her bag, cursing as she did so; just as she reached it the damn thing stopped. She took it out to check the number. Suddenly cross, Esme groaned, no caller ID. She turned back to the window and drank her coffee. The man next door had gone, Esme relaxed back into the scene outside.

Twenty minutes later, she walked toward Brigit's shop, peering into windows. As she passed a bakery, Esme blanched, almost vomiting. The smell disgusted her. She looked closely in the window. Thoughts scattered and collided as she wrestled with her stomach. The bread seemed too big, it was, no, couldn't be, the notion had to be daft. Esme stepped closer. It was no good, the bread pulsed, heaved, breathed.

She turned 180 degrees, looking into the dress shop opposite. The pavement buckled under foot. The dummies swayed as the glass bowed outward, the world turned violent shades of purple. The vehicles surrounding her hmmm'ed like swarms of bees. Esme tried to walk carefully to avoid the large black holes in the pavement. She tripped, going down, skinning her hands, but her knees were protected by jeans. She held her hands up to her face. The fingers went on forever. The blood looked like spots of black acid and it burned. Esme screamed and stumbled upright, trying to stop the acid from burning her hands, then her thighs as she scrubbed them against each other, again and again.

Bags forgotten, rational thought gone Esme stared at the heaving, noxious world around her. Every time she thought she managed to pinpoint an object, something would move around it and the whole lot would become one organic heaving mass. Pigeons became large enough to eat her. She tried to ask for help but everyone she approached grew fangs, turning into the evil creatures from the night before.

Then, it all made sense. That's what happened, the monsters had returned to kill her because she dared to stop them the other night. She ran, slipping and falling through a world that behaved like some giant, twisted bouncy castle. Huge purple mushrooms constantly forced her to weave manically, as they appeared and disappeared with each step.

Esme finally paused in an alley. Its darkness sheltered her from the disturbing, fluctuating madness outside. She breathed in air as though it smelt of roses. Mutant roses. Black mutant roses with massive thorns dripping black acid. Esme groaned the sound echoing back in the narrow alley. She twisted away from the daggers, which fell toward her as her cry died.

She huddled, trying to stay quiet and still, wanting the world to stop. Her ability to reason stripped away. She couldn't tell if this was illusion. For her everything had a sense of reality frightening enough to stop her breath. With eyes shut, Esme only saw huge star bursts of colour flashing behind her lids. This she could cope with and she began to calm, keeping her eyes shut tight.

However, her hearing remained unimpeded. A scratching, clawing and squealing began to penetrate her head. High pitched squealing. The sound took form in her mind. Just as the daggers flew from her cries, so these noises took on a life of their own.

Reality had to be better than the images forming in her mind. Her eyes opened. Unfortunately, she was wrong. Rats surrounded Esme. To her mind there were thousands. In reality, there were hundreds. A heaving mass of black fur and claws, teeth and tail. She froze. They grew still, forming a perfect semi circle around her, a breathing carpet of bodies. The circle started eighteen inches from her feet and spread into the darkness opposite. She slowly placed her hands flat on the wall behind her and pushed her way upward. She wanted to move very slowly toward the mouth of the alley. She could see it, it grinned at her. Rats in themselves didn't frighten her, but this many? The image plugged into fears so deep and ingrained in the human psyche there was no escape, no rationalisation. Esme whimpered. The rats toward the exit drew closer to her; she flicked her gaze elsewhere and noticed they drew her back in the direction of the rear of the alley. She moved that way. The mass of bodies and Esme made slow progress down the alley, deeper into its darkness. Every time she stopped they crept closer to her, corralling her deeper all the time.

The alley ended abruptly, the world outside no longer purple, just shades of black, night on night. The rats spilled outward, their cries becoming louder. It sounded like broken glass in Esme's distorted mind. She cried out, finally falling back on her faith, praying to God to get her out of this alive. Only to feel nothing, a void inside. The rats swarmed about her feet. Running over her shoes making her lash out. Then they began to clamber up her legs. Finally, she bolted. The rats ran with her, forcing her to their wishes. They opened a path for her to take among them, closing fast behind her, running at her and biting if she stopped.

A journey born of nightmares. Esme ran through a derelict warehouse district. It wasn't large, but to her it could have been the size of Australia and she wouldn't have been any the wiser. She ran through rats, through shadow, through what she thought were her worst nightmares.

The rats drew her toward the heart of the district, forced her toward a small door half way along the side of one building. The door opened. Esme stood, sweating and trembling. The rats finally silent. In the doorway stood a man, unremarkable in everyway. His face neither handsome nor ugly, old nor young. His features stayed thankfully neutral to Esme's twisted mind, relieving her fear.

"Welcome, Scion of the Prophecy, you arrived in good time, which pleases me," his voice held a neutral cadence and accent.

Esme found no voice to reply. She stood, frozen and confused. The rats were one quivering mass around her, all of them facing the open doorway.

"Thank you my little brothers, you may return to your lives," the man waved an arm limply toward the swarm, the rats dispersed instantly. To Esme's fevered mind, one minute they were there, the next - vanished in less than a heartbeat. A receding tide, disappearing back to its shadowy place of birth.

"You had better come in, Scion. I need to talk to you," he said softly.

Esme whimpered and tried to stay still. The panic induced such a dump of different chemicals into her body any form of thought, drug produced or not, became impossible.

"Dear, dear, it seems we may have already broken our young friend." He reached out, grasping Esme's arm, leading her into the darkness of the warehouse.

Esme's vision reverted to colourful shades of purple and small mushrooms began sprouting again through the floor. She took this as a good sign. Things were bad when the world went black. It made Esme compliant and she allowed herself to be towed to a chair in the centre of the large abandoned building. She gladly followed the instructions to sit. She felt tired and the voices around her were calm and quiet.

There were two of them, neither with an accent. Soft and gentle, so gentle she didn't notice the bindings around her wrists that stopped her arms moving from the armrests. Or the bindings on her legs, which attached her ankles to the chair legs, forcing her knees wide apart. Gratefully, she just listened to the two gentle voices taking care of her crazy world.

The voices and their shadows gradually moved away from Esme and she strained to hear their comforting sounds.

"We have to wait for her to come around a little. If we start pushing her mind now we will lose her," this voice and shadow seemed larger than the other.

"If we leave it much longer it'll be too close to dark. We can't afford to be found. If he does find us then all this is for nought."

"I tell you, the girl is still too sensitive. We will break her mind completely. She's had an extreme reaction to the drug."

"I really don't think we have to worry about whether we break her mind or not. The whole idea of this exercise is to take what she is and steal it from her body. We don't need her mind intact to do that and once the vampire accedes to our demands he won't want her back, unless to play with the shell."

"I am an artist. I did not come to destroy, only to dissect. Her essence is what the vampire will want, the thing that makes the girl unique. If we return her empty, he will know and act as we have planned. As our Master has planned for so long, so very long. He will return to the darkness," the larger shadow stated firmly.

Esme began to sweat. The words slowly took on meaning now she only had her eyes and ears to control. She whimpered, unable to control the fear response.

The sound dragged the two shadows closer, like vultures listening for the death rattle before moving in on their victim. Esme's heart raced, her purple mushrooms vanishing and shades of black on black returned. The bonds around her arms and legs became tight and hot, like hot wire, she tried to move.

"It's alright, child, stay still." She acquiesced to the quiet voice, already losing the thread of the threat. "Esme, I want you to close your eyes and I want you to listen to me, only me, do you understand?" She nodded, closing her eyes obediently. "Good girl, now I want you to relax and allow the pressure you will feel inside your head in a moment to flow through you. Think of it as a dam on the river that gently bursts and the water will flow throughout your being. Ready?" She nodded again.

Esme felt the pressure, like a reverse headache, coming from the outside, to the inside. She tried to do as she was told, to see the water flow through her, but the dam in her head would not burst. The pressure and the voice could not penetrate. Something within her held it back, something she didn't understand.

The larger shadow huffed, "This is going to be hard. She has massive internal walls, far more than most people. Either the vampire has interfered in her makeup already, or the Scions have strengths previously unknown. I will have to try violence where coaxing will not work. Unfortunate, but you are right, the vampire may find us if this isn't done fast and I can see his connection to the girl, it's strong, which might work in our favour."

The voice continued, "Esme, have you made love to the vampire yet?" She opened her eyes, shaking her head hoping to please. "Good, in that case I will allow him to make love to you now, as a vampire would. I want you to close your eyes again and keep them closed, all you are allowed to do is scream when you feel you need too. I want you to listen to my voice, and feel everywhere I touch on your body a hundred times more than the actual impact. Do you understand?" She did.

"Cursian is here with you and his hands are binding your arms to the chair." Esme whimpered slightly at the pressure, but enjoyed the pain. "He leans close to you, his lips and teeth touching your neck." Esme felt the sharp canines graze her neck painfully, the intenseness and speed stopping her true enjoyment. "Now, Esme everything you hear and feel from now is coming direct from your vampire lover."

Esme felt Cursian's hot mouth trail down her naked flesh as she lay, strapped down against the cold stone floor of what resembled a dungeon. His mouth hovered over her left breast, tongue flicking across its surface, raising the nipple. She groaned wanting to twist into him, she pulled against her chains, despite his instruction not to fight her captivity. As she twisted, he rose away from her and slapped her hard across the face.

"I told you to be still," he ordered.

She tasted blood, suddenly afraid of this lover's game.

He bent to her body once more, now sucking hard on her nipple, teeth digging in. It hurt. Esme screamed twisting away, unable to stay still. A whip appeared in his hand from nowhere, he brought it down across her stomach ordering her to stay still again. She began to ask to be let go, again the whip. She began to cry, he let her as he bit again. Esme felt him sucking, felt her skin give and her blood flow down his throat. He moved his body to cover her pelvis, his legs between her spread-eagled chained limbs and he sucked. Every time she begged release, she felt the whip pull back and its sudden snap against her skin, stomach, chest, thighs. Numb, quiet and still against the punishment, Esme endured. Cursian noticed her dumb acceptance, he grinned, her blood stained his face. He knelt across Esme's upper body, made a show of unbuttoning his trousers, made it plain what came next. Esme reacted badly, trying to turn and twist her thrashing body away. More pain lanced through her limbs as she struggled and the iron bit deeper.

Cursian pushed two fingers deep and hard into her, she bucked away, pushing her hips high. He pulled back and pushed again, with bruising force. Over and over. Esme drifted, disappearing, no longer fighting. Knowing nothing can last forever, she retreated further and further, even when his fingers were replaced by another more intimate part of him, so that all his vampire strength plunged into her over and over. Esme moved back deeper, touching the place that allowed her to burn the evil she had witnessed in her home. Esme fell into that pool of light, bright blue light.

As she fell, Esme became aware the light had a slight viscous quality making her descent slow. She moved her arms through the light, causing trails of silver phosphorous to trace her movements. The deeper she sank the darker the colour of her surroundings. Esme passed through every shade of blue imaginable and several no one knew existed, until the darkest glowing blue enclosed her and the descent stopped. She sat, becoming aware of the separation she accomplished by falling into this place.

Simultaneously, Esme heard the men talking about their plans for her, as the drugged part of her mind replayed again the monster in Cursian's form raping her. Repeatedly, she died under his hands only to be resurrected with the next breath and torn to sheds in increasingly depraved ways. Even her faith became a weapon used against her unwilling body in her minds eye. She knew the men who kept her captive were only waiting for her mind to collapse, before they stole in with their evil magic and drew out the part of her that would be reborn continuously. In this place of safety, Esme wept for the destruction of her spirit and mind. For the annihilation of her burgeoning love.

With every attack, Esme sensed the fractures appearing in her strong defences. She heard the men outside her body talk with confidence that it would soon be over. She stood in the strange glowing twilight becoming more and more resentful of the murderous manipulation of her captures. Her anger turned to rage and Esme rose upward through the blue light. Their actions would not destroy her relationship with Cursian. He was not her attacker.

As each shade crossed her body a film of the previous shade stayed with her, by the time she reached the surface, a thick covering of blue light a thousand shades deep surrounded her. Esme shot from the fluid, trailing silver behind her to retake her besieged mind.

Her eyes flew open glowing deep blue. Light pulsed from her skin. The coils surrounding her limbs fell away, charred to nothing. She heard the cries of the men as they stumbled away from her burning suit of armour. The sound came to her from a great distance. She raised her hand to attack. The men fled. She caught one with a glancing slice of flame, instantly searing his skin. The smell of burnt flesh filled the air. His companion dragged him up and they continued to run. Esme could not give chase, the light held her in a protective shield preventing her from controlling her surroundings with ease or grace. The need to be safe seemed to be all that drove her forward. She built an image of Brigit in her mind and found her body able to respond.

PURE INTENTIONS CAN DARKEN OUR DOORWAYS

Ever since he'd come to Glastonbury he knew there would be more to life than his city bred council house up bringing led him to believe. The small town did not let him down. More, more light, more dark, more love and lots more colour filled his life. His childhood consisted of a series of drab brown and grey images. Not his family's fault, but they didn't know what to do with a young lad who was described by an old neighbour as fey. That old neighbour eventually showed him a door, which led him to Glastonbury. He finally felt at home for the first time in his twenty eight years.

Ben smiled at the sky as he lay on his back watching the clouds float by on the light spring breeze. He smelt summer coming on a wind warmed by the sun kissing the famous Glastonbury Tor. He'd happily spend lifetimes up on the hill and never get bored. There were always folks to talk to if you wanted, or ignore if the mood took. He also watched the surrounding hills and Levels change with the days and seasons. Off one way were the Mendips, hazy in the sunshine today. Off to the other, the long stretch of Sedgemoor; full of old secrets, covered in just budding willow. The dragon's back lying dormant below him on the edge of town, leading to flatlands which didn't quite feel normal till you nearly reached the motorway. A sad carving up of Somerset that motorway. Before it s building, Ben felt the differences running through the county would have been easier to bear, between the lowland energy and the high feeling on the moors and hills in the West.

Ben shook himself and sat up slowly so the vertigo didn't get him, the way it did up the side of this hill if you weren't careful. He'd given himself the morning to think things through and he'd made his decision. He loved this town and all the crazy things it stood for, Christianity and Paganism. A lot of waffle all mixed in a great big pot of something slightly smelly yet wondrously unique. But the time had come to leave. He had a calling and he wouldn't let the old town down. His people would protect and guide him no matter how dark the path became and no matter how he'd be tested before the end. With his soul tangled into a story he had no right to stop, Ben knew he had to help control it, ensuring it came out right in the end. Believing that would keep him sane or he'd be lost before he started. For he could not avoid his fate, neither could the others, no matter how they might run. He'd rather face it than have it club him around the side of the head later.

He pushed himself up and began the controlled descent into the town. Walking past trees he gently stroked them when he could, storing as much light inside of himself as possible. He also studied each of the old buildings carefully, branding them into his memory so as never to forget this sense of calm and hope. Eventually, he arrived at the door to a small white cottage tucked discreetly away behind the magnificent remainders of the Abbey. The door opened before he raised his hand to the handle and Ben stepped over the threshold.

"Okay Ma, I'm ready to go. I'll do as you need me too," Ben puffed out his chest slightly, feeling small in the darkened cottage.

"Good lad, I always knew you was the one right from the moment you came 'ere. This journey will be hard on you and the others if I am any judge. That young lass you'll be helping will be going to hell and back before this is finished, indeed it might be the only way it can be finished. The Grail shows us many paths are possible and the line is a thin one right now. The vampire has no idea how close to the edge he really is," Ma said in the confines of her esoteric home.

CHAPTER TEN

"Brigit, the shop is quiet today can I cash up?"

Brigit stuck her head round the door at the back of her shop, "You might as well, May. I shall have to find out why Esme didn't show up today which means fighting my way across town."

The young woman flicked long jet hair over her shoulder and unfurled herself from the armchair they kept for customers. Long legs stretched, barely covered by a very short skirt, but what the skirt lacked the boots made up for, thick soles, thick leather, flames leaping up the sides. Brigit withdrew shaking her head. If May had not been naturally empathic, Brigit doubted she would put up with the more outrageous side of her student's nature.

May reached for the sign on the door at the same moment Esme fell through it landing heavily on her knees. Brigit rushed forward as May moved further back never having met the smaller woman.

"Help," Esme gasped.

Brigit grabbed Esme by the shoulders. Esme screamed making Brigit jump away from her. "What in the lowest parts of hell has happened?"

Esme's breath sounded loud in the silent shop. May stood frozen by the open doorway. Brigit tried again, "Esme, what's happened?" she noticed Esme's eyes were tight shut.

"Help, please, drugs, can't think, pain everywhere, please help," Esme said, her tone broken, harsh.

"I didn't think she'd be into drugs," May said, somewhat acidic.

Brigit glared at her, "Do something useful girl, lock the shop up and get me a large glass of water." Brigit didn't move toward Esme until the young woman had huffed her way to the kitchen.

"Esme, can you hear me?" A nod came in reply, followed by a whimper.

"Does it hurt to talk?" Another nod.

"That'll make life difficult. You said drugs, did someone drug you? Cursian mentioned you went through a phase when you were younger." A nod and a shake, Brigit realised she'd have to be more specific. "Someone drugged you?" A stronger nod. "And everything hurts?" More nods.

"Okay, sweetheart, we'll see what can be done. Was the drug a hallucinogen?"

Esme nodded. May walked back into the room.

"Acid? That's not good. Especially if she was spiked, anything might have happened to her." Honest concern creased May's strong face. They both saw Esme nod again.

"Someone has hurt you haven't they?" May asked. Again the nod, May sucked air through her teeth, "This could be messy."

"We can't afford to worry about that right now. Esme is obviously in a great deal of distress, all we can really do is wait until the drug wears off and hope Cursian turns up as soon as the sun sets. Let's get some water into her, then some detoxifying herbs if she keeps the water down. Dusk is in about an hour."

Brigit moved toward Esme, "Come on, sweetheart, the only way we can help is if you let us. Remember this is all created by your mind, our touch will not hurt and neither will the water you are going to drink." The two women managed to pick Esme up from the floor and half carried her to the large sofa.

"Lie down love," Brigit pushed Esme back. Just as they thought, she would relax Esme shot upright again.

"No, bad, don't like back, bad head," her breathing came in staccato hisses.

"She needs to feel stable," May said. "I think I've had far more experience of drug abuse than you, Brigit, maybe I ought to be the one to stay with her and talk her through."

Brigit thought for all of ten seconds, "Agreed, keep her sane I'll make some calls see if there is anything we can do."

"I can tell you now, there isn't a herb in the world to help this and it's going to blow a hole in her aura the size of Wembley Stadium," came May's optimistic appraisal.

Over the next hour Brigit and May took turns coaxing Esme to drink every time she vomited. Brigit concluded this had not been LSD, but one of the many natural herbs used to cause the same effect on the surface. Esme gradually began to relax, eventually talking without words forming knives. She brokenly tried to explain to the horrified women what had happened. Brigit soon realised Esme's attackers used the drug to infiltrate and break the young woman's mind. Despair filled her thoughts when she realised how this could permanently change both Esme and her relationship with the vampire.

May, surprisingly enough, repeatedly told Esme everything had been an illusion and nothing hurt unless she allowed it. Time toward dusk passed slowly, Brigit became increasingly nervous.

CHAPTER ELEVEN

Cursian woke as the last of the light faded from the edges of his very heavy curtains. His first thought, as always, sought Esme. He frowned finding nothing familiar as his thought returned unanswered. Again, he quested toward her, nothing but a haze and babble of shattered images. Cursian moved with lightening speed, his humanity forgotten as he sped across London toward Brigit's shop.

The lock broke on impact as Cursian kicked the door. He hardly noticed Brigit and her assistant jump away from Esme as he strode through the shop. Esme didn't move. She stank of sickness and fear. He dropped to one knee in front of her. His hand reached toward her head.

"Don't do that," one of the women said.

Cursian turned on his knee. He knew his eyes had fully dilated and shone like a feral cats. "She belongs to me, I protect her, you can not command me to leave her alone." He watched the women as they both gratifyingly blanched with fear. He pushed out further with his rage and hatred, the younger woman whimpered. Cursian smiled, humans were weak and easily destroyed. Especially if they allowed harm to come to his love, his charge, his reason for continuing to exist. He turned back to Esme shielding her from the anger.

"What happened?" his voice softened, cajoling, the tone he used to lull his prey.

Esme whimpered.

"Look at me, Esme."

Esme began to rock backward and forward, arms hugging the cushions she held tight to her chest. Cursian felt movement behind him. With lightening speed, he turned and grabbed the assistant around her throat, lifting her slightly.

"Well?" he asked calmly as she tried to claw through his hand. Cursian watched her breathing. He applied a little more pressure to stop her moving around, she obliged, staring at him defiantly. Cursian relaxed his grip and turned his head as he caught the older woman walking toward him, hands out in supplication.

His attention returned to the younger, he found her attractive and strong. He began to consider what she'd taste like, she squeaked, "If you touch her, you might send her over the edge. She's been abused and drugged. She needs your help not your rage." The assistant's voice cut through his thoughts.

Cursian blinked, another voice intruded, "Cursian, Esme is in terrible danger. You can only help her if you maintain some control. Please, release May and allow us to explain. We didn't harm Esme. You know that, just think about it."

Something flickering inside the vampire began to burn more brightly. Cursian released May who stumbled slightly as her feet regained the ground. He drew his first deep breath since entering the shop, forcing the monster away. The monster controlled to much of him these nights. He locked up his need and drive for death. Cursian closed his eyes and inhaled the stale air once more.

He heard both women breathe deeply as the pressure he created, released them from their primeval fears. "What happened? I woke to find Esme's sense of self in disarray and pain," he said.

Brigit, irritation plain on her face at his actions, stood in front of him as May moved back toward Esme, "She arrived in the shop about an hour ago, unable to talk. Eventually we found out she has been drugged with a powerful hallucinogen and her mind savaged." Brigit stopped, her hands on her hips.

Cursian looked away from Esme and toward the older woman, "What? Who would do this and why? Brigit you are not telling me everything, I am too close to the edge for games," he felt his anger rising again.

"Cursian, I..." Brigit stopped.

Cursian smelt fear, not something he was used to from his long time friend. He'd pushed her too far, threatened May and behaved like an oaf. Around Brigit, he tried to maintain his mask of humanity. If he wanted information from his friend, he would have to calm down.

He silently cursed his temper but said quietly, "Brigit, I apologise for my behaviour, I seem to have trouble controlling my reactions when Esme is threatened. Please tell me all or I can not help her and I can feel she is in great distress."

May spoke to him, looking over her shoulder as she stroked Esme's back. "Look, this is going to be hard for you to hear, and I don't know if you are going to understand how much damage they might have done to her, but from what I can gather Esme's been forced to think of you as a killer and a torturer. Her torturer."

Cursian froze, processing May's words. Pain blossomed deep in his gut. It didn't take a genius to work out what kind of torture they impressed into her mind. His body folded over. At no time did his own pain equal this torment. His Scion had been used. Rage began to seep outward again.

"Who are they?" his lips drew back exposing glistening needle sharp canines.

"Cursian, this isn't going to help Esme. She can't remember who they are," Brigit's words tumbled over themselves as she tried to force Cursian to concentrate on the situation at hand.

"Don't go after them." The vampire turned toward Esme, who raised her head if not her eyes. "It's what they did this for, don't go to them. I don't remember who they are but I do remember what they want and it's you. Please, Cursian, I need you to stop the pain in my head. I can feel madness beckoning. I can't keep control." She still did not raise her eyes to his.

Again, humanity asserted itself. Cursian began to feel slightly sick. Violence his first thought and action, rather than the cool logic he'd grown used too for the last few hundred years. He hadn't been this weak for centuries. He moved around Brigit and knelt opposite Esme.

"Esme, can you look at me?"

"Don't want too," she seemed exhausted after her explanation.

"Alright, but, Esme all I can do to help is take you out of your own self," he spoke slowly, carefully. "I can take the essence of you and that will close your conscious mind down, allowing your body to purge itself of drugs. You will be with me, within me. It should protect your sanity. The only trouble is I need time to feed. I have little enough control around you without having that demon to fight too. I will need time to find a volunteer."

"Don't have time. Cursian, please you have no idea how hard this is, it isn't like normal drugs, please." Esme's grip on the cushions strengthened.

Cursian turned toward Brigit feeling helpless. They both turned toward May as she said, "I'll do it. You can take what you need from me to stave off the withdrawal symptoms."

She sat on the floor, short skirt hiked up as far as it would go without showing everything she had to offer.

Cursian frowned, "Why? You know I can never be more to you than I am to Brigit don't you? Esme is all I shall ever want. This isn't some childish game?"

"Are you always this arrogant?" May laughed. "Listen buddy, I am far more likely to fall in love with this small brunette," she pointed to Esme, "than I will fall for you. Vampire or not, you are still essentially male and that doesn't interest me, unless you are very special."

Cursian opened his mouth and then snapped it shut. "Right, then I shall assume you are willing and I thank you."

"You look confused," Brigit said, amusement clear.

"I am not confused. I simply was not expecting such a beautiful young woman to be... I am not even sure what you call it anymore."

"That's because you're an arrogant man," Esme said quietly, obviously enjoying his discomfort too.

"Look, I think we need to move past the gender stereotypes as soon as possible or I will bottle out," May's tone changed. Her body thrummed with tension.

Cursian's blood lust rose to meet her fear. Memories of Matt's death surfaced. He shouldn't really be feeling this hungry, but a need is a need and fighting De'hevda had been hard. Besides, controlling Esme's essence inside his own mind would in itself be a great effort.

He moved like a cat around Esme's legs, curling his body and effectively trapping May against the other woman. "You do not need to be afraid. I can stop you from feeling any pain and I never take more than I need." He glanced up at Brigit, "I think we will leave London, all of us. If they know me well enough to take Esme, then you are both in danger too. We will go to the house in West Wycombe. It has strong shields I managed to set in place before the birth of Esme's mother and I have the keys. May will be weak, and I shall be barely able to function while trying to keep Esme safe. Get the car and get things organised to leave now, we will worry about clothes and food later. This city is a liability. At least in the country I have more chance of sensing the danger."

"I am not comfortable leaving May with you on her own," Brigit sounded defiant.

"I'll be fine," May's voice sounded slightly breathy. Cursian knew his close proximity to the girl left her feeling aroused, despite her sexual preferences.

Brigit looked concerned, "No, we do this together or not at all. Cursian has shown us he does not have decent control tonight, I will not risk you to his needs."

"Fine, we do not have the luxury of time to argue about this. May," Cursian turned and half pulled her toward him. "This is faster and more efficient from the neck, relax into me." Cursian kept his expression carefully neutral. Maintaining eye contact, he gently brushed thick black hair away from May's throat. As he bent his head, he tilted her upward slightly, holding her weight easily. His eyes met Esme's for the first time and locked.

Cursian lightly licked May's throat, disinfecting the skin. He opened his jaws just wide enough to encompass the jugular vein and carotid artery, then he pushed his upper jaw into May's open and willing flesh. The skin gave under the sharp points of his canines. His teeth were only millimetres longer than the average human's, the only real difference being the shape of the end.

As the skin broke May stiffened. Cursian flinched slightly suddenly expecting a fight. She stilled, his eyes never left Esme's gaze. Cursian pulled back to allow the wounds to bleed and as he drew the oxygenated blood from May's throat, they both sighed. Slowly Cursian drank, carefully gauging how much May could give without harm.

All vampires eventually develop another sense allowing them to feed from the same humans repeatedly without taking too much, without killing them. It developed as a safety mechanism so vampires could feed, making mortal's slaves, but not leave corpses lying around. Cursian tried not to feed from those he knew, it complicated his mortal relationships and he certainly didn't need any slaves.

For Cursian the world focused on two points. The warm metallic liquid filling his mouth, sliding down his throat filling him with renewed vigour and strength as it weakened his victim and Esme's green eyes. They were dilated from the drug. Cursian read so many conflicting thoughts fighting their way through her, horror, envy that he fed from May and not her, love, confusion, understanding, but mainly fear. This last confused him until he realised his vampiric nature would have been a part of the torture images she endured. As much as he hated an audience, he felt profoundly grateful she watched him feed from the girl with so little violence. The thought of her hatred and fear would have turned him from the Prophecy for good.

Finally, he pulled back, sated enough to be of use to Esme. May's strength meant she could give more, but Cursian had learned to curb his hunger many centuries ago. He lifted his mouth from her throat and licked the two tale-tell wounds more deeply than before, they stopped bleeding almost immediately. May lay in his arms in a swoon. Cursian reached for Esme's face.

"You see, Cariad. There is nothing to fear from me. Whatever they made you imagine I cannot cause those I care for harm." He never broke Esme's unblinking connection. "Brigit, come and help May up while I help Esme. I have just been allowed inside her." He felt the older woman gently help May to stand. Cursian moved around the two women, ensuring the bond between himself and Esme remained.

He moved closer and felt her barriers crumble further in her need to escape her own head. Cursian gently grasped her face and pushed his will into her mind. Esme rocked back slightly, fighting now as instinct overrode common sense. Cursian remained kind and strong in her mind. Like a fog made of steel, he encircled the essence of the woman he loved and separated it from the chaos of her conscious mind. Slowly he withdrew. Cursian breathed deeply continuing to centre himself to remain distinct from his lover. Esme's shell collapsed as she left her body and he felt himself become too full as he pulled her over. He saw, heard, smelt and touched everything around him twice. Not only with his predatory senses, but also with Esme's more prosaic ones. This would soon become difficult to manage.

With Cursian's mage training and metaphysical understanding stretched to the limit, he stood away from Esme's lax body. "Brigit, this is going to be very hard to control."

"Your aura has changed. I'm not sure this is going to be any good for either of you."

"It is simply a more complete and complex version of what happens during the feeding process. My essence dominates and subdues my victim's sense of self. I enter their minds and force them to stop fighting me, as I withdraw I can either return them to themselves or discard them. If a vampire chooses the latter then the victim is doomed to the life of an empty vessel, a zombie. This is deemed the cruellest way to deal with humans even among the most savage of us." He lifted Esme's body off the sofa.

Brigit grunted, "Good for you, but I don't think this is going to do Esme any good. However, I don't seem to have a great deal to say about things currently, so let's just get going shall we. Oh, and you are paying for the door now I have to nail the damned thing shut. Why couldn't you have knocked?"

"Sorry, I felt disoriented at the time." Cursian actually felt himself blush. That had to be Esme's influence.

"It seems to me you overreact rather a lot where that young woman is concerned. I think you need to learn to control yourself around her, or someone innocent will be hurt." Brigit turned smartly on her heel and stomped off, not waiting to see Cursian gently walk after her trying not to fall over the furniture.

CHAPTER TWELVE

Esme woke to gentle white light and a floor, which felt neither hard nor soft, just firm. She blinked several times wondering where the disorientation and purple mushrooms had gone.

"Hello, Esme," a male voice drew her around to face a young, slim, dark haired man. He looked to be twenty five years old or so, long dark hair down his back and very bright blue eyes. He sat with his arms locked around his knees, hands clasping his wrists. Strong, young forearms with a light skin tone, strong hands too. Esme shook her head, his supple strength distracting. A black loose fitting shirt with black baggy trousers gave the youth a relaxed attitude. Yet Esme noticed the alertness in his body and gaze, reminding her of a cat.

"Hello. Where am I?"

"You do not recognise me?" light laughter caused his voice to rise in a lilt.

Esme titled her head to one side, then rose onto all fours and crawled toward the young man. "Cursian?"

He nodded. "Sorry for the confusing appearance, but here we assume the form we think of ourselves to be."

"What? And where is here?" Esme frowned feeling herself slipping into another surreal moment.

"Here is inside my conscious mind, where I can keep your sanity safe until your body has been made clean again. What, is somewhat harder to explain. A vampire has the ability to enter their victim's minds and take them from the pain and stress a bite can cause. Rendering the victim pliant and easy to feed from, it minimises adrenaline, which makes some people unpalatable. Victims then stay alive during the feeding process, this being one of our requirements. Due to my additional abilities, I can segment myself completely, storing you and myself in another realm within my mind. We do not use all we are able of our conscious and unconscious minds. I have stretched the boundaries as much as possible."

Esme continued to frown while she sat back on her knees, as she would in the dojo, "Right, but why do you look so different?"

Cursian smiled sadly, "This is how I looked before I went to court so many centuries ago that I now need Brigit to keep count. Becoming vampire, mage and warrior made me fill out, grow harder. Have you ever looked in a mirror and been surprised at the face that stares back at you?"

Esme shrugged, "It happens occasionally."

"You expect to see a young urchin, with short tousled hair, strong limbs, slightly finer than your normal physical body. A face just slightly narrower and cheekbones slightly higher, eyes just a little greener?"

Esme nodded, supposing he was right, she'd never really thought about what should be there.

Cursian raised his hand and a mirror appeared. Esme moved forward and saw the urchin Cursian described. "Wow, though sometimes I see something much heavier and larger than I really am."

"This is because in reality you are slightly larger than you are in your own head, so that heaviness is emphasised. Esme, as a physical being you are beautiful to me, as a being of spirit you are almost irresistible."

Esme grinned, "I feel different inside too."

"You have lost all the baggage that being a thirty two year old human has given you, your spirit is pure you."

"Is that true of you as well?"

"Not entirely," a sadness swept over his features. "Vampire has infected my spirit. My form here is my attempt after many centuries to maintain a more human spirit, to never forget what I really am. It helps me to continue to empathise and participate in the real world you occupy."

Esme sat back feeling full of light, "So what now? We sit here and talk, or do we get to be a bit more adventurous than that?"

Cursian's eyes narrowed, "I cannot allow you to wander around inside my head. I will tell you anything you want to know, but I am not going to let you look for yourself. It is too dangerous and I do not think you would like to see all I have to offer."

"Well, it might take hours for my body to be clean again, what are we going to do?" she said mischievously. She couldn't remember a time when she had felt stronger, more alive. And considering she didn't currently occupy her own body this seemed very odd. Or was that ironic?

Cursian flicked and eyebrow upward, "I sense you are feeling vital?"

Esme grinned.

"Cariad, I would think any strong physical intimacy in this place may cause problems," Cursian looked seriously worried. It reminded Esme of how a male spider must look just before the female wants her eggs fertilised. "Besides, have you forgotten your recent trials?"

Her face clouded, she moved back, the light in the room dimmed. "No, of course not. I just, I want you. Is that so bad?" her voice thickened under the memories, which in truth, she had forgotten.

Cursian matched her move back with his own move forward, "I am sorry, Cariad. I did not want to hurt you, but you may regret your actions if I do not gauge them properly. I would not compound your pain."

"It wasn't you though, was it?" Esme held herself very still as Cursian came close, her eyes big with sudden unshed tears.

"No, but I understand what torture does to a person's mind. In this form, your original pain is now only intellectual. You know it happened, but you no longer feel as though it happened, it is just another memory. Unless stirred and given life. What you experienced today, if you were still in your own mind would be immediate, but here it is not and your instinct holds sway. I do not want you to regret your instincts."

"How do you know what that kind of abuse does?" Esme asked quietly.

Cursian looked down at his hands, "There should be truth between lovers, long term lovers, but some truths are hard to understand and harder to forgive."

"We are safe in this place aren't we?" Esme asked and Cursian nodded. "Then tell me what you need too."

Cursian took a deep breath, and held out his hand. Esme reached for him and they sat opposite each other, the energy between them calm.

"I am going to tell you about my beginning, the violence with which I was born. You know of the late Middle Ages. It was a time of change and death, from death came rebirth and the early Renaissance became my playground. I was sent from the borderlands of Wales to court and proved to be a favourite, especially among the ladies. However, one lady eluded me and so, when I saw her one day walking down a small side street in London, I followed. She entered the smallest shop imaginable. It contained a startling variety of goods, everything from sheep skulls dipped in silver to balls made of crystal. How it survived the religious persecutions, I could not fathom until much later. As I stood bemused, she walked toward me from the rear of the shop. 'What are you doing here?' She was petite and beautiful, just the way I liked women then.

'I watched you come here and thought I may be of assistance,' I told her smugly.

'I do not need your help, Sir, but I will teach you a lesson for making a nuisance of yourself.' And she took me to the back of the shop. In that place, I learnt about true magic and how we can manipulate the world around us. I soon forgot about pursuing the woman and strove only to learn more and more. My teachers, whom I outstripped easily, classed me as an adept student. When I ran out instructors in England, I travelled to Europe. I worked around the controls of the Church, not easy in those days, and made contacts everywhere. I gained my knowledge purely for my own benefit, rather than any higher purpose. As I travelled further and further into Europe, I began to hear stories of a powerful mage who had lived for centuries in a land full of darkness and myth. I travelled to this land of darkness. It is the place you know of as Romania.

"During my time there I met a band of Gypsies and asked them about this mage. They told me they worked for such a man and would take me to meet him. They did." At this point Esme felt the well of pain Cursian sank into while telling his story, she squeezed his hands reminding him he was not alone in this darkness. "I went to his castle, and gained an audience. His people appeared to me to be slaves, but my thirst for knowledge overcame caution and good sense. By the end of the evening he knew exactly how powerful I had become, but also how naive. I found myself in a dungeon by dawn. This is where the nightmare really begins. All that day I tried to escape the stone room, then as darkness fell men came, four in all. They chained me hand and foot to the wall. I threw everything magical I had at them, but to no avail. They had a form of protection I could not smash.

"Once true dark took hold the master returned and my life began to die. That first night he had three women dragged in, they were bound and gagged. He removed the gags one by one, beat them with a horse whip until they bled and then fed by tearing open their throats. All this he did while ignoring my screams and my begging. He told me what I would become under his guidance and how he would use my mage skills, combined with his immortality to take more land and spread his kind further afield. As dawn came, he left and the corpses were removed. I spent the day praying to a God I felt sure had abandoned me, in truth, it is I who had abandoned him, but it would take years for me to understand.

"The following three nights kept to the same pattern. I became almost deaf to his victim's screams. Each night more women or young boys fell to his monstrous desires. On the fifth night of my captivity, the pattern changed. The master returned with his guards, he brought three beautiful women with him. By this time, I had seduced and been seduced, by many women in my life. I never believed a woman could rape a man. I learnt the hard way. They were as he was, as I am. They stripped me naked, made me hard and used my sex.

They caused pain and humiliation until I grew soft, then once more forced me to hardness. My chains were removed and the guards held me down while they took their pleasure. Their master watched all the time. At the end of the night all four of them began the feeding process. All of them bit me and drank. And unlike the way I can protect my victims, I had no place to hide.

"They left at dawn. I regained what strength I could. That night he returned, this time with three handsome men. The process began again, but sodomy had never been my lust. I realise now it was part of his desire to make me his creature. If you destroy the person through cruelty and shame then rebuild them, they are always yours. They will always need you. I do not know if male on male rape is worse than it is for women, but it still burns, the shame, pain, helplessness. Up until that point, I had never understood why sexual degradation is used in war and in the home, but it is about dominance and power. If you rape your enemy's women you have power over your enemy's reproduction, you show them you are stronger and better. If a man rapes a woman in her home or on the street, he is showing he has the power to control and own another human being. It is the one way to show you are at the top of the food chain. It is the only way to demonstrate your power. In war, it is an amazing tool of propaganda and if our so called civilised countries do not openly use it, I am sure they do not discourage its use in the heat of battle." He paused once more as though surprised by his own vitriol. Esme stayed silent, a confessor by virtue of her presence.

"That night, once they fed, I felt broken and close to death. I became feverish as the day wore on and I began to truly embrace the end. When night came, he returned once more, the seventh night of my captivity, but only with one woman who happened to be very heavily pregnant. I cried openly when I saw her, for I knew it was just a matter of time before she met her death. I would have wept for myself had I known what would happen next. He told me I would be reborn. That my transformation would be completed by dawn and I would never see the light again. He came to me and held my torn body so gently in his arms I did not doubt he felt love as he took all I had left to give while still remaining conscious. Just as death walked toward me for the last time, I felt hot liquid caress my tongue. Upon opening my eyes I realised he had bitten his own arm and thrust the wound into my mouth. I struggled to escape, he pushed harder. I could no longer breathe, so I swallowed. Afterwards, I remember nothing except agony tearing through me for hours. I do not remember that last dawn but I do remember waking the following night to find the pregnant woman still chained to the slab where she had been left. She screamed as her contractions started. Seeing through the darkness as though it were nothing, I smelt her desperation.

"Everything around me changed. My vision altered, my strength, my power and over it all, the hunger. The master returned, he told me he was glad I had survived the day and now it was time to feed as I would every night for the rest of my existence. He moved to the woman ensuring I continued to have a clear view. She began to scream with more than pain. I soon realised why. The master held a large knife in one hand, blood still stained his mouth from previous feeding. As the knife came down, she continued to vent her anguish. Blood filled my mind, only blood. I almost felt the knife as he drove it into her abdomen. How it felt to hold it, not how she suffered under it. He drew it with great skill toward him, away from me and I watched with fascination as great gouts of her life force flowed toward me. Once the wound reached her opposite hip, the master reached into the woman and drew the baby forth. By this time she simply moaned, all fight and life dying. He held the baby high as he severed the umbilical cord, then he walked toward me with the baby still held at arm's length, blood and mess covering the child. A boy child. The chains holding me grew tight as I tried to escape this new, disgusting game. The futility of it made me pathetic. My hunger began to ride me hard. I cannot describe how it feels to need something so disgusting, so degrading. To need it so badly you will sacrifice everything to that need. He sat opposite me holding the child as though it were an offering to a god.

"I still had a huge part of my humanity during that first night. He had never witnessed a new born vampire resist so hard, it made him proud to have turned me. However, toward dawn I began to lose more and more of myself, the hunger overrode everything. I moved toward him and the child, who cried piteously. I did it. As the child's neck became exposed, I bit him and fed and fed and fed, I drank the child dry. My chains were released and I fed on the drying blood of his mother. After that came weeks of blood and gore and hate and pain. In truth, Esme I do not know how long I was kept in that dungeon, but I raped, murdered and fed on everything sent to me."

Cursian stopped, his voice thick and eyes downcast. Esme sat still holding his hands. She had no idea how to take away that much horror. Her heart quite literally ached for him, but what could she say? Nothing in the end, Cursian seemed unaware of her and continued with his personal horror story.

"Weeks, maybe months later I began to be able to think again. Small things at first. I pulled away from people as they began to scream when I came close. Not wanting to hear the sound of flesh tearing under a whip anymore. Not wanting to fight a woman for sex, wanting her consent for my lust. Eventually, I began to remember my life from before and my mage training. My new life began to horrify me more and more with each passing night, but I knew I could not stop the master. One night I walked out, I just strode from the castle. Nothing stopped me. I had the strength of the vampire. By that time, my ruthlessness had become legendry. For a countless turn of seasons, I existed in the mountains fighting for my sanity.

"As the time passed, the woman and baby I had first taken haunted me. I wanted control. I returned to the discipline I had learnt for my mage craft. I used it to help harness the monster. Through this, I learned the secrets of the vampire. Everything the master had not told me I found for myself. I also began to hunt those that had turned me over to him, the family who would betray their own for a large enough coin. Slowly I wiped them out, until only the twins were left, one of which was your last incarnation, Cariad. Unknown to me at the time, because of our links, I watched instead of killing them outright. I grew curious about these strong twins, who had survived my rage. They joined with another clan and the more I watched, the more reluctant I became to end their lives. One night, when they were alone I went to them. They knew me, but Isabeau was one of the bravest and most stubborn women I have ever met, she would not feel fear. I fell in love with her and she with me, despite her brother.

"Together the three of us decided the master had ruled the land these people travelled for too long, controlled all for too long. We hatched a plan. A night of slaughter ended at dawn, with the master chained down in his own courtyard. It filled with light as soon as the dawn broke. By this time I knew I could stay awake long enough to survive the dawn so long as I remained in deep shadow and did not see the sun. I revelled in his screams and curses as time ticked by. I laughed as he tried to escape the enchantments I placed in the steel of the chains. Isabeau stayed at my side the entire time. Blood dripped from our swords while he suffered, but a thousand deaths would not have satisfied me at that time. As the sun rose he began to burn, this is when the Prophecy first manifested itself through Isabeau. Through her love, I would find the strength to maintain the balance of power on the earth. I knew great evil already and I would also learn the gifts of love.

"I did learn through Isabeau and gradually our other incarnations were relieved. But she was a person of simple thoughts and needs. Her need and my common sense meant I saw her marry a man who provided for her and their children. From that moment, I became inextricably linked to your family line. Centuries later, here you are."

CHAPTER THIRTEEN

Cursian gazed at Esme. The calmness in his eyes showed an acceptance. She leant forward and lightly kissed his mouth.

"You are a brave man," she murmured quietly.

"I am a survivor, that is all." Cursian's young face smiled sadly.

"But I know surviving is often the hardest thing to do."

"How will you survive what I have told you?" again, acceptance. Whatever decision she made about their fate, he would abide by.

Esme remained still for a moment. Taking in what he had told her changed her perception of him and yet, these things made him the man she knew. Had he expunged his sins over the centuries since his days of slaughter? It really wasn't her place to judge, but she could accept what he had become.

"There is nothing for me to survive. It is a story of nightmare, Cursian, but you are not that monster anymore. If I hang you for what you did several centuries ago I'd have to be mad." She reached for his face, now kneeling before him, leaning in for a kiss. She felt his resistance, but he soon yielded to her pressure.

They kissed deeply, gently, a kiss of healing passion, of forgiveness and love. Cursian began to push into her, so Esme responded, their bodies rising up to touch and their hands exploring. His physical body felt so different in this place, softer somehow. Yet, still so strong and supple. She wanted to hold that strength to her as close as possible. Their clothes vanished due to some esoteric trickery. Esme felt the heat burning through Cursian as strong arms crushed her to his chest. She gasped, his passion raced through her. His hardness pushed against her strong stomach and Esme wanted that young, supple body inside her, filling her up and completing her, nothing else mattered. She began to allow her body to collapse backward pulling him toward her. Cursian responded, lowering her gently to the floor. He held himself off her body for a moment, the desire flaring through his soul. No words passed between them as he slowly lowered himself over her, kissing her neck making her writhe.

The heat rose further between them, Esme noticed the virtual room surrounding them becoming brighter and brighter. With every breath, their lust became stronger and the light grew. Esme finally screwed her eyes shut pulling away from Cursian. Her world shifted with a nauseating wrench. She heard a cry from Cursian so desperate it almost broke her heart.

Her eyes flew open, her breath came in short gasps.

"Esme? Are you okay?"

She noticed the body on the bed, the room gloomy compared to her virtual reality. "Brigit?" she asked softly.

Esme felt gentle hands push her down, "It's okay, Esme you're fine, your body has purged the poisons. You need to take it easy though."

"Where am I? Where's Cursian?"

"He's safe. He said he would not be able to hold you through the transition from dusk to night. Apparently, it's harder than the night to dawn change. I guess it's easier to die than to live again. We've brought you to your home. You're in your own bed."

"I'm in West Wycombe?" Esme asked, Brigit nodded, Esme flopped back on the bed. "Fuck, what a week."

Brigit chuckled, then turned at a light tap on the door, calling out, "It's alright, May, she's woken up."

May walked in carrying a tray. Esme struggled upright blinking hard as the room moved slightly and her head buzzed. "Bollocks, I feel like I have the hangover from hell."

"At least that's all you're feeling." May grinned at her, "The last time I had a trip even half that bad I was out of it for weeks."

Esme smiled, "Thanks, honey that makes me feel loads better. Seriously though, I want to thank both of you for saving my life yesterday." Esme's face crumpled as she began to remember.

May sat on the other side of the bed and pulled herself toward Esme laying a hand on the duvet covering Esme's leg. "Think nothing of it, it was the most interesting introduction I've ever had."

Esme cocked her head to one side studying May, "Who's Ben?"

May blinked, stiffening, "What do you mean?"

"Sorry, I didn't mean to intrude, but you need to phone Ben and let him know where you are, he's worried and still loves you."

"Right, well," May slid off the bed clearly flustered. "I've brought something for you to eat and a bucket of tea. I'll see you both downstairs later." Her trainers and jeans made her escape silent.

Esme turned to Brigit. "I've upset her. I didn't mean too."

"Ben is a sore point with May. She's claimed to be gay since she was fourteen, then a year ago she met Ben, who is a really nice man and she fell in love with him. They had an affair, he's married, her old girlfriend kicked off and it all ended. May even moved to avoid him, I had to ban him from the shop, it's all rather sad really. How did you know?"

"It just popped into my head when she touched the bed," Esme said with incredulity, not really believing herself.

Brigit moved back slightly her eyes changed their focus, "Hmm, your aura has changed. There are wispy bits waving around like antenna and lots of holes. We will need to get those plugged as soon as possible or you will start to suffer physically."

Esme's expression became rueful, "Oh, well we wouldn't want me to suffer physically would we."

Brigit's expression became hard, "Esme, none of us want you to suffer, but truth be told your mother and father haven't made things any easier for you. Cursian is doing all he can to protect you and has done for years. Believe me, if he could have found a way to exclude you from this Prophecy he would have done."

"I didn't ask to be dragged into this either. I don't want to be some kind of home grown super hero," tears pricked the back of Esme's eyes.

Brigit sighed, her face softening once more. "I know that, ducky, but your path was set long before the day you were born and it's going to be hard for you to accept. Esme, there is no escape from this life. It doesn't matter how far you might run, the darkness has to destroy you, so we need to teach you to fight."

"Will my faith help?"

"Undoubtedly, this is what Christianity has been created for, to fight the evil in the world. People are all too willing to believe they can call on the esoteric forces to help them in day to day life, angels, tarot, animal spirits, karma whatever, but rarely do they take the bits that require hard work and dedication within their chosen path. Ignoring the unpleasant and hard parts of a faith system will leave you open to negative influences and few people know how to stop negative influences from flooding in regardless. Christianity protects you from the moment you agree to try to follow Christ's rules. All the major faiths have been set up to stop the amateur from being caught by the darkness. If people believe they can manipulate their surroundings through their spiritual strength and they believe in negative and positive influences, they should believe in God and the Devil, but for some reason they don't. I'm sure it's a fashion thing, these names conjure up old fashioned ideas of spirituality, but this fight has been going on for aeons. Both sides have become more and more organised over the millennia giving us organised faiths with rules to protect and guide."

"But I thought you were a witch? Doesn't that mean you deal with things that should be left well enough alone?"

"Normally I'd say yes, but Cursian has guided and protected me for decades and I have been canny enough not to push the boundaries when he isn't around to help. Besides, don't forget he was a Catholic before he was anything else, he brings a well established faith with him too."

"But why don't you need a faith to protect you?"

"I have a faith, it's just not conventional and I don't need to sign my soul over to Christ or Mohammed or Shiva to maintain my integrity. Not having an organised faith means I am more able to stretch the boundaries and can manipulate things others cannot touch. Cursian appreciates my neutrality. I understand how not to delve into the darkness that is so easy to reach."

Esme frowned, "What do you believe will happen when you die?"

Brigit shrugged, "I'll haunt May to make sure she doesn't make mistakes with her life. Other than that, I shall return to that from which I was created and I am happy in that knowledge."

"What about me? What am I going to become?"

"Honestly, Esme, I don't know. I have never seen anyone be told in theory how to do something, then that person do it and extend it to the point they surpass all known barriers within moments. You have no idea what the rules are, so you don't seem to know when you are breaking them, they don't restrict you or your imagination. And it's the strength and confidence of your imagination that will take you as far as you want to go. Just believe in yourself and all is possible. Esme, the only thing you must remember is your faith. You must always come back to that and use it as the basis for all your actions. I doubt you have ever really studied your personal faith in depth, but now I think you should begin that journey. It will be your check and balance point."

Both women fell into silence. Esme considered Brigit's words and knew exactly how hard it would be to truly internalise her faith. How hard the path is for those who wish to become spiritual beings and live their lives on that path. She didn't doubt her faith was strong enough, she just doubted her willingness to hand her life over to the strictures involved.

"I'm not sure prayer and meditation are really my thing for the rest of my life," she sounded sulky.

Brigit grinned, "It's all right, Esme we aren't asking you to become a nun and meditation can take many forms. You don't have to sit in a cold church on your knees for hours giving yourself rheumatism and you don't have to live like a desert father on water and rice for sixty years. I don't think even your Christ would have wanted that. You know that your martial training for instance is a form of mediation. Just make sure that everything you learn and do you take to your God, ask for guidance and never shut him out. I think that will do for now, and if we need to do more I'm sure we will find out soon enough. Anyway, enough lectures." Brigit rose, "You need to shower and change. I expect Cursian will want to see you when he wakes."

When Brigit left, Esme finished her food and tea looking round her old bedroom ruefully. With the curtains drawn, she had to remember what many of the shapes in dark corners actually were, old mirrors, small cabinets, old martial arts gear propped up. It felt strange being home. She'd avoided the place since her parents had died, even employing a cleaning company to come in once a month and give the place an airing saving her the journey. Matt wanted her to sell the place, but Esme wouldn't, she'd never get rid of the house. It had been a part of her mother's family for over one hundred years. With six bedrooms, three bathrooms, two shower rooms, dining room, lounge, large entrance hall, huge kitchen, drive and massive gardens it seemed a tad over the top for one small family, but she had loved growing up here. The place existed for adventures in attics, cellars and tree houses. Even for a young girl who had no real close friends Esme found endless entertainments in her home. The one room her mother didn't like her to play in, had been the secret study. Esme's father hadn't been allowed in there much either; he'd had his own office in one of the larger bedrooms. She'd been banned from that too.

A secret door beside the large sweeping staircase in the hall gave access to her mother's office. It opened by pulling at an almost unnoticed carving in the panel, which looked like every other carved panel in the house. Inside a room full of treasure awaited a small child. It was the only time her mother really lost her temper with her inquisitive daughter. Esme had snuck into the room and been found playing with a large deck of cards, laying out all the pretty pictures in her favourite order. Her mother yelled that they should only be used by Esme's Knit Knit Nanny. After that, Esme curbed her curiosity because it caused a row between her parents.

Esme smiled sadly at the memory, missing her mother very much suddenly. Instead of wallowing, she rose and moved briskly to her own shower room, keeping her mind carefully blank.

CHAPTER FOURTEEN

Esme left the shower after twenty minutes of hot water burning her skin. A shift inside her occurred. She knew Cursian had woken, for the first time she felt him become aware of her in return. She gasped at the sudden alienness of feeling another being almost inside her. She also had an incredible need to be near him. Esme grabbed an old dressing gown and went downstairs. Turning around the newel-post toward the back of the entrance hall, she reached out for the hidden door. Air smelling of lavender rushed out at her as she felt for a light switch. Once the room filled with light, she saw Cursian emerge from a small door on the right hand side. He had bent almost double to walk through. Unnoticed, she moved toward him. When he straightened, she reached out to touch his shoulder. At that moment, he sensed her presence and lurched sideways to stop the contact.

"Cursian?" Esme asked, obviously wanting to know why he had moved away.

"Esme, I did not expect you to find me here. I would have come to you." Cursian's voice held a roughness she'd never heard before. Almost as though someone had taken a file to his throat. He also looked different, paler if it were possible. His eyes shadowed by darkness, his cheeks even more hollowed out, emphasizing his bone structure further. He moved further behind the desk, which filled the middle of the room.

Esme frowned, "What's up? I felt you wake and had to make sure you were okay, why move away? I'm hardly likely to hurt you."

They stared at each other for several long moments. Esme confused and hurt by his rejection.

Cursian broke the silence, "Esme, what are the chances of you leaving this room without argument and waiting until later tonight before we talk?"

She cocked her head to one side, intrigued by the note of controlled... fear? Was it fear she heard behind his calm words? She considered his question, "Umm, I'd say your chances are fairly slim in all honesty. Why?"

Their physical status quo didn't change, but Cursian's presence felt larger. Esme stepped back slightly. "Don't do that, I don't need you to try to frighten me out of the room."

The presence shrank slightly. Instantly contrite, Cursian said, "Sorry, I would like you to leave without question though. I will explain later."

"No."

Cursian closed his eyes and drew in a deep breath, "Very well. I should have known. Esme, I need to feed very badly. The reason you have come to me is because I called you the moment I woke aware of my hunger. It is something vampire can do, those we have fed from or are closest to us will be called to provide when we need them. I am closer to you than the girl May therefore you came. I do not wish to feed from you or May, so please leave and let me do what needs to be done elsewhere."

Esme felt strange, she felt very alive, as though her whole body vibrated slightly. "Why go elsewhere, why not me?"

Cursian's eyes widened in obvious surprise, "Esme, I saw in your mind what they made you experience under those drugs. I saw what they attempted to make you believe, how they manipulated the violence of which I am capable. And make no mistake I am capable of that level of cruelty. I can not expect you to be able to come close to me and trust me after experiencing that degradation." He then looked downward, away from her, "I would also keep the monster that lives within me hidden from you. If we are to be lovers, Esme, I want you to see me as a man, not as a vampire."

Silence prevailed once more, becoming the most powerful thing in the room. This time Esme spoke first, puffing air out nosily, "Well, what do I say to that?" she moved closer to the desk. "Cursian you're not a man, not just a man anyway. I don't feel like you've made me a victim, I have the hangover from hell, but that's it. It wasn't you doing those things to me, it was them in a Cursian mask making it happen in my head like a bad dream and since then I have been with you in a special place. You have shared such pain with me I don't feel my own anymore. Don't cut me out like this, please."

Silence again. Cursian moved around the desk, no longer using it as a barrier. But he didn't close the distance between them in the small room. "I will not take advantage of you and I will not feed from you. I want you too much for that. You may reject me once you have felt it."

"I am not some simpering virgin. I have had more than my fair share of lovers and not all them tender. Physical love can and does take many forms. There are many people who enjoy mixing their pain and pleasure sensations." She closed the distance between them. Esme watched the pressure in his eyes grow. The temptation she presented to him on so many levels. She wanted to fan the flames. She wanted to tempt him into carnal pleasure.

"Believe me, Esme, if you were a simpering virgin I would never be able to bed you. I am also losing this battle because I really do not want to fight you, but I warn you now, once this starts I am unlikely to be able to stop. Carrying you with me has weakened too many of my barriers and dissolved much of my control. It has left me hungry. Hungry for everything." He leaned slightly toward her, still not touching, his eyes dilated dramatically with his desire. Her lips ached to feel his skin under her tongue.

Esme caught sight of his wickedly sharp teeth and remembered watching him feed from May and how it had made her feel. "Am I enough to sustain you?" she asked, not wanting to share.

Cursian drew back, "Not alone, no. I would weaken you too much. But there are ways I can feed that would ensure we do not have to upset anyone."

"That's tactful," she smiled. Esme closed the distance once more, until all she had to do was take a deep breath for her small breasts to touch his rib cage. Her heart raced, everything trembled in anticipation of his touch.

Cursian shut his eyes against the sight of her visible nakedness under the, not so concealing, robe. Yet his hands moved of their own volition and slipped around her body lightly holding the small of her back. "Just say yes and if you need me to stop I will do all I can to allow you out of the room before this goes too far. But once it starts in earnest, Cariad, I will not be able to stop. I have wanted you for too long, far too long."

Esme smiled shyly, feeling suddenly very nervous. Half of her wanting out, the rest screaming at her timid side to shut the fuck up and enjoy. "Yes," she whispered as she rose onto her toes and slipped her hands around his neck pulling him down, already feeling her body react to his passion.

They kissed and it wasn't gentle. Both exerting strength, seeking dominance, they pushed their bodies together hard. Cursian's hands rode across and up Esme's back, holding her so tight escape became impossible. She grasped him back, desperate to feel his shirt gone so she could dig her nails into his flesh. When they had almost made love inside Cursian's mind, it had been with incredible tenderness. This became the antithesis of that moment. The passion between them rode them hard, too long denied and haltered.

Esme felt herself pushed backward toward the wall, but that wouldn't be enough for her, the height disparity, despite Cursian's strength, would leave her at a disadvantage, she wanted the floor. She twisted her body in his arms, as their mouths continued to explore each other and Esme hooked her right foot behind his left leg beginning a traditional hip throw. Cursian grunted and before she knew what had happened he reversed their fall. Esme landed heavily the wind whistling out of her lungs.

"Shit," she gasped.

Cursian looked down, reining back enough to look at her. "Oops, are you unharmed?"

Esme growled at him, "Just get your damned clothes off you bastard."

Cursian laughed, a deep masculine laugh finally sure of her commitment, "Whatever the lady commands."

Esme raised an eyebrow, "You might regret that sentence."

Cursian continued to chuckle, she'd never heard him really laugh before. Despite his heavily dilated eyes and otherworldly energy, Esme had never seen him look more human, like the young man she'd met inside his mind. As she gazed up at him, Cursian rose from her body, sitting astride her hips, effectively pinning her to the ground. He noticed her watching him and he grinned wickedly. Reaching for the top button on yet another soft black shirt, he slowly undid it. Esme instantly became impatient and grasped for the fabric.

"Oh no, Cariad, you can wait. Besides, I have not seen your gifts just yet," he said pushing her hands down.

"You're going to make me suffer aren't you?"

Cursian smiled at her again. Esme groaned feeling the tightness deep inside her increase with the delay. He reached once more for the buttons slowly opening each, exposing the hard chest muscles that swelled and dipped with perfection. No chest hair or blemish marked the wide expanse of flesh. She gasped as he slid the shirt down his back. Smooth muscle bunched and flowed with each movement, a true predator's body. Esme couldn't believe her luck. She ran her nails down his thighs where they pinned her down, tearing at the jeans. The sexual tension rose another notch. His chest heaved as he fought for control. Esme wanted the control to be stripped unceremoniously away. All her experiences led her to this point and she wanted it.

Cursian's hands reached for her chest, a small tremor in them making her aware of her own power over him. He closed his eyes for a briefest of moments, stilling his fingers as they touched the light fabric of her robe. Esme stopped breathing. Her hands tensed against his thighs. Cursian opened his eyes and pulled the robe apart with one deft movement, raising his own hips enough to leave her naked beneath him as he stripped the fabric away. Esme froze, feeling self conscious for the first time in years.

"My God, you are beautiful and perfect," Cursian said, his voice even deeper than normal, almost vibrating through her.

His eyes roved over her muscular form, strong stomach with well-defined form, strong thighs and arms. Breasts that were small enough to remain pert even at thirty, but large enough to enjoy. Once his eyes drank it in, his hands covered every inch of exposed flesh, even running down her legs, feeling all. Esme surrendered to his need to explore and writhed. Allowing him to turn her over when he wanted to trace the muscles on her back and arse.

"Yielding and soft on the outside, but so firm under the surface, everything I could have wanted," he muttered, turning her back over. Esme reacted to his touch and reached for his belt, wanting his trousers gone. "Esme, I need to feed before this can go any further."

She blinked at him, confused by the words, lust knocking out all other thought. Finally, the penny dropped, "Oh, you mean you can't…." She wasn't sure where to take the sentence.

Cursian actually looked embarrassed, "On this occasion, Cariad, no. I cannot finish this without you giving me what I need. However, it will not always be necessary."

Smiling at him, she said, "Well, get on with it then."

As the words left her mouth, he once more raised his hips and pulled Esme's torso upright, hard against his chest. The gentle exploration vanished. With one hand behind her back, fingers tight in her skin, he grasped her breast hard causing her to cry out slightly. His fingers manipulated her nipple exquisitely. Esme threw her head back, away from his kiss, catching her lip on one of his canines on the way back. She felt blood fill the wound and begin to fall down her chin. Her tongue flicked out automatically to stop the blood flow, but hard fingers grasped her jaw. Cursian pulled her face toward him. Esme's eyes widened as his vampiric nature swam before her, his eyes glowed and his lips drew back fully exposing his otherness.

"Allow me," he rumbled through her. His tongue flicked out, fast like a snakes. The wound on her lip smarted. Breath ceased as the anticipation increased. Cursian licked his lips, then brought his face close enough for a kiss, but took a long lick covering the area she'd felt the trickle of blood. He swallowed, for Esme time stood still, the strangeness of the act refusing to be accommodated swiftly. These actions lived a little outside her reality. There would be no going back. No backing down from this extreme form of eroticism. Cursian's hand slipped skilfully from Esme's jaw to her throat, his thumb pushing her head slightly to one side. "Breathe, Esme. I will not have you pass out on me."

She did as instructed. A hard loud breath filled her lungs, moving past the lump of lust in her throat. Esme briefly wondered if this is what a gazelle felt like the moment before having its throat ripped out, then her loins contracted almost painfully and she doubted a gazelle wanted to be bitten this badly by the lion.

With several deft movements, Cursian removed his jeans. How he released her to pull his belt off; undo his black jeans and slide out of his trousers; before once more holding her close to his full naked body, happened without her really registering the actions. Esme only noticed the smooth coolness of his skin before Cursian's energy grew, surrounding her, as his face lowered to her neck. He whispered against her skin causing her to writhe, "I will not be taking you inside of me, I may forget you are there, I need to be completely aware of my surroundings and you have stripped me of too much control."

Esme couldn't answer and didn't care if truth be told, she just wanted this done. The dampness between her legs grew with every wasted moment. Cursian held her so tightly against his body, she couldn't move against him to allow herself any form of release. Just as her frustration reached the point she'd fight him to regain control, Cursian struck.

Her skin tore, instinct took over. She began to writhe and fight him, her hands suddenly finding themselves trapped behind her, pulled tight with one strong grip from her lover. Cursian effectively pinned Esme to his body in an upright position, her head cocked to one side by his own, held firm due to her own skeletal structure. His one free hand slid under her behind, at the same moment his teeth withdrew slightly opening the small wounds in her neck. Esme cried out incoherently with fear and an unbelievable desire. The blood flowed into his hot wet mouth. She heard him groan into her neck. His fingers reached between her thighs. Esme opened them as far as possible, despite being trapped by his strength. As she felt him swallow against her neck, his fingers entered her, firmly and smoothly following the contours of her body. They both groaned. Esme pushed harder against him, wanting more of his hand inside her, wanting the pressure on her neck never to stop or the strength holding her hands to never be released. Before she could even detect it growing, the orgasm hit her, like a train. She screamed unable to move against wave after wave of energy spiking through her. Cursian's fingers drew in and out of her harder and harder, making her passion rise again and again.

Esme slowly became aware and registered Cursian's desire full and firm against her stomach. He released his grip on her throat, licking the wound clean while he waited with unbelievable patience for her to recover. Every movement he made against her body sent another tremor through her, but Esme wanted more. She wanted all of him. Once he allowed her hands to be free and he'd shifted his weight from her thighs, Esme wriggled out from underneath him, deftly turning her body over, rising onto all fours facing him. She tilted her head upward and saw his face for the first time since feeding. His flesh had filled out, his eyes shone with heavy sexual passion. The other hungers were chased away and his skin felt almost hot to the touch. Esme allowed her own lust to fill her eyes. Reassuring him, she may have had her pleasure but there was a great deal more where that came from, she lowered her head.

Esme felt Cursian throw his own head back and cry out as her mouth covered his erection. His length and thickness felt perfect in her mouth as she withdrew slightly flicking her tongue over his tip, concentrating on the flesh joining the skin and head. His fingers grasped her head and pulled spasmodically on her hair as he fought not to force her to take more than she was able. Esme's loins tighten, responding to his need. She groaned wanting to take more of him in her mouth with each push downward. The rhythm they created threatened to overwhelm the vampire. Swiftly, she withdrew her mouth completely and spun her body around. Her legs opened, straddling his own without conscious thought. Cursian held her hair tight pulling her head back viciously with one hand, while the other pulled her hips into the right angle for him to thrust. Which he did without ceremony; without control.

Esme thought he had split her in two. The full length and width of him too much to bear. She cried out as he hit her hard with his body, the relief as he withdrew. With the next push forward, she found her body suddenly able to cope. Cursian cried out as she pushed back with just as much force. Esme rode him as hard and fast as he came to her. Never had she felt such amazing completeness with another person. The tempo increased and the muscles in her arms burnt with the pressure he exerted. Her breath shortened due to the angle he held her head. Things began to change as their desire reached its peak.

Their bodies and souls joined as one, manifesting their power. Swirls of colour leapt around them forming a whirlwind spectrum, reds, yellows and oranges with flashes of light bouncing around. Her own energy rose higher, the colours blended before her eyes making her world look like fire.

Esme suddenly became aware of her own body as Cursian's fingers dug hard into her buttock. With his desire so close to the edge, she demanded he release his passion and he pushed hard against her body, only his grip on her hair stopping her falling on her face. Lights danced frantically. Esme felt the familiar tightening of her muscles as he filled her, the wave crested and an orgasm hit her again. Cursian held himself still against her body, while she allowed instinct to keep his rhythm going for him. They both peaked. Wave after wave moved through them as the colours danced and swirled in and round the couple. She crested the wave, knowing Cursian matched her, feeling him flood through her, feeling his sense of self fall through the top of her head. Esme's tears traced paths down her face. Her head dropped as Cursian released her.

CHAPTER FIFTEEN

As he withdrew Cursian almost collapsed onto Esme. He had never experienced such passion and power. Nothing he had ever done came close to what they created in that small hidden room. The flashes of the energy raised between them began to dim and slow. Fading back to the where they came from, he briefly mourned their passing knowing they would never again create such spontaneous beauty. His hands rested lightly on his lover's lower back. As he became more aware of his immediate surroundings, Cursian felt Esme shaking under his hands. The sensation cleared the last of the orgasm's impact from his mind. He shifted position moving his long body parallel looking at Esme without having to touch her.

"Cariad, are you well? Have I hurt you?" Cursian felt like smacking himself in the head for his stupidity.

Of course he had hurt her. Not only by bleeding the poor woman, but also fucking her so hard he was amazed he hadn't killed her. The vampire quickly realised Esme didn't just shake, she sobbed. Cursian backed away from her, wanting to have the last few minutes back. Wishing he had left her alone in the room. Cursian knew his desires were extreme. Although soft loving making made him content, an edge of violence always left him feeling more complete. He had constantly worried this would be too much for Esme. He did not want to have her hate him for loving her the only way he knew how. From the highest point of ecstasy, he plunged into despair. He did not want to see the hurt on her face when she turned and accused him of hurting her, of not controlling his needs sufficiently.

Esme slowly sank back on her haunches, tossing her hair away from her face. She winced while he warily watched her profile. Shame bit into his gut making him want to vomit all he had taken. Her hands ran down her face, wiping her tears.

Cursian could bear no more. He twisted away grabbing at his discarded shirt, wanting to flee. Obviously, it would be impossible to have her love twice in one lifetime. Not only that, but having the soul enhanced with Esme's personal twist, made her irresistible. Her passion and power, her strength and determination had driven him mad with desire for years as he watched her from a protective distance. That is why he finally lost control. Too much of a good thing, with no resistance from his heart's desire. Cursian kept his movements as small and careful as possible, so she should feel no threat. He slipped his shirt on. But his jeans were too close. If he reached for them, he would scare her. His hand stretched out, she turned to face him.

"Wow! That was the most amazing but scariest experience of my whole entire life. Did you see those swirly patterns? Or was that just me because I stopped breathing?" Esme's voice sounded hoarse and blood still trailed down her neck pooling slightly in the skin around her clavicle. "Are you alright?" concern made her face crease.

"Yes," Cursian said doubtfully.

"You sure? You don't look okay."

"You were crying. I hurt you," he said dumbly.

"Is that why you've put the shirt on, because you think you've hurt me?"

"Yes."

Esme looked surprised. But not half as surprised and off centre as Cursian felt.

She said, "Well that's daft. My love, I was crying because having someone's orgasm rip the top of your head off with its passion is an emotional experience. Cursian, you haven't hurt me, at least not in a bad way."

"I have not scared you away? Made you hate me?" Cursian continued to hold himself very still not believing her words.

Esme began to crawl across the room toward him. He flinched as she touched his arm, trailing her fingers over the fabric of his shirt. "No, you have not scared me away. Your desire is intense, but how can I hate you for a passion that matches my own?"

Cursian froze, her words should have lent him comfort, but fear of losing her meant he didn't know how to unravel his feelings. Esme must have recognised at least some of this chaos and moved closer. Pulling at his arms, pushing at his legs, she managed to open him up enough to curl her own body against his ridged form.

Esme touched his face, "Cursian, you feel as though you have been deeply wounded, what's wrong?"

The vampire grimaced with the bitterness consuming him because of her gentleness toward him. The scent of blood from her neck raised his hunger. He flinched away not wanting to show his weakness. Esme cried out slightly as her nails caught the skin over his cheek ripping a shallow wound. The sting caught him by surprise. He held still once more. Almost leaping out of his skin completely when Esme's tongue flicked up the wound.

Cursian twisted to face her, their noses almost touching. "What have you done?" he demanded.

"I am trying to get you to talk to me, that's all, or are you regretting what's just happened and wish me gone?" Esme's face clearly showed she was not amused.

"Do you know how much damage my blood can do to you? What I can create if you take it into your system?" Cursian found his anger reassuring, he embraced it.

"Oh bollocks, you can't turn me into a vampire with one lick. Besides, I wanted to see what it was like." She grinned clearly unable to stay cross, "And I like it, kind of kinky in a new and interesting way."

"Woman you are mad. Please, do not ever do that again. We are having more than enough problems trying to keep you safe without creating a whole new kind of creature." He paused, "Damn it, you are a sneaky wench. Seriously, Esme, are you sure you are quite well? I went a great deal further than I meant too." His concern for her subsumed his self pity, stealing his splendid isolation.

"Cursian, I couldn't be more okay. Listen carefully, lover. That was the most," she tilted her head slightly thinking, trying to find the words. "Connected, that's a good word for how it made me feel. Connected to you and too everything else at the same time. Yes, there are parts of me that feel more than a little bruised and my neck stings and I'm sure I am going to have some extremely interesting muscular strains in the morning, but I'm fine," she said earnestly.

Cursian studied her face and realised she actually meant it. She really did seem able to deal with who he had become over the centuries. The relief flooding through him made him take her in his arms and hold her close for the first time, as a gentle lover would. He breathed in her scent, from the shampoo she used, to the smell of her sex and her skin. He relaxed into her arms allowing her to hold him and love him and protect him. Cursian actually felt something he had not experienced for decades. He felt peace and hope for the future.

Gradually he became aware of voices in the hall outside their secret room. He pulled away from Esme, "We have company and they do not sound particularly amused."

Esme heaved a sigh, "Are we ever going to be left alone?"

Cursian lightly stroked her face, "Probably not, Cariad, but it might be fun trying to find some quiet time occasionally."

Esme grinned at him as she reached for her robe and threw him his jeans. "Are you sure you are well, Esme? You are moving very stiffly."

Her grin widened further, "I'm fine, Cursian, really but I want a rematch and a chance to make you feel this abused."

Cursian shook his head, wondering what he had done to deserve a woman who was capable of matching his potential in so many spheres of life. "Listen, I would like you to go downstairs, spend the night with me. I shall find you some food and liquid to replace what I have taken. I will also inform Brigit you are safe and explain what happened, they are bound to have felt the pull."

"Oh, you mean there's a room down there?" Esme pointed to the small door.

"What do you think, woman? I live in a closet shaped like a coffin when I stay here? This house still has a few surprises. It is one of the reasons your mother would not allow it to be sold," Cursian turned away, leaving Esme to find her own way. It would take her awhile to figure out how to open the small door.

He quietly left the study still buttoning his shirt, stopping in the hall as he sensed May walking toward him.

"I've found Cursian," she crossed her arms and hooked a hip as she stared at him.

Cursian sighed, he knew Brigit and May must have felt an incredible amount of power being collected and released by his lovemaking. He also knew it would make Brigit furious. This had been his main objective in stopping Esme from leaving the study. He hoped he'd be able to deflect the ensuing anger.

"What the bloody hell do you think you are playing at?" Brigit appeared from the lounge.

"Brigit."

"Don't, 'Brigit', me. You are either incredibly stupid or… no I think that sums it up, you are just plain bloody stupid! Do you know how much of an affect you have had on even the simplest plains of existence? You've caused a bloody great tsunami of power. Every one of our enemies is going to be able to pinpoint our location as soon as they pick up on the wave."

"Do you think we really need to discuss this in front of May?" Cursian asked urbanely.

"I think the poor woman has a right to know what kind of idiot she is going to be working for when I die. Which is going to happen a lot sooner than it should, if you pull another bloody stroke like that." Brigit actually shook with rage.

"Brigit, what has been done, has been done. You cannot think for one moment we would be able to put off our joining forever," Cursian remained calm.

"You've joined with her?" Brigit went quiet.

"Well, what did you think I would do? Esme and I are destined to be together."

"Cursian, what have you done? She knows nothing of this, she doesn't understand what this could do to her."

Cursian began to feel resentment toward Brigit. The woman had no right to doubt his decisions. All that happened with the bonding would be an extra level of connection between himself and Esme. She wouldn't even notice.

"This will not harm her. It is a natural process. A bonding between us is inevitable," his resentment began to reflect in his voice.

"I know that, Cursian, but Esme should have been made aware. The Prophecy is at its most vulnerable, the Scion's knowledge has never been weaker and our enemies are strong. You know this and in bonding to you, Esme is placed in greater danger."

"We are stronger together than apart."

"Are you? Esme still doesn't understand who and what you truly are and what her role is within your tangled web. Cursian, this bonding will kill her if something happens to you. And what if they catch hold of Esme again? They could have direct access to you. Every decision the two of you make will be affected by the other's emotional influences. You must sever this tie."

"I will not," Cursian's humanity began to fold away. He fought for control not wanting to give Brigit further examples of his current vulnerability.

"This bonding is a sacred thing. It can only happen safely when both are fully aware and have reached a higher level of spiritual understanding." Brigit walked toward him, hands outstretched, "Cursian, I know you have that understanding and you crave your match, but Esme is not ready. She may never be ready. The two of you are here to defeat evil in order to maintain the planet's spiritual balance and yes, the bonding can help that happen. But it can hinder too. You know you have to break this tie."

Cursian ground his teeth, "We are meant to be together, it is ordained." His fists clenched. He noticed May taking several steps back causing his predators instinct to rise.

"Yes, but you are left weak by Esme's weakness. She is naive and powerful. She is also stubborn and ignorant. Cursian, you must break this bond. With our enemies so active, you are weakened. They will use and destroy her to get to you. I beg you reverse what you have done, it is not too late."

"I will see she comes to no harm," he growled.

"Like you did when we were in London?"

"Arrg," Cursian threw his hands up as though to claw the sky down. "What would you have me do? Sacrifice myself to this Prophecy for all eternity? I wish the damn thing were destroyed. May humanity live in darkness forever, so I can have just a little joy. Why should I care what happens to you all? If my existence were discovered, I would be hunted, caught and torn apart by scientists or murdered. No one in this miserable world wants spiritual enlightenment, not really, and that is why my punishment must continue endlessly. Now I am denied the very thing I have waited for, for so long."

"Cursian, all you have to do is break the bond. Not end things with Esme," Brigit took a step back, his rage beating at her.

Cursian's control slipped completely, "The bonding occurred of its own volition. I could not have controlled it or stopped it if I had tried. Nor did I wish too. Do you really think making love to Esme would come without strings? And do you really think we are able to be together without physical intimacy? I have waited years for this moment. I will not be controlled by you or anything else including the Prophecy. I cannot be with her without the bonding becoming deeper and deeper. It is how it is meant to be and now you wish me to have a normal relationship with her? It is not possible. But if this cursed Prophecy demands it, perhaps I should sever the ties and may God preserve the Scion in the aftermath of such action. I will leave it to you to explain her loss and pain!"

He turned away from the two women, no longer able to discuss the matter. His drive for death and need to feed all encompassing. He wanted to rip out their throats for denying him his salvation. Cursian went back into the hidden room and opened the entrance to his private suite. He carried his anger like a cloak of darkness around him.

FROM BRIGHT, TO GREY, TO BLACK, PROTECT US....

The phone rang, "Yes. Good, you have done well, proceed." A man in his fifties turned to a woman who appeared slightly younger. Both had strong features and bodies, with dark hair shot through with grey.

"It seems the game is once more a foot, sister dear. They have been located and are making more noise than a room full of neophytes. It appears our erstwhile enemy has finally lost his control and our people have fully exploited the fact, as planned. We shall need to move operations to Wycombe." He smiled and raised a large glass of brandy to his lips.

"I am pleased to hear our efforts have not been in vain. I wondered what had caused such a magnificent wave of energy to wash through me earlier. I must say they are powerful, this pair. It has been hard to break him and keeping control will be harder, but worth the effort. I would rather that than have him dead." She also smiled and raised her own glass in return.

"The rite should be carried out soon, we do not wish to lose the power this wave created and I can only store it for so long," the man frowned to emphasise his words.

"Then we should spread around what we have gained, call others in, I wish for some companionship tonight. And we have not enjoyed each other for many days, brother, I miss your needs." She dropped from the leather chair and moved on all fours to push herself into his lap.

The man stroked her head, "I wonder if the Scion can be trained to enjoy our games, would you like to play with her?"

"Oh yes, all that power and strength broken and at my mercy. I can feed on her despair for decades, especially if we have her lover converted to our cause."

"Well, I would not wish to disappoint, we shall decamp tonight and bring the ties tight around our subjects. Now my vicious pussy cat, how many of our followers would you like to sample our delights?"

CHAPTER SIXTEEN

Esme stood dumbfounded at the size of Cursian's apartment. When she finally managed to work out how to get through the small door, she found a short set of stairs. These led down into a room of sizable proportions, in fact, bearing in mind her father's cellar, this must also go under the garden. There were no window's, which didn't really come as a surprise, but there appeared to be everything else a normal person required. He had a large double bed covered in a deep purple embroidered coverlet, with a wrought iron gothic bedstead. A wardrobe, chest of drawers and bedside cabinet of dark antique wood comprised the rest of the bedroom suite. This flowed into the lounge area, with large bookcases, old writing desk and huge old leather sofa. Esme found two doorways, one to a small kitchenette and the other to a large bathroom. This made her smile as it showed the obvious priority. A double ended corner bath with jacuzzi dominated the room. She did wonder how they'd managed to get it down the stairs.

Esme returned to the lounge area and stood looking round. Despite the books and plush rugs on the floor, the large central room felt devoid of permanency. There were few personal items and only two pictures. One, a beautiful watercolour representing dawn rising over the sea and another of light piercing a dabbled English wood. Harsh reminders of the unattainable.

It made Esme sad to think Cursian surrounded himself with so little. A more cheerful thought popped into her head as she looked at the bed. Should she strip and lounge on the bed erotically? Or be demure? She moved toward it tentatively, this room really didn't feel like it belonged to her house. She jumped as she heard the door slam at the top of the stairs.

"Hiya," she called. "I hope Brigit didn't give you to much of a hard time."

Cursian descended the stairs slowly, when he reached the bottom he looked at her.

"You are to leave," he said.

Simple words. No obvious violence within them, but Esme flinched, his words acting as a whip. Their impact licked like white fire at her soul. She saw the dark poison they contained and felt the cold rage boiling across the room.

She held her ground, "I think we've already had this conversation." Esme felt sick to the stomach and her knees were weak.

The stone wall at the back of the apartment slammed into her. Esme discovered stone is as hard as it looks when your head and shoulders meet it with the force of a train. She gasped, her vision spotty. Esme hung limply in the strong, cold hand crushing her throat.

"You will leave," waves of hate pushed into her body.

The hold on her throat tightened. All breathing ceased and she began to grasp ineffectually at the hand. The grip released just as suddenly as it started. Esme hit the floor in a heap. Lying still, she tried to breathe around the pain in her head and neck.

Slowly, she pushed herself onto all fours, mimicking the movement she had used such a short time ago in the study. Gradually, her breathing settled. Esme raised her head. Cursian stood over her, tall, dark and as far from human as she had ever seen him. Fear coursed through her, gut squelching fear.

"Why?" her voice betrayed her terror.

"I do not need to give you a reason, Scion," Cursian's words would have given a blizzard pause for thought.

Esme took a deep breath and despite the mind numbing terror of facing death, she rose to meet Cursian.

"Tell me why?" she managed, her fists rigid against her sides.

The futility of her situation made Esme even more stubborn, she wanted answers for her lover's bizarre cruelty.

There had to be a reason, no one, no matter how weird, behaved this strangely.

"That is the wrong attitude to take," he snarled.

The consequences of her decision became obvious as her feet lifted from the floor, again. She hit the mattress in a woof of purple silk. Cursian's legs straddling her own an instant later. He pinned her hands over her head. Esme began to fight. She twisted and cried out, but nothing gave. Fighting concrete would have accomplished more.

"Struggle all you like woman, I have had centuries of practice holding people still. Your fire and instinct will not serve you here. Stop and I shall not hurt you anymore than necessary," Cursian grinned, flashing his incisors.

Esme stopped moving. Instead, she hawked and spat at him, her eyes blazing with hate. Cursian didn't change expression as he calmly wiped the spittle from his face and neck. He backhanded her with a blow, which would have broken her neck, had she been standing and the blankets not absorbed the worst of the power. Esme's world switched off, folding into darkness.

Moments or hours later, everything rushed back in a wave of pain and sickness. Cursian's weight continued to pin her helplessly to the bed. The right side of her face screamed with pain. Her hearing returned slowly. The words filtering in made no sense, until she recognised some Latin. The vampire's eyes were closed, not that it made any difference to her being able to move. His lips murmured different sentences over and over. Esme sensed power begin to swirl around her, it gathered directly over the two of them, forming a dark forbidding cloud. Tears wet her cheeks. Cursian's voice rose louder, more commanding. His free hand reached into the cloud. His voice threatened to tear the walls down. From the cloud of darkness, Cursian drew a sword made from its essence. Esme screamed.

The medieval blade swept downward in a dark arc ending several inches above her chest. Intense pain flowered from her groin, abdomen, stomach, heart, throat, brow and head; she could no longer draw enough breath to scream. Colours began to swirl up the blade, dragged from her body. She watched Cursian draw the sword upward. Pain made Esme compliant. Cursian didn't have to hold her down. She tried to beg for mercy, but she could see nothing of the man she loved in his face, no flicker of compassion. The blade reflected no light as he plunged downward and drove it relentlessly though her heart. Esme bucked upward on impact finally finding the power to scream. The blade bit the mattress, her blood turned to lava in her veins, the pain enough to cause madness. She screamed repeatedly, her hands clutching the dark, cold metal of the sword. Cursian threw back his head, screaming. His weight no longer held down her writhing body, which tried to remove itself from the impaling weapon.

Her hands suddenly closed in on themselves and the pain ceased. The blade vanished. Esme turned her sweat soaked head looking for her tormentor. Blood soaked the front of Cursian's shirt, right over his heart. Brigit and May stood behind him transfixed with horror. Esme watched, struck dumb as he turned away.

"It is done as you requested, the ties I created have been torn asunder. But know there are some links I cannot sever. If she survives this night, she will recover. Goodbye."

Esme watched as Cursian's lean form walked past the women and rose up the stairs. He did not move with anything other than his usual grace and he did not look back. The door closed and Esme allowed the darkness in the corners of her vision to sweep forward.

CHAPTER SEVENTEEN

Her hearing returned first. The beautiful voice drifted through her darkness, so she followed it to the light. Her eyes flickered open and the singing stopped. The world moved slightly as a face appeared in her line of sight.

"Hi, Esme, you all there yet?" May asked.

Esme swallowed experimentally a few times, it hurt. She shook her head instead. The answering smile seemed the kindest and sweetest thing in the world.

"Okay, honey, don't worry. Let's sit you up and I'll give you a drink." May slipped her arm under Esme's shoulders raising her up.

Esme's world did more than spin, it revolved like some demon driven tumble drier. When everything became fairly still she opened her eyes once more.

"What happened?" she croaked, barely audible.

"It's a long story and one I'm sure you aren't going to like. Now is not the time. The main thing is he's left you alive, just, and didn't kill either me or Brigit, which is a minor miracle considering."

May held a glass of water up for Esme to drink.

"Please, I need to know," Esme's voice produced a whisper.

May sighed, "To be honest I'm not sure what happened. Cursian connected to you in a way he shouldn't have when you made love yesterday. Brigit went mental and told him it would kill you to be attached to him in that way. He then lost his temper and came down here. It took us ages to get in, Brigit's upstairs recovering due to the expenditure of magical energy she used to find the room. Anyway, as we arrived we saw the whole stabbing through the heart and blood flowing from him not you. Both of you screamed the place down. He more or less fell off you then the sword thing disappeared.

Cursian rose, covered in claret, told us you'd been separated and left. We haven't seen him since. It's now midday."

Esme began to weep. Overwhelming loneliness and a crushing sense of betrayal filled her heart. Every atom in her body hurt with his loss. May wrapped her arms around the other woman holding her gently. When the tears subsided, they sat on Cursian's bed side by side, holding hands. Esme hiccupped occasionally.

"How could he do this to me? I know he loves me, I don't understand," Esme sounded terribly small.

"I don't know, maybe it's the only way for the two of you to be together without this cosmic bonding getting in the way."

"But I can't feel him. For the first time in my life, I can't feel him. For years I must have had this part of me that was connected to him and now it isn't and I don't know how to breathe without that feeling." Tears slid down Esme's face again. Blankness stretched before her, a void.

"It'll be okay. I'm sure it'll be okay. Either he'll come back and you can have a more normal relationship or you'll recover, no one actually died."

"This is where I have to carry on as normal. Where my broken heart is made to heal over time," she said bitterly. "I suppose the Prophecy is still important?" Esme stated blankly.

" 'Fraid so, sweetie. There is nothing can stop that juggernaut. Come on, we need to get you out of this room." May jumped up, making the bed move violently again.

Esme took a deep breath. People survived broken hearts all the time. They had too, or there'd be lots of dead people walking around. The pain had to stop at some point. "I feel full of holes," she muttered as she followed May slowly up the stairs.

"I'm not surprised, the last few days have punched bloody great big motorways of negative energy through you, but we have some excellent cures so don't worry."

Esme couldn't care enough to worry. May's continuing cheerfulness and chatter gave her something to focus on, following the younger woman became Esme's goal.

The kitchen looked exceptionally gloomy in the dull autumn light. The emptiness of the house settled around her shoulders. That barrenness must have eked out from the vacuum filling her soul. She had never felt so confused or lost. What the hell had changed in such a short time? Esme noticed her hands still shook. She seemed to be suffering from shock.

The last few days blurred in a mess of the weird and wonderful, with huge doses of violence thrown in for good measure. She had overturned every notion of reality for a man she only remembered in dreams and glimpses. Yet he had taken over, completely. Esme barely believed her life had been normal. Run of the mill. Sane. She wondered if it would be possible to return to some kind of normality, to go back to work and meet another Matt. Carry on as normal. Normal, a normal life, that's what she wanted, she wanted to go back. To forget the last few days. Forget Cursian; forget magic and her family's nasty heritage. No vampires, mages, werewolves or demons. Tax returns, receipts, newspapers and the Stock Exchange should fill her life. Esme longed for the dullness.

May's voice interrupted Esme thoughts, "What?"

"I said, I've been in contact with Ben. He's coming over this afternoon I thought it might give you something else to think about."

"Ben?"

"Remember, you told me to contact him yesterday. He's an old friend, apparently he's left the wife and wants to talk to me. Anyway, he's coming over in about an hour, so we need to get you changed, I'd like you to meet him."

"May, I don't want to talk to anybody," plucking at the torn silk robe Esme's eyes filled with tears once more. "I don't want to see anyone. I need a shower," her voice cracked with taut emotion. She noticed her body stank of Cursian's scent, an earthy, wolfy muskiness.

Falling to her knees in front of Esme, May said, "You don't have to talk to him. I just wanted to give you a distraction, something else to think about." She grabbed Esme's hands as they compulsively plucked at the grey silk.

"Come on, we'll forget the food for the time being, we'll go and shower. I can always phone Ben and stop him."

"No, don't stop him," Esme's hands grasped May's with crushing intensity. "You must see him, it's really important. You should be happy and he will make you happy."

"Okay, Esme," May withdrew slightly, taken aback by the intensity. "But we really do need to get you clean."

"Yes, yes I want to wash him out of me, off me. Get rid of him." Esme began plucking at her skin.

Once more drawing Esme's hands away from her body, May coaxed the other woman upstairs to the en-suite. When they arrived, Esme shook so badly May wasn't prepared to trust her in the water on her own. Joining her in the warm water, May helped Esme meticulously clean her skin. Anguish erupted when the bite on Esme's neck started stinging because of the shampoo. May had her hands full trying to stop her friend from tearing her wounded throat while washing the soap out of her hair.

Forcing Esme to finish scrubbing, May wrapped her up in a towel and sat her on the bed. She then towel dried and brushed Esme's hair before bundling her into an old set of jogging trousers and sweatshirt. Esme sat dully throughout, not noticing and seeming not to care about the casual nakedness shared by the two women. Once clean and her neck wound covered in gauze and tape, May led her to the room the young witch used. There, May changed into clean tight jeans, running shoes and thick blue velour shirt. Being more fully endowed than Esme, May wore a bra that helped to further emphasise her cleavage, aided by several undone buttons on her shirt. She stood in front of a long mirror.

"Nice and not too tarty, also I don't look like a dyke." May shook out her damp hair, forming long black tails down her back. The colours brought out the translucent quality of her skin and the dark blue of her eyes.

Esme smiled, "You look lovely. Ben's just pulled up outside."

May frowned, "How do you know that, we're at the back of the house?"

Esme shrugged, uninterested. She rose and walked to the door, "I'll let him in, the kitchen's warmest, and I should eat. If you want private time I'll come back up here."

May narrowed her eyes, "I don't think I want to leave you alone right now. I can talk to Ben with you around, so we'll just stick together."

Esme shrugged again and went to answer the doorbell, leaving May to slide some mascara over her eyelashes.

CHAPTER EIGHTEEN

Esme walked downstairs as the doorbell chimed again, making her jaw clench. She opened the door and heard May appear on the landing. Esme faced a man in his mid thirties, with skin the colour of milk chocolate. He stood awkwardly on her doorstep, a worried expression clouding his dark brown eyes. Assessing him, Esme decided she approved. He stood just shy of six foot and seemed fit under his jeans and jumper. His hair flowed around him in long dreadlocks.

"Ben?" Esme said, feeling May stood close.

"May…"

Esme moved aside as Ben walked past her, he hadn't even registered her existence. Turning she watched them move together. For a handful of moments they stood at arm's length, just looking, simultaneously they folded into each other's embrace. Esme smiled sadly and closed the door. "I'll go and make lunch or something, see you down the back when you're ready."

Half an hour later May walked into the kitchen with Ben in tow. She wasn't smiling. "Esme, we need to talk."

"What's happened now?" weariness filled her void.

"Ben's been lying to me, he's not married and he didn't go back to his wife. He also knows about your abduction." May looked as though her whole world weighed a thousand tonnes and it sat on her shoulders growing heavier. Esme knew how she felt.

"I'm not going to like this am I?" Esme rose, losing the fight for her lunch, her stomach felt full of rats.

"I don't know to be honest. He won't tell me anything else without you or Cursian present and I don't think our friendly neighbourhood monster is going to be around for a while."

Flinching at the pain and bitterness in May's voice, Esme turned to Ben, knowing she had finally had enough and wasn't likely to be able to handle this new crisis.

The Prophecy

"Well?" resignation tinged with fear made her sound harsh.

"It's a long story," Ben said, as he moved nervously from foot to foot.

"Then I suggest you get on with it and sit down before I knock you on your arse for fidgeting." Esme pointed to a chair opposite her. Ben sat, May remained leaning against the kitchen cabinets.

"It started when I left home at seventeen. I moved to Glastonbury from a nasty Bristol estate. I'd always been thought of as fey and Glastonbury seemed like the right place for a Somerset lad to find a true home. And I did."

"Okay, very sweet, but you've been lying to my friend for months and you seem to know far more than you should about our situation. Who are you?" Esme's anger began to bubble.

"I'm getting to that," Ben anxiously fiddled with his own fingers. "When I arrived at Glastonbury life went a bit weird. Too many drugs and stuff, anyway, one day when I was wandering up the High Street from the Pilgrims pub I was accosted by this old woman. It turned out that Glastonbury, as well as being full of freaks and fools, also had some really sound spiritual groups.

"Go steady there Ben," May muttered. "Esme's a real Christian with a real faith and it's just about all she has left to hang on to at the moment. So no getting cosmic on our arses."

Ben, looking apprehensively at the two women, gulped and started again. "This group are party to the cosmic interconnectedness of our planet. They understand and use ley-lines."

Raising a derogatory eyebrow Esme murmured, "Ley-lines?"

"Don't dismiss them, Esme," May said. "It's what you tap into all the time. These lines run throughout the surface of the world and join up at different sites, Glastonbury being one of them. All that blue stuff you said you sank into, that would have been your mind seeing a line for you to use. You're a natural at it, most of us aren't." May finally sat down beside Ben.

Ben took up his narrative, "This group of people are very specialist. They monitor and assess the world's energy flows. They understand that the world is the manifest plane of existence in which the war between Good and Evil plays itself out. Part of what this group does, involves monitoring the flow of power being used by those with access to the ley-lines. Ensuring the balance is maintained. The forces for evil are always strong. It's easy to corrupt people and even a small corruption, turning aside when someone is bullying someone else, can lead to bigger and bigger problems. This corruption stops people from reaching a higher sense of spiritual understanding. Keeps us all in the harsh physical world we are in now, when we have the potential to make life shine and be beautiful."

Esme bit her lip. Ben really had taken too much LSD if he thought humanity could lift itself that far out of the pigsty.

Ben ambled on, flooding the dark kitchen with his enthusiasm. "Anyway, a part of this monitoring service is understanding all kinds of esoteric stuff to help maintain the right flow and balance in these lines. To do this we have been given charge of an ancient manuscript. Originally, it was a verbal text memorised by the elders of certain Celtic tribes. When the Romans came it was written down, then Christianity arrived and these texts were guarded and added to by the monks of the Abbey. Once they destroyed the Abbey, it then became the responsibility of our group. This grail, which is how many think of it, tells of the lines of energy that reach around the world and act as conduits for the light and dark through the many planes of the universe. It also talks of certain pairs of people who help to maintain and protect this world from the darkness and encourage the light.

"You see, there are seven pairs of people, one may be considered a creature who has turned their back on the dark and one human, who changes regularly," Ben no longer looked at either woman; he just rushed head long into his story. "The human partner is important because a human mind and soul are so precious. We all have an element of the divine spark and whichever side has the most divine sparks working for them wins. These pairs are known as Guardians and they defeat the big bits of evil that are created and allowed through the ley-lines from other spirit planes. Balance has to be maintained in this world until enough people are spiritually aware, allowing our world to reach a new plane of existence. Your curse and prophecy are a part of this massive story. Cursian and you, even your love for each other, have been foretold in this grail book."

Esme and May sat in stunned silence.

"You," May's voice cracked, "you knew all this and didn't tell me?"

"I couldn't, May and I'm sorry, really sorry. I was only meant to befriend you as a part of this group. What happened between us was never meant to hurt you and everything I said about how I felt was true." Ben looked at her beseechingly.

"Except the wife," Esme pointed out.

"Well, kind of, I might as well be married to this group of people and our cause. That's what took me away from you," he focused on May. "I had to go to Tibet to check something out. Most of the people who make up this group are too old to do that kind of travelling."

"So what's changed?" May asked.

"Everything," Ben sounded sad. His dreadlocks hung limply round his face. "Over the last few years the flux of this web of lines has changed and the world is currently headed toward a life of perpetual darkness. Dante's nine levels of hell are kind of true and we are going that way at a rate of knots."

"This is to do with these Guardian's and Tibet isn't it?" Esme felt the back of her head begin to tingle.

"Yes, I was sent to befriend you all if I could, because we have been worried about the changes. I met May and Brigit through the bookshop, hoping to meet you, the group had no idea you didn't understand your heritage. It wasn't my place to tell you either. So, we waited, knowing Cursian would have to do something soon because he couldn't hold the fort alone. But in the meantime things went pear shaped in Tibet."

"You're avoiding my question, Ben. I am not in the mood."

"You and Cursian are the last pair of the seven Guardians. He is the oldest and strongest. All the rest have been killed. Sacrificed. Our organisation has come out into the open to try to help stop the rot. The access points for the different planes are wide open and there is no control or balance. It's like a computer virus has destroyed the network of protection everyone's been working on. Personally, I think it might be too late, but this is why I need to see Cursian. I know the two of you have been joined. I think the whole damned planet must know after last night, but you are going to need help."

"So you didn't come here to see me?" May said, hardening once more.

"May, what I feel for you is real and honest and true I swear, but I have been directed to talk to Cursian and reveal the extent of our knowledge," Ben reached for her, but May backed away making her chair screech across the floor.

"I don't think so buddy. Now I know why so many straight women discover they're gay once they've been married for a few years. You lot lie to them so bloody much they want to try a different world for a change," May said, glaring at Ben so hard Esme expected him to combust.

Esme watched Ben's face crumple. The guy must have found it hard to lie to her all that time. He seemed to wear his heart upon his sleeve. And if Esme understood anything, it had to be men. She took pity.

"May, don't be too hard on him. He felt he had to do what he did and the two of you have a chance if you listen to him. Men aren't all bad, they just think differently and that's confusing." Esme rose, "Now, as interesting as all this talk is I'm off to bed and may never get up again. Please let Brigit know what's going on, I'll do what ever she says I have too."

"But what about Cursian?" Ben cried after Esme's retreating back.

"Don't know and don't care. You tell him, May, I don't want to talk to anybody else." Esme tossed back over her shoulder.

CHAPTER NINETEEN

Death breathed in her face. She smelt the metallic tang of blood and the grave. Her own breath filled her head as each inhalation struggled against the weight crushing her ribs, stopping her arms and legs from moving. Death sat, squatting on her chest and laughed. She tried to scream for help, to get rid of the creature, but no air came for the scream. She couldn't even open her mouth. She whimpered. Just as she thought she would die from lack of clean oxygen, she remembered the light. She drew a line of blue light sending a spear through the monster, through her own solar-plexus. The creature screamed briefly and vanished. Esme's eyes flew open. She gasped, shivering with the shock of waking.

Esme wiped her eyes ridding herself of the last remnants of the dream. Late night made her room a nest of shadows. She rose, washing her face in the bathroom. Still moving around in darkness, Esme threw on jogging trousers, trainers and hoodie. She quietly left the house to run a familiar path around West Wycombe. As she ran, Esme began an internal dialogue, trying to sort her confusion.

While allowing her muscles to pound to a strong rhythm, Esme's mind reached out asking for guidance. She wanted clarity, an acknowledgment she followed the right path. She replayed everything that had happened over the last few days. Laying it all out, she asked for forgiveness for some actions, while seeking approval for others. The further she ran, the more her legs burned with effort, the clearer her images grew. Esme realised she felt compelled to complete her fated task. For years, she had sensed a growing dislike and discomfort about her life. The modernity and drab reality dragged at her heels. No magic flowed, no passion, no vitality. Esme realised she craved the challenge of her new existence. How could a bricks and mortar world compete with the passion of feeling the whole universe flow through her blood? This change, this new dawn, Cursian had brought with him gave her focus, a purpose. Monks would have understood her sudden zeal to fight the darkness suffocating the world. It had driven them to live in isolated communities, working to create a balance between heaven and hell. The anguish and intense pain she had suffered over the last few days simply made her more determined. Besides, she now understood the nature of real, lasting love.

A crystal clear image of Cursian's own pain, as he drove the sword through her, caused Esme to stumble on the path. Fear overrode her enthusiasm. Why had he acted so strangely? Why talk of eternal love, then destroy everything, turning her world to ash? She burned with his loss. Over laying this image of Cursian's pain from the previous night came a picture of people in white. A thick chain of black foulness flowing from them and into him.

Esme stopped, panting hard. Closing her eyes, she sharpened the image. Not for one moment did she disbelieve the images in her mind's eye. How could she after all she'd seen in such a short time? Cursian appeared to be covered in the dark stickiness. It had swallowed her lover whole. This is what had caused her so much pain. Cursian literally disappeared under the weight. His replacement, the vampire, with no controls. The soul she loved and bonded with had vanished. Esme began running again. Her path set. Stopping the evil and retrieving her lover would be her new path. It may well be weird and undoubtedly painful, but Esme knew the mundane would kill her faster.

By the time she returned, sweaty and blowing hard, dawn bloomed. She stood facing the sun, watching the sky turn from grey, to red, to orange. The hollow feeling, where Cursian had sat inside her, ached but she felt calm at last. Esme turned, let herself in and headed to the kitchen in search of breakfast.

"You're up early," she said, when she noticed Brigit at the table.

Brigit smiled, "I needed to feel the sunrise. How are you?"

Esme began making tea, "Better, now. I had good long run. Things feel better. How are you?"

"Sad mostly, if I'm honest. And really rather confused."

Esme half chuckled, "Yeah, I know how that feels. Has May spoken to you about Ben?"

"Yes, frankly that's part of the confusion. How could this group exist and the two of you be a part of something much larger but Cursian never to have known?" Brigit looked down at her hands, "And what happened to him last night? How could he have hurt you so very badly?"

"Is Ben still here?"

"I don't know, is his car still here?"

Esme realised she had run past a Vauxhall Corsa in the drive. "He's still here. I'll go and shake them out of bed," Esme pushed herself off the kitchen units.

"It's a bit early, Esme. If they are together I shouldn't think they'll appreciate the disturbance."

"If I'm not bloody getting any I don't see why anyone else should. Besides, Ben owes me by the sounds of things," Esme strode out the kitchen, her new vitality making her almost run from the room.

"Right," Esme said, once May and Ben emerged from the same room. "We are going to sort this mess out."

"Esme, I don't know how you expect to do that," Ben muttered. "They have Cursian and they are going to try to destroy you by using him."

"But how have they managed to get to him?" Esme leaned across the table. "How have they made him turn so easily against me? What aren't we seeing? Brigit's right, our souls have been entwined for centuries, millennia. He couldn't give that up any more than I could."

May had her head down. She looked up through a thick tangle of black hair. "Are you sure? Esme, he's not human, not really, and he's not been normal for weeks according to Brigit. All these violent reactions, what he did to Matt. It bears consideration that he may have finally lost it."

Esme wondered how she knew about Matt and then looked at Brigit. May was the next generation; Brigit would have no secrets from her protégée. Besides, secrets had managed to get them into this situation.

Brigit said, "As far as I can gather the only time he's normal is with Esme, when they are alone. And under the circumstances I am not surprised he pushed for the bonding, but the violence of the breaking is not normal."

Esme grunted at the understatement, "Okay, Ben knew about the abduction and what it was meant to accomplish. We all thought it had failed, because I didn't come back a screaming zombie, but what if that wasn't the idea? Or they got it partly right? What if they have been attacking Cursian on a level unknown to us all? Please, Brigit, you must know more about this than you are letting on, even if it is speculation."

Brigit fell silent for a long time. The others watching her, finally she squared her shoulders. Esme held her breath. She wanted answers and she wanted Cursian back. She couldn't believe she had to live with this lump of nothingness for the rest of her life.

Brigit began slowly, "When your mother died, Cursian grieved as anyone would, but he wouldn't come close to you, wouldn't make himself known. He moved to London for the first time in decades, yet kept his distance. Every night for months, he would spend an hour after dusk and an hour at dawn watching you, if you went out he would follow, but never approach. When he wasn't with you he would come to me, if May wasn't there. When I asked him, all he would tell me was, 'I do not want to endanger her, and I do not wish to hurt her. Let her have as much peace as I can manage to give before bringing her into my world of darkness.' His sadness was almost palpable. As to the evil we have recently been subjected too, De'hevda is a given, he knew she would find you in the end, she always does. She's loved Cursian her entire afterlife and has vowed to destroy the Prophecy, turning him once more. He created her."

"What?" Esme gasped.

"I didn't think you knew," Brigit shook her head. "It was badly done. She was a peasant from the village near the castle. Cursian took her but wanted to keep her as a playmate, so he turned her, corrupting her innocence. He once told me she was his worst sin. Taking an innocent beauty and creating evil, but he couldn't destroy her and now she is too powerful having fully allied herself to the entity that gives life to vampire. So, when he realised she found you, he knew he had to act. That's when he approached. He knew he was doomed to love you from the moment it started. I think in keeping you at a distance he thought he could keep himself in check. I know he, how can I say this, deterred those that would harm you or had harmed you when he wasn't around to protect you, but he never allowed himself to get close. He came to see me the night he first made contact. Your smiling face, your drunken stumble, how he had held you in his arms. He trembled while he spoke of what happened in that instant." Brigit looked hard at Esme, "I think your instincts are right child. Cursian cares for you too much to have left you. What I saw in him that night took my breath away. He loves you with every fibre of his being, as a vampire, a mage and a man. And it's more than just the attraction of souls. He loves you for your strength, for yourself. That leads me to think something has happened to force this change."

Esme tensed when Brigit went silent, "Well, what? What happened? I don't want to have to guess." She stayed quiet about the image in her mind, wanting to know she hadn't created an illusion from desperation.

"I think I know," Ben said bravely.

"Go on then!" Esme exploded.

"Listen, our guys have spies in their ranks." Ben pushed the dreadlocks back, "I don't know who. They might not even be human, maybe just cosmic phone taps. I simply receive the relevant reports. That abduction wasn't the failure you guys thought and the bonding was the icing on their cake. Brigit is right about that, the two of you becoming so very close and creating such beauty left Cursian incredibly vulnerable for the first time in centuries. Esme, the drug they gave you and the invasion they perpetrated allowed them to steal some of what you are, kind of like voodoo. But instead of working with some of your hair and an effigy, they have a part of your essence. Through that, they could reach you and so through you, they reached him. His barriers were smashed by making love and bonding with you, so he wouldn't have even noticed. Besides, they have been throwing cosmic negativity toward him for years, wearing him down, getting him used to feeling them attack him constantly. They have a group working purely on destroying his psychic sensitivity. It seems they succeeded," he added glumly.

"So as soon as we made love he became vulnerable?" Esme asked, confirmation making her stronger.

Ben nodded, "But only because he took it too far himself. And don't forget, Brigit, tried to warn him. I should imagine they have attacked his humanity, subverted his mage sense and promoted his vampire nature."

"So how do I get him back?" Esme looked at the three people round the table.

Brigit reached out and grasped Esme's clenched fists, "I don't think you can, Esme."

Esme drew her hands away, "Yes, I can. I have too. If I don't, the last of the Guardian's have been destroyed, because we are a team and that won't do anyone any good. I've been informed that this is the only course of action, therefore, we are taking it. Now, I want ideas and I don't need any negativity."

"Esme, this is not a boardroom," Brigit made her indignation obvious.

"Yes, Brigit, it is and it is not a democracy. I have been run ragged by you lot. I am sick of secrets, I am sick of not understanding and not having control. I am also sick of things going wrong. It is time to be proactive. Now, forgive the ego, but most of this is about me. I am the relevant one, therefore I should be kept informed and the decisions I make should be for the good of all of us. So people - ideas."

"I don't see why we can't get him back," May said.

"We don't even know where he is," Brigit snapped scornfully.

"Well, where could he be?" Esme began to feel more confident. "Where is he likely to go? London? When will he need to feed and where does he feed in London?" finally, she had managed to drag her life into an environment she understood. Those around her might not appreciate her taking over, but leaving all their actions up to fate would end in someone dying, most likely her.

"He won't have returned to London," Brigit conceded. "He won't have any reason too. For feeding, he can find prostitutes close by who will give him what he needs."

"Prostitutes?" Esme gulped.

"How do you think he manages? Animal blood is a very poor substitute and the chemicals they use to preserve blood are bad for him. He's an old vampire. He needs the warmth and life of real blood to sustain him."

"Right," Esme grimaced, forcing the thought of him stealing so much from the vulnerable made her sick. Mind you, giving blood to him had to be better than some of the acts prostitutes performed and doubtless he paid well. "Well, apart from cruising the local red light district, where else can he be if he hasn't left Wycombe?"

"I can make a phone call and find out if my people know," Ben said.

"And I can go meditate and see if I can find him," May added. "He's fed from me so we have a link but it won't be strong, he shouldn't notice I'm hunting him."

"Don't be too sure, May, though he won't recognise you easily," Brigit warned.

"Good," Esme rose. "I'm going to follow a few hunches of my own on the internet. I think we need more information about this group of people who have been destroying everyone. Do they have a name, Ben?"

"The only name I know is Dominion. I don't know if that's going to be of any help. You might want to try Guardians and stuff."

"I'll tell you what, when you have finished speaking to your colleagues, come find me in the lounge and give me a hand. May, as soon as you find Cursian let me know. Brigit, could you use your contacts to try to help?"

"Yes, Esme, I'll do what I can if this is what you want," Brigit smiled sadly, obviously not convinced.

CHAPTER TWENTY

During the day, Esme learnt far more than was good for her about all things nasty. They found the Dominion, the one they wanted and found links onto other disturbing sites. Esme realised they were dealing with a well organised empire. This gave her pause for thought, it took a great deal of planning to destroy an empire and she had the feeling they didn't have that kind of time. She also discovered more about the Guardians. The seven pairs seemed to be a mix of sexes and races. The mortal elements all had spiritual backgrounds from different faiths and each pair existed in a set geographical area. Her family, for instance, had always been based in Europe; a pair covered Africa, the Far East, northern Asia, South America, far northern America and the Middle East. As with her family, when one of the human's died, another from the same branch took their place. It also seemed that Cursian and her family had been playing this game for longer than the others. This apparently, came from Europe's spiritual maturity (or lack), during a huge time of flux after the plague. Traditional methods of control no longer sufficient when it almost wiped out humanity. The darkness leaked through to many holes in the net. The 'powers that be', then decided to create the Guardians.

Certain souls were chosen and ties formed. The long term member of the pair chosen first. Those with the strength to resist the dark yet knowing exactly what its temptations were. Then, when that soul connected strongly with another, they selected the human element. In Esme's case, her family were chosen because of Cursian and how her soul had helped him chain his demons. It seemed the endless cycle of love they suffered provided the real trigger. Esme felt sad for her family. With no free will they had never known peace. Did she now have a chance for freedom?

She could walk away from Cursian, or fight for him, fight for his humanity, his sanity. The by-product of these actions meant she could stop the darkness spreading. Doing her bit for the Guardian's mission. Every time she thought about this she laughed at the absurdity of the idea, but if you believed in angels, why not devils?

They also found the vampire. It gave May the headache from hell, but as soon as dusk came she'd located him and he had not left the area. In fact, he seemed to be very close by and so did the Dominion.

"They're on the Dashwood estate?" Esme asked, incredulous.

"Yep, and the place seems to be really busy," May said.

"But all that garbage about the Dashwood family being devil worshippers is rubbish," Esme exclaimed. "Sir Francis, much like the rest of them, liked his booze and his women. He simply had too much time on his hands. The Hellfire Club weren't nice, but they don't seem to have been dangerous and why on earth would the current Lord Dashwood be involved?"

"It's not that simple, Esme," Ben said. "I don't think the Dashwood's as such, are involved. This Dominion have serious links to old schools of the occult, probably dating back before Cursian started his study, certainly from that time. The Hellfire Club might have originally been a rich man's drinking club, but eventually men such as Alistair Crowley became involved. This area has been strongly linked to the Golden Dawn. The Dominion will be using the estate and the caves because of the residual links to past power. For all we know the Dashwood's have been held against their will or aren't even in the area and have hired out the house."

"So, what do we do now?" Esme felt panic beginning to rise at the size and implications of this nightmare.

"We can't get into the place, so there is little we can do at the moment," Brigit said. She'd spent several hours that day helping Esme understand the history of Cursian's life and her part in the story.

They all jumped as the doorbell chimed loudly.

"Bugger," Esme rose. "I'll get it. Someone come up with an idea."

She slowly walked into the entrance hall, creating scenarios and then dumping them as bad movie script ideas. The doorbell chimed again as she reached the door. Annoyed now, Esme reached for the handle and instead of checking the spy-hole, she yanked the door open. Cursian smiled down at her.

Esme's gut reaction made her reach for him, which made her second action too slow. Just as she stepped back, Cursian stepped forward.

His hand encircled her wrist and before Esme applied any technique, he pulled her hard against his body. Twisting her around with the motion, she found her back pressed into his chest. Her own arm trapping her, Esme kicked out reaching for his softer body parts with her free hand.

"Oh, I do not think so, lover," his voice purred in her ear.

Cursian swiftly adjusted position placing dangerous pressure on her throat. A small amount of strength would render her unconscious in moments. The idea of being unconscious did not appeal. Esme forced herself to go limp. The whole thing lasted five seconds. She could have screamed in frustration. All those years of blood and sweat in the dojo wasted because her reactions would never be super human. No matter how good you are, there is always someone better.

"Come now, lover, we need to be leaving. I have something for you to do and if you come quietly no one will get hurt."

A shadow filled the corridor leading from the kitchen. Ben walked in, head down, studying a book, "Esme, we have found something interesting in one of Brigit's old books."

Esme watched Ben stop. He pushed a stray dreadlock behind one ear and looked up. His eyes widened as he took in the two figures filling the front entrance.

"Oh, shit," Ben said quietly.

Esme felt Cursian's breath against her ear.

"Replaced me already?" his voice was quiet, but she felt a whip of his energy flick outward.

Ben stumbled slightly.

"No, Cursian, he's with May. A friend that's all. Please, don't hurt him, he means no harm," Esme breathed harshly past her fear.

"Anything you say, lover," Cursian whispered.

Cursian began moving backward, she had no choice but to go with him. Her vision going spotty with the additional pressure on her neck. She stumbled down the small steps outside the front door. The cold of the night bit through her jumper, the air smelt damp and heavy with the threat of more rain. Her knees finally gave way. As the ground rushed up to meet her, Cursian changed his hold, throwing her over his shoulder, without apparent effort. One hand held her own hands firmly behind her back, while his other arm wrapped around her legs. Esme had to hold still, while Cursian carried her down the drive. There would be no point in screaming, the others knew what had happened and no one else would hear.

At the end of the drive, Cursian flipped her back onto her feet, once more encircling her throat with a single hand. She saw the dark Jaguar parked in the street. He must have been back to London to retrieve his car. She wondered briefly why cars were always so damned important to men. He unlocked it, Esme hearing the beep of the alarm. At no point did his gaze leave hers.

"You are not fighting," Cursian seemed amused.

"What's the point? You'll only hurt me and currently it serves no purpose. I am not in any immediate danger or I would already be dead," Esme sounded hollow.

"Hmm, I will concede that point." He leaned his body closer, "But I do hope you put up a fight later. Watching you struggle is a wonderful experience."

Esme's face didn't alter in anyway, but her hand struck out, covering the short distance from her hip to Cursian's throat in a split second. Her extended knuckles hit his windpipe hard. Cursian's grip on her own throat tightened rather than loosened, while his head shot forward and he gasped. The pressure on her windpipe increased to such an extent it drove Esme to her knees. She began to gag for air.

"Ooo, breaking you will be so much fun, lover," Cursian growled. "That was a good shot. Would have been a killing strike on a mortal."

Esme took a deep breath as his hand relaxed on her throat. "Or a human," she murmured.

"I am back to being a monster then?" he laughed, "That is reassuring, now please get into the passenger seat of the car, or do I have to force you?"

Esme felt a flash of anger through her fear. "No! And you will not force me. Cursian, for God's sake, what the fuck do you think you are doing? The last time I saw you we had made love and then you tried to kill me with some mystical bloody sword!" she stamped her foot.

Cursian's urban expression never altered, "I will break your legs to get you into the car, Esme, have no doubt about that."

"I have no doubt, but why? Why hurt me like that, what the hell has happened to you?" finally, her voice broke with the tumultuous emotional barrage she had suffered.

"Get in the car," anger threaded through his tone.

"The others have a theory," Esme began to rush her words as she saw his thin veil of humanity begin to disappear. "They think you have been targeted for months, weakened. When we bonded they noticed and snuck in through the back door, so to speak. Please, Cursian, this isn't you." Her legs began to tell her it was time to run.

"Get in the car," his voice filled out and dropped, his humanity vanished.

Esme stared at the creature before her and despaired. Her shoulders slumped. She moved around the open door and slid down into the low slung coupe.

CHAPTER TWENTY ONE

Cursian slowly regained some form of control as they sped through the streets. He didn't seem to be interested in reaching a particular goal, they soon left West Wycombe behind and began weaving through leafless lanes. The night was thick and dark outside the car. Esme noticed the wind whipped at the trees, their skeletal arms bending painfully. Surviving with Mr Hyde sat next to her would be hard. Esme prayed quietly, asking for courage. Her fear, anger, and loss, slowly began to fade.

"Do you not care where we are going?" Cursian asked eventually.

"Why should I? I can't stop anything that's happening. To fight fate right now is pointless. Besides, while it is just the two of us, no-one else can hurt me."

"How very prosaic of you." Cursian controlled the speeding car with effortless grace.

The scent of leather from the dark interior confused Esme. The smell made her feel safe. Her father's cars always had leather interiors and she wore leather all the time. But here, now, she should be feeling threatened, yet the comfortable elements of smooth driving, familiar smells and her lover lent the situation a surreal sense of safety. Esme pulled at that feeling, knowing it would be gone again soon, wanting it to last so badly she almost tasted the peace.

"Are we going anywhere special?" she asked, trying not care.

"Yes, tonight we are going somewhere special. And tomorrow you will be prepared for the ceremony."

Esme's stomach flipped at the mention of the ceremony. She knew what the Dominion had done to her mystical colleagues. The details were on the website she'd found, designed to look like a young person's sick fantasy, but Ben reassured her it had all been quite real. She felt nauseous. For

The Prophecy

the briefest of times she'd been complete, whole, two circles joining together to form an eternity together. And now? Now, she had to find a way to make Cursian understand his vulnerability. She had to make the monster acknowledge its weakness so she could find the man once more. Unless, he really had changed sides and she had to face her life alone, what was left of it. That is, until they turned her into a raving monster, forced into the madness of becoming a vampire slave. Could she really save Cursian?

The silence thickened as they travelled on, lanes becoming trunk roads, becoming the motorway. When they departed the M25 Esme felt her eyelids droop, she gave into sleep. What was the point in staying awake only to die tired? When she roused, due to the car taking a sudden fast turn, she saw a large sign welcoming her to the Historic Cathedral City of Canterbury.

Esme blinked, looked across at Cursian and said, "What the hell are we doing in Canterbury?"

"Did you sleep well?"

Esme frowned, "What do you care?" She noticed a hurt expression flit across his face, evidently he did care. "Yes, I slept well thank you. Are you going to tell me what we are doing here?"

"No, but I am not being difficult. I simply cannot tell you."

"And that's not being difficult?" Esme harrumphed and crossed her arms.

Silence descended again. They wove through the city, eventually parking outside the cathedral itself. By now, the dashboard clock said 10.05 pm. The study centre squatted in darkness and the spotlights on the cathedral lit up its ancient and beautiful stonework. Gothic arches made the building appear as a sleeping dragon, saintly statues and evil gargoyles stared coldly down as Esme slid from the car.

"Am I allowed a clue?" she said somewhat peevishly.

"Just follow me," and he strode off into the darkness.

Esme stood watching him. What now? To go or not to go. He clearly didn't intend to force the issue. He didn't seem interested in the previous casual violence and her curiosity began to win over common sense. If she was doomed, she may as well find out why, besides, if she ran they would hunt her down. The Dominion had to destroy her regardless, so running would only complicate things. Honestly, she wanted to have Cursian back. She wanted his arms around her body, not his hands around her throat. Pathetic really, this is the action of a domestic violence victim, she thought. Esme sighed and followed the departing vampire.

They went a circuitous route around the cathedral, Esme craned up to look at its technical, organic splendour rising high above them. The wind, this close to the sea breathed sharply over them. Esme shivered and jogged to catch up with Cursian. They walked around the outside of the cloisters, past the crypts and toward the main apse. He turned suddenly and began walking toward the houses surrounding the cathedral grounds. Their gardens backed onto the Cathedral green, but separated by a garden wall, which appeared to be as old as the medieval houses it protected. Cursian walked along this wall slowly.

He stopped and turned, "Make sure you keep your head down, there are no lights, so I will need to lead you." He stuck his hand out.

Esme looked at him, his hand and his face, which remained in shadow. She sensed his high level of tension.

"Why would I want to do this?"

"Because you want answers and I want to give them to you," his hand remained out, like an offering.

Esme growled and reached for him. Cursian drew a long shafted key from his inside pocket and inserted it into a lock. She noticed this part of the wall had a very small door placed in its base. The wall had thickened too, obviously to accommodate this door. Cursian bent double, then crouched. Esme saw stone steps as he began to disappear, dragging her with him.

He stopped a few steps from the entrance, "Shut the door."

Esme complied, "What is this place?" Blackness swallowed her whole. Stone absorbed all sound.

"It is a tunnel running from one of the houses in the cathedral close. They added this entrance many years later when the officials wanted to stop any secret kind of activity by the Church. They thought the tunnel destroyed."

"And how do you know about it?"

"There is little I do not know when it comes to old secrets in this country. Especially, where our esteemed authority figures are concerned. Besides, during the Protestant changes Canterbury happened to be a place I found most interesting at the time."

"Do I want to know why?"

"No," darkness filled his voice. "Now stick close and no screaming. I want to get into the Cathedral quietly."

They descended the stairs, following a low tunnel. The walls and floor were dry, but roughly made, as Esme discovered when she scraped her knuckles. Her back began to scream in protest because of the forced angle of their walk. Just as she was going to go onto hands and knees, she felt Cursian stand in front of her.

"That hurt," he muttered. "I must be getting old."

Despite herself, she smiled into the darkness. That inky blackness began to press heavily. Claustrophobia bit Esme's heels.

"Can we either keep moving or leave now?" panic tinged her voice.

"I have to find the lock," Cursian said, letting go of her hand. It felt as though he suddenly abandoned her to the dark. Esme almost yipped in fear. She reached out and touched the wall with one hand and his back with the other. The orientation of this action helped calm her nerves. She heard a lock go, pale light flooding the small room. Esme almost ran out into the body of the cathedral.

"My rufty tufty martial artist is afraid of the dark," Cursian laughed.

Esme frowned, "I am not afraid of the dark. I don't like small dark places, that's all."

Cursian continued to chuckle.

"Why are we here?" Esme asked, not looking at him, looking at the darkened beauty surrounding her. Soaring arches towered over them. The tunnel disgorged them at the head of the nave. Esme turned around and around in wonder and with a flagrant disregard for her safety.

"We are here because it is the only safe place we can talk," Cursian said.

CHAPTER TWENTY TWO

Watching Esme remained a favourite pastime and watching her fascination with this building caused a lump of pressure to build within his chest. Cursian blinked rapidly. How he wanted to catch hold of that long dark hair and wrestle her to the ground.

"No," he almost choked on the word. He could not touch her, he would hurt her again.

"What?"

"Esme, concentrate, please. I need to talk to you," he placed his hand over his midriff, his pain very real.

"Well, you certainly pick interesting places for conversations." Esme began to walk toward the altar.

"Esme, please," Cursian's legs no longer supported him. He sank into a pew. "We must talk."

She returned, sitting beside him. He smelt her clean skin. The blood from her knuckles assaulted his senses. Cursian pushed himself away slightly, his world spinning dangerously. He closed his eyes, his breath almost wheezing as he sucked in air.

"Is the church making you sick?" Esme asked.

"No, not the church as such. Esme, I brought you here because I needed to speak to you in safety. Somewhere we cannot be over heard. In this place I have dropped off their radar, so to speak." The pain eased as his energies readjusted to his surroundings. His control reasserted itself for the first time in months. Cursian took a deep cleansing breath, finally able to sit straight without pushing against the darkness surrounding him. He thanked God for powerful buildings.

Esme frowned, mystified.

He started from the beginning, once more forgetting how much she actually didn't know. "The Church has been around for centuries and has a collective goodness about it. These, the oldest buildings, store in their stone the sincere worship of thousands of souls. Canterbury is the nearest and most powerful cathedral in the area. That is why I brought you here. It acts as an amplifier for the honest and a barrier for the… not so honest."

"So you do know the Dominion has been attacking you," Esme stated.

"Yes, I have been fighting them for years. Gradually, the pressure has been building and as the other Guardians have fallen, it has become worse." Cursian stared at his hands, saddened by the loss. With every corruption his weakness intensified, he had felt their descent into madness, darkness. Although he knew it happened he could do nothing. His only goal to protect himself and Esme from the attacks and he'd clearly done such a good job.

"So, you know about it all? All the stuff Ben has been explaining to us. Why didn't you tell Brigit?"

"Esme, I have spent six hundred years gaining information. All I require of the record keepers is to train the Scions and keeping an accurate history of attacks, so I would be able to form patterns, recognise threats. There are some things humans do not need to know."

Esme shook her head, "That's just bloody arrogant. But I don't know what else I should expect. Why are you different here? You feel different."

"The Dominion has been corroding me for a long time. They give strength to the part of me that is vampire. You see, Esme, the essence that is vampire, the thing that we pass on, not only feeds on the blood of its victims; it also feeds on its host. The vampire essence is a parasite, it cannot exist without human hosts to feed on, but the energy that is vampire will consume the human it has been born into. Take De'hevda for example, she was once a perfectly nice young woman. Then she became infected and the parasite turned her into the homicidal maniac we know and hate today."

"Only because you infected her," Esme muttered.

Anger flared within him, "Brigit has told you a great deal. Yes, I killed her and I have paid a great price for it and will continue to pay."

"Alright, you say this is all some cosmic infection, which begs the question, what are you in all this mess?"

"I am unique, even among the Guardians. The essence of vampire filled me and consumed me. It destroyed the man within me, but never the mage. I have always had that strength to fall back on. That and you," Cursian looked up at Esme, hating himself for the emotional trap he planned. "Esme, your soul, as Isabeau, is the only thing that enabled me to reconnect to my true humanity. I may have begun the fight against my evil in the castle, but I would have lost if it had not have been for the love we have always had. That original connection can never truly be severed. It goes beyond the Prophecy, beyond the darkness, beyond it all. I do not fully comprehend its significance or how it functions, but it does," He looked at her beseechingly.

"Where is this leading Cursian?" Esme's suspicions radiated off her in waves.

Cursian could hardly blame her; he had given her no reason to trust him. "Esme, I know I have hurt you, deeply hurt you, but I had my reasons. While we made love, we bonded. Brigit must have explained its implications and meaning. We became one. In that moment, my barriers were finally breached. For the very reasons Brigit told me our bonding was wrong, but it was too late. The Dominion lay waiting. They pounced as soon as they felt me take you into myself and you took me. To my shame, I did not notice. It was during the conversation with Brigit that I finally felt them inside my soul. They attacked with great power. They grabbed the vampire and thrust it to the fore. I had no control to speak of, the harshness with which I hurt you is the creature that lurks within me. I wanted to punish you."

Cursian choked on his words as he remembered Esme writhing underneath him and how badly he had wanted to rip her throat out. Instead, the young Welsh noble within him, the man, managed to turn the vampire to one side long enough to attempt to sever the bond and divert the killing stroke. In severing that bond the human part of him prevented Esme from feeling the vampire. His madness would have become hers if that bond had not been broken. He manifested her pain at the moment he drove in the sword, taking her wound. The shock controlled his monster until he left the house.

Covering his face with his hands, Cursian openly displayed his shame, sadness and his fear of what the immediate future held.

A hand touched his head, "Cursian, we will run out of night. Whatever happened to us, whatever is going to happen, we have to move beyond the shit for the moment. We can deal with all this later. Don't flake out on me now."

"Typical," he said cynically. "Always deal with the crisis and leave the consequences for later."

"Well, there's no point in saying 'I forgive you', because I don't know if I can, but we obviously need to deal with this crisis. So, what's the plan?"

Her coldness shocked him; he wanted to hold her gently. He wanted to feel her melt in his arms and to feel her trust him with her world. To have back what he experienced just two nights ago. And now he would ask the impossible. He wouldn't blame her if she laughed in his face while driving Becket's sword through his heart. Part of him wished she would, just for the peace and quiet.

"You will have to trust me, that is the plan." His voice barely audible, "I will have to take you back to Wycombe and we will go through the ceremony. We will allow the evil to be made manifest. Allow the human worshippers to be full of their dark god. Then I will release you and we will fight them, using our bond."

Esme stood up and turned to face him. "You are joking? You're expecting me to be trussed up like a chicken and to put my head on the block? I know enough about all this to know that as soon as you leave here you are going to be at their mercy again. You will have to allow the monster within you to become dominant once more. I am then supposed to trust that our love will be enough to stop you killing me at the relevant moment? Are you fucking nuts?" She strode off into the dark interior of the cathedral.

Cursian let her go. He couldn't blame her for feeling angry. He wasn't even sure he would be able to contain himself when the time came. He could see her in front of the altar, pacing. He rose quietly, walking to the martyr's tomb. He had not prayed for centuries. As a young man he had been a devout Catholic, along with the rest of the country. He asked for many things in those days and begged forgiveness many times.

He stood in front of the distorted cross, wondering what kind of man became a martyr, to give everything to what he really believed. Cursian wished it could be that simple for him, to fall upon the ancient sword, even older than himself and end it. However, if he did that, the darkness would truly have won. The last of the Guardians gone. Esme would prove no trouble. She'd be dead or bent to madness within hours.

"You know what?" Esme's voice boomed out of the darkness.

Cursian jumped slightly.

"I went running this morning. And on this run, I discovered I was meant to help you, I was meant to find a way to save you and stop this all going to rat shit. And here, in this amazing place, I am being dragged the same way. I feel compelled to do this, to follow your plan. But I don't know if that is my desperately sad need to believe in you; outside influences making me want to help you; or my true path. I've become completely paranoid! I don't even trust my faith any more." The last came out as a cry from her heart.

Cursian bowed his head, unable to answer. Not truly able to trust himself. He felt Esme close at hand. Cursian turned toward her approach.

"Do you know what the sad part of this really is?" Esme's voice ricocheted off the high stone walls. "I want to do it. Because even if I end up completely deranged and start feeding on the flesh of those around me, at least I won't have to carry around this lump of nothingness anymore. A lump which used to be you."

Cursian heard the crack in her voice but remained locked away from her pain. He may never be able to cut her out of himself completely but he could stop them sensing each other. She stood close to him, too close. He wanted to back away. He smelt her blood pumping fast under her skin. Filling her up with strength and vitality. That strength, which he admired so much, promptly doubled him over. Esme followed the short range stomach punch with a low kick to his shin. Her opposite hand cracked him on the back of his head. Cursian fell to the floor, feeling as though his eyeballs were falling out of his head. His vision darkened, his brain stunned.

Cursian sensed Esme kneeling beside him. He couldn't rise to face her onslaught. She didn't attack him any further. Instead, she said menacingly.

"I want you to listen carefully, you fucking man. You hurt me, really hurt me, on so many levels I've lost count. You have taken my life from me and placed me in some kind of living hell. In this happy place, I am expected to kill or be killed. And I don't really draw a distinction between monsters and people. I have seen and heard things I never wanted to see or know about. And you, you have been central to it all. I have loved you for years. I have wanted you since the brief moment we met. And you took away everything. I don't care if it was your fault or not. You caved in to your rage. We all have demons living in our souls somewhere. We are all capable of hurting those around us, but most of us have some form of control. You've had centuries to sort your shit out, and you caved!"

Esme drew a shaking breath, "So, buddy, this is the plan. I will go back, and I will go through with this ceremony, but you will tell me here and now how I can destroy your sorry arse if necessary."

Cursian uncurled as Esme moved away from him. She had done no serious damage, but she could have easily broken his knee and damaged his spleen had he been made of softer stuff. He rubbed the back of his head.

Looking across the stone floor at her, he said, "Feel better for that?"

"Marginally, now bloody well tell me what I want to know."

"It will not help you."

"It might and that's better than not knowing."

Cursian looked out toward the cathedral's entrance. It all came down to trust, she didn't have any and he couldn't blame her. The darkest part of the night approached, they would have to leave soon. He had to get her back by dawn.

"I can give you a spell. But, Esme, I will remember I have done this and if it comes to it, I will try to survive. This spell disperses the soul of the human host, giving the vampire parasite nothing to hold onto in the host's body. It means the vampire has to leave as it becomes disentangled from the host. I will teach it to you and how you can set it up in your mind and hold onto it long before you might wish to use it."

"What does 'unravelling the soul' mean?" suspicion once more.

"It means exactly what I say," Cursian gave rein to a sudden irritation. "I give you my true mortal name and the spell, you can unravel me. I will cease to be."

He saw her frown, "What about the endless cycle of souls we have between us."

Cursian grimaced as he heard Esme's effort to stay away from the word love. "That will be gone too. My soul will no longer exist. It will become as nothing, returning to its finest elements within the universal pattern. We will no longer be reborn into each others lives."

"But," Esme's voice wobbled. "I don't want this to end. I have seen too much. Our love has been an amazing thing to all those surrounding us. We shouldn't have to sacrifice that."

"It is all I can offer you," he spread his hands. "It is all I have to keep you safe. Without my soul, the vampire will die and the Dominion's plans will be shattered. You might be able to escape and live out your life without interference from me. In fact you will live out all your lives without my interference. If you die, if they win, if evil is beckoned into our world, then perhaps it is meant to be. Perhaps it is time for change, for the Guardians to come to an end. Perhaps the plan will work, perhaps we will save the world and each other, destroying a layer of darkness in the process. I have carried this burden for so long and it has left me weary. I cannot see the path clearly."

"But you will be gone," she whispered.

"I thought you wanted me gone?" he said crossly.

"No, not like that. I want what we had before it all went wrong. I want that feeling of home back," Esme moved toward him on her hands and knees.

Cursian reached for her without thought, their love for each other once more making it impossible for them to remain separate entities. She curled up against his chest, while he leaned into one of the mighty stone pillars thrusting itself toward the heavens. He held her as if she were made of glass, allowing the cold stone and ancient peace to settle within him, to sigh through him. How he wished he could have stayed there forever, becoming one with the cathedral. Allowing its love to fill him forever, surrounded by love forever.

Stirring in his arms, Esme looked up at him. "This plan is not going to go wrong. I am not going to have to use that spell. But I will not let you destroy what is positive and good about our love. I will not let it be turned to darkness, even if I have to walk through the rest of eternity alone."

He saw she meant it. Cursian said, "My true name, the name I was given at birth, at my baptism, is Dafydd. That is the name you will use. And I am truly sorry this has fallen to you. All I have ever wanted, Esme, is to love you and be loved in return." He stroked her hair, laying a gentle kiss on her head.

Esme surprised him by pulling him down into a passionate embrace. When she finally relinquished her hold, she said, "We will make this work, or by God I will find a way to hunt you down and bring you back and kick you from here to kingdom come for leaving me."

Cursian laughed, "Well, I am confident everything will be fine then."

They untangled themselves, walking toward the secret entrance, hand in hand. Cursian turned before plunging once more into its darkness. "Esme, once we leave here I will again be under pressure and the closer to Wycombe the harder it will be for me to maintain control. When I take you to these people, I will have to allow the vampire to manifest. I will not be able to protect you fully from them or their games. If we do not allow this thing to happen they will chase us down and we will not have our current advantage."

Esme raised an eyebrow, "Shit, if this is an advantage then I'm not waiting for a crisis." Her eyes softened, "I understand, Cursian, just remember the feel of this place and remember what I can give you that the vampire can't."

He almost wept with the huge amount of trust she gave. Cursian only hoped he would be able to sustain that trust. He looked round the cathedral once more and silently asked, to whomever may be listening, for guidance, strength and help. He then turned, taking them back to a world full of madness, pain and grief.

CHAPTER TWENTY THREE

He drove back as fast as the journey down. Esme learnt the spell quickly. It seemed simple and utterly devastating. Cursian changed as the journey progressed. Esme could see his calm resolve unravelling. He became harder and harder. His energy spiky. Esme sank lower in her seat. Instinct telling her she had trapped herself with a huge and dangerous predator.

Driving into West Wycombe, the difficulty of this predicament crashed over Esme. Intellectually, in the safety of the cathedral, she had honestly believed it would be possible and may have even considered it a good idea. They would fool the bad guys into thinking they had succumbed to the ceremony, allow the demon to reach this realm, then defeat them all with the light she held within her. Sat in the car, on the way to the Dashwood estate, Esme's stomach felt full of lead, her mouth dried and her hands shook. The entrance loomed up out of the night. The idea of being imprisoned and at the Dominion's mercy, relying on Cursian's sense of control to pull this off, no longer seemed feasible. This had become her responsibility because of destiny, but she did not want to be a child of destiny. Cursian smoothly drove into the drive. The sleek dark car pulled up outside the huge house. Glue stuck her behind to the leather seat. Her legs lost all their strength. She shivered. She didn't want to move.

Cursian turned, "Get out of the car willingly. You do not want me to make you get out. Be quiet and still. Do not force me or the others to take action against you. Do not behave like a hunted rabbit, which will only encourage my predator and do not fight with me, that will make it stronger."

Esme took a deep breath, the last within the safety of the car. She centred herself and rose from the car. The words, 'This is madness', echoing in her mind.

The door clicked shut just as a man a woman walked from the house.

"Cursian, I knew you would return. My dear brother had his doubts, but I never doubted you."

The woman stood tall, naturally skinny and mature. Her contralto voice echoed inside Esme head, her familiarity with the vampire left a small ice-pick of pain in Esme's gut. She moved with an easy grace and wore expensive clothes, the trouser suit fitting her frame as though tailor made.

Esme turned next to her brother. Also tall and lithe, obviously older, but still strong, his dark speckled hair swept back from his face, blue eyes bright. His cream suit and open collar reminded Esme of Richard Branson. He stared carefully at Cursian, who lounged against the car, completely at ease.

"Your sudden disappearance worried us," the man had a stronger European accent than his sister.

Cursian raised an eyebrow and showed an open hand toward Esme. "You wished for the Scion in one piece, without drawing attention to what is happening here, this I accomplished."

The two people walked toward Esme. The Scion wanted to disappear into the metal of the car, which stood between her and freedom.

The woman spoke, "So, you are, Esme. My, my, hardly a conventional beauty, but then none in your line has been. And here without a fight, it must be love." The derogatory tone hurt.

"No, not really. I think it had more to do with keeping my friends safe," Esme tried to breathe deeply, through the fear.

"I think she is exquisite. I look forward to the cleansing ritual." The man turned to Cursian, "I am not surprised you guarded this one so very well, she is… simply… exquisite."

Esme did not like being thought of as a fine race horse, "Fuck off."

The woman moved in a flash, Esme's head twisted painfully as the slap resounded off her skin.

"You do not use such language to my brother. He will have your undying respect and unquestioning obedience. He now owns the very air you need." The woman's face contorted into a mask of hate.

Esme blinked, her cheek smarting, she resisted the temptation to rub it. She also felt her rage rise to meet this woman's madness. Her mouth opened to expel that rage, when Cursian smoothly slid himself between the two women.

"Please, Samantha, Duncan, do not harm her. For now she is mine and I wish for her to remain whole. She will be taught," Cursian flicked an amused glance toward Esme. "And she will be broken, but for tonight I want to enjoy the fight. Later she will be born anew and the months of madness that will follow shall make her unusable but for all the most brutal of magic's."

"Her cleansing must begin at dawn, Cursian," Duncan said mildly, as though all this was perfectly normal.

"And you may take her from my rooms at dawn. But until then she is mine. And I will not be argued with." Esme felt Cursian unravel the chains on his vampire. Although she could not see his face, she knew his eyes dilated and the monster hovered under the surface of his skin.

Samantha writhed. Esme thought she was going to orgasm on the spot, "Oh the power." She walked toward the vampire and leaned into him, "When will I have you in my bed, Master?"

Cursian reached for her throat and held her, as he had Esme. Samantha writhed again and then stilled. But not as Esme had done, out of fear of getting her throat crushed. She seemed to hold still out of anticipation of the possible violence Cursian might inflict. Her eyes glowed with the need. Esme grimaced.

"You are not yet worthy to call me Master, whore, and if you lay another hand on Esme until the ceremony I will personally slice it off." He dragged her face very close to his own, pulling the woman up onto her toes. "Are we clear? Remember I can smell you on her when I wake."

Samantha choked out a yes. Cursian threw her toward her brother.

"You are very protective of the Scion," Duncan said as he sidestepped his sister, who fell, he sounded cautious.

"As I should be, I have protected her and her kind for centuries. I will not see her harmed now, not by your twisted sister." Cursian reached behind pulling Esme out, "She has promised not to fight and she will honour that promise. I know you want her, Duncan. I know you want her for your games. But tonight she is mine. Her last night of sanity will be spent for my pleasure." Cursian ran a provocative hand of ownership over Esme's chest.

"And you will just hand her over at dawn?" Duncan obviously wasn't convinced.

"Duncan, you want to raise the darkness. For that to happen you need me in my current... mindset and you need to destroy the Scion. I really do not care one way or the other. The only thing I care about is ensuring my continuing pleasure with Esme. She will co-operate because she knows I will keep her alive, whereas your sister will send her mad with pain before I can turn her. Keeping her safe is my one selfish desire, so I suggest you allow me to continue enjoying her body for what is left of the night."

Cursian offered Esme his elbow. Esme looked from Duncan, to Samantha and decided discretion was the better part of valour. She laced her arm with Cursian's and allowed him to lead her into the house.

The inside of the house disappeared as one foot followed the other, which took too much effort. Paintings, statues, doors, corridors all seemed as nothing until Cursian stopped. The man in front of them loomed over the vampire. No mean feat. He'd obviously been carved from granite. Big, muscular granite with rough dark hair and dark skin. Feral energy came off him in waves.

Esme began pulling away from Cursian automatically, instinctual fear causing an overload of panic.

The man growled. Esme noticed a vivid slash of new stitches ran down his face, from his eye to his mouth.

"Jacob, this is Esme." Cursian once more placed her behind his body, without seeming too.

Again with the growl.

"Jacob, do I need to remind you who is master?" Cursian sounded weary.

The growl stopped, "No, Master."

"Good. Jacob, until dawn you will not allow another being over my threshold. When dawn comes, you will allow only one person into my rooms, you will accompany them and then you will stay with Esme until I rise tonight. If necessary, you will do anything to protect her. If she protests or is hurt at all during the day, you will stop them or your soul will be forfeit to me."

The granite man looked down doubtfully at Esme, who looked just as doubtfully back. But he said, "Yes, Master. I will not allow her to be hurt, unless you have ordered it."

"That's reassuring," Esme murmured, as Cursian ushered her into the room.

"It should be. He has sworn allegiance to me," Cursian swiftly moved away from her.

"The scar?"

"He challenged me. I beat him. He belongs to me."

"How wonderfully medieval. He's not human is he?"

"No," Cursian didn't elaborate.

Esme watched him as he moved around the small dressing room. His feline grace undeniable but she also sensed great violence. Esme's fear began to curl up her gullet once more. She backed into a corner.

"Control your fear woman or you will begin to suffer by my hand. That depraved witch Samantha would be a picnic by comparison," Cursian's voice sounded hard and brittle.

"It's hard. You scare me," Esme's mouth felt dry.

"Then talk to me," he sounded wounded. "Talk to me about anything. Remind me of what I am, not what they want me to be."

"Are you that close to the edge?" Esme asked in a small voice.

"Esme, I am so far over the edge it is all I can do not to rip your throat open and bathe in your blood." Cursian had managed to place as much room as possible between them, including an overstuffed armchair.

Esme stayed very still, "Erm, okay. So, we need to get you back on firmer ground. How long till dawn?"

"Just over an hour."

"Talking. I can do that," Esme swallowed hard. "Actually, maybe you should do that. If you talk your mind will begin to focus. Tell me something. Anything. What's your earliest childhood memory? Tell me about being human, Cursian." Esme mentally went through the spell in her mind once more. Concentration came hard with so much potential violence in the room.

"A memory?" Cursian gripped the armchair hard, the wood splintering. "I remember my first pony." He shut his eyes.

Esme didn't know if he did this so he couldn't see her or to help with the memory. It certainly made her breathe a sigh of relief. The fear it generated within her, watching his internal fight, obviously didn't help matters. His dark and beautiful voice smoothed out as he went on in detail.

"I must have been very small. The pony was named Cobweb and she was the fattest mare, but so gentle. My legs were so small I could not even broach her back. My father held onto the back of my tunic, while the steward led the mare around the field. I remember the sun shone, the grass was high and full of flowers. My mother's dress blended with the grasses, so it looked as though she floated through the field walking beside my father. Her long blond hair flowed loose, which is how she wore it away from the cities and towns. My father had my colouring. I remember how much I loved that small fat pony and how many miles we travelled together. When I became too big for her, I would not allow her to be sold. She spent her final years eating the summer hay and enjoying the sun."

Cursian opened his eyes. Esme relaxed. Normality returned, however briefly.

"I have not thought of my family for a very long time. I think my mother would have liked you." Cursian let the chair go. Its stuffing sagged.

"What happened to them?" Esme asked.

"Plague. I was in London. It hit St David's frequently. The pilgrims dragged it with them like a curse."

"I'm sorry," Esme said.

"So am I. If I had stayed and become the nobleman my father wanted me to be it would all have been so different." Cursian turned his back and walked into an adjoining room.

Esme followed at a discreet distance. "I don't think it matters how old you are, there are always times when you can think that about your family. Look at how hard my father tried to keep me away from you, for safety's sake. And all he succeeded in doing was making me a bloody liability." She entered a bedroom. Cursian had flopped out on the double bed.

He reached out a lazy hand, "I am tired, Esme, come sit beside me. I need to wrap myself up in you before dawn comes."

Sitting on the edge of the bed, with Cursian's arm resting over her lap, they filled the room with silence for a while. Esme heard people moving around the house, but fortunately no violence.

"When the dawn comes I will be alone, won't I?" Esme asked hardly daring to break Cursian's quietness.

He gazed at her, "Yes, Cariad. You will be alone."

"I'm scared." Tears pricked her eyes. Her throat filled. Her limbs were heavy.

Cursian remained watching her for a handful of seconds, "I know."

"I don't want to lose you. Here and now I know who you are, but I won't know who you will be when you wake up and I won't be here." It all spilled out in a rush. But the tears remained only in her eyes.

Again, Cursian fell into silence. "I know. I can make you no promises."

Esme's hand clutched his arm, "Will they hurt me, for the cleansing?"

"I believe not," Cursian rolled onto his side, spooning around her upright body. He stroked her hair. "No. The cleansing is literally that. They will clean you and leave you pure, before tonight." He paused obviously considering the wisdom of giving her more information.

"Tell me."

"You will be washed, dressed, prayed over and generally venerated. You are the last and most powerful of the Guardians they will respect that. Then you will be taken to the caves. You will be chained. You have to be. This ceremony will be hard. They need to create pain for the darkness to rise. I will be with you by then. I will need you to be strong. I will need you to project strength and love and every beautiful thing you can remember about our love, our history, your childhood. Then I will be made to strike, that is when we kick back at them."

Esme nodded. "Doesn't sound so bad. How far away is dawn?"

"About twenty minutes," Cursian's voice had softened.

"Right, well, what now? Quick shag?" Esme's smile hurt, her eyes betraying her.

Cursian smiled sadly, "I wish it were a good idea. But I do not trust myself, Cariad. You tell me something. Tell me what your earliest memory is of me."

"Oh, yes. That sounds nice. Okay, well, that'll be in the garden. Mum discovered I could get out through the dog-flap. I used to meet you out there, till Dad found out." She felt Cursian nodding, although she couldn't look at him. She continued to babble, she talked about every time she had seen him, even in the clubs as a student. She reminded him that she did this for their love, for peace, for safety, so people could stop dying at the hands of demons. That sometimes it felt easier to give into the inevitable, rather than fight it. Stream of consciousness stuff fell from her lips.

His arm and body went limp around her. Heavy and empty. Esme didn't move, she continued talking as Cursian died beside her. For a full five minutes she continued, rationalising her actions, her decisions. Eventually she had to stop, to wipe her nose. Looking down at him, fear rapidly took hold. He had gone, so asleep he might as well be dead. Esme rose.

She jumped at the knock on the door looking wildly at Cursian. Running into the other room, she grabbed the broken armchair pushing it to block the door. Someone tried the handle calling to her. She recognised Jacob's rumble.

Esme ran back to the bedroom. How should they be found? She must keep their secret. She was not to raise suspicion. She ripped Cursian's shirt open and undid his jeans, denying his corpse like feel under her fingers as she worked. She threw a blanket over him. Tangling her hair up even more, she took her jumper off and ripped her t-shirt. She even climbed out of her jeans, wishing she wore underwear more often. Esme then clambered over Cursian's body. The door gave under the pounding. She crawled into the corner of the bed, her back to the wall. Looking like a rape victim. It wasn't difficult.

Esme's heart pounded as Jacob filled the doorway and Duncan said from behind him, "Well, now it's our turn, my dear."

CHAPTER TWENTY FOUR

Duncan led the way, Jacob brought up the rear. Esme, jeans pulled back on, walked between, with fear in her heart. Her hands tingled and her knees were weak. She tried to remember the lay out of the house, but nothing would stay. She knew she should be dropping with exhaustion and hunger. Yet she felt strung tight, her mouth may be dry, but she knew she'd puke if forced to eat or drink.

This could not be happening to her, this could not be real. She supposed the process of shock had set in. The only time her current life did not seem utterly surreal was when she spoke with Cursian. Yet, he represented the truly bizarre. Irony. Great thing irony.

They stopped outside a room upstairs. Duncan opened the door and the three walked in. Jacob stopped once the door closed at his back. Esme stopped when she noticed the room. Duncan greeted the other people.

In the centre stood an old fashioned dentist's chair, heavy wood and dark leather. The carpet lay under the window, neatly rolled up. Esme noticed the weather had cleared at last, bright blue sky with large fluffy clouds offered an uncomfortable counterpoint to her fear.

She forced her eyes back to the room. The chair had adaptations, large leather straps at the arms and across the bottom. Esme noticed there were still hints of a colourful dawn left in the clouds.

The people in the room all wore long white coats, doctor's coats. There were four of them, two men and two women, all about her own age. If she moved closer to the window, she might be able to see more of the trees and the gardens, the gardens were lovely here.

Next to the chair stood a large table, it had stuff on it. Esme's eyes wouldn't stay on the table long enough to understand its contents. She wondered how far from the ground the windows were, they didn't look double glazed.

Duncan turned toward her, Esme wanted to be sick, really sick. Hot flushes and cold trembling sped across her skin.

He smiled, "Please, Esme, you look ill. Why not sit down? We are in no real hurry. We have all day to prepare you."

She ignored him, the nausea finally winning. Turning her back, Esme bent double. Very little but bile and water came up, her appetite had not been strong for days. She urged over and over, sinking to her knees. When her stomach muscles felt torn the urging eased. She rocked back on her heals and used the bottom of her ruined t-shirt to wipe her mouth. Now she understood sick with fear. Drawing a deep breath, she closed her eyes. As she inhaled, the fear retreated. She retreated. They would not destroy her; she would not scream and beg for help. She would make this hard for them. Esme drew her courage from deep within, she had always been strong, had always survived. They needed her alive, so she would fight.

She stood and turned back, "I don't seem to be ill anymore. So I won't be needing to sit thanks," Esme planted her feet.

Duncan narrowed his eyes, "Are we about to have a problem?"

"I'm not, but you are," Esme stuck her chin out defiantly.

"We will not hurt you if you co-operate. But this process must be completed whether you wish it or not," Duncan spread his hands as though offering a peaceful solution.

Esme laughed, "Don't patronise me. This will hurt regardless, one way or another I am going to hate you and this… cleansing." She daren't say too much, or she might end up screaming.

"Very well. Jacob, will you ensure the Scion reaches the chair in one piece please. Our vampire will not be happy if you break her," Duncan turned his back and walked to the window.

Esme turned ready to face Jacob. The granite mountain looked down. He moved smoothly toward Esme, who backed off guessing he wasn't going to be a kicker with the weight he carried. She stayed light on her feet, hands open and defensive. Jacob rushed forward, aiming to sweep her up and off her feet. Esme neatly turned ninety degrees, suddenly no longer in front of the big man, as he continued passed her she reached for his right arm. Grabbing his wrist and elbow, she swung back toward his body and continued his forward momentum. Jacob hit the floor, scattering white coats and banging his head on the chair. Esme's body hummed. She twisted easily away and began to look for a weapon. She heard Jacob begin to push himself up. Like most big men, he had relied on his size and strength. Esme knew she could use that against him. More respectful now, Jacob took stock of the situation before rushing her again.

Esme kept her guard high, waiting, thrilling in the moment of power. She noticed Jacob's hands clench and his shoulders tense, the right one began to draw back. Just as the punch flew to her face (and this was his idea of keeping her in one piece), Esme twisted her hips pulling her head out of the way. Simultaneously, she brushed his arm past her head and sliding into his body delivered a powerful reverse punch to his liver. Esme's arm went numb at the impact. Jacob fell over. She turned ready to deliver a knock out blow to the back of his head, when someone switched the lights off in her own head.

Esme came too fighting. She couldn't have been out for any longer than a few seconds, but they had lifted her into the chair. She bucked and fought as Jacob dug his fingers into her shoulders and the other four pinned down a limb each. They all struggled to keep her under control. Esme yelled the room down, creating a long chain of expletives, concentrating heavily on their sexual preferences.

After she'd split one lip and caused a bloody nose, the white coats subdued Esme enough to get the leather straps done up. Jacob had her head in a crushing grip between his hands, stopping her from biting anyone else. Esme felt murderous, her chest heaving with fury and exertion. Duncan appeared in her line of vision.

"Goodness me, but that was fun. You really are very good. Of course, now I cannot trust you, so things will be harder from this moment on. I shall be retiring for the day, I must be fresh this evening and that sleep spell should have kept you under for hours, not minutes. You cost me much effort. But tonight I will have boundless energy to call on for all eternity, once our dark Lord has arrived."

Esme ground out, "Bastard, I will have your heart for this."

"No," Duncan leaned across Esme's body, "I will have yours. I already have Cursian tucked up downstairs, and soon you will be mine. By the end of today you will not want to fight me."

"Cursian said you wouldn't hurt me if I didn't fight," Esme's eyes were wild.

"I won't, physically. And I promised I wouldn't hurt you, physically, but the cleansing rite has a way of humiliating people into submission," he smiled and disappeared from Esme's vision.

Esme screamed and fought once more as she heard the door close behind the nasty, evil, little man.

They let her fight, obviously confident the bonds would hold. They did. As she began to calm Jacob stood beside her, careful not to be bitten again.

"You were told I should not be hurt!" she yelled.

"You haven't been hurt. They are not hurting you. You are hurting you. You are the one fighting, not us." His face remained distant and bland.

Esme stared at him for a long time, then relaxed, finally realising she couldn't win and even if she escaped how the hell would she a) rescue Cursian and b) stop the bad guys? This is why she was here after all.

The white coats sensed her passivity and moved in.

"What's going on?" Esme's senses twanged at having them able to touch her, while she couldn't stop them.

"We are to cleanse you," one of the white coats said quietly.

"This I know," Esme spat. "What's it going to involve?"

"You must be clean for the ceremony. Therefore we are going to clean you," said a man's voice and as he stood straight Esme saw a cut throat razor in his hand.

"What the fuck are you going to do with that?"

"We will ensure your skin is clean," his face looked passive, almost happy. "You will be clean for our dark Lord's entrance."

Esme felt someone pouring water on her head. It flooded her eyes and soaked her t-shirt, making it cling to her body. The people in white coats began to sing quietly. Esme shook her head trying to clear the water out of her eyes. Someone took hold of her hair, she couldn't move her head. And then she could. Again someone took hold of her hair. Esme realised what they were doing, she watched as a long, thick tangle of her hair fell down her chest. Stunned she lay still as cut after cut took her hair, as much a part of her as her belly button and just as unchangeable.

The squirt of an aerosol spurned her into thrashing once more as she realised what the razor would do to her head. Jacob grabbed her face as foam covered her scalp. He kept telling her to hold still, or she would be cut. Esme did hold still, but only because her body locked rigid as the cold steel touched her forehead and the blade dragged back to her crown. Over and over she felt and heard the scrape of the blade. Tears of rage and frustration trickled down her face, as she listened to the litany they sang while she lay, still unable to stop them touching her. The women cleaned her fingernails and took her shoes off, cleaning her toes next. Esme hated being fussed with. She vowed she would destroy these people no matter what the cost. And she hated Cursian. Hated him for leaving her here. For abandoning her to this humiliation. But it didn't stop with her head.

Once her toenails had been cleaned, and none to gently, they began to cut her jeans off. By this time, Esme understood what cleansing really meant. Had Cursian known? Had he lied? Was he setting her up? Her fragile confidence in their plan began to shatter. What a fucking idiot she'd made herself, had she really thought he would come good? She began to panic.

"Wait, please, wait. You're not going to use that cutthroat razor on my pubic hair are you? Cause I wax, full Brazil, there won't be anything to cut." Esme felt desperate, she did not want to be naked in this chair.

They ignored her and carried on singing. Esme flung her head back and squealed as cold, hard leather met with sensitive skin for the first time. She retreated inside herself as all her clothes were cut from her body. Esme did not want to be a part of this, not anymore. However, no comforting blue light came to her rescue this time and she couldn't even begin to reach it. Every time she tried she became lost in a web of sticky blackness. Now she could no longer fight, her last refuge and power base stolen or hidden, Esme had nothing. No resources to pull from which would help her understand this situation. No way of assimilating the actions inflicted upon her body. Never had she felt this vulnerable, humiliated and alone. All this to save a lover and to stop a demon, which she didn't really believe in anyway.

The white coats released a limb in turn and shaved her legs, her armpits, her groin. Esme couldn't bring herself to fight. Over and over the blade kissed her skin. They never drew blood, they didn't hurt her, but Esme felt each kiss as though it were a blow from the mightiest sword.

The day wore on. At some point an older woman arrived and gave Esme a rough internal examination. Swabs were taken, the woman declared Esme had never been pregnant and wasn't currently carrying a child. Esme thought that maybe having a child would have been worth it if it had stopped this from happening. Then images of Cursian's first victim swam up from the darkest parts of her memory. Nausea hit and she began to puke again.

Esme found herself taken from the barber's room, to a large bathroom. Jacob remained with her, holding her wrists together with a thick length of rope in front of her body. Esme walked stiffly, her limbs rigid from the stress of fighting her bondage and the continued drip of fight or flight hormones.

Bruises began to show on her naked skin. Her back itched where her hair should have brushed her shoulders.

The bath squat like a toad full hot water. Esme watched the steam rising. The people in this room sang too, Esme switched the meaning off, not willing to remember the words. Pushing her toward the bath, they forced her to step into the hot water. Her skin blanched at the heat, but she welcomed the sting, at least it felt familiar. Jacob yanked the rope down, obviously enjoying the control. Esme scowled at him, imagining how beautiful his blood would look sprayed all over the walls. She lowered herself into the water. The man and woman who sat at the head and foot of the bath instantly moved into action. They reached for Esme, who flinched but held reasonably still and began to scrub.

The scrubbing wasn't hard, but over and over again with small pumice stones, soon left Esme feeling raw. Jacob lifted her onto all fours, while they scrubbed her buttocks. Esme knew her face flushed red with more than the heat as Jacob took up position behind her, the threat of Cursian depriving him of his soul now a distant memory.

Repeated scouring left Esme squirming to escape the nasty little stones. The wet ropes bit into her skin. Dizziness swept through her as the heat of the bath, along with the constant pain, tiredness, hunger and dehydration combined to deprive her of her senses. The white coats began to take turns holding her upright while they continued to scrub. Esme felt her mouth being prised open and her tongue scraped, along with her teeth. Then back on all fours. She came around with the shocked realisation they were going to clean all of her, inside and out. First, they pushed a wide tube into her vagina and hot water flowed into and out of her. Esme made a desperate attempt to escape, calling brokenly for Cursian for the first time. Jacob grabbed her hips and held her under the water until she stopped fighting. Still the singing went on. The next thing, inevitably, had to be the anal enema. Esme endured. Telling herself, women paid hundreds of pounds a month for this kind of diet treatment. At least they knew what they were doing.

Connecting to the world became increasingly difficult and Esme simply became a rag doll under the white coats care. Once the bath ended, they raised her up and dried her off. They left the ropes binding her wrists, clearly not willing to risk her temper. Esme though, had no fight left. She could neither see nor think clearly. She surrendered.

CHAPTER TWENTY FIVE

The white coats and Jacob led her to a smaller room. White walls, no windows, and a scrubbed wooden floor, with a bare light bulb hanging alone and desolate. They left her there, naked. They told her she should pray to their dark Lord so she would be accepted by Him. Esme said nothing. She stood limply, feeling numb. She heard the key turn in the lock and she was truly alone for the first time in hours.

Raising her bound hands to her head, Esme ran her palms over her scalp. Her knees began to give way as her fingers dug into her skull. She curled into a small ball, in the middle of the room, protecting her head and sobbed.

Sleep must have taken her at some point. She woke up cold, stiff and covered in bruises. The first few seconds were horribly disorientating, until she touched her head. Esme's bottom lip began to quiver, but she stopped. Why, why cry because someone had shaved off her hair? Scrubbed her raw and forced her to have internal examinations?

Esme stayed close to the floor, on her knees and asked for the strength to go through with this, to stop them succeeding. The spell to destroy Cursian filled her mind for long moments, the temptation strong. She endured this pain so she would have her freedom from the Prophecy. Maybe he had not known what was to happen to her and watching his face die, as she cast the spell, would be far better than doing the job here. Moving past the anger she prayed and finally received a response, peace.

Esme so enjoyed the feeling of being alone and quiet, after days of frantic activity, she rose and began to try to iron out the stiffness in her limbs. She attacked the rope with her teeth and after some serious struggling she managed to free her hands. Esme then explored every part of herself in minute detail. Everything felt sore, overly clean. If she thought about the last few hours in any detail she began to lose control, but physically she seemed okay.

Once she'd determined her body worked and she kept her hands away from her head, she looked at the room in detail. This didn't take long. She had one way out, the door. The door didn't seem to be a sensible option as she had no doubt Jacob stood the other side. Esme did not want to give him an excuse to hurt her. She paced the small room. She didn't want to become bored. Boredom would lead to thinking and thinking would lead to madness. She began to try to focus on her kata. The series of martial arts movements flowing safely through her, reminding her of who and what she was, regulating her breathing and encouraging concentration. Unfortunately, the day's events had taken their toll. After only the second run through of all thirteen traditional kata, her thoughts began to drift, her movements were hard and ragged, her focus gone. Hunger, thirst and damaged joints soon made her sit on the floor in a heap.

"Okay, so if I can't move much I can talk. I can remember things," Esme began to recite all the Japanese she could remember. Then historical dates, trying for as much detail as possible. Whenever her mind wanted to give up and ponder the nasty stuff, she screwed her eyes tight and started again. Time, without a watch, stretched endlessly. Without food or water, it became a torment.

Esme never sat still and did nothing. She never gave herself a chance to think too much about anything, she lived her life constantly moving toward the next goal. The hard floor set her body off aching again. Walking seemed to help, so that's what she did, and when the walking became too hard because her knees began to tremble, she sat and began counting. Time did pass. But Esme became increasingly more brittle, her confidence from earlier eroding again. Her sense of peace dissolved, dread taking its place.

The key turned in the lock. Esme rose from the far corner, where she had finally succumbed to exhaustion. Fear shot through her, making her tremble. Duncan, Samantha and

Jacob walked in, followed by people in white robes. Jacob hadn't changed, but the other two had.

Samantha's hair rose in a pile made of hundreds of small plaits, held by shiny pins. Esme thought it looked like a nest of snakes. The woman's clothing seemed to consist of layers and layers of cream silk hanging from large metal clips at her shoulders and down her arms. When she moved, the silk wrapped itself around her body.

Duncan had simply changed a grey suit for a cream one matching his sister's robe. Their eyes were heavily dilated irises and they exuded confidence.

"Your resources are astonishing, Esme, I felt sure you'd still be a babbling mess," Duncan sounded like a proud father.

Esme stayed silent, not wanting to spoil the image of control they seemed to think she had.

"When the ceremony starts, she will not be so calm. I have to say, you look stunning in your nakedness," Samantha began to sidle toward Esme.

Esme tried to push herself further into the corner. She'd forgotten her nakedness and now felt too conscious of it, too vulnerable. Still no words would come. She felt empty of smart remarks, empty and alone. Terribly alone in front of all these people.

"Samantha, darling, we don't have time for this. Cursian will rise soon and we must have Esme ready," Duncan sounded slightly cross.

"She's covered in bruises!" Samantha cried out, as though her favourite doll had been scratched.

"She fought much of the time, Samantha. Jacob has already explained," patience now from Duncan, who waved one of the robed figures forward.

A small woman approached Esme with a long white cloak in her arms. Samantha walked back to her brother, clearly cross. The woman held it toward Esme, bowing as she did so. Esme looked at the cloak, looked at the other people and reached forward. She tried to lift the heavy silk cloth around her shoulders, but managed to become knotted in the mass of fabric. The woman reached out to help. Esme yelped when the woman's hand made contact with skin. She pushed the woman over while continuing to struggle against the cloth. No one moved to help or said a word. Eventually, the cloak hung straight, held by an old fashioned fabric clasp. Esme reached up and pulled the hood low over her face.

"Now we are ready to present you to our acolytes and begin the procession. Come, Esme, let us show them what a wonderful gift we will be giving our dark Lord this evening," Duncan held his arm out.

Esme grabbed handfuls of the robe, determined she would walk and not be carried by any of these monsters. Slowly she moved past Duncan and Samantha, following the white robes in front of her.

CHAPTER TWENTY SIX

Cursian woke hungry and disorientated. His hunger sang through his body like a junkie craving crack. As with the last few nights, he did not think toward Esme, the hardest of habits to break after all these years. He hoped it would stop the others from realising how deeply they were still bound to each other. He noticed Esme's jumper, discarded on the floor and curled around the pain blossoming within him at the thought of her helplessness. What had he done to her, bringing her here and expecting her to survive without him? Cursian breathed deeply around his anguish. The faster he could find a way to be with her, the sooner she would be no longer be alone.

He rose, then stopped. His sharpened senses picking up something in the corner. Cursian turned, a woman had her faced pressed into the floor, genuflecting toward him.

"Who are you?" he asked on guard.

"They thought you might need me, Master, before you began tonight's rituals," came a small and tremulous voice.

"What? Sit up, for Gods sake woman." Cursian had not been offered flesh in this context for centuries. The thought an unhappy one.

The woman rose to her haunches, "Do you need to feed, Master?"

Cursian, until that moment, thought he had complete control over the vampire. He had woken calm and sane. However, as the woman offered herself to him, his need rose like a thunderous wave of lust. The man inside him screamed and vanished under the torrent. Cursian moved across the room in a single leap, picking the woman up and pushing her head back in one practiced motion. She cried out in terror, as well she might and he hesitated. His teeth were pressing into her flesh, but he stopped short of slacking his thirst. The woman smelt of Esme, smelt strongly of his Scion. Even the vampire within him hesitated because of that scent. The vampire knew that scent was the sweetest feeding ground in the world. Images of Esme, with him at her side, happy and laughing in her flat, drew the drowning man out of the tide of hunger.

Cursian dropped the woman to the floor, "Get out. Now!" He turned away as he heard her scramble for the door. Cursian ran his fingers through his hair, clenched his fists and pulled, groaning in frustration. He lashed out and a small area of the brick wall between the two rooms crumbled under the impact. The pain focused his mind, driving the need back slightly further, so he could think.

He walked through to the bathroom and showered quickly. He also found clean clothes laid out for him. A dark red shirt and leather jeans, even his boots shone. Cursian shrugged and changed, concentrating on human memories and emotions. The dark web surrounding him, suffocated his humanity, making it hard to be normal.

He heard a footstep outside his door and he finished dressing. He carefully locked away his thoughts as the person knocked.

"Enter."

The door opened to reveal two men in white robes. One said, "Master, you are to follow us. It is time. The Scion is ready."

Cursian's heart pounded at the mention of Esme. His instinct to rip through these pathetic humans to reach her almost overpowering. However, he followed the men, silently.

They went up the back stairs and began to walk along a long gallery. Cursian saw a group of people moving toward them from the other end. Both groups met in the middle. Cursian could only see the siblings from hell and Jacob, yet he started to sense Esme close by. Duncan smiled at him. Samantha looked as though she would throw herself at him and drag him off to her own version of damnation.

"You appear rested," Duncan said blandly.

"Yes, but I did not appreciate being left breakfast. I have no wish to feed on weak humans who would give themselves up willingly," Cursian didn't hide his annoyance.

"I am sorry if we gave you offence. She was more than happy to satisfy any of your needs."

"Maybe he's saving himself," Samantha stepped close to the vampire.

Cursian looked down at her disdainfully and brushed her hand from his shirt. She stank of dark magic and drugs.

"If I am, woman, it will not be for you. Where is Esme?" Cursian asked, agitated because he couldn't pick her scent up from any of the people present. They all seemed to smell of her, Jacob more strongly than the others.

"Patience," Duncan turned and placed his hands on the banister running along the edge of the gallery.

Cursian noticed the heaving mass of people below them for the first time. White robes moved and rustled, large crowds never able to be completely silent.

Duncan raised his arms, Samantha standing on his left side, Cursian on his right, more by accident than design. "Brothers and Sisters," Duncan began. "We are here tonight to witness the final step toward a new age. We will soon be making our way to the Hall of Ceremonies, where it all began so long ago. Ours began our path, and we have inherited the right to finish it. The last of the Guardians will be accepted into our family and the gates will be opened to our dark Lord." The crowd erupted.

Cursian gazed down with loathing and disdain.

Once Duncan had managed to regain the crowds silence he continued, "I have the last human Guardian here. She has been cleansed and is ready to accept the dark Lord into her, so he may be born through her suffering."

Alarm shot through the vampire. Born through her suffering? What had they done to her and what were they going to do?

Duncan turned and pulled a fully cloaked figure forward. Cursian's heart raced. The priest reached around and undid the frog at the cloak's neck. In one deft move, he took the cloak away and Esme stood there. Naked, trembling and bruised. Cursian stood only three feet away from her, but she seemed so locked up inside herself, he could have been on the moon. She stared out, over the crowd, obviously refusing to be baited by her naked vulnerability. He groaned as the crowd screamed their approval. Her denuded body shone in the artificial light and her humiliation sliced through him. This reminder of her frail humanity brought his vampire simmering upward. This time he welcomed the darkness and the suffering it bred. Cursian's humanity slowly folded itself away as he gazed with love and ownership upon the one thing uniting his vampire and his manhood.

"What have you done to her?" Cursian growled.

"She has been cleansed," Duncan seemed almost vacuous on his drug enhanced high.

"You took her hair. And where did the bruises come from?" Cursian tried to keep an emotional distance.

"It is a part of the process. This has to be our best offering. She is the most powerful of the Guardians." Duncan swept his hand over the crowd, "They worship her. She will give life to our dark Lord. The bruises are simply because she doesn't understand her place in our world, she resisted."

Cursian turned away from them and faced Jacob, "You stink of her. You did not keep my Scion safe. You are not worthy to call me, Master." For the first time in centuries, Cursian allowed his vampiric nature full control.

The decision had to be the wrong one. Cursian knew he could be sacrificing his control permanently. When the time came for the ceremony, with all the dark energy baiting him, it would be hard enough not to bring Esme into his world completely, without giving himself this luxury of violence now. Yet, someone would pay for her pain. And Jacob held no importance.

Everyone surrounding Jacob moved away from the hulking man. The rest of the gallery were unaware of the small circle of contradictory energy in the corner. Cursian stalked the bigger man who backed off. Jacob turned his retreat into attack and sprang at the vampire, clearly desperate to escape his death. Cursian sidestepped and grabbed a wrist as Jacob began to pull back. The giant man lashed out, but Cursian maintained tight control on the wrist and twisted it away from Jacob's flailing body. With Cursian's hips fully committed to turning such a small joint, Jacob had no choice but to hit the ground. And still his wrist snapped audibly. Jacob screamed. Cursian pushed his knee into the elbow of the arm he still grasped, the elbow suddenly bent in the wrong direction, the shoulder held high from the ground. Jacob screamed again.

Everyone turned, including Esme.

"I will not have my Scion hurt, in any way. She belongs to me," Cursian's blood lust rose to the point were he could barely speak.

They all moved as far away from him as they could, except Esme. Who stood alone.

The crowd noises began to break up, confusion clear.

"This pathetic fool has not only betrayed his kind by mixing with humans in such a way, he has also betrayed his, Master." Cursian turned toward the banister, effortlessly dragging the struggling beast behind him. Now Jacob stood in the middle, with Esme to the left and Cursian to the right. Duncan and Samantha stood behind, enjoying the scene.

"I want you to witness what betrayal in this world will give you," Cursian revelled in the crowd's disturbed silence. It had been so long since he had allowed himself to terrify humans.

Jacob began to babble apologies.

The vampire pulled on the broken arm and Jacob screamed as Cursian forced him to his knees. He turned slightly. Esme moved to stand next to him. He gazed down into pain filled green eyes, larger now without her dark hair framing her beautiful face. Her small breasts brushed his arm as she breathed into his ear.

"I want to see him suffer, Cursian. I want to kill him. Give me this before the end, please," Esme sounded broken and hoarse. He knew what screaming endlessly did to a voice.

Finally, united as one, the man and the vampire inhaled her hate, rage and pain. Cursian pulled Jacob's head back, pushing his neck forward. With his free hand Cursian delivered a hammer blow to Jacob's sternum, it splintered. All the years of control, of forcing his capacity for violence away, vanished. The intoxication of feeding on fear and blood filled Cursian. He must keep this creature alive long enough for the real suffering to be Esme's reward. Still gazing at his Scion, Cursian caught the now loose skin over the man's chest and pulled one side. The skin tore. Still Jacob stayed aware. Killing monsters had always been fun, they lasted so long. If he'd done this to a human, they would be dead. Only knives worked on humans; they could not sustain this kind of impact. Blood began to pour over the gallery, covering Esme's bare feet, and down onto the acolytes below. They began to sing their nasty song. Cursian reached into the hole in Jacob's chest, pushing splintered bone aside. He grasped the franticly beating heart and began to pull gently. The heart came, making sucking noises as Jacob gurgled in response. Cursian pulled it out far enough for Esme to take hold. He offered it to her.

Esme gazed at the beating heart and at Jacob. She reached forward and then hesitated, fingers not quite touching the beating organ. Jacob swayed against Cursian's legs. She looked up. Cursian could see himself reflected in her eyes. Blood splattered his face lightly. His pale skin glowed with power and lust. His eyes were fully black and utterly dreadful. Her own expression reflected the normally torn nature of his personality. She clearly wanted Jacob dead, but actually causing that death filled her with horror. He filled her with horror. With a moment of understanding, Cursian threw his head back and howled at his own disgusting behaviour. He did not want to corrupt Esme in this way. He had spent decades ensuring she did not become a creature of hate and vengeance. He thrust the heart back into Jacob. Cursian lifted the huge, dying body, covering everyone in blood and hurled the hulk over the banister into the waiting crowd below.

Cursian turned to Esme, both of them were painted with red streaks. She stepped toward him, closing the distance and wrapped her arms around his body, burying her head in his soaked, gore covered shirt.

"Thank you," came the broken whisper.

Cursian wondered why she thanked him and then didn't care as the vampire took physical hold of his property. He relaxed, possessing Esme, along with the blood soaking into his skin took the edge off his hunger. He no longer needed to rip any ones throat out. He merely wanted too. For now, with Esme in his arms, Cursian could claim his vampire and human personalities were at peace with each other.

"That was incredible," Samantha said with awe.

Cursian turned toward the siblings, holding Esme tight to his chest. Samantha's glee at Jacob's demise made Cursian sick.

"The Scion will need to be cleaned again," Duncan frowned slightly, sounding perturbed. He waved several people forward.

"No, I am not trusting her to your care. I shall clean her. If you want her sane and whole you are going to have to be careful. She is dangerously close to losing her mind."

"I think you care for this woman too much," Duncan's expression flitted from drug hazed stupidity, to Machiavellian devilment.

Cursian grew wary. Protecting Esme, if you could call it that, only remained possible because the siblings did not expect him to join them willingly. If he made too much noise about protecting her, the Dominion would know their bonds were not severed. A bad case of, 'the Lady doth protest too much'.

Cursian forced Esme away from his body slightly. Her naked form hung limp and blood stained. He carefully turned her toward them.

"Fine, you take her. But Jacob's fate is as nothing compared to my vengeance should she be harmed again. And if she dies before or during your ceremony your dark Lord cannot make his entrance. She has fought you most of the day. And she will fight you again if she thinks her death will stop this from happening. However, she loves and trusts me. Despite it all."

Samantha cocked her head, fully lucid, "Why would she trust you?"

Cursian smiled, "Because she has no choice. And I am vampire. I can force her to trust me without her knowing it. Just as I can force her not to remember this conversation. So long as it is brief. Now let me get her cleaned up. I do not want her having hysterics when she realises she is covered with blood."

He watched as the two lost their fight to stay fully aware when the drug washed back over them. Thank God for drugs. They made people stupid and pliable. Duncan waved a hand.

"We will be down in among our people. You have a short time to make yourselves ready."

They walked away from Cursian and Esme, leading their elite group down the stairs, toward the waiting throng.

Cursian swept Esme off her feet and carried her to one of the many bathrooms. Once he found one large enough to accommodate both of them, he placed Esme on the floor and began running a bath.

"No, no bath. Shower, please, Cursian," she told him quietly.

He looked down at her. She slumped against the wall, like some broken rag doll. Her bald head covered in a sticky skull cap of blood.

"All right, Cariad, no bath. But I cannot leave you in the shower alone."

Esme tried to laugh, "Funny, May, said that when you beat me up."

The words delivered a mortal blow to his heart. "Oh, Esme, I… I…"

"Just get me clean and get this over with," Esme straightened herself up, the effort it took pitiful.

Cursian pulled off his leather jeans and shirt, switching on the shower.

"Is what you said true? About being able to manipulate my trust?" Esme looked at him with a mixture of pure hate and fear.

He gazed down, his vampire and human elements still in quiet accord. "No, Esme, no it was not true. I can no more force you to love and trust me, than I can stop loving you myself. But I have to keep control of your situation."

Her expression turned to flint, "Shame you couldn't have controlled it earlier."

Cursian opened his mouth to apologise and realised the futility. He bent and picked her up, carrying her into a gentle stream of warm water. Lowering them both to floor, he watched the dark sticky mess begin to turn the water pink around them.

"They hurt me. They took my hair. They cleaned me inside and out and that creature held me still, all the time," Esme whispered into the water.

Cursian bent his head over hers. "Cariad, I am so sorry. You of all people I would not see hurt. I did not think they would go to such extremes. Their madness is strong. With each pair of Guardians they have destroyed, they have become more powerful and therefore, more unstable. But I will see them dead," the last came out as a growl.

"Why not make me vampire, Cursian?" Esme asked blinking as water filled her upturned face.

"What?"

"If I were vampire I could survive this and keep the gates closed on their dark Lord."

"Esme, as a vampire you would want to usher in their new dawn." Cursian felt deeply disturbed by her logic and calm.

"So? We would also be together for all eternity. We would never have to go through the pain of separation."

"No, we would not."

"I would not be as De'hevda, you could stop that."

His vampire began to writhe at the thought of having her forever beside him, the Mistress to his Master. Oh, the temptation.

"Esme, it would send you mad. I might be able to bring you back, but we can only defeat these people with your light and humanity. Your purity and connection to love and God is all that can save us and stop them."

"So my weakness is actually my strength," she sounded depressed at the thought.

"Your weakness keeps me sane. While you are human and vulnerable, I have discovered my vampire and human elements are happy to work together to protect you. The vampire within me understands and wants you. I must admit to the thought of keeping you forever is almost too much of a temptation, but I need you to be who you are. Not a creation of mine."

Silence. Then, "I don't know if I can forgive you for this."

"I am not certain I expect you to be able to forgive me. However, I will spend the rest of your life trying to gain that forgiveness," Cursian smiled slightly.

"I shall die long before you, get all old and I have to have children." Her thoughts seemed broken and fragmented.

"Esme, I think we need to solve one problem at a time. We do not know what God or the Fates have in store for us." Cursian noticed the water ran clear, time to leave.

"I'm not pregnant, they checked."

He stroked her face. Empty of hair he realised exactly how fragile, how perfect she really was and now he would take her back to them. Hand her over once more to allow the dark Lord to rise through her sacrifice. Then use her to stop them and destroy them. At that moment, he hated himself so much he couldn't bear to look at her any longer. He screwed his eyes shut, brushed his hair back, turning to let the full stream of water fall over his face.

"We must leave," he said to the ceiling.

"I know," Esme began to move in his arms.

CHAPTER TWENTY SEVEN

As he dried her off he asked, "Do you remember the spell?"

"Yes," she seemed quiet and calm.

"Good. Esme," he looked at her for the first time in five minutes. "This is about to become harder. You will have to go out there without my support. We need to appear separate."

"Right."

"Esme," he took her by the shoulders, pulling her around to face him. He feared the coldness in her eyes. "I need to prove to them that we are not involved. It needs to look as though we have fallen out."

"You want me to hit you, don't you?" Esme looked weary beyond belief. She'd never been stupid.

Cursian didn't even have a chance to nod before Esme's fist slammed into his jaw, then her opposite hand raked across his face. The welts from her nails filled up quickly. She turned away, a look of disgust on her face.

He reached toward her, to reassure her everything would be okay. But what the hell was the point? They would probably die a painful death regardless. The look of hate on her face as she struck him shook Cursian. He wished he had more time to steady her mind before the rest of the night's depravities. Their previous plans and optimism were a cruel joke. The Dominion had almost broken his Scion. The likelihood of her surviving this ritual dwindled by the hour.

"Can you leave here under your own steam? It would be better, emphasise our separateness."

"Fine," Esme's voice sounded too quiet. "Can you pass me that cloak they want me to wear?"

He handed it to her. She took the cloak, without looking at him, walking out voluntarily.

He followed her out, watching as she swayed with every step. Her aura looked dark and shrunk tight to her body. She'd cut herself off from her energy source. She must reattach or their plan would never work. They would never defeat this crowd of darkness without her gifts. Walking slowly down the stairs, the crowd at the bottom parted as though watching a prom queen glide through them. Cursian noticed the bloody hands of most of those in the crowd. Jacob's corpse seemed to have been put to good use.

"I see the tiger still has claws," Samantha sashayed toward them as they finished their descent.

"I told you she would continue to fight. But she is not going to make the journey to the caves unaided, she is too weak and I do not trust your people to keep hold of her," Cursian said.

"If she is so weak she should be easy to control. I can see how pathetic she's become. Our dark Lord should be able to enter her easily," she said with glee.

Cursian's jaw flexed, "Do not allow her current position to fool you. She is more than capable of dragging strength from her source or someone here. I will take her with me. She cannot take what I shall not give."

Samantha's eyes narrowed, showing suspicion, "Vampire, you walk a dangerous path. Why care so much?"

"You people are becoming tiresome. I care because I have waited decades to shed my responsibilities and take Esme into my life. I wish to be her Sire, to have her with me forever. But if you or your dark Lord break her mind before I turn her, like you did with the others, I will not be able to salvage her. She will not be suitable as a lifetime's companion. Now get out of my way and we will proceed with this ceremony."

Cursian walked swiftly toward Esme, who sagged again, sweeping her off her feet once more.

He led the pageant, Samantha's eyes boring into his back. They passed singing neophytes lining the walls and the procession grew. This plan turned on a knife's edge. They clearly doubted his loyalty but whether they doubted his commitment to their plan because he wanted Esme to himself or doubted his turning from his Guardianship, it had become hard to tell. His only trump card lay with the knowledge they needed both Esme and himself alive, for their dark Lord to be made manifest. Faking his own corruption had not been hard. Indeed, he walked the tightrope too well, losing himself on occasion. His instinct for keeping Esme out of harms way maintained his sanity but gave them fuel of their doubts. Even in their fuddled state, they would soon realise the truth. He just hoped to act this out long enough to save himself and Esme during the final summoning.

The Scion relaxed into his chest and surrendered herself without a word. He didn't know if it was trust (unlikely to say the least), or exhaustion leading her to relax so completely. The temptation, in that moment, to begin running and never stop, made his legs ache. If he ran far enough, maybe, just maybe they could escape all this, maybe.

"Ah, Cursian and your Scion," Duncan stepped toward him from the doorway at the end of the hall. "Glad you joined me. Shall we begin our journey to the caves?"

"As you wish, though the girl is stupefied with exhaustion," Cursian held Esme out slightly.

"Oh, I'm sure she'll find the strength to scream before the end. I wouldn't want to deprive you of that pleasure," Duncan smiled and led the way.

He opened a large door, with stairs leading down in an even, broad expanse. The ceiling reached at least seven foot forming a smooth arch. Duncan and Cursian walked side by side, plenty of room surrounding them. Torches lit their way with a flickering orangey glow and dark smoke. Cursian's mind began to sink into the ground, calling forth his power, slowly and carefully. He had to win this fight if he wanted any kind of future.

CHAPTER TWENTY EIGHT

Esme shivered as the cold from the tunnel penetrated her cloak. She heard Duncan telling Cursian about the formation of the tunnels and caves, the link between the Dashwood estate and the Hellfire Caves. Esme suspected Cursian knew about these tunnels since their conception. He would have ensconced her family here around that time. Crowley and the caves, motivation enough to ensure her family remained in West Wycombe. She shivered again, tunnels were always cold and Cursian didn't waste energy on creating body heat. Esme allowed her mind to wander off. She didn't want to be a part of the next few hours, however they turned out.

Her dazed state continued even as Cursian stopped and the sounds around her changed. The auditory quality improved, its resonance becoming more rounded and synonymous with church acoustics. Esme didn't want to open her eyes and become a part of this larger sound. She didn't want to continue with this game. She began to struggle against the iron hard arms, which held her softly.

"Please, do not fight me now, Esme," Cursian whispered over her head.

But Esme's need to escape this haunting chant, which began to make her skin tight and her scalp tingle, became stronger. She finally started really struggling when the sound of chains being moved infiltrated her haze. That haze vanished with the speed of Concorde when the chains came into view and Cursian lowered her body to the floor. Esme lashed out at those surrounding her, trying to escape the two men advancing with the chains.

"Cursian, if you don't control your charge and get her chained we will have to do it for you," Duncan snapped.

He and Samantha were watching the performance from some distance away. The people from the house began to fill the cavern. The only other exit lay clean across the large cave.

Esme sprang for the exit. Instinct driving her, common sense telling her she would never make it. One of the men holding the chains grabbed an ankle as she propelled herself forward. Esme hit the ground but twisted as she did so, landing on her back. She kicked out, exhaustion rendered the kick wild and lacking power. Cursian came toward her, hands out in supplication. The man who had her ankle pulled her toward him. Esme's naked back scraped painfully against the rough stone floor. Her attacker stood up, preparing to haul his prisoner upright. Esme rolled toward him, grabbed his ankle and slammed the palm of her other hand into the side of his knee joint. She heard and felt a sickening crunch as the joint dislocated. He collapsed screaming and writhing in surprised agony. Esme began to struggle to her feet once more.

Just as she thought she'd have a fairly clear run at it, arms like steel wrapped in velvet surrounded her and lifted her off her feet.

Cursian's voice filtered through her panic, its rich sound calming her, "Please, Esme, do not fight," he whispered. "Now is not the time for us to fight. I need you to concentrate on your power, on your faith, on your spiritual strength, not your physical strength. Please, hear me, my love."

She continued to fight for a few heartbeats longer, eyes firmly on the exit tunnel. Then people began filling up that part of the cave and its welcoming darkness vanished. Esme slumped. Cursian released her.

Duncan stood in front of her, "When are you going to stop denying your part in our dark Lord's rising? This cave has been used for our ceremonies for centuries and you are the pinnacle of that sacrificial history, why do you deny this?"

Esme squared her shoulders, noting that the small scrap bloodied her back. She glared at the white suited mad man in front of her, "I will never willingly give myself to your path, or any one's path. I am a child of my Lord, the only one that really counts and he will deliver me from this, one way or another. I cannot be used by you!" her panic made her rhetoric sound fundamentalist.

"Your adherence to your faith is the very path our dark Lord will use to reach us. Your purity is what will feed him and that purity's defilement by our favourite creature of darkness will be your final undoing. You will welcome him in the end," Duncan said smugly.

Esme hawked and spat at Duncan's feet. His hand lashed out, whipping her head to the right, stars blossomed in her eyes and blood filled her mouth. She felt Cursian stiffen.

"Respect, Esme, dear," Duncan continued.

Her body began to move forward of its own volition, hands aching to strangle the bastard, when other hands grasped her wrists and pulled backward. Esme turned slightly. Cursian replaced the man holding the chains.

Her eyes widened in shock, "What?"

Cursian's face appeared empty, "The ceremony must begin. We cannot allow any more delays due to your foolishness. Do not fight us, Esme."

His rich voice fell like shards of darkness through her body. Esme couldn't bring herself to fight or scream as he forced the cold, hard iron onto her limbs. Her skin screamed in response to its touch.

Her wrists were contained behind her back, a metal bar separating them by eighteen inches or so, the centre of the bar held a ring that led to a chain. This chain clipped to a ring in the floor of the cave. Cursian pushed Esme to her knees to make the chain reach the ring. Once secured, the human removed her stained cloak. Esme found herself sitting in a tragic imitation of her traditional martial posture. The chains so heavy behind her that her shoulders were pulled back, leaving her nakedness thrust forward. Without her hair to cover even her scalp and neck, Esme felt indescribably isolated and exposed. Her brief display of bravado vanished in a wave of fear and shame.

She tried to breath around the fear, Esme took in her surrounds for the first time. The hall, for it appeared to be a hall rather than a cave on closer examination, had a high domed ceiling. The walls sloped down from that dome forming a perfect half sphere, as though the floor cut the sphere in half. Despite the ground having sliced Esme's back, she saw in the flickering orange light that the chalk had been made as smooth as possible. The dark flecks of flint adding pits of scar tissue to the white smoothness of the walls and floor. The acolytes congregated right around the edges of the room, at least three people deep. There must have been several hundred bodies in the room, all singing their creepy song. The centre remained clear, except for herself, Duncan, Samantha, the human who helped Cursian and the vampire himself. The space they occupied at least fifty feet in diameter, making the room huge. Cursian stood to Esme's right, Samantha to her left and Duncan in front. The guard stood to Esme's back once he helped his broken comrade out of the central circle. Her whereabouts established, Esme glared at Duncan.

He smiled at her, "Beauty finally chained by the beast. Our vampire must want your blood a great deal, Esme, his willingness to have you here has been heartening."

"He wants you dead," Esme heard her voice crack with fear.

"I don't doubt that, my dear. It's in the nature of vampires to want humans dead." Duncan turned away from her, to face his crowd. "It is time. My beautiful sister will be the one to lead our dark Lord into our world."

Samantha stalked to centre stage, madness and an unnatural high making her strangely beautiful. The witch stared at Cursian with an expression Esme could not interpret. A mixture of lust, greed and fear seemed close to the mark.

Following the witch's gaze, Esme turned to look at Cursian herself. Having lost his shirt to Jacob's blood Cursian's broad, lean chest glistened in the orange glow. His white skin contrasted with the shadows, which seemed to hover around his form. The effect threw his body into soft relief. Esme's desire rose, she wanted to trace the path of every muscle under that firm white skin, and follow them down under the black leather of his jeans and boots. She shook her head. Not sure these thoughts were her own. A few moments ago, she could have happily ripped his heart out.

Cursian stared back at Samantha, whose heels clicked softly on the floor of the hall. The woman drew Cursian toward her and led him back to centre stage. Esme watched as Samantha's hands played over that white skin. Cursian continued to look impassively into the other woman's eyes.

Samantha dug her nails into the skin covering the left hand side of Cursian's chest and slowly drew her hand downward, toward his right hip. Blood welled immediately, Esme winced, Cursian hadn't even blinked. Only the energy between them changed, the sexual flare unmistakable. Samantha's violence clearly turned the vampire on, he reached for her. The snake headed witch slipped from his grasp and strode to her brother. Duncan held out an object that resembled a wooden chalice, she took the plain cup and held it against the vampire's chest. It caught the blood flowing from the nail marks. Esme watched as Samantha smeared the blood over the vampire's chest. She caught the sigh coming from Cursian as he threw his head back clearly enjoying the situation. Esme's mind drew a blank at this game, she just watched in horrid fascination.

Esme saw Samantha's lips moving. Her eyes were unfocused. The litany tripped from the woman easily. Cursian closed his eyes. Esme realised he wanted take this further, right there in front of all of them. The murmuring chant from the audience quietened considerably.

"Dow eanish formenta," Samantha finally cried out.

A blur of reality stung Esme's eyes and a cry from Cursian made her want to focus fast. Clearing her confusion, Esme realised the vampire now stood before her in chains. They were as white as his skin and appeared to come from the floor of the hall. Made from the earth itself.

"Betrayal will no longer be possible vampire. You are now mine and my Lord's. We are not as stupid as you suspected. You will be a part of this and you can not escape." She smiled and stepped out of reach.

Esme looked directly up into Cursian's dark blue-black eyes as they faced each other, only five feet apart. Cursian's rage burst forth.

His face contorted and his body bucked against the restraints, he bellowed his frustration. Esme shrank back, fearing the monster before her, but her own chains made escape impossible. She cowered. Cursian became vampire. His age and power flowed out of him, his strength unbelievable. The shadows hovering around him in the hall swept outward. Tendrils of darkness flicked against anything or anyone they touched. Each time one touched Esme, she flinched. Their vampiric energy harsh and ugly. Cursian began to glow with his power, the bones on his face and the muscles of his straining chest becoming more and more defined. His eyes bled to pits of blackness. Each time he cried out, he fought the chains, but all Esme heard was the dull clank of stone on stone. She tore her eyes away from the demented figure before her and noticed the siblings from hell were watching the show. They held expressions of enraptured delight.

"Let him go!" Esme screamed over Cursian's cries.

Samantha walked toward her, flicking the tongues of darkness away.

"Esme, dear, if we do that you will have to face his madness. For it will be you he sees first."

"What have you done to him?" Esme looked up into the dilated pupils of a mad woman.

"We have hurt him of course, pain is necessary for our dark Lord." Samantha tutted, "You don't understand do you?" She stroked Esme's head, "You see, this hall contains the blood and suffering spilt into its walls and floor for the last two hundred years. We are surrounded by the pain of hundreds of our victims. I have made that pain, fear, hate and death a part of the chains binding your vampire. He underestimated me, to his cost. This anguish is what hurts him, stopping the control he has over his vampiric nature. He feels the pain of every lash laid on a human body in this room. Every knife wound. Every sexual depravity. Every death. And it is sending him mad. And when he feeds from you and then feeds you in turn, you will either die, or become his human slave, or vampire. None of which matters to us, by that time we will have what we want. A mother for our dark Lord."

Esme's horrified gaze slid back to the raging beast. His fangs were clear and glistening in the torch light, Esme feared their sharpness. In fact, she watched Cursian's teeth with such concentration she didn't notice the triple edged blade heading for her neck, until far too late. Esme pulled herself away but she became entangled in her chains and nearly yanked her hands off in the process. Samantha just pursued her; the black athame pierced the skin in the hollow of Esme's throat. Blood flowed quickly. Samantha pressed the chalice against Esme's sternum. The Scion of the Prophecy could do nothing.

As her blood mixed with Cursian's, the chanting became louder. Samantha and Duncan now stood together, the cup raised high over their heads. They walked the circle making the chant faster and faster. Esme sensed the coming change. The torches no longer held the darkness back. Shadows, not just the ones emanating from Cursian, danced through the hall. The atmosphere thickened, hardened, rendering the air almost unbreathable. It felt as though an electric storm should burst through the room. Harsh white light provided the shadows with form. These shadows started to weave and move around the crowd, resembling contorted ghosts. Each person they touched or passed through, shuddered, yelled in brief pain, then continued as before, but their eyes held only emptiness. With each emptied human, the shadows became more manifest. Esme glanced once more at Cursian. The shadows flew around his body, yet they never actually touched him. He yelled at them in a language Esme didn't recognise. His body continued its futile fight against his bonds. The shadows converged around him. The siblings approached the captives. Esme heard Duncan and Samantha begin to chant a counterpoint to the horde. The air made her gag.

She struggled to draw breath. Cursian pulled hard on his chains and they shifted. Esme flinched, another loop of stone formed and another. The vampire's madly snapping jaws moved toward her naked, weak, human body. The chant, the shadows, the flickering light became faster and faster. The floor began to give way, dizziness overwhelming her, Esme shut her eyes. Cursian reached his destination. Esme screamed as his teeth dug deeply into the flesh over her clavicle. He bit and the shadows which gathered like a dark cloak around him, swept downward, through the floor of the cave and up, up, into Esme. They used the only entrance they could if she was to give birth to the dark Lord. Esme screamed again, pushing away, frantic to release herself from the chains, from the bite and suck of the creature at her throat, from life itself. She screamed and felt herself topple inward.

CHAPTER TWENTY NINE

Esme hit her core and bounced off a disc of blue energy. This place of safety no longer resembled the one which saved her from the drug abuse, it looked dirty and thin. Nothing remained for her to use. Crying out, spinning in circles Esme knew despair. The only thing which existed in this place sat in large letters. The spell lay in quiet malevolence ready to destroy her lover. She could end all this now, end Cursian's existence if she said those words aloud. But in ending that, she would end all. She screamed into the emptiness within her and pushed upward, outward with her misery. Esme pushed so hard she found herself pushing through the blackness woven into the fabric of the cave. Layer, on layer of sticky, web-like, nastiness gave way under her rush for the surface. Each layer became weaker as she rose, until the chalk around her spirit form became natural.

Esme shot like a bullet out of the earth, a ghost of insubstantial blue and white light. She stopped, she breathed pure night air and found her form within the church on top of the hill above her village. She faced Brigit.

"Esme? I've been looking for you both for hours," Brigit's silvery hair formed a mass of fluffy, bright, cottony stuff around the older woman's head.

The old woman's aura also shone bright and strong. She appeared replete with crystalline energy. She wore her age like a cloth of wisdom wrapped carefully around the soul of a child. Esme reached for her friend.

"Esme, you cannot touch me. You're not really here. I knew, if one place existed on earth you could reach, it would be this church. This is the most powerful place in the area. I have asked for help and it has been granted," Brigit's eyes held a wealth of sadness. "Esme, duckie, listen to me. May will help you, she knows all she needs too; she just has to have faith. Cursian will need your forgiveness; his love for you might just kill the both of you. And, Esme, I am now going to teach you your final lesson. Reach out toward me child and I will give what we have been granted, use it as you see fit."

Esme, despite her incorporeal form, reached out and brushed Brigit's colours. Her weak blue light sprang into vivid life as the contact pulled on Brigit. Suddenly, Esme could see the multi-hued river of power that Brigit contained. The dam broke and the wave of light engulfed Esme. For a moment she thought her spirit would be torn to shreds by the power, but fighting for control, she won. Esme looked into Brigit's smiling face. Then she turned and dived for the floor. She raced through the chalk, pulling the light behind and within her, burning holes through the layers of nasty blackness.

Esme shot down into the body waiting below. A matter of seconds seemed to have passed. Cursian did not yet drink and the pain in her womb remained weak. She knew she needed to regain control of Cursian. She pushed into his mind. Using the same paths he used to saved her. Following her instincts, Esme found herself in the white space from her earlier visit. In the centre of this space, she found a crumpled heap.

She rushed over and pulled the young man onto her lap. His eyes flickered, his face drawn and ashen. He lay in her arms, dying.

"Dafydd?" Esme shook him gently. Mystified, she stared down at the young man. How did an illusion die?

"I am draining him of life."

Esme raised her eyes slowly, knowing who would be staring down at her, Dafydd's evil twin. The other half of Cursian. The vampire.

Her jaw jumping, Esme tried to stay calm. Demanding things from vampires didn't work. "Why are you draining him?"

The vampire grinned, his features hard, his eyes black, "I am draining him, Esme dear, because I am about to be released and the power the Dominion has given me is setting me free."

"So, you are killing him because you think you will be more powerful without him?" Esme spoke to Dafydd.

"I will be free of his damned conscience that will make me more powerful than you can ever imagine."

Esme watched the fevered glow on the vampire's face and despaired.

"Cariad," Dafydd stirred, his blue eyes opened. "I am man and mage, if you want me to live, you must make him understand."

Esme very much wanted Dafydd to live. The light bulb switched on, she smiled gently. "Okay, I understand the monster wants his freedom. After all, that's exactly what the world needs, another psychopath killing innocent people."

"I am not a psychopath, I am a vampire. A vampire so powerful the world will quake."

"It's not the fourteenth century anymore, big boy," Esme snapped. "There are worse things out there than you."

"There is nothing worse than me," said the vampire. He lunged at Esme. She yelped and jumped back, dropping Dafydd off her lap. "I am death, Esme." Pinning her to the floor she felt his long hard body press hard against her as she froze.

She believed him too, he lived to feed. His whole existence revolved around feeding and attaining satisfaction. Holding still, she gazed up into soulless eyes, his cruel mouth twisted into a smile of male knowing. Esme realised he sensed her body's reaction to his presence.

"Damn it," she huffed. "When am I going to learn? Bad boys are not good for me."

"So, you do want me, Scion?" the smug vampire infuriated her more than the dangerous one.

"If I do it's only because I'm a sick and twisted puppy. The one I love is over there," she flicked her head toward Dafydd, the only part of her the vampire didn't hold down.

"In this moment, Esme, Cursian has his fangs deep in your neck. I am about to take your life and turn you. We will become one. I have waited centuries for this. I want your power inside me forever." The vampire's lust lay hard between them. Esme felt herself drawn into his mesmerising power.

She forced herself to continue talking, hoping to control this beast in her own way, "Just one problem, if you turn me, I might lose my magic. If you kill Dafydd you lose your magecraft and it's that which makes you a truly powerful and a feared vampire."

The monster stilled, his eyes narrowed, "What are you talking about?"

"You must understand?" Esme asked. She really thought he should, "As powerful as you are as a vampire, it's the mage the other monsters really fear. It's your control, your magic, your humanity that leaves them powerless against you and the same goes for me. If you turn me now, you will be helping to release a real demon on earth and you will be weak beside it. You will lose everything if you don't help me and Dafydd overcome the power the Dominion has given you."

He continued to hold her as the wheels turned and the monster ran through all the connotations of her thought processes.

"They will destroy me, enslave me, just as my Master did before we slaughtered him."

Esme nodded, wondering what the vampire saw in his mind's eye.

"I need a gift in return for letting you live."

"Cursian can feed from me any time he likes you know that," Esme said, rashly.

The vampire smiled slowly, he lay down closer to Esme's body, murmuring in her ear. "My darling girl, you do not understand. Every time I feed from you as full vampire, you come closer to me. If I feed from you here, in this reality it will be my way of bonding with you just as magic boy over there did when you were making the beast with two backs," he nodded toward Dafydd.

Esme, her heart pounding, wondered if she had understood the vampire properly. "You want me for a bonding of some kind?" A part of her wanted desperately to escape from the monster holding her, but another part wanted him just as desperately. Cursian's dark nature came from this creature, the part that had fed from her, made love to her, taken Matt away. She groaned softly.

He smiled, "You know what I want. I want you to entwine yourself with me as much as the mage. I want you to need me as much as you need him. I want you to crave my touch, not just his. It will drive him mad knowing you desire the monster as much as the man." The whisper close to Esme's ear made her tremble under the vampire. He ground his hips against her, not to hurt, just so she could feel his desire.

"If I let you feed here, I will come closer to the vampire in Cursian, to you?"

He nodded, his dark hair brushing against her face. He smelt of her lover. She could almost feel his teeth on her neck.

"If you feed you will release Dafydd and help me destroy the dark Lord?"

"I will help you any way you need me too, Scion. I have no wish to be enslaved by the demon they are summoning."

Esme flexed her arms against his hands, testing his hold. He held her completely still. Twisting her head she caught sight of Dafydd, he'd begun to fade. The power she had from Brigit's sacrifice, the suffering she'd gone through to help destroy the Dominion would all be for nothing if she did not consent to the vampire's desire.

"You could force this," she said, trying to give herself a few moments protection.

"If I wanted you against your will I would have already taken you. I want to hurt the mage and you will not desire me if I force you. You have to do this willingly."

Esme laughed, "This deal is clearly only your version of willing."

"Nothing in life is perfect, Esme. I will take what I can for now, later, when you understand the monster in Cursian you will come to me willingly." He kissed her neck, "Now, time grows short, even here. Make your choice. My bite and we save the world, or you leave this place and we all die."

"Alright," Esme said. "I agree."

"Open yourself to me."

Esme forced her right shoulder down and twisted her head to give the vampire full access. She saw Dafydd moving, coming back to life. His eyes opened and met hers just as the vampire bit. The pain, without sex, made her want to scream. She bit her lip and just gazed into the sad blue eyes of her soul mate.

After a long time, the vampire removed himself from Esme's neck. He pushed himself upright, but stayed on her hips, letting her hands free. Her blood dripped down his chin, his dark eyes watched her as he licked his lips.

"It is time you left, Esme, my love," he said, almost cooing with pleasure.

"May I speak with Dafydd?" she asked. Esme found herself trembling. The vampire swung himself off her hips without obvious effort and rose.

"Talk away, just know that the longer you take to return to the real world the harder it will be for Cursian to win." He began walking away from her, then turned, "Oh, and I look forward to tasting you again, lover. You never know, the next time you may give yourself over completely."

"I wouldn't count on it, buster," she muttered, pushing upright. Brushing herself down, she finally raised her eyes to Dafydd.

"Sorry," she said.

"For what?"

"For that, I think." Esme realised she felt as though she had betrayed him, which she supposed had been the point from the vampire's perspective.

Watching Dafydd struggle with his own emotions Esme realised she needed to leave. Cursian could talk to her about this if they left here alive. She realised her lover contained the monster and the man. This is what she wanted. Dafydd alone could not understand her or her personal darkness. Cursian would though.

"Look, I have to go."

Dafydd smiled, "I love you."

"Can you deal with this?" she asked, meaning the vampire bite.

"I have dealt with far worse."

"I love you too, you know."

"You would not have done it if you did not love me, Cariad."

Esme wanted in that moment to feel his arms around her, making the world disappear and their love to be real in sunshine and flowers. She walked toward him but the world containing Dafydd disappeared and Cursian's reappeared.

CHAPTER THIRTY

She screamed as she flew back to her own body. The time that had passed inside the vampire, only lasted a few seconds, but Esme forgot the pain to which she would return. She cut the scream off as Cursian withdrew and the power her soul dragged into this pit of hell burst forth. It drove down through her head and out from the middle of her chest into the waiting vampire.

Cursian's chains snapped as he gently raised his arms in supplication to the gathering light surrounding them. He became a living torch as Esme watched. The multihued light flowed through her, into the waiting mage, out through his crown and then swept down and around his body, like a huge loving snake of power. Esme watched Cursian's mouth moving, his eyes closed, but she couldn't understand the words. When he opened his eyes, they glowed an iridescent blue.

"Someone loves you a great deal, Esme, this is beautiful," Cursian whispered.

"Fine," Esme said, feeling sick with the pressure channelling this weird light put on her body. "But can you please do something with it. I don't think I can keep this up and I think my belly is growing." Her voice rose an octave with hysteria as she looked down and saw that indeed, her belly swelled.

"Take some of what you are giving to me and push down, through your womb. Make it leave." Cursian sounded so bloody reasonable, as though she should just know how to abort demons. Esme would have hit him if she wasn't still bound.

She felt movement, like some vast parasite within her and had the strongest urge to get up and run from her own body. In panic Esme reached into herself and pulled on the rope of light she channelled. A section broke away, she pushed downward and into her womb. Her minds eye saw the light hit a barrier of black swarming tendrils. If Esme could have taken a knife at the moment and opened her own guts to get rid of the foul creation she would have done. Instead, she forced the arrow of light into the heaving mass of demon energy made manifest. The thing exploded into action. As it moved within Esme's mind, she felt the mirror action within her body. The tendrils leapt up to surround the light. Almost as though they were trying to pull it apart. The writhing action within her lower abdomen horribly real. The light slowly descended into the tendrils, Esme finally saw the thing they were trying to protect. A small foetus shaped body, lay within the heaving nest. Its blackened body and elongated limbs wriggled as the light slowly approached.

Esme felt unholy terror that such a creature could use her womb to generate its earthly body. Just as she was about to send the light in, to impale the monster, its eyes opened. Eyes like coals of molten lava looked deep into Esme's mind; ravished it, trying to tear her from the light, stop her from continuing its descent. Esme laughed. Nothing would stop her from killing this abomination. She speared the creature, with all the colours of the known spectrum, pushing into the foul thing and out the other side. She could see its fear and hatred. She could feel its desperation to hang on to its manifest life. She felt the pain as her body expelled the creature, causing it to reform back to the black misty substance from previously.

Opening her eyes, Esme watched as the darkness attacked Cursian. He laughed. The light grew around him, forming a shield, covering his pale flesh in thousands of dancing lights. Esme fancied she could see the lights pouring from the very pores of his skin as they wove around and into him. The dance a thing of magic and beauty. She felt humbled by the sight.

He looked down at her, "But it is your gift too, Cariad." As though he read her mind. "And now we must destroy this place and all within it."

He reached behind Esme and held the iron bar containing her hands. The locks simply opened and fell away. He pulled Esme to her feet.

"Now, Cariad, open yourself fully and allow the love to flow between us so we may defeat our enemy."

"I thought it was," she said. She honestly didn't think she more existed, but looking into the soul entwined within her own for millennia, Esme realised she must now open herself to the love of an eternity. She must reach into that connection and use it to end this fight. She relaxed and as she did so, the light flew through her a thousand times faster. Esme felt herself become the living torch she witnessed in Cursian. She embraced her love for him and he guided that light out from their centre.

The energy poured from the ceiling, through them and out into the crowd. It mimicked the ghosts of darkness sweeping through the room. The light appeared to chase the dark shadows, weaving into and out of, the mass of chanting neophytes. Those who were touched by the light collapsed. Esme realised Cursian looked behind her; she turned in his arms and saw Samantha and Duncan. Together they appeared to be trying to do with the spectrum of darkness, what Esme and Cursian accomplished with light. But evil is more unpredictable. It consumed Duncan and Samantha.

"What's happening?" Esme's concern clouded her pull on the source.

"They are dying, Esme. It cannot be helped nor should it. Each of those souls has been kissed by their dark Lord and he can use them if they stay with us. This way he is denied their strength and worship."

"Okay, but how the hell are we going to get out?" Esme felt her body weakening as the strength of the light became stronger.

"You aren't, you are going to give birth to our Lord!"

Esme saw Samantha drop her brother to the floor. His skin blistered under the pressure of dragging that much energy into himself and out again. The Scion also noticed the witch held the athame in her hand. Esme's reaction came from instinct.

She switched, one moment a being of pure light, the next a warrior, designed to stop Samantha in her tracks. The light stopped flowing through the Scion of the Prophecy. The wrench felt terrible as she fell back into the world of the purely physical. Cursian cried out from behind her, collapsing from the shock. But nothing stopped Esme from concentrating on the witch.

They circled each other. The connection to the source of light gave Esme strength, but she had no idea how long it would last. Dealing with the bitch and running seemed to be the best plan. She sprang forward, feigning an attack to the knife hand. The witch pulled back, leaving her left side open and the knife a fair distance from Esme. The Scion aimed a low kick to the knee, but Samantha turned, obviously having done some kind of training herself.

They circled once more. The dancing shadows gathered speed, pulling a wind into the hall. The torches guttered and sparked. Esme noticed small fires breaking out because of robes caught up in the conflagration. Esme dropped her guard, faking vulnerability. Samantha took her cue. The witch rushed Esme with the blade low and tilled upward. Esme sidestepped at the last minute, pushed the arm down that held the knife and brought her left arm over the weapon, sweeping upward toward the witch's head. Her hand arched over Samantha's right shoulder. The witch found her forward momentum stopped and switched suddenly to compensate. With her head tilted too far back Samantha lost her balance and hit the floor. Esme followed her down, twisting to grab the knife hand. She took the athame without difficulty, surprise being the best form of attack.

Esme raised the knife and plunged it toward the woman on the floor beneath her.

"NO!"

Cursian's cry caused Esme to glance upward as her hand thrust downward. The knife struck, but missed the intended target. It entered Samantha's upper arm, just as it joined her torso. The witch screamed. The knife flared red hot in Esme's hand. She cried out, leaping backward.

"Esme, run," Cursian scrambled to his feet and held a hand out for her.

"What have I done?" Esme whispered. The glowing blade still stuck out of the witch, who writhed under its agony. Out of the blade poured a swarm of winged insect like creatures, a creation of nightmares.

"You have released the thousands of souls who have been kept within the blade." Cursian cried. "We have to leave. They are going to want to feed! Only with the right knowledge can you use a knife like that and not have the souls retaliate."

For the first time Esme heard real fear in the vampire's voice. She ran toward him as the tide of bug like nastiness flew to the ceiling and began to disperse.

CHAPTER THIRTY ONE

Cursian pulled Esme toward the tunnel entrance she had tried to reach previously. As they ran across the room, a sound like a thousand dried wings beating franticly circled their heads. Esme jumped over fallen bodies, the whispery beat overhead increased. She turned to look back just as Cursian dragged her into the darkness, yanking a torch off the wall as he went past. The distorted souls started to descend on the people, alive and dead. Just as locusts will devour a crop of wheat, so these fiends began to devour human flesh. Screams filled the hall. Those still in religious ecstasy fell under the onslaught without even batting the creatures from their faces, their flesh torn from their bones. Esme lost sight of many of the people who had tortured her during that day, as they were covered in a wave of heaving, moving, flying, black hell. The images spurred Esme on to run faster.

"Are we going to get away?" Esme panted as they hurled themselves up the tunnel.

"I have no idea, Esme. Those things are more dangerous and unpredictable than anything we have faced."

Esme pulled Cursian to a stop, "Listen, my feet are bare and starting to bleed. These tunnels are miles long. Is there a way we can stand and fight, because I can't run forever? I'm at the end of everything, no more resources."

"Esme, now is not the time. We have to keep moving," Cursian pulled on her arm again.

She held firm, "No. Cursian, I'm not going to make it if we get lost in these tunnels."

"Esme, we will not get lost. I know these tunnels well enough. Besides, I can carry you if needs be," he pulled again.

Esme opened her mouth to argue and then nearly bit her tongue off as the pull turned into a yank. Cursian wrapped his arms around her body and turned his back on the space she'd occupied. His body jolted and she heard him grunt when something impacted with his back. His grip relaxed frighteningly quickly. His body dropped to the floor. Esme, responding to the implied threat, prepared for the fight. Samantha stood over the vampire's crumbled body. She held the athame in her hand, blood dripping from the blade.

"You will die here!" the witch screamed, lunging at Esme.

Esme briefly thought, why can't this bloody woman stop behaving as though she's in a horror movie, when she fell back allowing Samantha to ride her to the ground. The nice white suit and snake like hair had become a bloody torn mess. Esme's own body continued to take the brunt of floor and wall as she wrestled with the demonic mad woman. The witch's own blood made her almost impossible to hold onto and fight. Esme's strength began to ebb. The knife began to move closer and closer with each push. However, over the struggle, Esme heard the whispery wings. The thought of being devoured by swarming masses of tortured souls did amazing things for Esme's strength. She squirmed under Samantha, losing more skin on her back. Esme planted a foot against the other woman's hipbone and pushed. The witch lost her hold and fell. Samantha may have been demonic in nature, but she didn't have Esme's physical strength. Esme scrambled to her feet and reached for Cursian on instinct as the swarm rounded the corner.

A black mist descended on the nearest fleshy being, Samantha. The witch screamed as she became covered in the souls of those she and countless others had murdered. Esme froze with the need to gloat and the need to watch the horror, but as Cursian stirred, she pulled and he rose. Blood covered his naked back and ran down his jeans. They turned, stumbling together up the tunnel.

"Esme, Cursian."

Esme pulled herself up. May, beautiful, strong, healthy May stood in front of them as they rounded the next bend. Without another word, May tucked herself under Cursian and the two women began to run as well as they could.

"What's the sound?" May yelled, as they ran.

"Trust me, you do not want to know. Just get us somewhere safe," Esme yelled back. The tunnels acted as an echo chamber for the whispery wind behind them. The swarm became louder and louder. Esme had never moved so fast, she was not going to be eaten alive.

The cold night air suddenly caressed her bare skin and the car park opened in front of her. She almost went down out of pure relief but the sound continued to pursue them. Esme spotted Ben fifty yards away. He stood in the centre of a silver bubble.

"We have to reach Ben. He's channelling his group. They're forming a protective shield." May looked as dishevelled as Esme and just as bloody.

Esme didn't have the energy to speak. She merely nodded and set off toward Ben. She felt Cursian's weight shift as she continued to carry him.

"Holy shit!"

Esme looked toward May then toward the space May stared at. The swarm erupted from the tunnel. They massed in the entrance, seemingly disconcerted by their new surroundings.

"RUN!" Esme screamed. She lunged for the sphere of silver light.

The swarm sensed their victims and descended.

Esme hit the bubble of light first. May followed half a breath later. They both pulled hard and managed to haul Cursian in just as the flesh eating fairies from hell hit the barrier. Ben grunted and went straight down on one knee. Esme watched him with very large, frightened eyes. He rallied.

"Tough little bastards. This could take awhile," he grinned at her.

Esme watched as little black bodies covered the white orb. The bodies began to burn where they touched the light. Cursian groaned.

"Are you all right?" Esme asked, now focusing on the vampire.

"Esme," he smiled up at her. "I thought I would be the one to save you. And no, Cariad, I am not all right. My heart has been damaged. It is only my great age that is keeping me going," blood bubbled from his mouth as he spoke.

Esme didn't move, she couldn't. If she did, it would acknowledge what he said and she wasn't going to let that happen.

"Esme, Cursian's dying." May touched her hand gently.

Esme shook her head, "No, no you aren't dying. You promised me, you promised you would always be here. I'm not losing you. You can heal this." His blood covered her chest as he coughed, denying the truth of her words.

"No, Cariad. We…will have to wait until next time…maybe then we can be together. Let me go, I am tired." Sticky goo matted his dark hair.

"You selfish bastard," Esme whispered at him. "I went through all this for you to leave me now? And what about De'hevda? Am I supposed to deal with her on my own? I will not be left here alone," Esme reached for a stone near Ben's boot. Tears coursed down her face and her heart burned in despair.

Pain lanced through her arm as skin tore. May's cry of disbelief and shock was worthy of an Oscar. Esme thrust the wound into the vampire's stubborn mouth. His instinct took over. Esme continued to mutter about men being selfish bastards who gave up too easily, until she fainted over his body.

CHAPTER THIRTY TWO

Strong hands shook her. A voice repeated her name continuously. Cracking an eye open Esme groaned. A harsh red sky made her blink. Undulating black clouds formed a stark contrast. She closed her eye again.

"Oh no, no, Esme I need you to wake, I need you up and moving. Come, listen to me woman. Damn you, ignore me at your peril!"

She finally gave in. Cursian knelt beside her in leather jeans and red shirt once more. He blended with his surroundings beautifully. His long dark hair and pale skin….hmmm… Esme pulled him toward her.

"Damn it, woman, not now! Desist will you. We do not have time. Esme, please look around and let your reality sink into that fuddled mind of yours. Honestly, do you think of nothing else?"

She still hadn't spoken, but did as commanded. She lay none too comfortably, on black lava pebbles. Harsh, jagged blackish rocks surrounded them. The pebbles lay in a crevasse of these rocks. No, she realised sitting up, the pebbles formed a path through the high rocks. She rose, carefully. The landscape opened out before her, the black rocks continued. They formed tortuous shapes, resembling water frozen at the very moment of a devastating flood. This flood appeared to pour from the sides of huge stark mountains. Everything around her consisted of these sharp rocks. Looking up, the sky really had turned a thousand shades of red, with great ugly black clouds obscuring the highest peaks of the distant mountains. The air stank of dry land and dust, with an undertone of sulphurous pollution. Esme coughed. The hot searing, smelly wind made her squint. There were no plants in the vicinity, no water, nothing. She found herself dressed in leather jeans and black shirt, no wounds. Her long hair fell around her shoulders.

"What the fuck?" Esme stamped her old trusted boots testing her reality.

"Esme, we are in trouble," Cursian said, turning her to face him.

"No shit, Sherlock. What the hell is going on?" bemused, Esme didn't know quite how to react. One moment she lay in the car park of the Hellfire caves, naked. The next she woke fully clothed, looking around at a land which didn't exist.

"Very observant," Cursian said looking around him anxiously.

"What? Could you be any more obtuse?" Esme stamped a foot again, the ground crunched.

"We have been dragged to Hell." His sharp blue eyes penetrated her, "Esme, we are in a version of Hell I hoped never to see again. I fear we may have died after all. I may have killed us both."

She paused trying to understand, "Hell? I can't go there, I'm baptised."

A whooshing noise filled her ears. Cursian pushed her to the ground. Esme caught sight of a creature with wings spinning over her head. Needless to say its skin colour blended with its environment, it had claws on its hands and feet. The torso appeared all ribs with sunken skin. Its face resembled an elongated pixie. The wings were large and leathery. It screamed at them before diving off. The tongue forked.

"What was that?" Esme cried.

"Lesser demon. On patrol, come we must leave or it will bring others to us." Cursian dragged her up pulling her toward an opening in the rocks.

Esme followed, more through not knowing what else to do than obliging the vampire. The further they travelled the more Esme determined her surroundings. She found herself inside a world stuck between Dante's Inferno and Tolkien's Moria, but with none of the benefits. The red sky bled to the colour scarlet at its height, toward what could be seen of the horizon it approached purple. The lighter clouds were stratus, grey strips at the sky's zenith, but in the distance a deep black thrown up against the dark amethyst. The land itself had only one colour, black. Not the uniform black of ebony, but all the shades black could be when it melded into other colours. The path Cursian dragged her along continued as small beads of porous rock, with large ones thrown in to trip over. All she saw of the countryside reinforced her first impressions. Brown black or jet black outcrops stretched away creating fields of jagged, sharp, tortured rock. Occasionally she could clearly see, melted into the rock, smooth shapes resembling water forever locked into the stone. At one point, she hauled Cursian to a full stop to peer at faces buried beneath the surface. Screaming faces. Cursian simply grunted and pulled her onward.

The air made Esme feel sick, its heat stole her breath, yet she didn't sweat. It blew into her face unrelentingly, making her eyes sting and her nose sore. The sulphur smell combined with the dry heat from scorched earth, remained continuous, but also something indefinably foul lingered unidentified. Rotting corpses maybe?

Just as Esme wanted to give in to her aching legs, Cursian found a large cavern. The instantaneous relief from the heat and the sudden lack of noise from the wind made everything preternaturally loud. Cursian sat her down on a rock. He moved to the cavern entrance keeping his eyes on the sky. After a few minutes, he returned.

"I believe we should remain safe for the time being, they are hovering over where we were. They are unused to their prey moving this fast. It takes time to adjust to this world." His hands shook and his eyes darted about nervously.

This more than anything else scared Esme, "Where are we?"

"Esme, you are going to have good cause to hate me for this, because it is my fault. I have acted rashly, without thought, once more placing you in grave danger. This time it is your soul, not your life that is in jeopardy, as is whatever is left of mine."

"At least I have my hair back," she joked, but seeing the sadness in his eyes she conceded, "Okay, what's happened and I promise not to yell until you've finished telling me everything."

Cursian took her hands, but looked at the floor. "When we were in the caves, destroying the Dominion, we were bound together through love, sacrifice and need. The bonding I attempted to destroy between us with the sword recreated itself through the light we channelled. That and your insane bargain with my vampire." He frowned, clearly concerned over her decision but too pressed to pursue the matter. Continuing he said, "Never in the history of humanity have two souls been so much a part of each other. If we spent time in your world we would know each other's thoughts, feel each other's actions. We have blended two souls in two bodies into perfect harmony," he stopped.

"However?" Esme knew a catch when she heard one.

"When we reached the safety of Ben's shield, I knew I was dying. And in that moment I wanted to let go. However, I had underestimated the power of our ties. I did not understand what we have achieved. At the moment you thrust your arm into my mouth my instinct took over, yet still I knew death waited. In that very instant the vampire within me lashed out in desperation, using your connection. It is old and powerful, more so since the Dominion's interference. I understood its intention. It wished to return with its knowledge of you, of us, to its fountainhead. I pursued the creature with my mage craft, wanting to stop it reaching its goal. You also held images of De'hevda and her destruction in your mind. Due to our spiritual ties and our physical contact, along with your own need to hunt vampire, I brought you with me. Our physical bodies are just where we left them. I have dragged your soul into the place that spawned and contains the vampires Creator."

"He is the one that forced the vampire virus into mankind. He is the one that uses vampire to kill and manipulate humanity. He and his children are the ones that want, above all things, to destroy those who can stop them from entering your world. The Dominion's power derived from them, guided their actions and murdered the Guardians. I know the demon leader created men such as Crowley and my Master. He made men believe blood sacrifice would appease gods. He feeds on the wars of religion and greed."

"He's our Devil?" Esme asked her voice small.

"Yes and no. The Devil of your faith and of mine is partly this monster, but he is also an amalgamation of many others. He is evil. Humanity cannot and should not try to recreate each separate demon. They should just fear them all. God made many mistakes before creating mankind and some of his biggest are kept here, in these alternate dimensions, safely locked away. But even God cannot stop them from leaking out. The rules in your world were created to help contain this evil. It is why you have codes and why Christ, or Abraham or Mohamed or any of the others ask mankind to follow those rules. It gives people a chance to defeat the evil in the world. It is the part of 'free will' that you like so much."

"How do you know so much and recognise where we are?"

"Because, Cariad," Cursian's haunted gaze made her tremble. "Because I have been here before. This is where I battled for my freedom from the evil holding sway over my vampire. I could not eradicate the virus from me, but I thought I had severed its ties to this plane. Obviously, my control has not been omnipotent. The Dominion and the games I played with them have left me weak, tying the vampire to this source more strongly than I realised. They have been harassing me for years and I failed to act. I have been distracted from my vigilance for some decades."

"Let me guess, about three, right?"

Cursian nodded.

"So what now? Now you've almost sacrificed my body to the Dominion and dragged my soul into some version of Hell, what's next?" Esme took her hands away from Cursian. Rising she began pacing the cavern.

Cursian remained still, continuing to watch the floor. "I did not know you could be dragged here with me. Uncalled souls have never been made manifest in this place before. I thought I was dying. All I wanted to achieve was an end. As I felt the vampire flee, I wanted to stop it from reaching its Master. I did not want the thing to be able to give the Master any clue as to you, your whereabouts or your capabilities. It was my sole intention to protect you, but once more I have miscalculated."

"Damn right, and now what? I am not staying here to become fish food for some demon," Esme allowed her fear and frustration to take hold. It caused her voice to rise.

"Please, Esme, do not make too much noise. We are not safe here." Cursian rose and walked toward her, catching hold of her shoulders when she tried to move away. "Listen to me. Maybe we are meant to be here, this is the one place we can end this cycle of war. The Dominion wanted to use your body to create a demon in your world. That demon will still want to be born. They can still use you. If we stay and fight, we may be able to stop them completely. We have the possibility of some kind of peace."

"And the down side?"

"An eternity trapped in this place as playthings."

"And the, not doing anything apart from escaping, option?" Esme asked earnestly.

"We will be dooming humanity to the inevitable rise of the demon, through you or another innocent. And we will be forced to continue the fight against the Dominion without the other Guardians."

Esme closed her eyes, "Why, oh why, couldn't I have met the man of my dreams and lead a normal life? Having sex on Sunday mornings and reading the paper till noon, then walking in the hills all afternoon with the dog."

"You do not own a dog, Esme and besides you bore easily. You were never meant to be 'normal', whatever you consider that may be," Cursian said, frowning in exasperation.

Esme harrumphed, "Fine, whatever. I might just like the chance to find out though." She kicked at the gravel, "So, what do we do now? And before you say it," she held up her hand. "I am not going to be the sacrificial virgin again. You are not hanging me out somewhere for the big nasty monster to be tempted out of his cave."

"I do not think I ever made the mistake of asking you to be a virgin, Cariad," Cursian's tone held a hard point to its edge.

Eyes narrowing, hackles raised Esme prepared to attack Cursian for being a chauvinist. Suddenly, however, she threw her hands in the air, puffing the anger out of her lungs instead. "Bollocks, I can't be bothered. Just tell me what needs to be done, because I'm damned sure I am not going to convince you to walk away from this without a fight. Besides, if we are dead I haven't got a body to go back too and there's no one left to stop the Wicked Witch of the West, because she had them all killed."

CHAPTER THIRTY THREE

Sitting none too patiently, Esme listened while Cursian gave her instructions on how to survive this new world. With her soul removed from her actual body, which remained in the wet car park, Esme's essence recreated her body. This form reacted to its surroundings with the same weaknesses and strengths as it would in her own dimension. The only difference being, here she couldn't die, as such. Her soul would continue to manifest its physical form for as long as it existed. Each time she fell to injury she healed, continuing the suffering Hell demanded from its inhabitants.

After experimenting, Cursian realised Esme retained her connection to her spiritual source. Confusion followed, how could a piece of Heaven exist in Hell? Cursian finally decided it meant they followed their fate by coming to this dimension. When he mentioned this, Esme hit him. She'd had more than enough of being destiny's child. They agreed they would not use this energy unless necessary. It would flag their power and presence to the wrong people. It would also be a waste of the gift.

Cursian checked the sky once more and led the way out of the cavern. Running smoothly through the strange world, the vampire continued to explain the rules. The deserts were populated by the lesser demons that flew and walked. They sought the souls who had been dragged down here to begin their torment. Cursian told her these creatures were of limited intelligence but had great skill in causing pain. Their primary goal was to feed from the fear and agony they created, partly by keeping the souls separate. Loneliness when in pain made the torture worse. This pain then fed back to their Master. As Esme fed on her source, he fed on the emotions created within his domain. Cursian told her the bite of these lesser demons connected the soul to the Master. If she remained unbitten he remained unaware and unfed. Once bitten she'd join the ranks of the enslaved. Fighting the demons on their own terms, without the use of energy manipulation, would be the only option. In hiding her gift, Cursian hope to reach his goal without revealing their strengths. If the Master gained access to her soul, he gained access to everything.

The vampire went on to tell her that the Master lived within a city fashioned after the earliest of humanities civilisations. Its streets overflowed with the souls of the tormented. They were beaten and abused. The lesser demons eventually allowed the souls to congregate when more could be gained from punishing them en masse. The city maintained a hierarchy of demons, all of which should be studiously avoided. The strain of demon, which created vampire, were the highest form. Their bite meant instant and eternal agony. The soul they bit enslaved to them personally. Every whim and fancy played out on the manifest form all souls took within this place. The victim would not be able to help but stay with their tormentor, their slavery would feel self induced.

If they were to stop the vampires Master and prevent him breaking into Esme's world, they would have to find a way through. Cursian managed to do this previously by giving his vampiric nature full control, the demons thought him one of their own and had not hunted him. However, with Esme in tow, this would undoubtedly lead to disaster. Besides, Cursian didn't think the Master would be stupid enough to fall for it twice. At the moment, Cursian thought they were both relatively undetected. If he could keep the vampire within him from gaining the upper hand, maybe they would remain so. If they lost the advantage, they would have to adapt to their circumstances.

Removed from her world, Esme gave up being afraid or surprised. Her goal became survival and stopping the nasty things invading her life. If it took this form of reality to do it, then so be it. She'd fight to the last.

They moved with a fair amount of speed through the twisted labyrinth, keeping watch for the flying demons.

Several hours passed, the constant light making it hard to judge, when they struck their first serious obstacle.

The scream echoed around them. Esme stopped dead, tiredness making that part easy. Cursian only halted when he realised she didn't follow him.

"Come, we cannot afford to stop," his voice sounded gritty.

"Didn't you hear that?"

"Of course I did, but we can do nothing except place ourselves in danger. Please, Esme, come, we will be caught if we stay still."

She moved off again but the scream surrounded her once more, much closer this time. They both stopped. Cursian turned, clearly about to pull her into the black morass when a man rounded the bend ahead of them. He screamed as he saw them, maybe presuming they were another torment, Esme never found out. Her instinct drove her away from him. He appeared to be an older man and clearly led a debauched life. He looked Indian by descent, though it was hard to tell as every inch of his skin writhed in blue flame. Everywhere it touched blistered and burned to blackened flesh. Then the flame moved on to a new area. While Esme watched him run toward and then passed her, his skin healed while the next lot exploded into blisters. Pursuing him on long legs, making them around eight feet tall, came two demons.

They had no wings, but were covered in the same leathery mottled hide as the others she'd seen. Their legs worked backward, like a flamingo's and ended in clawed feet, not cloven hooves. Their torsos were too short for the legs. Their arms were too long. They carried swords on belts at their otherwise naked waists and long staffs in their hands. Their genitalia were as out of proportion as their limbs, dangling long and free and semi aroused. They noticed Cursian and Esme instantly, swinging their bald pointy heads toward the pair. Long noses, ears like a bald Alsatian and sharp needle teeth with no lips made them really ugly. The sight froze Esme more from stupidity than fear. They were too unreal. The demons froze in turn. She could see the surprise only in their red eyes, black pupils elongated as a cats dilated at the sight of new prey.

They had nowhere to run. With legs that long the demons would catch them in seconds. She didn't waste time glancing at Cursian but launched into an attack. She aimed a powerful side kick through the knee of her nearest opponent, shock made the thing squeal. It went down, joint shattering easily. With a speed she never knew she possessed, Esme turned the side kick into an axe kick. Bringing the heel of her boot down on the back of demons exposed neck. A sickening crunching sound meant her boot caved its skull. It didn't even try to get up. Just lay in the black gravel blinking and gurgling. Looking toward Cursian she realised he must have attacked at the same instant. He too had maimed his creature.

"Strip the body of weapons, you will find them of use," he bent pulling the belt and sword off his demon. "Hack its head off. They heal fast, faster than me." He saw her hesitate, "Do it woman, or we will have to fight them again."

His tone brooked no argument. With surprising ease, Esme hacked off the thing's head. She kicked it away the eyes still watching her, making the task truly surreal.

"Why the hell was that so easy? Should they have fallen that fast?" she panted as Cursian began to run once more.

"It seems you have my strength and speed now, as well as your skill. It is a part of our bonding. We are closer than any two creatures have ever been. Only someone with my abilities should have been able to despatch them that fast. We fought as one unit. I take it from your silence you did not notice."

"No, well, it's easier. Everything is easier here. I just assumed it was me. And I can feel you, sense you more." Esme kept pace with his stride easily, which with their height difference should not have been possible. They lapsed into silence.

This didn't end their adventures. A short time later, they stumbled across a larger group of demons. Some of this group were winged. These were smaller than the land based creatures but just as ugly. Cursian and Esme moved in as one.

From the previous skirmish, she'd taken a sword and several knives. She'd discovered, after a short practice, its longer hilt and wider blade gave her no trouble. In fact, Esme revelled into the excellent craftsmanship and balance. Some kind of leather covered the hilt. Esme didn't want to think about it as cows must be in shortage in a land of rock. Silver studs helped her to maintain grip. Overall, it made her smile. So, when she and Cursian were faced with a dozen opponents, she drew the blade easily and fell back on years of training.

The sword became an extension of her body. Her feet glided over the pebbly surface finding purchase without unnecessary thought. Her hips and arms moved with power. A relaxed grace reflected years of practice. She parried blows by blending with each strike, using the perfection of her weapon and her own smallness to her advantage. With each defence, she formed a counter strike taking chunks out of her victims. Even the flying demons stood no chance as she sliced her way through them. All too soon, the monsters lay in small, bloody pieces. She looked up dazed, the adrenaline vanishing in a rush. Cursian leaned against a wall of black rock, grinning, unusually even his elongated teeth were in evidence. Sexual heat replaced the battle madness. Esme shivered in anticipation.

"I knew you were good, Cariad, but that was beautiful. I could love you forever just because of watching you fight," his voice poured through her.

Esme walked toward him, utterly focused. The sword still dripped gore from the monsters. "I am good at all sorts of physical activities, if I like them enough."

Cursian pushed himself away from the wall as she approached. Their bodies touched. Esme looked up into his rapidly darkening eyes. He growled in response to her heat. A moan from behind them broke the spell. Esme turned and raised her sword, ready for the attack. She saw Cursian step to her side, his own sword already drawn.

A small man, covered in sores and dirt emerged from under the slaughtered demons.

"Have mercy, please help me," he begged as soon as he caught sight of the armed pair.

Moving forward Esme went to help as her nature dictated but Cursian placed a restraining hand on her arm.

"All the souls who are here are here for a reason. Trust in nothing," his voice held deep disgust.

Esme pointed with her sword, "How on earth can he hurt us?"

"Maybe he cannot but I still would not wish you to touch him."

"Cursian, we have to help him, besides I'm hungry and very thirsty, maybe he can show us water," Esme moved forward.

"There is nowhere here for you to drink or eat. We must find other ways for you to satisfy your body's needs. Please, leave him alone," Cursian was cross now.

Esme turned to argue. The man dragged himself closer. She flinched, jumping sideways as Cursian leapt toward her, a cry of rage escaping. She turned, watching as Cursian collided with the man. They fell to the ground. Cursian soon gained the upper hand and held the squirming human, removing a lethal looking dagger from the revolting creature.

"Nothing here is as it seems," exasperation clear, Cursian continued, "These are not innocent people, no matter how their bodies appear to be abused. Do not fall victim to this again. However, from a purely practical point of view, you are thirsty and I need to feed before we are caught up in the city. I think he will do well enough."

"You're going to feed from him?" Esme stood shocked, her previous elation gone.

"There is nothing for you here and to be honest I do not know if you need sustenance or not. I doubt any human has been here under these circumstances before. I do know I can take your needs away if I feed. It will not sustain your physical body but it will help your supposed needs in this realm." Cursian rose effortlessly, dragging the poisonous little ferret with him.

The ferret began howling, "You can't do that to me! You are not one of these monsters, she won't let you! I can see she doesn't understand or want you to do this. Do you lady? You don't want him to hurt me, let me go!" He babbled through lips covered in blisters. His face appeared to be a mass of open sores. Cursian held him from behind, an arm locked behind his back pulling his shoulder out of true.

Esme winced, "Listen mate, you don't know me and you don't know what I'm capable of. If the vampire needs to feed he feeds, I ain't going to be getting in the way."

The man opened his mouth to argue, Cursian yanked his head back and struck. He used none of the softness he did with Esme. She watched in fascination as a large wound opened and blood began pouring into Cursian's mouth and down the man's chest. Esme began to experience something new. A fine tremor ran through her body, a craving she'd never known. A very small part of her knew she should find this revolting, but the majority wanted to be there beside her lover, sharing the spoils. As Cursian drank, watching Esme react to the scene, he must have sensed her desire.

She found her mouth open in response to his need. Pleasure, deep penetrating pleasure, swept through her almost causing her to faint. Wave on wave hit as her own teeth seemed to rip the side of the man's throat open, with a long known dexterity. She sank to her knees, no longer able to contain the sensations. The hot liquid burned through her body giving life to limbs and organs, which had begun to tire and weaken. Her mouth felt full, her throat open, an endless stream of power poured into her flesh. She knew the pulse and love of life, the intimate secrets of time and energy. She finally understood the love of the chase. The inevitability of death. The deepest form of satisfaction it gave.

With tears coursing down her face, she watched Cursian pull away from the now empty body. Suddenly, he became all tenderness in his great strength. Cursian lay the empty body on the ground. He walked toward her, knelt before her, held her face in his hands.

"Cariad?" his voice contained deep contentment and love.

Esme gazed into his dark eyes and fell. She tumbled into his soul, swam in his adoration for her and his peace at feeding so well. She blinked finding herself back. His eyes slowly withdrew from the black of his feeding, to the more usual calm blue.

"Cariad?" he asked again, concern showing on his beautiful face.

"Wow," she breathed quietly. Esme's limbs hummed with strength and vitality, "Is that how it feels every time?"

Cursian smiled, "No, Cariad, the edge is denied us when we do not take the life of our victim. But here he will be reborn. I can do no harm so have nothing to fear."

Esme drew a deep breath trying to come back down from the cloud she'd been floating on, "Is that why vampires usually kill? They need the edge?"

Cursian nodded, "Eternity is a long time when one denies ones self these pleasures. I had almost forgotten myself how incredible a death feed can be until recently. Are you certain you are quite well?"

"Don't I look okay?"

"Esme, you are quite beautiful and ironically, more alive than I have ever seen you." He reached for her and they kissed.

Esme tasted the metallic tinge of blood in his mouth, she pushed harder against him desperate for everything he offered. His hands cupped her leather clad buttocks pulling her into his body. The kiss grew within Esme. She never wanted to let him go, their danger and surroundings vanished. Just as she reached for his waistband, Cursian withdrew. Panting, he gently pushed her away.

Shaking his head as though trying to clear his mind, he said, "No, Cariad, not here. We do not have the luxury of time, it is not safe."

Esme pushed her hair back, also breathing hard. "I guess not, but bugger me if I'm not as horny as hell. Can we go and find some more demons to kill instead?"

He laughed, "What happened to the unbelieving woman I approached barely a week ago?"

Esme smiled, "She disappeared under an onslaught of the strange and bizarre. There is more life in me now than all the normal days of my life put together. I feel free for the first time. My actions hold no consequences." She rose, breathing the putrid air as though it were the finest of spring days.

Cursian grinned lopsidedly, "I think you are punch drunk and will hate me when you begin to rationalise."

He rose. They ran off into the black desert once more, following a maze of paths Cursian knew would bring them to the city.

CHAPTER THIRTY FOUR

Time passed, it must have done as they covered miles at a gentle loping pace. They had small skirmishes along the way but nothing they couldn't deal with swiftly and easily. Esme felt wonderful. Her whole body tingled. The pair seemed to think and move in perfect harmony, everything flowing with instantaneous perfection. She tried to question Cursian as they travelled. She wanted to understand why they were so conjoined, why she felt so fantastic. But he had no answers. He couldn't tell her if the feeling would remain forever, or if it only occurred in Hell. This bonding they had undergone remained an unknown quantity. Unique, it only existed as a theory, a myth. Esme wasn't sure she wanted to return if she lost this sense of freedom and power. There were no rules and no responsibilities in this place. No laws to abide by, no one to question her actions or thoughts. Nothing related to her previous life, nothing felt quite real. Everything seemed carved from a world, which only abided by harsh natural laws.

They reached the top of a long rise, offering a fine view of the city for the first time. Cleaning her weapon after yet another fight, Esme glanced upward. She stopped moving. Cursian noticed her stillness and followed her gaze. His breath hissed out. A fast approaching battalion of monsters appropriated their full attention.

"Oh shit," Esme breathed.

"Well, they seem to be aware of our presence," Cursian sounded completely calm.

Esme turned aghast, "Shouldn't we be running?"

"It is pointless. We cannot hide from them, this is not our world, it is theirs. See," he pointed, "it is not just the demons. There are others come to welcome us." He stood tall, completely in control.

"You weren't this calm when we arrived," Esme couldn't help but step away from the brow of the hill.

"Our path is now set. I can do little to alter it, the only thing I can do is work toward a positive resolution. There is nothing left to fear." He held out his hand, "Come, Esme we do not want to meet these people full of terror. We are warriors and will meet our enemies as such."

Esme wished she shared his confidence. Nonetheless, she walked toward him. They stood shoulder to shoulder on the crest, waiting for the approaching army.

The mass of the throng made the air and ground heave with pressure. The wind grew around the pair on the hilltop, as did the stink of rotting bodies. Each creature carried weapons, clearly with one objective in mind. At the head of this swiftly moving mass, Esme soon made out the 'others' Cursian mentioned. They rode horses across the sky, ahead of the winged forces. The horses were blood red in colour, with manes and tails of sooty blackness. Their eyes and open mouths glowed like hot coals. Truly, beasts made of nightmares. A man controlled one of the beasts. Another appeared free, the last held a demon of a different shade. He towered over his mount, with skin the deepest royal purple and a mane of deep green hair flowing in tangles. He carried only a mace, but it must have weighed more than she did. His long hands and feet ended more in dagger sharp points than claws. And his eyes, once he came close enough, looked like a snakes.

Cursian held her hand as the horde encircled them, drawing to a halt. For the first time Esme saw the man clearly. Smaller than Cursian, he appeared just as well formed. His body hard and beautiful under his long robes of white cotton. Esme noticed the swell of his chest from between the edges of the cloth. His skin glowed almost blue it was so black. His dark eyes held a laugh deep within them. Long hair fell in cornrolls to his waist. A fine rapier hung from his hip. He and the large beast walked toward Cursian, eyeing him as they approached.

"Salis, it has been many years, brawd," Cursian said.

"Don't 'brother' me, Cursian. You left me to rot," Salis drew to a halt, well out of swords reach. He had an accent Esme couldn't place.

"It seems as though you have managed to make the best of the situation. It must have been character building." Cursian's arm wrapped around Esme's shoulder, pinning her to his body. "And I see you brought Caiaphas with you. Do I still make you that nervous little brother?" Cursian nodded toward the large purple beast.

Esme couldn't decide which to watch more closely for potential attack. Both made her nervous, though Salis was a great deal easier on the eye. The army held their ground, apparently awaiting orders.

"Let's say I've learnt to be cautious," Salis's voice sang like the cello. He held himself with a swordsman's poise. Esme liked him, despite the fangs he didn't bother to conceal. He continued, "What are you doing here, Cursian? And why have you brought an uncontaminated soul with you?"

"Such direct questions, you surprise me. You are not known for being direct, Salis. I shall return the compliment. I am here to stop De'hevda and your Master. Esme is here because she is my future, my past and my forgiveness."

The large purple monster, Caiaphas growled while stepping closer. Cursian let Esme go matching the beast.

Raising a languid hand Salis said, "Stop, we have our orders and you will not disobey. They're not to be harmed by you."

Cursian continued to watch Caiaphas but asked Salis, "So, if we are not to fight, why are you here?"

"I am to take the strongest of our Master's children to him. He wants to see you, as do the rest of the court. Your protégée is to ride with me." Salis turned to Esme for the first time.

Esme looked back with equal frankness. She found herself surprised by the sadness in Salis's eyes. The laughter gone. She thought he looked tired. Deeply weary of his role in this game. However, this did not mean she would mount one of those red horses and ride off into the sky.

"I don't think so," she said, standing her ground.

"I will not have her ride with you, Salis. If you find yourself unable to resist temptation, I will lose her to you. That I will not tolerate," Cursian still sounded calm, as though he were asking for a latte.

"I cannot allow her to stay with you. Together on one of our Master's horses you could create even more havoc."

Esme looked at the slavering mounts, "I tell you what, I'll walk. Never was one to ride demon bred horses."

Salis smiled, "If you walk, you will walk with the army."

Esme looked at the surrounding horde of black demons, then back at the horses, pawing the ground.

Cursian answered, "No. We will have an arrangement."

Salis nodded his acquiesce.

"I will have your promise that she shall become victim to no demon or vampire while you are responsible for her soul. You will protect her as though she were your own."

Esme watched Salis's face becoming increasingly incredulous. He said, "You may be the most powerful among our kind, Cursian, but you have no right to dictate terms like these."

Cursian stepped toward Salis. Esme noticed the quality of the air around the two vampire's change. A sharpness, a thickness swirled around them, raising small pebbles from the ground. Caiaphas moved toward the pair. Esme closed the distance to Cursian, though what she could do to the huge purple beastie would be down to inspiration and luck.

Cursian's voice deepened, booming over the army, "I will have my Scion protected. Only your Master may have the right to try to take her from me. I shall not allow you or your pathetic horde to attempt to enslave her soul. And if I find her harmed I will bring down the full capacity of my wrath for vengeance."

Esme watched Salis shrink into himself as Cursian dominated the smaller man. His fear seemed completely out of proportion and very real. Esme wondered how well she knew her lover if he inspired this kind of fear, in this kind of place.

"Do I have your promise?" Cursian asked slowly and with great emphasis.

Salis nodded, "You have my promise, Cursian. I will see her kept safe, I will not harm her. I will lay my life down in order to protect her soul from harm. My word upon it, hombre."

Esme sensed she missed something important between the two men.

Cursian stepped back, the atmosphere around them dissipating.

"You trust him?" Esme asked.

"He has given his word and that is his bond. He has no choice. He will protect you as best he can and not harm you himself." Cursian turned to Esme, "It is the best I can do for you if something happens to me." His voice dropped, his gaze intent, "Cariad, you and I are closer now than ever before. Salis will not hurt you, but he does not love you either. Always leave yourself open for me. Even if we are parted I shall find you."

Esme nodded. Turning to the other vampire she said, "Right, let's go for a ride."

Salis mounted his horse effortlessly, swinging up onto the beast bareback. He pushed his seat backwards holding out his hand. "Come, querido de mi hermano, we will journey together to the city of the damned."

Esme glancing once at Cursian, grasped Salis's hand and allowed herself to be pulled up in front of his body. The horse moved restlessly making her tense.

"Relax, Esme, you will come to no harm here. The horse will not throw you. The journey will be infinitely more enjoyable if you and I become one with his movements." Salis's arms wrapped round Esme's body grasping handfuls of mane.

Esme squirmed. Being pushed up against the dark vampire's strong body and having the heat of the horse between her legs made her want to groan aloud. Closing her eyes for a moment, she almost fell off the horse when she opened them. Caiaphas had stuck his face in hers. She swallowed her scream pushing harder into Salis but for all the right reasons.

Caiaphas growled something unintelligible. Salis laughed causing Esme's body to tighten in response to the vibration.

"What?" she asked irritated by her reaction.

Salis's breath whispered against her ear, "He says he can smell sex on you like a blanket. Thick and warm. It appears my brother has not been keeping you sated. Your needs are clear."

Esme shivered, "I may have needs but believe me, Cursian is more than able to deal with them when given the opportunity." Her reply fell a long way short of the sarcasm she needed for defence.

"Perhaps our Master will see the need for a floor show later to rid you of your needs," he hissed.

Esme stiffened, threats such as these cut to the bone. Salis found her weak spot instantly and wanted to milk it for all it was worth.

Another horse's head appeared beside her, Esme looked toward Cursian.

"I heard that, Salis," he drew up beside them. His hand lashed out grabbing Salis around the throat, so fast a blink could not have happened in the time it took. Esme heard Salis choke behind her as Cursian continued, "If you scare or threaten her again I will tear you apart and feed on your liver. Do you understand?"

Slightly stunned, Esme watched as Cursian's hand withdrew from Salis. His gaze shifted from him to herself, "Cariad, do not allow them to fill you with fear through their words. Words in this place mean nothing. It is a way to control the weak, you are not weak. They will all know what you fear, it is in their nature to see it but I will not and cannot be made to see you hurt like this, not here."

She smiled trying to show she understood and she believed him. But for the first time the doubts in him the Dominion created began to haunt her confidence in her lover.

"I see," Salis said slightly hoarse, "that casual violence is still strong in your nature, Cursian." A hand stroked Esme's back making her shiver. He continued, "The medieval period made brutes of us all. This place does little to cure us, I apologise for my cruelty, hermano."

Without another word, the three horses leapt forward rising into the air.

The horde rose into the air around them and through it Esme began to appreciate the magnitude of the world she now inhabited. In every direction the harsh black landscape continued. She realised the path they followed wove a complex pattern through fields of fossilised lava. In fact, a maze of paths covered the terrain. The beauty of the scene made Esme long to capture it, she had never seen such desolate and terrible splendour. It reminded her of the endless sands of the Sahara stretching toward the end of the world. Only this held all the shades of darkness, not gold. They began to angle themselves toward a wider path, the army on the ground easily keeping pace with the leisurely flight of their winged brethren. They neared the broad road. The traffic along its length fairly heavy considering there didn't seem to be another town or city within visual distance making trade unlikely. But trade in the traditional sense didn't come into it.

"Oh shit," Esme rocked back into Salis, almost forcing both of them off the horse. It took a while for her mind to grasp what her eyes had seen.

Along either side of the road, like some sick parody of one of Rome's worse atrocities were crucified bodies. This demonic Appian Way did not just have one form of cross upon its banks. Esme realised they used the cruciform cross; a traditional cross; wheels; empty squares where hands and feet were nailed to the edges but no support existed in the middle. Every form of wooden structure contained damned souls, their bodies hanging listlessly in the dry heat. Only moving when a demon drew close enough to beat the victim.

"Impressive isn't it," Salis sounded empty. Esme turned wanting to see his expression, but found it impossible he held her so tightly.

"Why? It's awful," she exclaimed.

"These souls want to enter the city. They cannot bear to be alone any longer. They must stay on these crosses until they have earned the right to join the throng in the city. If they take enough punishment, they are eventually allowed to become one of the slaves we have in our palace. Personally, I'd rather stay out in the fields, but then I am sick of being social."

Esme glanced at Cursian who rode easily on her right hand side. He appeared to feel as she did, his face set in hard lines. Caiaphas rode on Cursian's right, clearly pleased with the view and the souls' discomfort. She closed her eyes trying to disappear to a softer place inside herself, full of green hills and blue skies.

Sometime later, she heard Salis whisper, "It's over, you can look now, Senora. We have entered the city."

CHAPTER THIRTY FIVE

The city rose before them, dark and austere. Esme, despite her studies, had no idea whether this place really did resemble one of the oldest civilisations on earth but it did look like a city ready for war. The walls were made of great blocks of lava towering upward and at least eight foot thick. The buildings inside the city resembled the houses of the early Greeks. Built around central courtyards with black colonnades and simply tiled roofs. Esme noticed meeting places and areas that could have been parks. Everywhere she looked, she witnessed pain and suffering.

Animals didn't pull carts; teams of people did with demons lashing them into greater efforts. In places, she saw the walls being torn down, then next door they would be rebuilding. At one point they flew over something which resembled an arena. Here she saw men and women fighting against savage dogs like beasts. They were being torn apart. Her initial fascination soon waned when all around lay anguish.

Heartily sickened by the sight of one small woman trying to move a block of rock three times her size and being goaded the whole time by sharp sticks, Esme said, "Why? Why is it like this? There is no joy, no peace, no beauty without suffering."

Salis replied, "This is hell, Esme, why should there be? We are killers, they are sinners. It is what we do unless we can all break the cycle. These souls do leave, once they have understood how too. For some it may take moments, for some an eternity. Some grow to love the pain and will never leave. They end up with us in the palace." He pointed upward over Esme's shoulder.

Crowning the hill in the city rose the palace. It shone in the perpetual red light of the sky. Every aspect of its black façade burnished mirror bright. It was huge. Esme gasped. It rambled all over the hilltop. Vast open courtyards contained the first evidence of free flowing water, gushing from complex fountains. There were hundreds of statues as pillars. The walls towered overhead, far higher than they needed to be and evidence everywhere of pain. Esme saw within every courtyard they flew over elements and instruments of torture. Every conceivable cruelty humanity created must have its genus in this place. Stocks, guillotines, cages, gallows, scolds bridle, iron maidens, garrottes, whole benches covered in small iron spikes on which people were held down tightly by iron bars.

She soon had more than enough and wanted to weep for the agony she witnessed. It put her own experiences into proportion. The smells also made her feel sick. The anguish these souls went through made the air thick with sweat, vomit, faeces and the stench of fear and agony. Despite Esme never having seen food or water in this place, people were still surviving. She supposed it must have been a part of the punishment. Their bodies still able to show fear and pain even in a metaphysical reality.

The horse descended, preserving Esme's sanity as the visions of pain disappeared behind their high walls. As soon as the beast hit the ground, Esme slid off the side and ran to Cursian. She buried her head into his shoulder.

"I can't do this. This place is foul. It doesn't matter how bad someone is, this isn't right."

Cursian's hand came up to stroke her hair, "Esme, this place has been created by man's evil and his need to be punished. We all create our own Hell, our own torments. It is the Master's job to make our fears real. There is nothing we can do for these souls and if you truly understood their crimes you may not be so forgiving."

Esme pulled away, "So what have you got to do to end up in a place like this?"

"I will not tell you such things and I would ask you not to enquire too closely of other people. Let me just say, a soul has to be the blackest and darkest of all to end up in a place like this. The Master specialises in making unrepentant sinners, repent." Cursian had held her tightly while he spoke into her hair.

"We need to make our way to court, Cursian," Salis said.

Cursian released Esme, but only so much that she simply turned in the circle of his arms. She took the offered comfort and leaned into his strong body. Salis stood near Caiaphas, dwarfed by the large purple beastie.

"I would ask you to lead us the kindest way possible, Salis."

Esme watched Caiaphas's face darken. He said something to Salis who frowned.

"No, I will not permit that, Caiaphas," Cursian interrupted. "And as powerful as you are you do not have sway over me. I will not have myself or my companion dragged through endless rooms of entertainment."

The beast stepped toward Cursian, now shouting in his guttural language. Cursian pushed Esme behind him. She continued to back track making enough space for them both to draw weapons. Cursian stood still, relaxed. He did not reach for his blade. Esme wanted to scream as the huge monster towered over the vampire, weapons waving and forked tongue spitting venom. She sensed a change in Cursian and herself, a shift, a pull. She heard her lover ask for her pure light to be given to him to use. Esme opened her heart and pushed the ethereal blue light toward him. Cursian pulled it into himself and created a spear of power, energy and light. Pushing it toward Caiaphas made the beastie burn. His skin began to bubble and blister, turning black and charred. A stink filled the hot air surrounding them. The demon's legs buckled as smoke rose from his mouth. Salis doubled over as the excess vibration hit him. Cursian stepped toward the demon.

"We are not of this realm, Caiaphas. I will not be cowed by the likes of you. I am and have always been your superior. I have not been gone long enough to lose my place here. My companion is a creature of light and love. You will not hurt her or I will have her burn you slowly until you disappear entirely, never able to return to your world." Cursian flexed his right hand, cutting Esme off.

She staggered slightly, not yet able to control what she did, only able to summon the energy to blast things. The supple power Cursian exhibited fell completely beyond her capabilities. Cursian turned his back on the demon and walked to her, offering her his arm.

Over his shoulder he said, "Well, Salis? Do not keep your Master waiting. I am sure after that little display he will be even more anxious than before to see me."

Salis walked passed them, but took a wide berth to do so, "Hombre, you have more tools in your armoury I see."

"Esme has lent me certain advantages, I cannot deny that. But, Salis I have never meant you harm, you know this," Cursian said with softness.

Salis turned, "Does this mean I am safe from your vengeance, Magi?" he laughed. Esme could almost taste the bitterness on her tongue from the sound. "Well, I thank you brother and I will sleep well knowing I will not be one of your victims."

The venom behind Salis's words shocked Esme. She looked up at Cursian, she could see how they had hurt.

"I don't understand," she said.

Cursian's hand once more stroked her hair unconsciously, "You are not meant to, Cariad. It is Salis's bitterness and in sending him to me, his Master is having a fine joke upon him. He will tell you if he wishes you to know."

Esme looked at the dark skinned vampire as he barked a laugh, "More like you don't want your precious love to know how cruel you can truly be."

The obvious pain wrapped up in Salis's bitterness made Esme move toward him. She lay her hand on his sword arm. Sensing his anger came from a deeply imbedded betrayal Esme gave herself over to compassion. They stood at almost the same height. Tears filled Salis's eyes.

His beautifully full mouth smiled, "Ha, Senora, you have unmanned me with your love. Now I know what Cursian's greatest weapon will be here, your passion for easing pain."

Esme smiled at him, "Salis, give me the guided tour of this miserable place." Linking her arm through his, Esme began to relax slightly now the purple beastie left them alone.

CHAPTER THIRTY SIX

Cursian's eyes widened, his mouth actually hung open as Esme turned her back. She simply walked off with Salis. Snapping his mouth shut Cursian glared after the pair. Resentment curled in his stomach. Watching her tight leather clad behind roll as she walked, giving Salis her full attention, made his blood boil. Powerful rushes of energy filled his head. He paused, unable to move. The physical distance between them grew and so did the pain Cursian felt. The agony of their separation stopped him from being able to think. Sinking to his knees, he looked toward her, watching helplessly as she collapsed into Salis's arms.

Salis's corn-rolls whipped around Esme's body as he turned to face Cursian, "What the hell is going on?"

"Bring her to me," Cursian gasped, barely holding his head up.

"She's fading in my arms, Cursian. I can feel her dying, that's not possible here." Salis didn't move.

"Salis, please. Bring her to me," Cursian pulled on his magecraft, trying to use it to enable him to walk. But it slipped from his control, sliding back to its origins.

"I've never seen you weakened," Salis sounded curious.

"Please, Salis, now is not the time to gloat. I will make it a compulsion if you do not return with her," Cursian found his voice reduced to a whisper. He seriously doubted he could force a compulsion on the lesser vampire, but he had to get Esme back.

"Ha, I doubt you could manage that, hombre. However, I do want to find out how you make each other so weak."

Cursian flinched as Salis appeared in front of his nose with Esme's limp form held easily in his arms.

"Give her to me," the pain inside Cursian eased, but could not be called bearable.

"Shit, Cursian, you look as though you are dying too." Salis bent to peer more closely, "Come, whatever is going on for you both I will not see you die here in the open." The smaller vampire switched Esme from his arms to his shoulder in one move. Years of learning to move dead or dying bodies making it graceful. With his free hand, he wriggled under Cursian, hooking his arm over his other shoulder. Cursian tried helping as Salis dragged him to a stable door nearest the exit of the courtyard. Nothing witnessed their broken journey to safety.

Salis dropped Cursian onto the empty rough stable floor, lowering Esme with infinitely more care. Cursian dragged his aching body toward her still form. Knives drove into each joint as he moved. His breath quickly grew painfully ragged. Finally, he pulled her into his arms. The whole time Salis leaned nonchalantly against the wall, watching them as though they were a science experiment.

"You could offer us aid," Cursian spat.

"No. I don't think so. Not after everything you have put me through. What's happening to you both?"

"If I knew that I would be able to control it," Cursian whispered. He lowered his head to Esme, "Cariad, I need you to wake. I need your faith. My magic is destroying me."

She gasped noisily in his arms, her eyes flying open. "Cursian, feed from me." Strong fingers pulled his mouth down toward her neck.

He resisted, confused, "What?"

"I feel our connection wither. We must sustain it. I am being pulled back to my world," Esme's green eyes glowed with need and insistence.

"How can our connection wither?"

"Now is not the time to ask. Either feed from me or fuck me, my love." Esme tried to smile, indicating either option would work for her.

His arms convulsed around her body. Lust rising through the pain. He had actually only been inside her once. Just once in all the years of watching and guarding.

"My God," a soft sound from the corner.

His head whipped around, his senses on overload as Esme filled his mind. A growl escaped as he saw another male, another vampire, in the stable, within reach.

"Cursian, the two of you look so beautiful," Salis's voice softened Cursian's blood lust.

The air around the pair shone a soft iridescent blue as his need rose. Esme moved in his arms, pulling again at his hair. Her eyes were hugely dilated.

"We have spent too much energy without giving back. We need to do something to give back the energy we have used. Our physical love is a great way of creating that energy. We have to maintain the balance. My body will die and my soul lost," Esme used the hand she tangled in his hair to pull herself toward his mouth.

Cursian sank deeply into the kiss. Time and place ceased to matter. He cradled her head in his hand as he plunged into her soul through her warm, wet mouth. He flew through her memories, barely seeing her thirty year history as she opened and welcomed him to her core. There the elfin representation of Esme waited, naked. She rose. All lithe grace and gentle smiles. Her strong body walked toward him, small breasts jutting outward. Her dark hair spiked around her head. He admired the flat, strong stomach that lay clean and clear between her hipbones. The small mound and dark slit unashamedly clear. Without words, she went to him and on tiptoes kissed him, pushing her tongue deeply into his mouth. He sensed her body's need as she leaned against his chest. Cursian's hands cupped her buttocks and pulled her pelvis hard against his groin. He hadn't noticed his own nakedness until now, but having her hot flesh pressed against him made him moan and stiffen, as he tried to bury himself in her through her skin.

Pulling back slightly he paused, wanting to control this moment for as long as possible. He lightly stroked her face. She turned her head into his palm, first kissing then nipping the skin. Cursian groaned again as his imagination wondered what those teeth might feel like on his neck, or chest, or thighs. To distract himself he cupped a small breast in his free hand. Esme responded, her swollen nipple hardened immediately when he flicked his thumb over it. She began moaning, biting his index finger as she drew it into her mouth. Cursian almost lost control in that moment. Feeling her hot wet mouth sucking on any part of him made his knees weak. Gently pulling his hand away from her control the vampire decided she needed to experience six hundred years worth of practice. He returned her mouth to his and made her drink deeply of his lust pulling away just as she decided she could take all he had to give. He moved on to lay soft lips and kisses against her cheek, jaw and down her exposed neck. Feeling her pulse jump in his slightly parted mouth Cursian imagined tasted her power and purity running into him, down his naked chest. He moaned again as she writhed under his kisses digging her nails into his back, wanting the sweetest of his kisses now.

No, Cursian drew a breath and moved on. In doing so he realised he held her up, apparently Esme decided standing had become inconvenient. Cursian smiled as he nibbled her clavicle. Lowering her to the white floor below he allowed the soft ground to take her weight, while his hands found new jobs on her body. He kissed across her chest and lowered himself to her breast, carefully holding the other in his hand, while his elbow supported his weight. He glanced toward her face, Esme's head arched back, her eyes closed in anticipation of his touch. He held off until she moved and opened her eyes. Blazing green need shone from the look she cast toward him, he grinned in response. Holding her gaze, he lowered his head. His mouth and hand pulled on her sensitized nipples simultaneously. Breasts should be handled well if they are going to help arouse a woman. After the initial harshness, Cursian used soft movements of tongue and fingers to trigger Esme's desire. She began to push her breasts toward him wanting him to suck harder again, he removed his hand from one breast and trailed it down her stomach.

The change in his concentration altered Esme's response. Once more, she grew still in anticipation of his journey. He bit her breast hard enough to hurt, drawing her attention back to where he wanted it. After the pain in her breast, he gave instant pleasure, making her forget the roving hand. Her eyes closed. Cursian grinned against her skin. He would have to be quick, but having a hairless body would make life so much easier. Her legs opened and her knees rose. He began to flick his tongue hard over her rigid tip also sucking and biting into the soft flesh. His skill as a lover meant he could make Esme reach her climax easily, however, Cursian had his own needs to satisfy and they demanded knowledge of her dark interior.

Just as she arched her back to push herself further into his harsh mouth Cursian forced two of his long elegant fingers deep inside. He heard her cry out in surprise as he buried himself in her body. The heat, the engorged flesh and sheer wetness made him feel very welcome. Almost instantly, before he even drew his hand out, he felt her spasm around his fingers. Her body held him so tightly Cursian gasped in surprise. She pushed harder onto his hand. He bunched the muscles in his arm to hold himself still while she used his hand and fingers to continue the orgasm. Wave after wave stroked his fingers, which pushed and twisted inside, hot liquid spilling out to cover his hand. Eventually, the spasms slowed and Esme opened eyes still full of lazy heat. He grinned at the apology written plainly on her satisfied face.

That was enough consent for Cursian to begin again. He pulled his fingers from her and smiled as she sighed. Her hips wiggled slightly as she adjusted to his absence. Cursian knew that would not be the state of play for long. His whole body ached. But he wanted Esme to need his fullness as much as he needed her, so he lowered his head and began the journey downwards. Licks and nips made Esme's recently relaxed body begin to writhe and tighten. Cursian changed position with vampiric grace and power. As he moved his body effortless over, then down hers, he allowed the head of his penis to trail down her body. Esme groaned and pushed her hips upward. Cursian ignored the demand, much to his aching regret. As he settled his long body inside her smooth thighs, he kissed the flesh covering her pubic bone and did something he hadn't allowed himself to do in centuries. He tilted his head slightly, grazed one sharp tooth along the smooth skin and opened the flesh just above the beginning of her labia. He watched as Esme pushed her hips upward in response to the pain of the cut. The wound filled, then spilled blood.

Breathing deeply, Cursian allowed the hot scent of blood and sex to fill his senses. The dark red stain slid through the wetness Esme created. It travelled down one side of her engorged bud, becoming diverted on its course by her inner petals. They kindly guided the life giving stream over the dark wet entrance. Cursian closed his eyes in thankfulness for this glorious woman laid out before him.

Before a drop could be wasted, he lowered his head. If her scent made him dizzy, the taste of blood and sex made Cursian want to faint. He drew into his mouth as much of her as he could, forcing his tongue deeply into her body. Esme's hands grasped his head and her legs widened to help him accommodate as much of her as he could. He gladly complied. His tongue moved from deep within her hot wet body to flick and rub against her. She bucked underneath him and he found he had to ride her, as she demanded more.

Moving his mouth away from her entrance, he sent shivers through her by licking long and hard, cleaning her own juices from her body. Satisfied her desire matched his once more, he moved slightly higher up and kissed the wound. Checking he understood Esme's compliance, Cursian sucked, knowing it would sting as the salty juice on his tongue entered the small hole.

Blood slowly filled his mouth as his fingers once more, slowly infiltrated his woman. She felt bigger this time, more able to accommodate his need, which would fill her to capacity. She was nearly ready. He could sense her body wanting to orgasm, but each time she drew close, he would hold himself still inside and outside of her until the wave subsided. Cursian held the mouthful of blood enjoying the tingling sensation it gave as he began absorbing it into his own system. When he eventually swallowed, he knew he could not put it off any longer.

With fingers still inside, he pushed his long body up hers. Esme cried out inarticulate with need. Cursian kissed her, making her taste her sex and her blood on his tongue. She surprised him by licking the inside of his mouth, clearly wanting everything. As she kissed, Cursian slowly, arms trembling with effort, drew his fingers out of her darkness. The moment he left her, without a breath drawn between he began to push his throbbing sex into her tight, young body. His skin gave on his back as her nails expressed her desire and desperation. Still he pushed slowly. The only time they had managed to get this far in the real world Cursian slammed into her so hard he thought he'd broken her pelvis. This time he wanted to experience her ridges and enveloping softness slowly, until his willpower broke. However, Esme would not be controlled. Her body pulsed, fluid once more gushing as Esme writhed in the throws of her second orgasm.

Cursian drew a sharp breath in, determined not to come himself, but the temptation to drive into her as the muscles surrounding him rippled and gripped him drew his resolve close to the edge. The orgasm passed and he found her even larger and wetter than before, taking the edge off his own need as his stimulations changed.

Pulling almost completely out he felt Esme's fingers dig into his buttocks. So he pushed smoothly into her, and she rose to meet him. Burying his long thickness inside her meant he brushed against her cervix. Silently he asked with his eyes if he proved too much for her to take. Her answer came with her hips pushing him even deeper, if such a thing were possible. Cursian cried out and lowered his body over hers, burying his face in her neck. He pulled out but unable to go far in their current position, he no longer cared. With short thrusts, Cursian finally allowed his own lust to build. His stomach tightened with need, his balls rose high and sweat beaded his flesh. He smelt blood and lust and sex and need. Esme tightened around him and her body began to go rigid with another climax. Faster and harder, they rode each other with an equal desperation. But Cursian wanted more.

The orgasm began to build, he reared back, slowed slightly, altering their rhythm. He thrust hard into her with all his male power. He watched as her face twisted briefly in pain, the pain in turn raised his blood lust further. Still pounding her body mercilessly, Cursian struck. He bit hard into her neck. Wanted to hear her scream in pain. And she did. He groaned as hot, salty blood filled his mouth and he gulped it down. Too much spilled from her for him to drink it all. It spilled over his face, down her skin. He groaned again as the change in his position allowed Esme to pick up their previous drive. She rode him hard as he drank from her and willingly impaled herself on his body. Cursian now craved his own explosion. She cried out, scalding hot juice spilling from her willing body and he finally lost control. His body pulsed and he pushed deep into his lover. Both continued to remain tightly joined as wave after wave flowed through them. Cursian pulled his mouth from the wound in Esme's throat and arched over her body, thrusts instinctual and still deep while she tore open his back in long scratches.

Slowly they came down from the incredible high. Cursian licked Esme's blood off her neck and closed the large holes. Still inside her, he cradled her body tightly against his own while awareness returned. He woke in the darkness of a stable. In a world of pain and hate. He still held his lover as he had before becoming a part of her. Cursian silently wept over her unconscious form.

A small, soft hand brushed tears from his face. He opened his eyes and looked directly into Esme's.

"I'm not sure what is more amazing, the real thing or metaphysical sex?" she smiled.

"Rwy'n dy garu di." Cursian, feeling all his strength and power rush back, pulled her close.

She squirmed slightly, "Urgh, breathing is necessary I'm not that evolved!"

Cursian laughed and released her, pulling her upright as he stood. Turning he saw Salis pressed into a corner. "It seems our friend here has a problem."

"Salis?" Esme asked.

"I didn't believe such a thing were possible. I saw you become one, I saw your bodies melt and join in a dance of light. I felt your…your…todo," Salis's eyes looked haunted. He actually shook. Cursian took a step toward him, concerned.

"No, no brother, do not touch me. I can't afford to be any more a part of this than I am already. You were wrong to come here. They will destroy what you have. You should not do that to Esme, she deserves better."

"We didn't have a great deal of choice," Esme said.

"Cursian, whatever you are doing here, please don't finish it. Leave, they will have felt you, they know how strong you are, how strong both of you are. Please, brother, I know there is no love loss between us, but I would not see you torn apart by their malice," Salis's voice held an edge of panic.

"Why the panic, Salis? What has been planned? He will know why we are here." Cursian began to pull on his renewed strength, filling the small space with power.

Salis choked, "Don't, Cursian. There is no need to threaten me. I have told you I will protect Esme as though she were my own. I cannot give you more and you know why. You maybe ruthless but you ran your cruel streak dry many centuries ago."

"I will stop them."

"I know you will try, even if it means your soul's destruction. But what of the mortal? Does she not deserve to live in peace?" Salis sounded as though he would beg his old companion if he thought it would do any good.

Cursian hesitated. Salis had lived in this place for longer than any vampire would choose too. Usually they moved between dimensions. But Salis was stuck, yet he had stayed sane and profited despite his lack of power. For Salis to want to protect them, things must be very bad. He of all the immortals in this place had reason to see Cursian suffer.

"If I could find a way to send her home, Salis, I would," Cursian said quietly.

"I appreciate the gallantry, gentlemen," Esme said. "But I am here for a reason. Has it occurred to you that the 'powers that be' might well want me here? It might well be necessary for me to be a part of this fight? Besides, if I were not here would you be as powerful as you are now? I complete you in a way nothing else could, we have always been one, Cursian, always. Why are you fighting this now? Right from the dawn of time we have faced danger and evil together, what makes this time so different? Your chauvinistic desire to protect me?"

Her clear gaze pinned him to the wall. She had a point. They were designed for each other, honed over centuries and many lifetimes, to become this powerful fighting machine. They had already destroyed a great evil in their own world. Now they would face one here, which may well be worse. He had no right to deny their destiny, just as he had not allowed Esme to avoid the Prophecy. He knew, through years of suffering and study that if they succeeded in fulfilling their joint destiny they might have peace together. If they split, and he found a way to send her home, he would fail, all their suffering would have been for naught and he would have gained nothing but the destruction of Esme's life.

He drew in a shuddering breath.

"It breaks my heart, but you are right." He turned away. He didn't have to like it.

CHAPTER THIRTY SEVEN

Esme watched Cursian walk away, not far enough to trigger a reaction in either of them, but it didn't stop her feeling sad. Their journey through the labyrinth of hell bizarrely helped her accept her destiny. Esme used the time to consider her options, think about the true meaning of her existence and the terrible things she'd suffered to reach this point. She began to see the patterns, she began to understand Cursian's terrible dilemmas, she began to see how intrinsically linked they were to each other. Cursian had no choice but to follow this terrible path and defeat this evil. If she did not stand at his side, he would fail and she would be lost. If she gave him her strength, they might just succeed and she might just have a chance at happiness. She might also find a way to save him from eternal damnation in this place when he did die.

She looked around the dark stable. The chances of living to a ripe of old age seemed slim suddenly. Far too slim, her resolve crumbled. She reached for Cursian without really thinking about what she was doing, he instantly responded on a new level. Turning back toward her, he smiled. He caressed her mind like a warm blanket threaded with the finest steel. She relaxed.

Nothing will stand in our way, Cariad. We will either die together or live together.

I hope to God, you're right. I don't think I'd survive losing you now.

She looked at Salis, who she would have described as ashen, if his skin wasn't so dark it hid any visible weakness. His stance and eyes told her all she needed to know. Salis felt afraid, deeply afraid. She pushed her gaze further, wanting more information. His fear lay in losing his one way ticket out of this place. Cursian could, should have, freed him centuries ago. Esme pushed further into Salis's unresisting mind.

Scenes from Salis's past flashed through her head. He lay in De'hevda's arms, her blood filling his mouth, his family slaughtered around him. Cursian appeared full of rage with De'hevda's as she attempted to make her own vampire companion. The older vampire, his sanity returned and his control over De'hevda weakening, took the smaller man in his arms and finished the change. Salis woke as a vampire, but weak, due to his unusual method of creation. He became Cursian's companion, not De'hevda's. They lived together for decades, all of them unfurling before Esme's mind. Salis became a vampire capable of compassion, helping Cursian control his own bloodlust, until one night it all came to an end. De'hevda, in an attempt to regain Cursian, tricked Salis and drugged him, forcing him to help her destroy a small village somewhere in Italy. Cursian found them near dawn, covered in the blood of their victims. In his rage, Cursian finally decided to sever his links with his vampiric fountainhead. His mage craft opened a channel into the hell dimension. Grabbing Salis and De'hevda, Cursian pulled all three of them into hell. Once there, Cursian abandoned Salis and because of his weakness, Salis could not escape without De'hevda's or Cursian's help. De'hevda wouldn't help and Cursian left once he had own his freedom. He abandoned Salis in this place because Cursian believed Salis could not be saved and should suffer for his sins.

Cursian denied Salis's pleas for mercy, his claims of innocence. Salis remained locked in hell for almost four hundred years. A weak vampire among the cruellest beings in creation.

Esme cut the connection as visions of what Salis had done to survive began to surface in her mind making her stomach crawl. She gazed into his brown eyes and realised having witnessed her bonding with Cursian he'd been reminded of true love, of salvation, of redemption. She knew he saw her as his only way out of this place, if he could convince her of his innocence. His enmity toward Cursian vanished under this desperate need to gain his freedom. He would do anything to find a way out.

"Salis? We aren't going to hurt you," she spoke as though to a spooked horse.

Wide eyes swivelled to face her, "The two of you could crush me like a cicada."

She smiled, "Yes, but why would we want too? Salis, we can give you your heart's desire."

Careful, Cariad, he is vampire and not as I am. They are clever and ultimately fuelled by evil.

Oh, and you know him so well, do you? she snapped. Angry with him for the pain Salis suffered because he couldn't believe another vampire had the self control he demonstrated.

"Do not think such things here. He will know," Salis said. Meaning the demon controlling the vampire.

"Not from me," Esme replied. "Salis, I can help Cursian become your fountainhead once more and I can help you out of this place."

"What?" both men gaped.

"Cursian has controlled and abandoned me before, why would now be any different?" Salis asked suspiciously.

Esme sensed his desperation, "Because he has me and I know the truth of what you have suffered."

Esme watched Salis close his eyes trying to deny what she said. She stepped toward him, drawn to him like no one else except Cursian. She felt her lover reach through her and once her hand touched Salis's chest, into the smaller vampire.

She lay a soft kiss on dark lips, "Salis, I am sorry." They were not her words, or not hers alone.

Salis didn't move. He didn't look as though he were breathing. His voice whispered, "Please, stop. You will break what is left of my soul and my heart. I am loyal to my Master and I will help him destroy you." His lips whispered the words into Esme's mouth, yet her mind heard his plea. He agreed to help them if he could.

Esme smiled. She felt Cursian's confusion and pain over his emotional connection to Salis. She took her lover's hand.

I hope you know what you are doing, Cariad.

We need allies. Esme replied, *We will need our backs covered at the very least. He loved you once. He deserves this chance. Compassion is as important as forgiveness, Cursian. You have a habit of forgetting both.*

She heard Cursian grunt and felt his lack of belief wash through her.

"Well," Cursian muttered. "This has all been very diverting but we really need to accomplish our task." He moved to open the stable door.

Salis walked out, warily keeping as much distance between himself and Cursian as possible. Esme sighed. She needed them to trust each other.

Esme, you need to shield your thoughts if you are exasperated with me.

"Don't give me a hard time. You're the one that got me into this mess in the first place." She held out her hand, forcing her irritation away, "Come on, we need to stay close so let's not fall out."

She felt odd, to say the least. Her skin no longer fit, because it now contained a part of her lover's soul, which would never return. Esme guessed something of her own soul now resided within him. They had melded, become one and separated again. Just as the yang contained the ying. One thing rose like a hydra from their experience. Esme glimpsed a dark part of Cursian's soul as she'd separated and come back to her own body. A weight of desolation, isolation, age and the knowledge necessary to manipulate the Universe lived inside her lover. That and the hunger. The terrible hunger and not just for blood. Then barriers came crashing down, allowing only certain information through, such as their immediate thoughts and emotions. Over time, Esme suspected she'd be able to dig deeper into her lover's soul, the thought both scary and exhilarating.

One of the more interesting side effects seemed to be the enhancement of her physical facilities. The world appeared sharper, as though in hyper focus, her body stronger, more fluid. Her hearing now caught the sound of Salis walking. His robes of silk rubbing against his bare skin, reminding her of small streams of water. The very walls were alive under her hand. In fact, the more things she touched the more she understood how they were formed. Even to the point where she knew how to blend and alter each part of herself, absorbing the world surrounding them. Underlying this sensation lay the hunger. Esme really didn't mind being dinner, but experiencing the drive that made her dinner, began pushing things too far.

Not wanting Salis to know too much about how things had changed she silently asked, *Can you stop me wanting to taste blood? I'm finding it hard to deal with.*

One of the more unpleasant aspects of my life. I will do what I can to help, Cariad.

The sensation vanished, but so did so much more. Esme realised Cursian cut off as much of the link as possible. She'd hurt him, rejected his nature.

"Oh, bloody hell," she turned and stamped a foot. Salis stopped just ahead of them. "For pity's sake, Cursian, all I wanted you to do was stop me from craving blood. It's really disturbing. I wasn't rejecting you!"

Salis smiled cynically, his barriers once more surrounding him. "He's always been touchy, Esme. He is ashamed of his own nature."

She frowned at Salis's pleasure, "Shut up, you're not helping. He isn't ashamed, he'd simply rather I didn't have to put up with it."

"Just keep thinking that…" Salis said.

"Quiet, Salis," Cursian snapped. "I apologise, I have yet to control our connection properly."

Esme gasped when he flooded back. Her eyes widened. Her lower abdomen clenched tightly as her mind sprang into full sexual arousal. "Oh, shit."

Cursian smiled, amusement plain. *Wrestling those needs ought to keep you quiet woman.*

Esme couldn't think coherently enough to reply. She just turned and wandered off after Salis thinking of vampiric strength in tight fitting leather.

She wrestled with Cursian's other needs, as she tried to focus on the palace.

They entered the edifice itself through a plain Romanesque archway. The outside of the courtyard and the arch maintained the roughness lava has naturally. The inside however, glowed. Everywhere Esme looked the stone shone. Braziers and torches lit the way reflecting off the walls. The blackness of the stone appeared to be miles deep due to the reflections, creating many illusions. Each step made you feel as though you were walking off the edge of a cliff. It took some coaxing by the vampires to convince Esme everything would remain solid. She found she couldn't concentrate on the illusion while she walked. It made her sea sick to have her senses deceived so easily.

Along each corridor, there were regular doorways and arched windows. Each resembled the early medieval period architecturally.

"I thought you said this place resembled the cities of the earliest civilisations?" Esme said.

"It did," Cursian peered around almost as much as she did. "I assume he grew bored."

"He's been redesigning," Salis said. "He thinks this is more up to date. He likes the heavy churchiness. I can't stand it myself."

Esme leapt back and yelped as though charged with an electric shock, "Shit! What the hell?"

She had approached one of the stone doorways, curiosity driving her to look through a small window. With her face pressed up against the glass, Esme almost died of shock when another face threw itself into view, screaming. She couldn't hear the scream, but the face she would never forget. Bald head, with tattered ears, no nose and a toothless mouth pushed forward in obvious pain. The eyes were blind, once they may have been blue. They stared right into her being. Opaque skin had the look of the starved.

Cursian answered her, "Vampires who were not strong enough to win their independence from their Master when they challenged him."

Esme heard the emptiness in Cursian's voice. That very lack of emotion answered many questions. The horror of knowing the creature in the cell couldn't feed as its teeth had been pulled, couldn't smell its food, couldn't see its prey, but could live an eternity starving and raving, made Esme admire Cursian all the more. His determination to break with his Master meant facing this horror and he had won. After seeing the creature, Esme made sure she didn't peer through any more glass. If she did hear any sounds, she ignored them. This was the world of the damned. Pity in her heart would doom her to madness. Survival her only priority.

They walked further and further into the palace. Esme became completely lost inside its maze. More corridors, more light, more grandeur, more art. Statues predominated, beautiful in their darkness and sinuous in their grace, but tormenting in their context. They depicted men and women cavorting with beasts of myth, from all cultures. In each depiction, someone was always in pain or being humiliated. Where statues usually represented faces in repose or serenity these, when examined closely, reminded Esme of Munch's Scream. Buggery, mutilation, orgies, whipping, everything on view an antonym to the beauty of Renaissance art. Every sadistic possibility portrayed. Even the tapestries were covered in scenes of hate. Hunts, where the victim wasn't a fox, covered the walls of one long corridor. Salis tried, by diverting their path through every conceivable twist and turn, to take them through the least unpleasant places. Still Esme wanted to stop walking and bury her head in a bowl of water to wash her eyes and mind clean. She'd always enjoyed erotic art but she now doubted she'd ever be able to look at Rohdan's Kiss again.

Finally, Salis stopped. He lightly touched her arm, eliciting a growl from Cursian. They both turned glaring at him.

Quietly Salis said, "We are near the main ballroom. The Court will be waiting for our Master and you. I do not want you to go in there unprepared."

Esme looked at Cursian, "What should I know?"

"Almost everything I have not wished to tell you." Cursian touched her face, "Esme, the Court is not just made up of vampire and Salis is correct, you need to be prepared. The vampire are just a part of the Master's Court, those that gave us life are also a part, the stronger part. These creatures are the equivalent to your archangels. They gave the Master the virus, which makes man vampire. They feed as the Master does, on death and pain. They are banned from your world, which is why they helped their Master create vampire. Only our kind can move between the worlds. We feed on life blood, they want it too and they will be helping their Master find a way through."

"So," Esme said slowly. "I'm not just trying to defeat the Devil I have to get his henchmen too?"

The vampires nodded, looking like bookends. Esme chuckled, "Oh, what fun. And if they're enough to make you two hesitate, they must be really scary."

"I like this woman, Cursian," Salis said. "She catches hold of things very quickly."

"That may be so but she often refuses to see exactly how dangerous things are," Cursian answered Salis but frowned at Esme.

She grinned up at him, "There is bugger all we can do about it, sweetie, so let's go meet the bad guys."

CHAPTER THIRTY EIGHT

Cursian knew Esme couldn't possibly understand the dangers she walked into by following the vampires, yet he couldn't force her to see them. The trouble started when she realised she could kill things with immunity. Watching her face change as he wiped the blood and gore off with the edge of her shirt frightened him at first. A veil descended, but at the same moment, a light switched on. Her natural warrior's soul, no longer bound or contained by society, flowered in this violent world. Setting her free for the first time, but overconfidence killed more warriors than bad training. With more of his own power and knowledge filtering into her, Cursian worried about her sanity and self control. If they, or in fact she, ever returned to their world Cursian feared she would no longer abide by the rules of that place. But by God, she was impressive walking down the long dark corridor, sword at her waist, leather jeans hugging a fit backside and black shirt just blood stained enough to make him want to throw her to floor.

That's an interesting turn on. Esme lightly brushed his mind.

Cheeky wench, what gives you the right to peek?

You! You're broadcasting your lust thick enough to drown me!

Cursian grinned, jogging to catch her up. If they ever managed to reach a place of safety he promised himself he would spend hours reminding Esme of every nerve ending in her body.

He realised he would simply have to trust in her ability to cope. All this must seem like some weird Daliequse film. Just so long as he protected her from the worst of this places abuses, he might just get her out and retain her sanity. So long as her body survived the Hellfire Caves. The lightness Cursian enjoyed through his link with Esme fled under his natural sense of desperation. He'd been playing this game for too long to think it could end positively. He also knew his new found optimism would be beaten from him sooner or later. This place specialised in destroying people's souls.

Cursian, you can't think like this. You will doom us all if you do.

Cariad, I should be shielding more efficiently than this. I am sorry. Please, ignore my dark nature.

Dark I can handle, my love. What I can't think about is how much this might hurt. Please, some things should be ignored. I need my bubble. I can't afford to go back to the place I found in those Caves. I need this to be a dream.

Cursian found himself unable to reply and left a void hanging between them. A void filled with their own personal demons. He almost grabbed her hand in that moment and ran from the palace. Be damned of the consequences. Maybe that is what he should have done in Wycombe after all, but Salis coughed and he found they had reached the final doorway to the Ballroom. Cursian went cold, cold and hard. He knew this place and its games. He brought his vampiric nature forward, pulling on the lashed demon within his soul. It rushed to the fore. Esme gasped beside him, stepping back obviously sensing the change through the link.

Cariad, as you can harness the mage within me, reach for my beast. It will help protect you from them.

Let's just hope it doesn't turn me into a complete sociopath, I'm having a hard enough time as it is controlling my new desires. Despite her jocular thoughts, Cursian felt her fear.

It won't, so long as you remember who and what you truly are, Cariad. You are light and love to me. I am the darkness and death. We need to maintain that balance and the monster within me will understand it must work within our own natures or it will be destroyed in this place. It has no desire to control you, it wants to leave because it now knows its only real strength is staying separate and independent from the power in this place. It should not have returned.

I hope you're right.

Cursian sensed Esme move physically closer as though this would encourage her to embrace his demon. She stiffened as he allowed his vampiric essence to flow between them. Its disgusting alienness must have felt like a wave of putrid darkness.

"Wow, this is what being a vampire feels like?" Esme asked the men.

Salis looked confused. Cursian replied quickly, "Yes, Cariad." Hoping she'd have the sense to stay quiet.

"No wonder you all think we're stupid. This is amazing."

Cursian stared at her. How could it be amazing? Then he understood. He had siphoned off the strength and abilities of vampire. Esme only received these positive parts. The downsides she would not understand or feel thanks to his age and experience. And the blood lust? Esme seemed to be enjoying her own version, so doubtless didn't notice his so much. Cursian mentally shrugged. Nothing for it but to give Salis the signal, leading them into the pit.

Salis pushed the huge black doors open with ease. The three of them strode onto the upper gallery surrounding the large room below. Cursian almost winced as Esme's hand convulsed. The view disturbed him too.

The walls and floor of this place were constructed of the same black lava as the rest of the building, but here veins of green gems wove through the fabric of the rock. The light came from an indefinable source and unlike the rest of the palace gave a soft glow to the room. Long sweeping stairways descended from the gallery at even intervals, four in all. The perfectly round room held a mass of bodies. Cursian blanched, every vampire and arch demon within the realm must have congregated because of their arrival. Silence descended as the three approached the first stairway. It reminded Cursian, horribly, of their recent conflict.

Shit, these things aren't real are they?

Esme's initial sense of terror rapidly wore off as she pulled on Cursian's memories and strength. He let her take everything she needed. Even with his memories she couldn't quiet believe her eyes. Over half the congregation were vampire, beautiful, arrogant and powerful; the other half consisted of beings so perfect they made you want to weep. Translucent skin, perfect almond shaped eyes, high imperious cheekbones, sleek hair done in complex styles, full sensuous lips. Limbs formed for power or pleasure. But the illusion of beauty ended with the eyes. Death filled their gaze. Cursian firmly closed his mind on his memories when Esme wanted to know more about these creature's habits. They reminded Cursian of the worst of the warriors he had known. Those who enjoyed the bloodletting, the death, the rape and pain. A vampire killed for blood, for food, had a compulsion to do so. These things killed only to feed on the terror of their victim's.

They reached the bottom of the stairs, still cloaked in silence. Cursian paused, sweeping his gaze over the crowd. He read hunger, curiosity and in some, fear. This did not surprise him. During his last visit he caused chaos. Using any means to hand to accomplish his goal. Many paid dearly for helping him or hindering him. The crowd began to part, from the centre. Once the wave of movement reached the stairs, Cursian noticed the diminutive figure of De'hevda. His breath caught, as it always did when he first saw her, before she opened her mouth. She had to be the most beautiful creature he had ever seen and he could not forget how the small body responded to his carnal needs. She dressed simply, as always, but the sheer fabric hinted at all the soft pleasures she might bestow. Her long pale hair gleamed in the defused light. For the mass of creatures to have parted like this, they must be hoping for a fine spectacle.

"Hey, remember me?" Esme asked, pulling lightly on his hand.

Cursian looked down into green eyes. The dusty and bloody black shirt, scuffed leather jeans and practical boots emphasised Esme's whole attitude to life. Tangled dark hair reminded him of when she was five years old and he'd pulled her from a tree she'd climbed into one night.

He smiled, "I really do love you, you know."

Esme's eyebrow went up, "Bloody good job. Looked to me like you were about to change sides."

He bent, took her head in his hands and before the whole assembly, kissed her lightly on the lips. "Esme, you remind me of the beauty of innocents. I will always want you more than any other being, remember that."

Turning away from her, he stepped onto the floor. Esme walked two steps behind. Salis flanked him on the other side.

De'hevda would be one of the most powerful vampires in the room, but why the arch demons were giving her the floor Cursian needed to discover before any challenge could be issued. It had been a long time since he had played games quite this dangerous.

Stopping out of arms reach from his nemesis, Cursian asked, "And how have you been, my dear?" He used the same tone a mortal would use to an aged aunt. It galled De'hevda.

Her crystal blue eyes narrowed imperceptibly, "I am vexed with you, Cursian. You have been causing me an awful lot of trouble. And now you bring your witch here. You really are becoming quite impossible." Her eyes shifted to Esme. Cursian dare not ignore the hunger embedded there.

He moved attracting her attention. De'hevda's characteristics resembled those of a cat.

"Well, if you will persist in forcing my hand. I must say though, your latest efforts did offer us some trouble," Cursian said.

"Hmmm, you still managed to defeat me though. And I thought using your own passion against the witch would cause at least one of you to betray the other."

"Guess you don't understand the nature of loyalty and trust," Esme muttered from behind Cursian.

He did wonder how long she would remain quiet.

De'hevda's silvery laugh glided over his skin. "Oh dear, witch, I don't think you understand your master very well. Cursian is loyal to no one but himself. Did he not show he was willing to sacrifice you to our little scheme?"

"De'hevda, what happened to Esme and I only served to strengthen our connection." Cursian opened his mouth to say more, but the smile on De'hevda's face gave him pause. His chest heaved, "This was a part of your plan. You wanted us to be so tightly bound that by killing one you would rid yourselves of the other. Thus destroying the last of the Guardian's. You want to nullify the Prophecy and think the only place you can really succeed is here." Six hundred years old and he had been completely duped.

"I don't understand," Esme said.

"No, you won't mortal," a new voice penetrated Cursian's dismay.

CHAPTER THIRTY NINE

Esme's body responded to Cursian's fear and shock by making her stomach clench and breathing stop. She gasped, too confused to follow the conversation for a few moments. When her eyes focused, as Cursian regained control, she noticed a man standing behind De'hevda.

"Nicolaitan, I shall not submit to you," Cursian said.

Esme lightly touched his back, to regain a physical connection. This person, creature, frightened Cursian deeply. Despite not knowing half of what was happening, Esme realised why. The man stood half a head taller than Cursian. But where the vampire was handsome and well formed, Nicolaitan had been handcrafted by the gods. Thick blond hair fell down his back. Blue eyes, a perfect shade between De'hevda's crystal blue and Cursian's dark blue, shone with intelligence and powerful arrogance. His form and face must have been chiselled from living marble by the most gifted of artists. Flawless, he too dressed simply in a cream silk shirt and trousers. Esme wished for cloven hooves and woollen legs. She also decided she'd never wear white or cream again. All the bad guys should be in black hats at least. She giggled involuntarily.

All eyes turned.

She stopped giggling, but didn't stop grinning.

Nicolaitan marred his face by frowning, "Is the witch a fool?"

Esme bit her lip to stop the next giggle, "Sorry, as you were. Just thought of something silly. Couldn't help myself."

"Are you an imbecile?" Nicolaitan asked.

"No, I just happened to be wondering where the horns and tail had gone?" Esme sounded light and far away, even to her own ears.

Esme, you are in shock. This is my doing. I have forced my fear into you to rid myself of it so I may face this situation with a clear head. Please, Cariad, try to stay silent until I find you somewhere safe to discharge this emotion.

Esme blinked several times.

"Erm, my Lord," Salis said from beside her. "I think the mortal is overwhelmed by your presence. Perhaps we should remove her?" he placed a hand on her arm, positioning himself between her and De'hevda.

"Is this the best the Prophecy can offer? I thought she'd be worth the fight," De'hevda drawled, stroking a hand over Nicolaitan's chest and Cursian's face at the same time.

Esme shivered with the contact. Hate for the female vampire surged over the fear and confusion Cursian had dumped.

She pushed against Salis and growled, "We've discussed you touching Cursian before. Get your fucking hands off."

De'hevda let her hand drop slowly. Esme stepped forward enjoying the release of energy. The journey down the stairway and across the floor made her tense because of its passive nature. As a creature of action, this polite game of chess made her weak, unsure. Hate for the vampire bitch she understood. She pulled on her source of power, ready to blast the cow. Instead of blue light, pain shot through her skull so fast and with such screaming agony Esme dropped to the floor clutching her head.

Within a breath, the pain vanished. However, it left her weak and trembling.

"She's not an imbecile. In fact she is powerful," Nicolaitan said. "But you have left her untrained, Cursian and you have not bound her to you as a vampire would his slave. Why?"

"You wouldn't understand," Esme grated, still on her knees head in hands.

"She is right, you would not understand," Cursian said. He gave Esme space, wanting to maintain contact with the enemy. It didn't stop him sending her waves of peace.

Esme rose, "Listen, I want to rewind. Why are all these things," she gestured around her, "being so patient? And why does Cursian think we have fallen into some kind of complex plot?"

"My people are waiting to see how we deal with you. Cursian has long been the most powerful of vampire and he is the most unruly. If I fail they will see an opening and grab it, standard courtly procedure," Nicolaitan smiled. Esme watched the slightly pointed teeth. "As to the plot? Ah, well, De'hevda has fought Cursian for a long time. My father punished her for each of her failures. It makes her mind sharp. If a little erratic. She laid so many traps that your fall was inevitable. If the drugs hadn't worked, then the Dominion would, if they failed as they did, then your own need to keep each other alive would work. There have been other snares along the way you avoided. I have to say, the Dominion were fantastic. I really enjoyed the death of each of the Guardians. De'hevda showed her true flare with that one. She has spent decades setting this up, weakening your position, learning about your bond. She has earned the right to be my consort. Are things clearer for you witch?"

Esme looked up into the beautiful face and watched an abyss open. Nicolaitan's confidence drained her. "So, you're saying you have us exactly where you want us and we are as emotionally close as you wanted us?"

Careful, Cariad they do not understand everything. They cannot, they are not mortal and that means they cannot fully understand you.

Alright, but what can I do? It really does look as though they've won!

Esme, we are meant to be here. I do not fully trust this plan they say they have, De'hevda is not patient and we can do more harm to them here than when we are in your realm.

Are you mad? We are completely fucked! This bastard is going to tear us apart.

Cariad, we are meant to feel despair. Do not allow it to conquer our courage.

Esme cut him off, the Greek god spoke again.

"We will take you from here to finish what the Dominion started," Nicolaitan waved a hand.

Esme watched with dismay as solider demons began to run from the openings around the gallery above them.

"Not without cost." Cursian said calmly, "Cariad, it is time for battle."

She shrugged, pulling the wicked blade out. It shone in the soft light. "Now, that I understand."

She turned her back to Cursian. A wider circle opening around them as the crowd responded. It seemed violence made them animated. Salis disappeared from her side, blending with the rest of the crowd. Esme felt a small prick of sadness. Looking into his eyes as he departed Esme witnessed deep loss and overwhelming fear. This kept him from fighting, there seemed no point in blaming him for his fear, she was afraid too.

"This is foolish, Cursian," De'hevda said, standing with them in their circle, Nicolaitan at her side. "You cannot hurt us."

"I simply want to make this as hard as possible. You cannot kill us here. It lacks the ceremony your magic needs. Therefore, our capture will cost you lives instead. Did you really think I would allow you to take us willingly?" Cursian replied.

The Court spread itself up the stairs. The soldiers came down. Esme knew their numbers would be infinite. Surrender loomed before them despite Cursian's words. Defeat and capture inevitable. However, displays of power impressed all beings, the law of the jungle predominant. Going down fighting had to be better than suffering as she had before. She took a deep breath and blended her thoughts with Cursian. His hyper reality and strength filled her. A maniacal grin spread over her face. She locked eyes with Nicolaitan for a moment. Despite his physical humanity, Esme understood he knew nothing of human strength. She decided to aim for him. Let him see what havoc she could cause.

At a silent command, the army of demons, their black skin shining, began to approach. The moment the nearest were in swords reach both Cursian and Esme began to fight. They stayed tight together. Their swords wove through the throng. Each foot and arm motion timed to perfection as they sank into each other's battle frenzy. Esme found herself able to sense everything he could see, responding to threats she would never normally have been able to defeat. Her instinct for fighting took her to a place of white light and calm confidence. Her body flowing from one bloody contact to the next. She drove her blade though one demon, her opponent's face screamed in her own and kicking it off her blade, turned to the next to slice through a neck. Viscous blood sprayed. Limbs twitched and heads rolled. The pair continued to dance. Wave after wave succumbed to the fight. Esme's blood sang with elation as she thrust into another demon burying a knife up to its hilt. She and her partner approached Nicolaitan and his consort.

From the periphery of her vision, Esme saw Salis. He held his rapier in hand and began to cut a swathe through the demon army to reach her and Cursian. He fought with a grace so profound and desperate she found herself caught up in his dance and not her own. He joined them in no time. The two vampires shared a moment of silent understanding. The horde breathed in shock, as one of their own sacrificed himself for Cursian and his witch. A blade swung toward Esme's head.

Ducking, while Cursian swept his blade through the space she occupied moments before, Esme circled him at ground level. She hacked at another attacker's leg. Rising, she pulled the sword upward with her own momentum. The two halves of her victim spilled guts onto the wet black floor. Soon there would be no stable footing and she knew they would begin to tire. Cursian's stamina the only thing staving off her exhaustion. Once more, the defenders danced around each other and Esme found herself just out of reach of Nicolaitan. Salis and Cursian flanked her. Neither he nor De'hevda seemed concerned. Only two more demons and she could have a crack at the fatuous bastard. She took a harsh parry on her sword, tiredness making her unable to blend with the attack. Ignoring the pain in her shoulder, she asked the blade to find its own path around her head. Redirecting the attack Esme's sword fell under its own weight and dissected the demon's clavicle. Cursian turned, the other demon across the stomach. Esme's nose wrinkled at the stench as guts spilled to the floor. The battle stopped with his final stroke. The soldiers suddenly receded on a silent command.

The three stood, side by side. Esme only heard her own harsh breathing. Trembling limbs threatened to give up the ghost, the adrenaline vanished. Blood matted her hair, running over her chest and down her arms.

Cursian stood still full of fight beside her, he said, "Have we the right to duel?"

Nicolaitan smiled, "Impressive as you are, no. I will not offer you a way out and a potential defeat for myself by allowing my ego to fight for me. Now, either submit or I will have my soldiers use your witch once she loses the will to fight."

Esme lost her exhaustion as the threat penetrated. "Fucking try it," she snarled, wiping blood off her face.

"Don't worry, witch, I expect he will before he sends you into madness." De'hevda smiled holding out a handkerchief. Esme ignored the offer. In this place with death denied her, she could be truly hurt. Not an option really.

If we surrender now, we may have a chance later, Cariad. We need to entangle them to snare them.

Cursian, I'm afraid. I can fight, I can't let them hurt me voluntarily. Not again.

Do not let your panic rule you. Have faith, Cariad. Surrender your weapon. Time will see to our final fate and their own.

Fear gripped Esme. It didn't seem to be a great consolation.

Nevertheless, she threw her sword to the floor. Cursian did the same. As the blades clanged against the polished stone, which absorbed the blood, soldiers rushed forward. A great cry rose from the crowd. Esme found herself grabbed by dozens of black skinned creatures. Their hot leathery flesh and sharp nails jarred her mind, making her fight.

The demon held up his hand for silence. Esme noticed Salis still stood free of restraint. Nicolaitan smiled at the black vampire, "It seems you have decided to throw your lot in with your old Master, Salis. I am surprised, he gave you to us after all."

Salis bowed his body trembling, blood staining his white robes, "My Lord, the witch has shown me compassion and love. I will follow her to the ends of the earth. Regardless."

Esme froze, the implications of Salis's words shocked her to the core. All he had ever wanted was to be loved. She gave him a glimmer of that love and he would suffer for all eternity to protect it, nurture it.

"Then you will share their fate," Nicolaitan waved his hand and the soldiers caught Salis just as they held her. Esme began to fight. They lifted her struggling form off the floor. Holding her aloft they started to run toward a stairway in a darkened corner. From victor to victim in such a short space of time made Esme cry out and flail.

Nicolaitan's voice rang out over the noise, "And before you think you shall have a chance to defeat my father. Know this, Cursian, I rule here. You belong to me."

Esme fought harder.

Softly, Cariad, let them take you. Remember they cannot kill you.

It's not that which is scaring me….

Empty your mind, join with me and reach a place of safety.

I CAN'T.

The connection snapped, unable to survive Esme's fight. Those hot dry hands pulled and tore her clothes and skin. Turning her around again and again. Foul breath making her retch. They continued to travel into darkness, down, further down steps, endless steps. Esme struggled, fought, fell, and was lifted, over and over. Then a long dark corridor, large openings and screams from everywhere filling the air. Rough hands pushed her harshly. Esme stumbled through a doorway. Colliding with a wall and sliding down to land on a rough floor. Cursian pulled up short of the wall, punching one of the soldiers who made a lunge at Esme. The creature shrieked and ran off. The door slammed shut, thick darkness fell. Esme howled.

CHAPTER FORTY

Cursian bent and wrapped his arms around the shivering, sobbing bundle. He uttered a small incantation. Soft light took the edge off the black. Esme began to calm. He pulled her further into the circle of his body. As her wracking sobs softened he realised he had begun to rock them both and she gave him as much comfort as he gave her. They stayed silently holding each other for an age. He allowed soft, quiet tears to fall on her head, while her small hands stroked his back.

"We're in deep shit aren't we?" Esme finally mumbled.

"Yes," Cursian couldn't think of anything comforting to say. Nicolaitan's final words made his fear deepen. This place served up experiences for extreme appetites.

"Where's Salis?" Esme asked. Her heart felt concern for the other vampire touching Cursian deeply.

"I do not know, we became separated, Cariad." Cursian tried very hard not to think about what would happen to Salis.

"Two questions. What are we going to do? And what is going to happen to us? You can lie to me, I don't mind." Esme pulled away from him slightly.

"I am unable to lie to you, you would know. All I can tell you, Esme, is that we will know what to do when the time comes. It is the way of things. As too what is going to happen? That bit I am not looking forward too. They will try to defeat us by playing us at our own game. We may have a slim opportunity by over reaching their goals. But I am afraid it will mean a great deal of suffering. It always does." He held her close once more as Esme buried her head into his chest.

"I need a plan, Cursian. I work best with a plan," she shivered. "I'm not even sure I understand how they can use us to get themselves out of this place."

"That part I shall explain. As with the Dominion, they can destroy the safety net the Guardians created by killing us, but that alone will not allow them power in your realm. That can only happen if they gain entrance to your realm through you. They will try to make you accept their plan, submit willingly to their needs. Nicolaitan will use your soul and its connection to your body to gain access."

"So, if I don't summit to them, they're stuck here?"

"Yes." Cursian felt the weight of that one small word crush his heart. Esme could not know how hard they would push to reach their goal. It would make the Dominion a picnic.

"If it's that simple, why are you so afraid of Nicolaitan?"

"You are too perceptive, Cariad. I duelled with Nicolaitan to win through to fight my Master for the right to my soul. The fact that my Master has yet to put in an appearance means Nicolaitan has even more power. It seems as though everything is being left to the son, while the father learns to let go."

"I'm guessing this duel was not a happy experience for you," Esme said.

"No, Cariad, it was not. I won, eventually, but he has learnt from the experience. His arrogance was his undoing before, I doubt it will be again."

"But if I am not connected to my body they can't get access can they?"

"No, but then your soul is stuck here for all eternity. And I would not wish for that to happen. The plan is simply to resist for as long as you can. With luck Ben and May are able to detect what is happening to a certain extent and will cause your body's death at the right moment, thus freeing us both."

"Cursian, that's a shit plan," Esme struggled away, turning to face him, her back propped up against the wall. Her face a mask of streaked blood. It made her look like some kind of demon herself. What had he done dragging her down here?

"I agree it has more holes in it than a rusted skillet but I honestly consider it our only option."

"Why can't we use what we have? This link of ours has to be useful for something other than great metaphysical sex and violence. Maybe Salis will help?"

"Salis cannot help. He knows, unless he leaves with us, which is unlikely, he will be tried as a traitor. Not a fate you want him to suffer."

Cursian looked at her, really looked and noticed a thousand small changes from the woman he had 'bumped' into in the street. He considered. They might have a small chance, but it would be dangerous, to their soul's destruction dangerous. Esme had the power, but did she have the courage?

"There is one way we may be able to prevent them from gaining access through you. But I will need your complete submission and agreement."

Esme raised an eyebrow, "Submission? Like, I'd have to do as I was told. To the letter, kind of submission?"

"Yes." That one little word again.

"Tell me first." Always the negotiator.

He smiled, "If you wait, wait for as long as possible before giving in and then ask to be alone with me for the last time. I will turn you. This stops Nicolaitan from having immediate dominance over your soul. You will belong solely to me. I can then use your connection to the light to pull us from this place. This will leave De'hevda and her master stuck here without us."

"By turning, you don't mean - facing the wall or anything do you?" Esme sounded scared. "Well, it's one plan. But why can't you just turn me now?"

"The power and energy have to be right for me to harness your gift. If we accomplish this with them connected to us through their lust, hate and need, we will weaken them both to the point of their own destruction by pulling them apart. They will be binding themselves to us to hurt us, it is how the demons feed, they have too. Otherwise, they will gain nothing from us, no power and no strength. Once they are at the height of their lust, we turn the tables on them. It will take a huge amount of energy for Nicolaitan to reach your realm. He will be feeding so much he may not notice anything until too late. De'hevda we may have to distract, it depends on how she will involve herself."

"So, that's the plan. You turn me into a vampire, depriving the bad guys of our pain and my power. This then pulls them apart because they will be feeding on us as we return home and you use that energy and mine to get us there?" Esme sounded blank.

Cursian had no idea what she thought. For the first time since their lovemaking in the stable, he did not feel her. Disconcerting to say the least. She learnt far too fast. Turning Esme into a vampire, if it worked here, had to be the most dangerous gamble of their lives. Her power, combined with her lack of discipline might make her a monster with no possibility of control. Esme's will currently remained intact. His own had been broken for such a change. This would make a difference, one he couldn't anticipate. He might even be forced to see her destroyed. It was also a selfish act. He would not have a watch her die, but he would have changed her irrevocably. Too many thoughts chased themselves through his head. Apart from anything else, would her gifts allow her to be changed?

Esme interrupted these morbid thoughts with a question, "I wouldn't see the light again would I? Or watch birds feeding on the lawn? Or walk through springtime woods with the air warmed by the sun?"

Cursian let out a small breath, "No, Cariad."

"Night is the only time you know. And I would have to feed from people." She sounded as though she were shrivelling up.

"Esme, we do not have to do this. I do not have to change you." Ice stabbed Cursian's heart. She hated the idea. She didn't want to be tied to him like this.

"But for you to suggest it, it must be something that can happen anyway." A small, small voice.

Cursian paused.

"I'm right aren't I? That's what you're really worried about. If I become infected from the demon's bite I'm lost. Forever. Whereas if you get me…well…you get me. You keep me. Forever." Panic made the words blur.

Cursian watched her small body shiver, the shock manifesting. All he wanted was to enjoy her company, listen to her laugh, teach her of the beauty of life. He rubbed his hands over his face. De'hevda was right, he was ruthless when necessary, but he wouldn't have Esme used by these creatures, even if it meant destroying her himself.

"Yes, Cariad, it will happen. I think Nicolaitan will use your esoteric soiling to gain access. The Dominion wanted your body, he wants your essence. Your choice is him or me."

"What's the difference?" so quiet. But the shards of ice in his heart twisted with her words. He gasped, could she not see the difference?

Silence. The words left hanging.

A key turned in the lock. They continued to stare at each other as the door opened.

"My, my. It seems our lovers have had a tiff," De'hevda drawled sensing the atmosphere. "Come along, Cursian, we want to instruct you on the finer points of revenge."

He didn't turn, didn't care and didn't want to break contact with Esme. Rough, sharp hands grabbed him but nothing mattered except his lover and her possible rejection. He couldn't resist as they began to drag his heavy body away. All the flowing energy between them lay dead. All he had were his eyes, which he filled with love and compassion. How could she think he would be like them? Did she know nothing? Was her fear so great she couldn't trust him? All these questions he asked although he knew she wouldn't hear them.

Confusion and loss laced Esme's gaze. Cursian tried pulling away. He wanted to make her understand.

"I choose you." Softly, so softy the words bled from her lips. Unless you were listening for it under the scrape of boots and feet on stone, you missed it.

Cursian closed his eyes. When they opened the veil he used to face the world descended. He punched one demon in the spine and snapped the arm of the other, saying, "I will walk. Thank you."

The Prophecy

As the door to the cell slammed shut behind, he heard Esme scream for him.

CHAPTER FORTY ONE

Esme howled as the foot steps receded. The light Cursian created stayed though, mercifully. What the hell had she just agreed too? And what were they going to do to him? Was there another way she could get them out? Could her instinctual use of mage craft help? She stood up and paced the cell. Frustration hid deep, deep fear.

Reaching out for Cursian, wanting to know he understood her change of heart, left a blank. He'd cut her off. For the first time Esme was alone. Alone in hell. Screams from other cells began to fill her mind. Her pacing grew more frantic. There had to be another way. This couldn't be what was intended. This couldn't be the answer. Three choices, all of which would leave her cursed in one way or another. She would die here; it had simply become a matter of how and by whose hand. Being told you would die is one thing, but actually understanding its inevitability is something else. Could this really be her destiny? Was she really meant to become vampire? Why would they want another creature out in the world? What would be the sense? Would they allow it to happen? Would her body manage the change her soul undertook? How the hell did this kind of inter-dimensional stuff work anyway?

The light in the cell began to dim. Esme stopped. The implication clear. Cursian no longer had the concentration spare to maintain it. The thought of the light going out, the cell becoming a black pit and Cursian...

No. No, don't think about it. What was the worse they could do? No. Don't think about that either. Concentrate on life. Concentrate on what it will be like when she returns as vampire. Cursian must know a way of doing it that will stop her from going mad. That's a bonus. A positive. What else is positive? She'd be stronger, heal faster, live a really long time. She'd be with Cursian forever. That's a good thing.

Right? He'd be her master. That's a weird thing. Best not to touch that. Blood, what about the blood. Esme wasn't sure she'd really managed to understand Cursian's needs. Never mind deal with her own. But when Cursian fed from the man in the desert. Wow. To have access to that vitality for all time? She stood still, with her head cocked remembering how the blood poured down her own throat though her link with the vampire. To feel another person's heartbeat filling your head, giving you life. That was power.

The light dimmed again.

Esme flinched. Was she ready to say goodbye to sunlight? Really ready? Did she have a choice? Her heart raced. They say it takes but a moment to make a decision, even a life changing one. If you wait to make that decision, you are only second guessing yourself because you already have the answer you want. So what was her decision and when had she made it?

She heard something moving outside the door.

Remembering this adage, Esme knew the answer. When she'd looked into her lover's eyes, watching him beg for her understanding, while they dragged him away. If death awaited her, she demanded it from her lover, not her captor.

The door to the cell swung inward and Nicolaitan stood there.

"Esme, my sweet mortal. I have need of you. Come quietly please," he smiled holding out his hand.

She stood, watching the arrogant creature for a moment. Rather Cursian as her master than this monster.

"What do you want me for?" damn it her voice cracked.

"I want to take you to your current lover," he smiled. The insinuation making her stomach twist another knot. The hand remained outstretched.

Esme breathed, closed her eyes, surrounding herself with swiftly conjured memories of sunlight and love. She slapped his hand away, "I don't need your bloody help to walk to my doom, thanks very much."

He chuckled as she passed him, "Oh, I will enjoy you so very much. To have all that energy willing to accede to my every wish. Delicious. I can see why De'hevda hates you so much."

Esme's jaw clenched as he fell into step behind her. She continued to stride, despite her shaking legs, down the corridor. Concentrating solely on placing one foot confidently in front of the other, forcing the sounds from the other rooms out of her head, Esme walked. Far too soon, she came across two demons that resembled Caiaphas. Nicolaitan stopped and called her to a halt. She turned, like an automaton, toward the door. One of the large purple beasts flung the door open. Nicolaitan pushed her inside.

The room wasn't large, almost the same size as their cell. The walls and floor were rough, sticking with the general theme. Their cell however hadn't contained a table of medieval looking implements and didn't have Cursian hung by his wrists in the centre of the room. Or Salis chained to a wall on her left. They gagged Salis with a chain forced into his mouth and attached it tight to the wall. Her eyes flinched away from his still form and returned to the table.

So, this was it, the beginning of the end game.

She couldn't raise her eyes to Cursian's face but she smelt the blood.

A movement dragged her attention from the table, which seemed comforting and safe compared to the hanging body. A small white hand snaked around Cursian's ribcage. Esme belatedly realised they'd torn his shirt off. De'hevda smiled at her from under his stretched arms, almost as though she were playing hide and seek. The vampire's hand caressed Cursian's strong chest. His breathing changed, speeding up and the chains holding his arms jerked, clanking. Esme couldn't move.

"Cariad?" a breath of a name.

She looked up. Up into the face she loved more than life itself. They hung him high. Cuffs were around his wrists and neck, blood already trickling down his arms from their savage bite. He could barely open his jaw the cuff around his neck held his head so elevated. Cursian fought the angle to be able to look at her. Dark blue eyes, almost black in the torch light, shone with compassion. The ground rocked under Esme. He had allowed himself to be strung up like a Christmas turkey so she maintained the control. In becoming the sacrifice, Cursian made sure she held all the cards. She could make her own decisions, no manipulation. By goading Nicolaitan and De'hevda he brought their hate down on his own head. Removing her from jeopardy for as long as possible.

Esme stepped toward him, a hand clamped down on her shoulder.

"I think not. Not yet. My lover has yet to finish her fun. De'hevda likes to keep pain simple and she has wanted Cursian for many centuries. Each stroke is a loving reminder for her." Nicolaitan dug his fingers into Esme's shoulder so much her knees buckled. He stood close to her right shoulder, the pain keeping her still for fear of breaking bones.

"What do you want from us?" Esme ground out. She watched De'hevda take small licks of blood from Cursian's stretched arms. His muscles flinched and his eyes tracked her movements with hate blazing forth.

"We want you to suffer. That is all," Nicolaitan sounded content with the thought.

Esme wanted to know their plan. She wanted to know Cursian had guessed right. Did Nicolaitan want to change her himself? Did he want to use her to reach her own dimension?

The demon said, "Let us make the mighty mage scream shall we, my dear? We so enjoyed the look on his face when he realised what we had done to his child. Let's see if we can make Esme feel the same horror." The urbane gent smiled sweetly forcing Esme to look more closely at Salis's still body.

Esme felt sick. They had torn at Salis. She now realised his skin lay in ribbons. Blood spilled from his torn mouth, they had taken his eyes, his teeth, his fingers and legs lay at odd angles, joints broken. He groaned softly.

Esme squirmed, wanting to help the broken creature on the wall. Nicolaitan held her tight, "No. If you fight me mortal I will have every bone in Cursian's body broken. And remember he will survive it." Iron under the tone now. Esme stilled.

De'hevda smiled at her, "Watch how I make Cursian flinch. I bet you can't make him move in such a way."

She disappeared behind Cursian. Esme looked franticly into his eyes, wanting a sign to fight, wanting to know how to make this stop. All he gave her were the eyes of a patient penitent. The first crack sliced through the air before she felt ready. Esme watched, as Cursian's body twitched away from the three headed, studded whip. He uttered no sound. His eyes closed for a moment. Reopening them, he sought her out. Esme realised she would have to watch as each lash landed, she couldn't leave him with the pain and humiliation.

Ten more cracks. Tears bled from her eyes but she would not look away. Sweat poured down his skin, tingeing it slightly red. He began to grunt under the pressure as each blow found its mark. Nothing else in the room mattered to Esme but letting him know he was not alone.

Five more cracks. Her body sagged as the blood flew from the whip's end.

"Please, please stop. I can't watch any more," Esme folded. She pushed her hands against her face, refusing to believe this was real. This level of torture did not happen. This had to be some kind of game.

"You will watch, Esme," a manicured hand grabbed her hair. The shock and pain pulled her to her feet. "If you don't open your eyes I will have my guards come in and make you open them."

Esme's eyes snapped open. Her mantra, 'be strong, be strong', no longer having a meaning as the blood pooled at Cursian's feet. Another five lashes.

"I want the witch to see what I have done to him," De'hevda declared. "I think it maybe some of my best work." The vampire glided around from behind Cursian, her diaphanous gown blood splattered. Grasping Cursian's waistband, she pulled.

He turned. Esme shut her eyes. Nicolaitan shook her head until she responded by looking up.

The back of Cursian's leather jeans were slick with blood. His breath coming in shallow gasps. His long dark hair lay in tangled rats' tails across his shoulders, the ends covered in blood or pushed into open wounds. Esme moaned. The twenty one lashes she witnessed were not the only ones. Red wields on his skin gave evidence of earlier abuse. Each one of these twenty one, they had torn his flesh open. Across his ribs areas of white under the dark pink flesh peeked through. Ribbons of skin hung limply from his shoulder blades. Esme wanted to scream and fight. Neither would stop his pain.

"Why?" she asked. "It's me you want isn't it?"

Nicolaitan replied, "Yes, my dear, it is, but I want you in a certain frame of mind. And I think you are beginning to get there. I have to say, you are the only one who can make this stop. De'hevda here can do this to him for decades without becoming bored. She plans on flaying all the flesh from that beautifully strong back at some point." The demon released the hold he had on Esme's hair.

As though a piece of elastic were tied between them Esme walked stiffly to Cursian's hung, trapped body. Placing her hands gently on the firm skin just above his waist, she turned him back. His loose feet brushed the floor. The cuffs the only thing keeping him upright. His blood stained her hands. Even on tiptoes she couldn't reach his face with her kisses and she didn't want to push against his body for balance. All the places De'hevda touched Esme lightly ran her own hands, laying soft lips to cold flesh. Cursian groaned, far more loudly than when receiving his punishment.

"I have to say, watching the two of them is one of the most erotic things I have ever seen," Nicolaitan announced gaily.

"I wish to make her suffer like this," De'hevda drawled.

Esme turned her back on Cursian, one hand holding his firm thigh to act as ballast for her tumultuous feelings.

"We wouldn't get anywhere, De'hevda," Nicolaitan said. "He's going to be able to watch Esme suffer far more easily than she is able to watch him. This is bread and butter stuff to our kind. Esme's humanity will be her undoing. Besides, I don't want to have to wait for her to heal before I take her to my bed as a willing guest," he smiled like a courtly lover.

"Would fucking you make this stop?" Esme asked. Her pitch and tone surprisingly even. Cursian gurgled something.

Nicolaitan grinned showing lots of small sharp teeth. "Not entirely, no. Once I have you give yourself over to me, willingly, to save this poor wretch I will make you mine in a way he doesn't have the strength to do. Then I will show my followers exactly how compliant you have become. I do love an audience when I'm being deviant."

"If I agree to your whims I can stop this? Cursian and Salis can leave without any more pain?" Esme forced herself not to think of their plan. There had to be no hope. The bastards must not guess.

"I shall certainly stop this pain and if you serve me well I may release Cursian but not Salis from our custody, I will not have traitors rewarded. However, I would love to watch Cursian's face when I take you to my bed. So you will have to earn his release over time."

"She…will not…be willing," Cursian ground out.

"Think what you like, Cursian," De'hevda goaded. "You are unable to witness the look on her face. My lover will have his way with the witch." She turned and pouted at Nicolaitan, "I want to give her a taste of what it will be like for him, when he watches her with you."

Esme's mind didn't process De'hevda's sentence. What was the mad cow wanting now?

The demon brushed a drop of blood from De'hevda's cheek and licked his finger. "Hmm, I think it would be a fine aphrodisiac to watch you play him a little more. We are not quite full enough for the next stage to be complete."

De'hevda actually squealed with delight. Esme found herself willing to die to stop the bitch from touching him again. Anger raised its head within her body. Esme readied for a fight.

"Oh no, witch, you are with me." Nicolaitan waved his hand. Esme's feet left the ground. Her body turning in mid air she slammed into the wall nearest the door. Her back took the brunt. She collapsed onto the floor. Nicolaitan dragged her back to her kneeling position. "You are going to create more emotion for me before this ends. You are rich to feed from. Now watch."

De'hevda pressed her body against Cursian. Her arms stretched high, her hands holding his forearms tight. Her weight almost completely supported by his wrists in the cuffs. He grunted as his muscles were pulled even tighter. The vampire licked his throat, small, light licks. The kind a lover makes. Then she bit. Blood poured down his chest as she worried at the wound, her hands and nails digging into his arms. The small blond body licked and bit her way down Cursian's chest and stomach. Esme found herself watching in horrid fascination. It didn't hurt, because it was too surreal. Until she heard his belt buckle chime.

"Fucking cow, that's mine!" Esme exploded, pulling against the hand holding her hair.

Nicolaitan chuckled, "Oh, no my sweet, I'll not have her interrupted now. She would kill me. She has wanted Cursian for far too long."

De'hevda pulled Cursian's waist free of his jeans the action yanking on the chains. He cursed in a language Esme didn't know. Looking at his bloody body Esme grimaced. His flesh hardened. Cursian's eyes were closed, his breath coming in very short gasps. The bitch turned him on. The pain De'hevda inflicted made him respond. The female vampire left his trousers handing loosely around his backside. She grinned at Esme, knelt before his body like a supplicant and lowered her head. Cursian moaned, loudly. De'hevda took the full length of him in her mouth.

"I do not wish for this to happen," his most coherent sentence for ages.

De'hevda pulled her head back, "Yes, you do. You remember and you want." Her head pushed forward.

Esme's mind exploded with the rage she felt. This was rape. A part of her knew she shouldn't try for it, that they must remain submissive but Esme wanted this farce to stop.

She reached for the light within her and found the channel blocked.

"Do you really think I wouldn't have thought of that?" Nicolaitan said. "You shan't have access to that energy again until you join our ranks."

Unable to move, Nicolaitan holding her body with his magic, Esme roared with rage.

De'hevda rose, slowly, her hand replacing her mouth. Turning to face Esme with gloating eyes, she clicked her fingers. The chains lowered, clanking through a hole in the ceiling. Cursian's form folded to the ground. Blood seeped down his erect penis. She'd grazed him with her teeth. He should have started to fight as soon as the chains relaxed, but he wouldn't. He'd allow the evil hag bag from hell to have her way. He wanted to catch as much of her and Nicolaitan as he could in his suffering.

Esme caught sight of Cursian's face just as he lowered his head. She realised, to her horror, his submission was real. He wasn't trying to trick them. His eyes remained blue, not the black of vampire, the colour they bled to when he became angry. Behind those beautiful, soft eyes, Esme only saw retreat. He vanished inside himself. The pain, the humiliation, the actions which he knew were inevitable made him retreat. Esme remembered his description of how his Master created him. Rape. Cursian may have inflicted it on others in his madness but as a sane being, rape defeated him. To her shame Esme knew this would hurt him far more than if she were the victim.

Esme felt violated and defiled as she watched De'hevda pull her gown over her head. Naked, perfect, pale skin, long white blond hair, ice blue eyes. The only real colour Cursian's blood staining her mouth. The vampire pulled her nails down his chest as she stepped astride his body. Her nails dragged at the bites she'd inflicted, further opening the wounds. Cursian twitched. Esme willed him to fight. He half rose. De'hevda waved a hand. He collapsed back to the floor. The same power which held her still, kept him pinned down.

De'hevda stepped across his prone body, then stepped astride him once more. Now facing Nicolaitan, she smiled, blowing him a kiss. De'hevda lowered her body. A hand on Cursian's member guided it with practiced ease into her body. With her legs wide Esme saw how wet the bitch had become through torturing Cursian. The vampire began to pump her body up and down. Closing her eyes to enjoy each stroke all the more, she leaned back, her hands resting on Cursian's chest, giving her demon lover more to look at. Faster and faster, she pumped forcing Cursian's length into her small, perfect body.

Something snapped inside Esme. She reached toward him with all her power, no longer able to bear his glazed expression. Again she hit a barrier. Sobbing she tried again and again. What fucking use was magic if it didn't work when you needed it too!

"Oh, yes," Nicolaitan breathed in her ear. "Fight me my beautiful whore. Let me feed off your pain and his. Your love is so extreme, his anguish so real. I have no idea which of you is arousing me more."

Nicolaitan had managed to cut them off from each other. Why had Cursian allowed this to happen? All Esme had left was every foul curse she could think of and all she received for her efforts was laughter.

Not soon enough the bitch began her orgasm. Her cries of release filled the room. Nicolaitan groaned in response, heat radiating off him. The air felt thick with violence, blood, magic and sex. De'hevda dismounted.

A sensation of release washed through her, Nicolaitan's binding gone. Stumbling, she scooted to Cursian's body before they raised it again.

"I think we will leave the happy lovers to each other for a while. I want Esme to say goodbye while we enjoy what they have given to us." Nicolaitan placed a hand of ownership on De'hevda's naked buttock.

"How do you know I'll give in?" Esme cried brokenly after their departing backs.

"Because you cannot watch another session like that. And if you don't I shall have you in the chains with Cursian watching," Nicolaitan threw at her.

CHAPTER FORTY TWO

No tears and no pity. He hoped he would see neither when he opened his eyes. Anger, rage and jealousy he could deal with. But hurt? No.

Cursian's arms and neck were still chained together. His back replaced by sheet lightening. Every breath pushed open wounds onto the rough floor. He tried to struggle upright. Small, but strong hands pulled on his arms. He grunted. They let go. He cried out as he fell backward again.

"Oh shit, sorry," Esme pulled again. Ignoring his soft whimpers.

Once she managed to pull him straight, he folded his legs closer to his body. Only then, opening his eyes. He sensed the tendrils of energy Nicolaitan and De'hevda pushed into their auras. He knew he had enough of those tendrils to carry out his plan, but he would have to look at Esme to do it.

He did not want to raise his eyes. He did not want to know what she thought of him. The hollow feeling in his chest scared him.

"Cursian, we have to get on with this. We have to finish the plan. He's right I can't watch that hag bag hurt you again." Esme lightly shook his shoulders, "Damn it, don't flake out on me now. I want to go home."

The desperation in her voice finally made him look up.

"Esme...I..." Numb. He felt numb.

"Don't, just don't. You hurt, you're probably in shock and you don't want to remember what just happened." She brushed his hair out of his face while she spoke. Cursian didn't think she was aware of the wobble in her voice, or the tears staining her face. Esme hurt, but he saw no pity, no shame.

"I really fucking well don't deserve you," he said, sounding more normal than ever before. Esme used the last of his shirt to clean some of his smaller wounds.

She smiled, "Ha, see, it's catching. You sound like me. Come on, sweetheart, I do not want to be a show piece for Nicolaitan and we have to help Salis."

Cursian could not turn to look at his old companion. He had wept when he'd seen the damage done to Salis. The black vampire's courage meant he made not one sound as they pulled his teeth from his upper jaw. Salis finally found something worth living for and it would be his destruction.

"The key to Salis' chains is on the table. Bring him to me, Cariad." Cursian took his weight off her arms and watched her scramble to do his bidding. He heard chains clink, he heard Esme swear and Salis groan in agony.

"Esme, you know this may not work?" Cursian had to warn her, they might not be strong enough.

"It will," she grunted. She pulled Salis's broken form across the floor toward him, laying down the black vampire over his legs. For the first time she held still. An arm braced his chest once more so he didn't have to support all his own weight.

The last of the demon's barriers which kept them apart, crumbled. Esme's love and confidence flooded through him. A broken sob escaped him as he realised she would submit to his plan.

"Cariad, you will need to surrender to me utterly." His shackled arms rattled as they rose to hold her face. "For me to take your life and give it back, you will have to trust and love me completely. If I create you in pain and anger, as I was created, I will only hurt you and you shall awaken deranged as I did."

Esme looked at him with huge green eyes. She nodded understanding.

"I dare not take you to a place of safety to do this. As we have agreed, we have to stay in the moment, completely here to make the most of our chance to harm the others. I have only ever made De'hevda and Salis. I made neither with love in my heart. Salis was a necessity after De'hevda bungled his original change. I made De'hevda in a fit of madness while under the control of my Master. You, I make with love, to save us from hell and to stop Nicolaitan from using you to reach our home," Cursian's voice softened. He had begun to weave the web, which would have Esme lying willingly in his arms.

"I guess your vampiric nature will finally get what it wants," Esme quipped, nerves plain.

"All it wants is to leave here. It made a grave mistake in trying to return. It knows that now. It is no longer a true creature of this dimension. It enjoys its power and freedom. But yes, it is anticipating the feel of your heart in my mouth." Cursian raised his aching arms. Esme slipped under the chains. He held her close. "No matter what happens, try not to panic. I have no wish to fight you. Just remember, Cariad, I am going to take your life and I will be your Master when you wake. I will have control of you until you are strong enough to pull away from me. Do I still have your agreement?"

Cursian watched this piece of news filter through. Esme wasn't a feminist, but neither did she believe one person held rights over another.

"I am not sure I understand but so help me, I trust you. I must be mad."

"Well, at least you are honest. I will ask you to follow my lead for as long as you can. This is about magic and the vampire virus. If we wish to help Salis he will need you too." Cursian gauged Esme's reaction to this piece of news.

"You want him to feed from me so he can heal?"

Cursian nodded. Esme moved and pulled Salis's barely breathing form onto her own lap. "What do I do?" she asked, fear laying under the decision she'd made to save Salis.

Cursian softly pushed Esme's dirty tangled hair away from her neck. He watched her pulse frantically trying to claw its way to safety. His blood lust rose at the sight. The energy changed between them. Esme shivered in anticipation.

He lowered his head. Pulled back his lips. His sharp incisors touched Esme's skin. Hot, rich, alive skin. He closed his eyes as she sighed, surrendering her life. Cursian's heart pounded with bitterness, he realised he took from Esme the very thing he loved the most. Her life. Her zest for it, her lust for it. He knew a part of him would die the moment her heart stopped. For thirty two years he nurtured and loved this woman, but in a few short weeks, he destroyed everything, to save a world he wasn't convinced was worth the effort. Cursian felt his conviction slide. He didn't think he wanted to live with the guilt if he took her, changed her, but no longer loved his creation. And if he couldn't control her, death waited regardless.

"Don't pull away from me. Love me and trust I will become what you need," Esme said, sensing his reticence.

Kissing her neck, Cursian flicked his tongue over her pulse and sank his teeth into her live flesh for the last time. The wound opened. His need made him draw on the blood just as he heard Salis moan in agony. Cursian paused then pulled away from Esme's neck. He grabbed Salis and pulled the smaller vampire into Esme's arms, laying his head against the blood flowing from Esme's neck as her heart pushed her life out of the large wound. Blood filled Salis's mouth, he swallowed. Esme gasped as Salis moved on his own account. Cursian felt her push against him as Salis covered her body with his own. He murmured to her not to be afraid while he watched Salis drink deeper and deeper. He heard Salis cry out as he healed. Finally, dark brown eyes gazed upward into Cursian's.

"Let go of her, brother. I need her now," Cursian said. This was the test, could Salis release Esme? If not, Cursian would end his life by leaving him here forever.

Salis blinked and moved back. His lips stained with Esme's blood. "Thank you, Master," he whispered.

Cursian leaned over Esme's quiet body and licked Salis's mouth clean. The dark vampire trembled more violently at Cursian's gentle caress. "You are welcome," Cursian said, hoping Salis would hear more in those words than the older vampire felt able to express openly.

Salis smiled, "She needs this to be finished." He moved off Esme and helped Cursian move her with more grace than the still chained vampire would manage alone.

Cursian once more bent his head to his beloved's neck. Blood filled his mouth, searingly hot and spicy. He drank. He moaned as she clutched at him, pulling him closer. Mouthful, after mouthful he swallowed. He wanted to drown in the oxygen rich liquid. The feel of her torn skin against the end of his tongue electrified his senses. The iron rich taste of her life pouring down his thankful throat. He found he wanted to take the final heartbeat of his lover. He wanted to absorb all of her, pull all of her into his body. More than he could when they made love. More than he had ever dreamed possible. She filled every sense he possessed. Her life flowed into his veins and his soul.

The screaming pain in his back receded as he healed. Strength returned to his limbs as she filled him. Esme's uncontaminated blood intoxicated him, making his consciousness fly with renewed power. A clear path opened to Esme's prone body. He saw exactly how to drag their souls from this place of damnation. Cursian revelled in his knowledge and power as Esme's arms slipped from his own.

Her heartbeat fluttered lightly in his mouth. Cursian slowed. Concentration and mage power focusing entirely on the small body in his arms. He pulled back. Esme's head lolled to the side. He moved to cradle her in his arms.

"Esme? Esme, can you hear me?" his voice soft.

She opened her eyes, "Hi," barely there.

"Esme, I am about to finish this and then draw the veil back for your return. You will be mine forever and always. I do this with love, not desire, or hate, or power, or lust. Do you understand?" he watched as her eyes dilated. Her breathing became erratic and shallow, organs closing down.

Cursian studied her dying face. He would never again look into those green eyes and see the remainder of the sun's light glowing deep within.

Esme nodded.

"Do you agree?" he paused, wondering if he had left the final incantation too late.

"Yes," she breathed the last word on her last breath.

Esme's heart stopped. He bowed his head over her body. Allowing himself a small breath of time to mourn his actions.

"I am so sorry, Cariad," he felt Salis lay a hand on his head and hers as though to share in his grief. He appreciated the silent understanding. Salis knew only to well how Cursian felt about making children.

The moment gone, Cursian pushed his sadness away. Now he must revive her body. Grief a luxury he didn't deserve.

Reaching awkwardly for the whip De'hevda discarded, Cursian pulled the edge across his chest. Its metallic end sharp enough to cut his skin. His virus laden blood rushed out.

The prayer for her resurrection came easily to his lips. "With my blood I bind thee. With my strength, I shall protect thee. With my love, I bring thee home to me. Hear me immortals. I create life with love and bring love back with the life I create."

Cursian raised Esme's lifeless face to his chest. Pushing her lips to the wound in his flesh, he repeated his chosen mantra over and over. Words and blood would bind them. Their souls would bind them. Their fates would bind them. The magic flowed.

The thick air around their still forms began to move. Faster and faster, from breeze, to wind, they sat in the centre of a sudden whirlwind. His dark power and her light energy began to blend. The frantic shining ball of power within the whirlwind whipped at their bodies. Esme heaved against his chest as he bent over her to protect her from the chaos surrounding them. Another spasm. Cursian drew back. Their anarchic power drew up, high above their heads. It formed two thick channels, each containing parts of the whole. Cursian held Esme still, watching the power peek above them. Then down it plunged, filling Esme through head and heart. Giving a new existence.

She rose, clutched his chest, pushing her mouth hard against the only wound left open. Cursian howled as he felt her tongue fill his broken skin. The wind pulled the sound from his lips. Pushing her head against his chest, Cursian forced more of him inside her mouth. Her now sharp incisors meant she opened her own wounds. He concentrated on the locks holding his chains. They gave under metaphysical persuasion. With his arms and neck free, Cursian helped Esme climb up his body. He guided her to his neck. Teeth, sharp teeth, grazed his skin, sinking into him. Cursian cried out, full of the power spinning around and through them.

Esme fed. He could not remember feeling so blissful. A sense of peace descended over him and soaked into his essence. She pulled on the wound, filling her mouth over and over. Life, his life animated his lover. Cursian surrendered utterly to her feeding.

Vaguely, he began to hear someone battering at the door to their sanctuary. Salis called to him from a great distance.

Another wave of their combined magic hit him, rocking his body backward, Cursian gave in and collapsed. The movement dislodged Esme, who stayed upright. Their eyes met.

All timidity, all fear, everything that made Esme human vanished. A being of sentient awareness and great power looked back, Esme, terrible in her supremacy. Cursian reached for that beauty. Just as his fingertip brushed her shirt, Esme's back arched. The vampiric hunger caused her to cry out with need.

"Fight it, Esme, gain control as fast as you can, I know you will conquer this." Cursian's voice rose over the magic, which persisted in forming and changing around them.

Esme shut her eyes and screamed. The darkness of vampire filled her aura. He could do nothing but watch her fight. Spears of white, blue light shot through the darkness of the virus. Esme fought for control. Amazed, Cursian watched while Esme dominated the darkness. His faith in her power held true, she caged the beast. At least for now.

The next stage of their plan began. Cursian reached for the magic flowing around them, drawing the power within himself, then pushing all he could into Esme. In no time, he felt bloated and Esme's face held the flushed look of the sated. He asked for the rest to hide within the stones of the palace and, to his amazement, it did just that. Suddenly vanishing, leaving the cell a dark, still place.

Esme grinned, sharp teeth glinting, "Hello, Master."

Cursian laughed. Grabbing her, he hugged her close. Just as the door caved in.

CHAPTER FORTY THREE

Nicolaitan and De'hevda filled the large door shaped hole. "WHAT HAVE YOU DONE!" the demon bellowed.

Esme watched in fascination as his demonic nature shifted over his beautiful features. His skin went a funny shade of purple. De'hevda looked truly scared and even paler, if such as thing were possible. She noticed Salis rise next to her, healed and strong.

Cursian smiled, confident. Powerful in front of the enemy. "She belongs to me, Nicolaitan. This time your lust and greed have undone your advantage. I did not think you would let me defeat you twice."

Esme's still heart swelled as she watched the demon realise his error and the consequences.

"The other mistake you made was in underestimating Esme's power. She has been gifted with abilities even I do not yet understand. She is also very angry with you," Cursian ran a finger down her cheek.

Esme couldn't help but push her head lightly against the touch. Her Master's pleasure made her warm inside. Deep contentment, a kind of peace and simplicity filled her mind. The world now seemed incredibly simple. And the power. The power hummed through her body. Every nerve ending tingled. Each cell within her body pulsed. Everything around her radiated its essence, making the world so alive it bordered on pain. All her senses were full. The rough ground textured by infinitesimal troughs and peaks, even through her boots. The room rank with magic and old blood. Her hearing picked up the sound of despair in De'hevda's breathing. Her sight saw past the mask Nicolaitan wore. She saw the demon.

"She is mine," Nicolaitan strode into the room. De'hevda stayed in the doorway.

"Esme, what to do you want my love?" Cursian asked.

Esme cocked her head on one side as though pondering the end of the universe. "I think I would like us to destroy these two and leave here, Master."

De'hevda flung herself into action. "He is my Master witch!" she screamed flying at Esme.

Esme's heart jumped once in response, her body twisted slightly off the line as De'hevda reached with clawed hands. In missing her target De'hevda swiftly pulled back, Esme neatly followed the movement. Her arm and hand pointed to the ground just behind the vampire, lightly encircling her neck. De'hevda went down, Esme rode the fall. The vampire's back hit the floor, Esme made contact with her knee on De'hevda's chest. Ribs splintered. Salis appeared beside her, a knife from the table in his hand.

Still calm Esme smiled into the pain filled, twisted face. "He is mine De'hevda and I am his. Always have been, always will be."

The two men watched as Esme and Salis pulled De'hevda, who yelped in pain, to her feet. Esme held her still as Salis dragged the knife across her throat and allowed the blood of his evil sibling to cover his body. Together as one mind, they flung her across the room. Nicolaitan didn't move to help his fallen comrade. He continued to try to find a way through the barriers Cursian created to protect himself and Esme from dark magic. Those barriers also stopped the demon from taking back the part of himself he left within Cursian and Esme, in order to feed from their pain.

"I win again, Nicolaitan. I wonder what your father will say when he realises what I have done. What you allowed me to do," Cursian actually grinned at the now still and silent demon. "I think it is time we left. Esme, come to my arms."

She turned obediently to his embrace.

Think of your home, your flesh, the place we left it and the people waiting for us. Fill your mind. Take Salis's hand and hold him close to your heart. Also, maintain the links you have which may be our demonic friends. I want to drag them with us but give them nowhere to go.

Esme nodded, concentrating on home, clearly seeing the dark, wet, cold car park they had reached when leaving the caves. She pictured May, beautiful thick black hair, long legs and shapely body. Next, Ben, his dedication to his cause a beacon in the darkness. Dreadlocks flowing like thick rivers down his dark skin. The autumn trees, the autumn sky. Night, the only time she would now know. The smell of wet leaves and wet earth filled her head. Finally, her body and Cursian's folded over each other in the centre of the tableau.

Back in the cell, she felt Cursian pull on the power he'd hidden within themselves and the palace. Esme's strong blue light, now clearly shot through with Cursian's darker energies and a strange tangle of sheer black, pulsed in her head. She opened to him again. Cursian accepted the offer. He pulled on her deeply, she gave willingly. Together they recreated the whirlwind of power. She watched Nicolaitan and De'hevda start to scream. The power the two vampiric mages created pulsed through the evil in the room, tearing at it, dissolving its integrity. She pulled Salis into her arms as she felt Cursian wrap himself around her body.

Take us home, Cariad.

Esme pushed for her flesh. Pushed hard. Wanting to feel its solidity surrounding her once more. She, Cursian and Salis rose together. Rose from darkness, rose through a whirlwind of light, their light. They tumbled through the channel he created. Barely separate in the manic rush to fill the void inside their empty bodies.

The sheer blackness, tangled with her own energy and Cursian's, tried to separate. It wanted to return to its own dimension. It didn't have a place to live within Esme's. The demon could not manifest in her world and De'hevda did not have enough of her essence inside her victims to accomplish the same task. Esme watched the evil desperation of demon and vampire being torn apart within and behind them as they travelled.

From a long way off Esme heard.

"He's killed her. We have to call an ambulance. She's drained of blood," May yelled at Ben.

"Just wait, May, I can feel something, please concentrate on them."

Cold hands on cold flesh. Naked and cold on a tarmac floor. Owls and foxes watching, rain coming again. A body moving under her chest.

Esme bucked, taking a huge gasp of natural, clean air. Cursian reared up simultaneously, also breathing deeply. She watched as Salis's body manifested out of the tarmac of the car park.

Cursian grabbed her face, "Esme?"

Cold hands on her cold, naked scalp. She gazed into the most beautiful blue eyes she had ever seen.

"I'm hungry," she told her Master.

Lightning Source UK Ltd.
Milton Keynes UK
12 November 2010

162783UK00001B/16/P